PRAISE FOR DONNA GRANT'S BEST-SELLING ROMANCE NOVELS

"Grant's ability to quickly convey complicated backstory makes this jam-packed love story accessible even to new or periodic readers." *–Publishers' Weekly*

"Donna Grant has given the paranormal genre a burst of fresh air…." *–San Francisco Book Review*

"The premise is dramatic and heartbreaking; the characters are colorful and engaging; the romance is spirited and seductive." *–The Reading Cafe*

"The central romance, fueled by a hostage drama, plays out in glorious detail against a backdrop of multiple ongoing issues in the "Dark Kings" books. This seemingly penultimate installment creates a nice segue to a climactic end." *–Library Journal*

"…intense romance amid the growing war between the Dragons and the Dark Fae is scorching hot." *–Booklist*

SKYE DRUIDS SERIES

Iron Ember ~ Shoulder the Skye ~ Heart of Glass
Endless Skye ~ Still of the Night ~ Blood Skye
After Midnight ~ Kiss of Skye

DARK KINGS SERIES

Dark Heat ~ Darkest Flame ~ Fire Rising ~ Burning Desire
Hot Blooded ~ Night's Blaze ~ Soul Scorched ~ Dragon King
Passion Ignites ~ Smoldering Hunger ~ Smoke and Fire
Dragon Fever ~ Firestorm ~ Blaze ~ Dragon Burn
Constantine: A History, Parts 1-3 ~ Heat ~ Torched
Dragon Night ~ Dragonfire ~ Dragon Claimed
Ignite ~ Fever ~ Dragon Lost ~ Flame ~ Inferno
A Dragon's Tale (Whisky and Wishes: *A Holiday Novella*,
Heart of Gold: *A Valentine's Novella*, & Of Fire and Flame)
My Fiery Valentine ~ The Dragon King Coloring Book
Dragon King Special Edition Character Coloring Book: Rhi

DARK WARRIORS SERIES

Midnight's Master ~ Midnight's Lover ~ Midnight's Seduction
Midnight's Warrior ~ Midnight's Kiss ~ Midnight's Captive
Midnight's Temptation ~ Midnight's Promise
Midnight's Surrender ~ A Warrior for Christmas

CHIASSON SERIES

Wild Fever ~ Wild Dream ~ Wild Need
Wild Flame ~ Wild Rapture

LARUE SERIES
Moon Kissed ~ Moon Thrall ~ Moon Struck ~ Moon Bound

WICKED TREASURES
Seized by Passion ~ Enticed by Ecstasy ~ Captured by Desire
Books 1-3: Wicked Treasures Box Set

HISTORICAL PARANORMAL

THE KINDRED SERIES
Everkin ~ Eversong ~ Everwylde ~ Everbound
Evernight ~ Everspell

KINDRED: THE FATED SERIES
Rage ~ Ruin ~ Reign

DARK SWORD SERIES
Dangerous Highlander ~ Forbidden Highlander
Wicked Highlander ~ Untamed Highlander
Shadow Highlander ~ Darkest Highlander

ROGUES OF SCOTLAND SERIES
The Craving ~ The Hunger ~ The Tempted ~ The Seduced
Books 1-4: Rogues of Scotland Box Set

THE SHIELDS SERIES

A Dark Guardian ~ A Kind of Magic ~ A Dark Seduction
A Forbidden Temptation ~ A Warrior's Heart
Mystic Trinity (a series connecting novel)

DRUIDS GLEN SERIES

Highland Mist ~ Highland Nights ~ Highland Dawn
Highland Fires ~ Highland Magic
Mystic Trinity (a series connecting novel)

SISTERS OF MAGIC TRILOGY

Shadow Magic ~ Echoes of Magic ~ Dangerous Magic
Books 1-3: Sisters of Magic Box Set

THE ROYAL CHRONICLES NOVELLA SERIES

Prince of Desire ~ Prince of Seduction
Prince of Love ~ Prince of Passion
Books 1-4: The Royal Chronicles Box Set
Mystic Trinity (a series connecting novel)

DARK BEGINNINGS: A FIRST IN SERIES BOXSET

Chiasson Series, Book 1: Wild Fever
LaRue Series, Book 1: Moon Kissed
The Royal Chronicles Series, Book 1: Prince of Desire

MILITARY ROMANCE / ROMANTIC SUSPENSE

SONS OF TEXAS SERIES

The Hero ~ The Protector ~ The Legend
The Defender ~ The Guardian

COWBOY / CONTEMPORARY

HEART OF TEXAS SERIES

The Christmas Cowboy Hero ~ Cowboy, Cross My Heart
My Favorite Cowboy ~ A Cowboy Like You
Looking for a Cowboy ~ A Cowboy Kind of Love

STAND ALONE BOOKS

That Cowboy of Mine ~ Home for a Cowboy Christmas
Mutual Desire ~ Forever Mine ~ Savage Moon

* * *

**Check out Donna Grant's Online Store at
www.DonnaGrant.com/shop
for autographed books, character
themed goodies, and more!**

AFTER MIDNIGHT

SKYE DRUIDS

SEVEN

NEW YORK TIMES & USA TODAY BESTSELLING AUTHOR

DONNA GRANT

AFTER MIDNIGHT

SKYE DRUIDS

SEVEN

CHAPTER ONE

SKYE DRUIDS

May
Outside of Ullapool

Rain pattered steadily against the windows and onto the roof, beads of water running down the panes of glass highlighted by moonlight to form patterns on the floor. But Kurt wasn't aware of any of it. He kept seeing his brother's face on the screen right before he set the warehouse to blow and made his escape. He and the Druids with him had also managed to escape.

It had been so long since he'd had contact with his family that he actually began to believe they had released him. He should've known better. His mother didn't let anything go. Ever. He had become complacent, had gotten too confident. And he would pay for it. *If* Parker found him. His little brother was as ruthless and uncompromising as their mum. Maybe more so. The difference was that Parker didn't have the intelligence or control Diana Barclay did.

Kurt rubbed his eyes, wincing at the discomfort it caused. He'd gotten in a few cat naps throughout the day but didn't dare allow himself to really sleep. He couldn't. Parker and the Druids had been on his heels for days. Kurt would lose them, only for them to pick up his trail. This cat-and-mouse game was draining and tedious, and the lack of rest was taking its toll. At this rate, it would only be a matter of time before Parker found him.

Kurt rose from the table, his body protesting. The only light in the kitchen came from his open laptop and the green light on the coffee maker. He shuffled over and poured another cup. Was it his sixth? Seventh? He had lost count.

He stared at the dark liquid before placing his hands on the counter and hanging his head. His eyes were so heavy. He lost the battle and let his lids close. He only wanted a second to rest, but the next thing he knew, he was falling. Kurt jerked awake and hastily righted himself. He shoved his hands into his hair, still damp from the shower, and blinked his weary eyes several times to try to wake up. The coffee was hot and bitter, but it was the only thing keeping him awake.

After half a cup, he made his way back to the table and sank into the chair, punching a button to wake up his computer and check for any signs that Parker and his associates were getting close again. Kurt was ready to leave at a moment's notice. He'd been in the small flat for a day, and that was usually when he had to go in search of somewhere else to hide. However, he wasn't sure how much longer he could keep it up. He should've been able to shake Parker by now.

He sipped his coffee and scrolled through the CCTV footage he'd hacked, searching for the unnamed faces of those with his brother. Unease crept in when he found no trace of Parker or his cronies. Ice slid through Kurt's veins as he set down his cup and hastily typed the address of where he'd stayed in Aviemore to scour more video footage.

It didn't take him long to find the sleek, racing-green Jaguar F-Pace turning the corner under the streetlamps and coming to a halt outside the house he had stayed in. Parker exited the passenger side, and the driver and two others followed. Two other SUVs pulled up, and more Druids climbed out. They swarmed the house while Parker stayed back, his hands in his pockets, watching as others did the dirty work.

Kurt shook his head. Some things never changed.

He should've viewed this hours ago. If he had been thinking clearly, he would have. He clenched his hands and took a deep breath to focus, blinking to ease the discomfort in his dry eyes. He observed Parker's men exit the house and shake their heads. His brother straightened and looked at the man on his left. Words were exchanged, and the Druid got out a map and spread it over the vehicle's bonnet as everyone gathered around. Kurt had seen them perform the locator spell before. He had countered it each time but couldn't remember when he had done it last.

"Bloody fucking hell," he muttered and shoved away from the computer.

As he did, his shirt rubbed against his chest, making him hiss in pain. He unbuttoned it to look where he had tattooed a warding emblem. He was in a bad way if he had forgotten that.

Every time he blinked, it was like someone rubbed sand into his eyes. His stomach growled, but the thought of eating another protein bar turned it. Instead, he drank more coffee and settled in front of the laptop again. He hadn't paused the video, so he had to rewind to get back to where he'd been. Little things like this would do him in.

Little things that shouldn't be happening.

Little things he'd never done before.

He returned to the recording and watched Parker's group repeat the locator spell several times. His brother couldn't get a good lock on him, but Parker *could* get a generalized location. Kurt couldn't zoom the video, and with it recording at night, the shadows and shine of the streetlamps made it challenging to see specifics. Luckily, he could make out one Druid circling a section on the map.

Kurt's gaze shifted to Parker, and he waited for his little brother's temper to flare. Surprisingly, he remained calm as he spoke. The moment he finished, everyone climbed into their vehicles and drove away. Now that Kurt knew the direction they were headed, he tracked the vehicles through Aviemore but lost them where there were no cameras. Several tense minutes later, he found them again on the A9. He looked at the timestamp and then searched the footage of the Longman Roundabout. Just as he suspected, they took the second exit to stay on the A9 before heading to the A835 exit on the Tore Roundabout.

"Fuck," he muttered, dread filling him.

He'd been fighting sleep when he should've been leaving. He started to rise, only to sit back down. There was no more room for mistakes. Before he headed out, he needed to know exactly where Parker was.

Kurt jumped to another view and scanned the recording until he located the F-Pace. Following it as best he could, he suddenly lost it and the SUVs trailing Parker.

Panic thudded in Kurt's chest. His instinct was to run, but a thread of apprehension kept him seated. He shoved the heels of his hands into his eyes and took a couple of calming breaths.

"Focus," he told himself. "You have to focus. The next place you go, you can sleep. But you can't do that now. You just need a little more time."

Kurt lowered his hands and lifted his head. His fingers flew across the keys. When he found his brother this time, he followed the Jaguar from camera to camera, watching in horror as it took an exit he was familiar with.

His stomach churned with fear. His brother could be headed anywhere, but Kurt knew that for the lie it was the moment Parker got on the A87. Kurt didn't need to look at a map to know they were headed to Skye.

To Sabryn.

He leaned back in the chair as he hit pause on the footage. He didn't trust himself, so he replayed every recording to ensure his mind wasn't playing tricks on him. A look at the bridge entry into Skye confirmed his suspicions when he saw the Jaguar.

Parker was a London Druid and forbidden from setting foot on the isle, but his brother was ignoring that directive. Parker was the perfect soldier, doing whatever it was their mother, Diana, told him. If he was on Skye, it was because London—or Diana—had decreed it.

But there was only one reason for Parker to go to Skye: to draw Kurt out. He shouldn't have told his brother or Diana about his feelings for Sabryn. He'd hoped that part of his life was dead and buried, but he should've known he wouldn't get away that easily.

Kurt stood and slammed the laptop shut in one movement before stuffing it into his rucksack and hurrying out of the flat. Parker and his Druids were already on the isle. It would take

Kurt a little over two hours to get there. That wasn't good enough.

With his blood pumping and more awake than he had been in days, he kept to the shadows and looked for a car to steal. He sent a prayer of thanks when he found a mid-nineties Volkswagen Golf sitting by itself. To his surprise, the door was unlocked. Kurt slid behind the wheel, popped the cover on the steering column, and reached past the battery and ignition for the wire bundle. He stripped the wires and brushed them together. The moment the engine roared to life, he put the car in drive and sped off. He pressed the accelerator to the floor as he wove through the village to the motorway. He didn't care about the cameras that caught him speeding. He'd return the car and pay any fines he incurred once he reached Skye.

The thing he had both yearned for and dreaded for the past six years was nearly at hand. Sabryn wouldn't take discovering his true identity well. She would be furious, and he deserved everything she would say and do to him. Elias, Carlyle, and Finn would take her side and would likely be just as angry. All of them had that right since he had deceived them for years.

Kurt glanced at his speed as he flew down the motorway. He couldn't remember the timestamp of Parker reaching Skye. Had he already found his way to Carwood Manor and confronted Sabryn? The house was sentient. Surely, it would sense that Parker couldn't be trusted and keep him out.

"What was the fucking time?" Kurt asked as he slammed his hand against the steering wheel.

His mind was jumbled, his body spent. He was running on fear and caffeine. There was no time to think about sleep as he wove through the light traffic and pushed the car faster. The needle on the speedometer couldn't go any further, but he didn't let up on the accelerator. Too much depended on him stopping Parker.

He needed to warn the Knights. They could prepare before he got there. Kurt reached over to the passenger seat and blindly dug around in the front pocket of his rucksack, searching for his mobile. When his hand brushed everything but his phone, he yanked the bag onto his lap and fished around some more, but still couldn't find it. He gave up and began to take items out of the pocket until it was empty. He kept his eyes on the road and opened every compartment, looking for the device, only to remember it had been plugged in on the kitchen counter.

"Fuck!" he shouted, furiously tossing the rucksack aside.

Another bloody mistake. And this one could cost someone their life. He could pull over and contact the Knights via his laptop, but he'd already lost hours because he hadn't checked his brother's whereabouts. He decided to keep driving and prayed it was the right choice.

All these screwups could get his friends killed. Kurt gripped the wheel tighter and wondered if there was a spell to propel a car faster. Even if there was, he didn't know it. Parker wanted him. All Kurt had to do was find his brother before he located the others. Most of their group would be at Carwood Manor, which meant no one could get to them—at least those within its walls. But what about the others *not* at the house?

Everything fell away as he focused on the road and the cars around him. He had always loved driving, even before he'd gotten his license. He'd taken every driving course there was out of sheer enjoyment for learning how to handle a vehicle. Now, he poured all he had absorbed into getting him to his friends.

He wove around cars with expert precision and took turns like he was on a racetrack. He blasted down straightaways as if on the Autobahn. All the while, he prayed the magic of Skye would protect his friends. Especially Sabryn.

If Parker found her…Kurt couldn't even finish that thought.

He didn't take his foot off the accelerator until he crossed the bridge from the mainland onto Skye. A brief look at the time on the dash showed he had reached the isle in just over an hour, but there was no time to relax. Not when Sabryn was in danger.

Kurt kept having to take his foot off the pedal because he was going too fast as he drove through Kyleakin. With his thoughts still on Sabryn, he turned and headed to the manor. The Knights called Bronwyn's house home for the moment. It was also where everyone gathered—everyone except for him.

He debated going to Rhona as the leader of the Skye Druids for a moment, but this was Knights' business. He owed it to his team to come clean about who he was and why he had kept his identity a secret.

Before Parker found them.

After an hour of over a hundred miles per hour, it was nearly impossible for Kurt to keep his speed down. The numerous winding curves didn't hamper him *or* calm the urgency to reach Carwood as quickly as possible.

"I should've called for Balladyn," he muttered.

Why *hadn't* he called for the Reaper? Balladyn could've teleported him to the manor in seconds. He inwardly berated himself for one more screwup. Kurt would never forgive himself if someone got hurt because he hadn't been thinking straight. He should've thought it all through instead of reacting—even if it was warranted after what'd happened in Washington, DC.

Finally, Kurt reached the drive to the manor. He turned on the blinker and pressed the brake to slow, only to discover his leg shaking. Adrenaline coursed through him, making his heart beat rapidly, and sweat break out on his forehead. He parked next to a black Range Rover, feeling numb and more scared than he had ever been in his life.

His brain was on autopilot, and before he knew it, he was out of the car and headed to the front door. His heart beat like a drum against his ribs with every step, hard and fast. This was it. *This* was when he told Sabryn. Of all the ways he had imagined this moment going—and there had been thousands—it had never looked like this.

He stopped before a door softly lit by sconces and adjusted the rucksack he didn't remember grabbing. Briefly closing his eyes, he rapped his knuckles on the door. No sooner had he knocked than he remembered it was three in the morning. Everyone was asleep.

He turned and looked out over the land. The best thing to do would be for him to look for the F-Pace until a more reasonable time. Maybe he could confront Parker, and Sabryn would never need to know.

"Bloody fucking hell," he muttered.

He should have searched for Parker first. One more mistake. Fortunately, with it being so late, no one had to know he was here. He took a step toward his car when the sound of locks turning reached him, followed by the soft squeak of the door's hinges as it opened. Years of hiding were ingrained in him, and he almost ducked behind one of the cars. But it was too late. He had been seen. Maybe it was time he came out of the shadows and faced the consequences of his past.

"Can I help you?"

Of course, Elias would answer the door. Kurt took a deep

breath and turned to face the Scotsman. Elias's bright blue eyes were filled with curiosity and wariness as he held the door and stood just inside the manor in a tee shirt and sweatpants, his blond hair tousled from sleep. Kurt had stared at the pictures and watched videos of the Knights for so long that he knew them as well as they knew each other. The problem was, *they* didn't know *him*. He'd always kept a barrier between them.

"Mate? Are you all right?" Elias asked, a worried frown creasing his brow.

Kurt shook his head. "Not even remotely. I have a lot to divulge, but you need to know that London Druids are on the isle and coming after all of you."

Elias's face went hard as Kurt spoke, and suspicion hardened the Scotsman's gaze. "Is that so? And I'm supposed to believe, even with that posh accent of yours, that you are no' one of them?"

"I was. Once. I haven't been for a long time. And you know that, actually."

"I doona know you."

His legs grew weak. Kurt wished there was something he could hold on to before he collapsed. "You know me as Sabertooth."

Elias searched his face for a long minute. "Bollocks. Saber would never show up. He would've contacted us another way."

"I would have if I hadn't left my mobile behind."

"I doona believe a word you're saying."

Kurt nodded slowly. He should've expected this. All the responses he had put together went right out of his head the moment Elias opened the door. He removed his rucksack to take out the laptop and opened it. Kurt had to forcibly blink his eyes to focus so he could find the footage of the warehouse explosion where he had been found. He pulled it up and spun the computer around so Elias could see, then hit play.

He watched Elias's face as the video showed Parker and a group of Druids busting into the warehouse. Just as it finished, Kurt played the second video that showed him escaping seconds before the warehouse blew.

"As you can see, that's me. That was where I had set up. I never wanted any of you to know where I was, but I was always close. Just in case." Kurt slowly closed the laptop and held it at his side. "I have other videos and recordings I can pull up to prove how I've helped the Knights."

Elias remained silent, his stare on Kurt.

"The Druids are after me," Kurt continued. "And my brother is leading them. They've been after me for days, growing closer each time. Tonight, they stopped coming for me and headed here."

"Why?" Elias demanded.

Kurt really wanted to sit down. No, what he needed was to close his eyes. Just for a second. "Parker knew I'd show if he went after Sabryn."

"Sabryn?" Elias repeated, his brow puckered. "She knows who you are?"

"Not in the way you think. She knows me as Kurt Barclay." There. He'd said it. His real identity was out. There was no going back.

There hadn't been before, but once he spoke his name, there was a finality to it.

Elias glanced behind him as he braced a hand on the door, a look of shock on his face.

Kurt inwardly winced. "She told you about us, then. That

makes sense with as close as you all are." He would have thought about that if he were thinking straight.

"I doona know the whole story. She doesna speak of it. But I know you hurt her."

"I did. And I knew she wouldn't allow me into the group if she knew who I was. But I had skills that could help you all."

Elias grunted. "So, you put them to use while deceiving us."

"I wouldn't be here now if it wasn't important. I wanted to alert you to what's happening." He needed to get back to the car and sit before he fell over. How many hours had he been awake now?

"I suppose you want us to take care of this problem for you?"

Kurt returned his laptop to his pack with slippery fingers. "It's my problem. I'll handle it." He held out the rucksack to Elias. "The password is Sabryn. It'll get you into everything. You'll find a folder with a list of safe houses. I've been moving them into aliases each of you has used in the past. There's also a contact in there to the only other white hat hacker I trust."

"I'm no' taking that."

Kurt set the bag at his feet and turned to go. He focused on the car and how many steps it would take him to reach it. He had pushed his body past its limits, but he only needed a little more time. Elias would make sure Parker didn't get close to Sabryn. Maybe then Kurt could sleep for an hour or two before he started his search for his brother.

"What are you planning?" Elias asked.

"Parker won't stop coming for me. Ever. He has orders, and he always carries them out."

"Orders? From whom?"

Kurt glanced at the stars. "Diana, our mother. I'm glad you

know the truth about me. I should've done this from the beginning."

He started for the car again. The muscles in his legs shuddered, causing him to stumble forward into the side of it.

Gravel crunched behind him. "You're in no shape to do anything but climb into bed. When was the last time you slept?"

"I can't remember." Kurt opened the door. He was so close to sitting he could almost taste it.

The door was shoved closed before he could get in.

Kurt swiveled his head to Elias. "Remove your hand, please."

"You're a Knight."

Kurt squeezed the bridge of his nose. Now that he had delivered his warning, exhaustion settled over him like a heavy blanket. He wavered precariously. If only he could sit. "As soon as Parker has me, they'll leave."

"You doona know that."

"They want me. Now, remove your hand from the door so I can go."

"I'm afraid I can no' allow that."

Kurt parted his lips to respond when everything went black.

CHAPTER TWO

"What the bloody hell is on his chest?"

"It's a fekking ward. He tattooed a fekking ward on himself. I don't know whether to be worried or impressed."

The voices, one British, one Irish, penetrated his brain. Kurt knew those voices. He had to force his exhausted eyes to open, and when he did, he found Carlyle and Finn standing next to Elias, who had his arms crossed over his chest. And all three stared down at him as he lay on a couch. By the way the other two regarded him with interest, Elias had apparently filled them in. The only Knight missing was Sabryn. Had they left her out? Or had she refused to see him?

It was probably the latter. And fuck, that hurt as much as he knew it would.

Kurt shoved aside his fatigue and pushed himself into a sitting position. He rubbed his sore jaw and glared at Elias. "Did you punch me?"

"You were no' listening," Elias said with a shrug.

Carlyle sat on the arm of a chair, his bare foot propped up on the sofa cushion as he locked his turquoise eyes on Kurt. Recently combed auburn waves and the sweats adorning his body said that he, too, had recently woken. "Took us ten minutes to wake you. I didn't think Elias hit that hard."

"I hit verra hard," Elias stated with a smirk directed at Carlyle.

Finn, with his dark brown hair and even darker brown eyes, was in his usual jeans and a tee. "It wasn't the hit. Look at him," he said, jerking his chin toward Kurt. "He looks like shite."

Kurt felt like it, too. He swung his legs over the side of the couch and got to his feet, only to have Elias drop his arms and stand in his way. Kurt ran a hand down his face, trying to chase away the brain fog. "Your best option is to let me leave."

"Not until we know everything," Carlyle said.

Kurt threw up his arms and let his hands slap against his legs. "Doesn't Skye have enough problems? I can take at least one away."

"Why do they want you?" Finn interjected.

Kurt felt himself weaving and sank back onto the couch before he fell. If only he could shut his eyes. "I didn't follow the plan. Diana doesn't like that."

"Diana?" Carlyle asked.

"My mum. She prefers to be called Diana rather than Mother." Kurt worked his sore jaw.

"How deep is she in the London Druids?" Carlyle asked.

Kurt turned to meet his gaze. "Deep. Diana has always set her sights on the top."

"Good luck with that," Finn murmured.

Carlyle blew out a breath. "Which means she's likely working with Thomas."

The group on Skye had just learned that Carlyle's father,

Thomas, was running the London Druids—not a group of elders as others in the organization believed.

"She might be," Kurt conceded. "But Diana always has a plan."

"And what is that plan now?" Elias demanded.

Kurt scrubbed his hands over his face and blinked several times, trying to stay awake. "Your guess is as good as mine, but it must have something to do with me. She wouldn't send Parker to Skye otherwise."

"We're going to need more than that," Finn said.

Kurt leaned back against the cushion. "Diana wants a dynasty. It's why she married my father. She did her homework and looked at the lineage of every male London Druid until she found one that fit her schemes. My father, the poor sod, fell in love with her. He thinks she can do no wrong. Whatever she wants, she gets. Diana doesn't just run the house. She dictates the lives of everyone around her."

Carlyle quirked a brow. "But not you?"

"She did for a long time," Kurt admitted. "Too long, actually. It was drilled into Parker and me from birth. She is the matriarch of our family, and she takes the role seriously."

Carlyle sat up straight as he murmured, "Bloody hell. Your mum is Diana Barclay, Viscountess Bridemere."

"The very one," Kurt replied.

"I knew the name Barclay sounded familiar." Carlyle looked at Finn and Elias. "Lady Diana doesn't take no for an answer to anything. She's beautiful and charming and, from what I've heard, very persuasive."

Finn swung his dark gaze to Kurt. "A lot of mums are like that."

"You don't understand. She wants a dynasty, and you only get that when you're at the top," Kurt said.

Carlyle grinned. "What he's saying is that Diana is going after Thomas."

"Then we let them duke it out," Elias said with a dismissive shrug.

Kurt shook his head. "If only it were that easy. She'll work with Thomas until the very end. She's gained a lot of trust in the organization. She might be able to pull it off."

"How do you fit into those plans?" Finn said.

Kurt rubbed his palms on his thighs. It would be so easy to lean back and close his eyes. He'd be asleep in a second. "Parker might listen to her, but he's got a wicked temper that he does little to control. On top of that, he's not smart enough to be the leader she needs."

"And you are, I take it?" Elias asked.

"I'm the safer bet." Kurt shook his head as irritation swelled. "She let me think I had escaped. I should've known she'd pull me back in somehow."

Finn grunted. "Are you sure your brother is here to bring you home?"

Kurt frowned and looked at each of them. "What do you mean?"

"He's asking if Parker is here to kill you," Elias said.

Kurt shook his head. "Family is too important to Diana. That isn't an option."

"How long has it been since you talked to your family?" Carlyle asked.

Kurt said, "Six years."

"That's a long time. People change," Elias pointed out.

Carlyle twisted his lips. "And you won't know until you and Parker are face-to-face."

"Why not just call him?" Finn asked with a shrug.

Elias's brows rose in astonishment. "That's actually a good idea."

Finn cut him a flat look, affronted. "You say that as if I don't have good ideas."

"They are few and far between," Carlyle said with a chuckle.

Finn made a sound in the back of his throat. "Both of you can fek right off."

Kurt watched it all, fascinated with the dynamics and comradery between them. It was something he'd longed to have from his earliest memory. And he might have been able to have that with Parker, but Diana's need for power ensured it never happened.

"What do you think?" Elias asked him. "Do you want to call Parker?"

It was the last thing Kurt wanted. "I can. I'm not sure if we'll get any answers, but it won't hurt."

"He needs to sleep first. He can barely sit up," Carlyle said.

"Who can barely sit up?"

They all froze at the sound of Sabryn's voice. It was Finn who stepped aside, giving Kurt a view of her standing in black pajamas and fuzzy pink socks with lime green aliens. His breath left him as he gazed up at her, starving for a taste of her, aching to hold her. It had been six long years since he had stood in the same room with her. Six lifetimes of going over his mistakes and seeing all the ways he'd hurt her.

He'd stared at her picture for so long that seeing her in the flesh was almost surreal. She hadn't changed much. If anything, she had gotten more beautiful. Her inky hair was cut at her jawline, showing off her long, slender neck. She had always had an amazing body with legs that went on forever. He had once caressed a finger over her high cheekbones. Had kissed her lips and heard her moans of pleasure. Had gazed into her fathomless, deep blue eyes.

Those gorgeous orbs locked onto him now. He tensed, waiting for her explosion of anger.

"I'm making coffee. Who wants some?" she asked as she walked away.

Kurt had prepared for every conceivable reaction Sabryn might have—except being ignored. It left more of an impact than any words she might have said.

CHAPTER THREE

The moment Sabryn's eyes locked with Kurt's, it felt as if the very world had been snatched from under her feet. Her brain refused to acknowledge what she was seeing. At first, she'd believed she had imagined him. After all, she had done it countless times before. But he didn't vanish this time.

Remaining in the same room with him was impossible, so she turned and walked out. Her legs felt wooden, and her feet weighed down while blood pounded in her ears, drowning out sound.

Kurt was here.

Inside the manor.

Talking to the boys.

How? When?

Why?

Every question made her bristle, roiling rage growing in her chest and shooting through her body like lightning. She ran up the stairs to her room, shutting and locking the door before rushing into the bathroom and closing and barring that door, too. She leaned against it, fighting the dismay and shock.

The seething, smoldering indignation.

A scream bubbled up. She clenched her lips and frantically grabbed the hand towel, burying her face in it as a scream of denial burst free.

All the pain, heartache, misery, and despair crashed down on her with the intensity of a tsunami. She crumpled to the floor, her legs no longer able to support her as the dam broke in a torrent of tears. Her body was racked with sobs. Harrowing memories barreled back from their incarceration deep within her mind where she had cast them. They slammed into her, one after the other, in quick succession, ricocheting around in her head on a loop.

There was no rejecting them, no disregarding them. The memories were there to stay now, compelling her to face the endless silence that had met her when she needed Kurt the most. The boundless confusion regarding what she had done wrong that made him turn away from her without an explanation. Those recollections forced her to recall each unendurable, gut-wrenching moment of emptiness after he'd left.

And all it had taken to drown in the abyss of misery once more was coming face-to-face with Kurt again.

When the tears eventually dried, she found herself curled in a fetal position on the floor. She was raw and numb after the emotional hurricane, her nerves frayed. The carefully constructed walls she had built around her heart were wobbly but still standing. Now that the worst of the internal storm had passed, she could think rationally. With that came two more questions: How had Kurt found her? And why was he at Carwood?

It wasn't a coincidence. She was positive of that.

He looked like he'd been through something terrible, given the dark bags under his eyes and his drawn face. A part of her wanted to uncover what it was. But the other part, the incensed part that couldn't forget—or forgive—didn't care.

She hugged the towel against her and brought her knees to her chest. She might have only glimpsed him for a heartbeat, but she had *seen* everything. He looked older, wearier. More cynical, perhaps. Like he had seen or done things that had irrevocably changed him.

Yet the bastard had the gall to be as handsome as ever. His sun-kissed brown locks were longer and disheveled, but it looked good on him. He sported an unkempt beard as if he hadn't had time to shave. Unfortunately, it only enhanced his striking jawline and chin.

His nose had a bump that hadn't been there before, confirming it had been broken at least once. The asshole's lips were just as full and sensual as ever—the kind of mouth no man had the right to possess. His baby blue eyes were as startlingly pale and hypnotizing as they had been the first time she'd seen him.

Sabryn shut off thoughts of Kurt's looks. Not only did they have nothing to do with why he had come to the isle, but thinking about how good he still looked only caused her outrage to grow. She sighed and pressed her hot cheek against the cool tile. She couldn't stay in the bathroom forever. One of the boys would eventually come looking for her, and she didn't want anyone to know that Kurt's arrival had affected her so badly. No one needed to know the depths of her pain. Especially not Finn, Carlyle, and Elias.

She'd find out what Kurt wanted and then send him on his way. All without giving in to the emotions that had crippled her in the privacy of the bathroom. She had been caught unawares. It wouldn't happen again. She had lived through him leaving her. Had even grown stronger. This momentary lapse was just that. A lapse. She was made of sterner stuff and wouldn't allow one man the power to bring her to her knees a second time.

With that, she picked herself up off the floor and purposefully kept her gaze away from the mirror. There was no need to see her swollen eyes or red nose. She washed her face and dabbed it dry, only then daring to look at herself. There were still traces of her meltdown, and that wouldn't do.

Sabryn stripped out of her pajamas and took a shower. The hot water soothed her tense muscles and erased any evidence of her tears. Once she'd dried off, she walked into her bedroom and to the closet, where she had hung up the few items of clothing she owned. She needed to wear something she felt great in because it would be her armor.

She chose her beloved, long-sleeved black shirt that showed off her curves while also hanging softly against her. Her hand hovered over black jeans, but she opted for stonewashed black instead because they were newer and fit amazing.

Sabryn returned to the bathroom and put some gel in her hair before running her fingers through the chin-length bob to let it dry naturally. At one time, she'd had an intense makeup routine. Now, it was just tinted moisturizer with the occasional mascara and lip gloss. She returned to the bedroom and the small jewelry box with various earrings for her many piercings. She spent time choosing specific ones to adorn her ears before slipping her feet into her Dr. Martens lace-up boots.

Only then did she inspect herself in the full-length mirror. Her face was no longer pale, nor was her nose red. She shook her head so the ends of her damp hair swayed, then turned from one side to the other to inspect her clothes.

"I'm not the girl from DC," she told her image. "I'm not the girl he knew. I'm stronger, smarter. I have a new family now. I'm a badass who doesn't need a man. I don't need *him*. He can never hurt me again."

Sabryn took a deep breath and walked to the door. The moment she opened it, she found Bronwyn, her shoulder-length brunette hair gathered in a low ponytail. She held a cup of coffee as she leaned against the wall.

She held out the mug to Sabryn. "Are you okay?"

The petite owner of the manor was also Elias's lover, which made Bronwyn part of the Knights' family. "Thanks," Sabryn said, taking the steaming cup and bringing it to her lips.

"I saw you on the stairs earlier," Bronwyn continued, her hazel eyes watching Sabryn closely.

She inwardly winced. "Ah."

"I've never seen you wear such a look."

"I'm…" Sabryn was going to say *fine*, but it would be a lie. She looked into the dark liquid in the mug and shrugged. "I'll be okay."

Bronwyn leaned back against the wall and bit the side of her lip. "I'm here if you need anything."

"Thank you."

"Elias, Finn, and Carlyle have all been up here—separately, mind you—to see you."

Sabryn sipped the coffee, hoping the caffeine would fortify her for what was to come. "Did you send them away?"

"I didn't need to. They knocked once, and when you didn't respond, they left."

She eyed the pretty Scotswoman. "It seems you're going out of your way not to say anything. I take it Elias told you who's here?"

Bronwyn's chin dipped. "He did."

"Did he, ah, say anything else?" Sabryn hated herself for asking, but she needed details. The problem was, she couldn't actually find the words to say that.

Bronwyn shook her head. "He said he needed to talk to you first."

It must be serious if Elias didn't tell Bronwyn. Anxiety churned in Sabryn's stomach.

"The house will remove him. All you have to do is ask," Bronwyn stated.

Sabryn's eyes prickled with tears. Bronwyn knew nothing of Kurt or their past, but she was showing her support, which meant the world to Sabryn. "I love you."

"I love you, too," Bronwyn replied with a soft smile. "We have your back. I hope you know that."

"I do. But thanks for the reminder."

Bronwyn adjusted her shirt as she pushed away from the wall. "They're waiting for you."

"No. They're waiting for *us*. We need to get Song. This is family business."

Bronwyn nodded. "Then let's go."

They silently walked down the hall to the room Song and Carlyle shared. Song answered the door bleary-eyed but took one look at the two of them and hastily put on some clothes as she gathered her long, luxurious black hair into a messy bun. Then, the three of them walked down to the main floor. Sabryn's knees threatened to give out with each step.

Her apprehension became so great that her hands shook so

badly she couldn't drink her coffee without spilling it. Bronwyn took it from her and set it on a table in the foyer, then turned to the left where the double doors to the library sat closed. Whatever Sabryn learned on the other side would change things.

It seemed Kurt upended her life anytime he was in it. She knew what to expect this time. She knew *him*. The only way he would hurt her is if she allowed him to get close. He'd had his chance with her and had chosen something else. It took Sabryn a moment to realize that the doors hadn't opened. She looked at both Bronwyn and Song, who each had a hand on a knob, waiting for her.

"Let's get this over with," she said.

The women opened the doors and walked in ahead of her. Sabryn scanned the cozy room—one of her favorites. She inhaled the scents of books, leather, and fire as she entered. The walls were stocked with books, the floor-to-ceiling bookcases only broken up by the large hearth, double doors, and the stunning window overlooking the front of the estate.

The room was quiet and lit mainly by the flames dancing in the fireplace. The sconces were on yet dimmed to their lowest setting. Elias sat on the sofa facing the hearth, perched on the edge of the cushion near the arm. Finn stood near the fireplace, one arm resting on the mantel as he stared into the flames. Carlyle was at the window, gazing out to the dawning new day.

And Kurt sat in the chair to the left. His head lifted as the doors opened. She purposefully kept her gaze from meeting his. She'd seen enough that morning. The problem came when Bronwyn sat next to Elias and Song beside her. That left the only other chair—the one facing Kurt.

Sabryn briefly thought about standing but didn't want anyone

—especially, Kurt—to think she was bothered by his arrival. So, she lowered herself into the chair and turned her head to Elias.

His blue eyes, usually bright and engaging, looked troubled. Elias parted his lips as if to speak and then closed them. Carlyle walked to stand behind Song, his fingers on her shoulders as if the very act of touching her calmed him. Bronwyn nudged Elias as Song looked up at Carlyle, a question in her eyes. It was Finn who finally spoke.

"I'm sorry, Sabryn," he said, turning his dark eyes to her. "We should've handled things better this morning."

Elias nodded. "We were no' trying to keep anything from you."

"Absolutely not," Carlyle agreed. "We were attempting to acquire the facts."

Sabryn rested her arms on the chair and endeavored to calm her racing heart. It was futile as long as she could see Kurt staring at her from the corner of her eye. "And what are those facts?"

All three looked at each other as if expecting one another to speak.

Kurt blew out a breath. "That's a question I should answer. I didn't show up out of nowhere. I knew where you were because I'm Saber."

Sabryn had expected something drastic, but not this. Her stomach dropped to her feet as she dug her fingers into the leather chair arms. She glared at Elias, expecting him to laugh and say it was all a big joke, but he didn't. Instead, he dropped his chin to his chest. She felt another scream welling.

"Saber?" Bronwyn asked Kurt. "As in the fifth member of the Knights? The hacker?"

Leather creaked as Kurt shifted in his chair. "The very one," he replied in that highborn British accent she had once loved.

"You went out of your way to make sure no one knew your identity. What changed?" Song asked, wielding her refined British accent like a blade.

Sabryn still couldn't bring herself to look directly at Kurt. Instead, she focused her gaze on the coffee table between them, where she could still see him in her periphery.

He ran a hand down his face. "If I had been thinking straight, I never would have come here. I'd have gone straight to Parker."

Sabryn's eyes jerked to him at the mention of his brother. Kurt stared at the floor, slowly shaking his head. She thought back to the warehouse attack. He'd said the London Druids had tracked him. It had never entered her mind that he had connections to them or might even be one. Everything was starting to make sense.

"He's been tracking me since the warehouse," Kurt continued. "I'd lose him for a short time, but he always found me again. I hacked a city's CCTV system and saw one of the Druids with him using a tracking spell. The wards and protection spells I used weren't working effectively. So, I made adjustments."

Song quirked a brow. "What kind of adjustments?"

"He fekking tattooed a ward on his chest," Finn stated.

Kurt grimaced and shifted in the chair. "Three wards, actually. It did the trick. I thought I had shaken Parker. Then I tracked him and saw he was headed toward Skye. The problem is, I've not slept more than about fifteen minutes in four days and wasn't thinking clearly. Which is why I didn't track him in time. He had four hours on me by the time I realized he was coming here."

"London Druids don't travel to Skye," Bronwyn said. "Why would you think they'd head here?"

Kurt's baby blue eyes slid to Sabryn, his gaze pinning her to her chair. "Parker knew I'd come if they went after Sabryn."

CHAPTER FOUR

Kurt's heart missed a beat when Sabryn finally met his gaze, but only because he had surprised her. She showed no outward emotion otherwise. The same couldn't be said for Finn, Elias, and Carlyle. The atmosphere in the room changed the moment they realized he was the man who had hurt Sabryn.

He felt their furious looks, sensed their rage. The tension in the room grew, and he fully expected all three to give him the pounding he deserved. But their attack didn't come, at least not from their fists. It came from expressions that could flay him alive and a silent promise for recompense later.

Kurt couldn't tear his gaze from Sabryn. He didn't care that she thought less of him than the dirt beneath her shoe. He was in the same room as her after years of wondering if he would ever get the chance again. The red-orange glow of the fire bathed the right side of her face in fiery light in direct contrast to her icy regard. Yet still, he burned for her. Ached with a soul-deep hunger that would forever seek a connection to her.

Song looked from him to Sabryn and then back again. Her eyes narrowed slightly before she crossed one leg over the other, a new frostiness in her demeanor. He hadn't expected a warm welcome from anyone. The fact that he was inside the manor still shocked him. He'd anticipated the house tossing him out and barring him from ever seeing Sabryn again.

Kurt cleared his throat. "I left the safe house without grabbing my mobile. I thought about pulling over and sending a message through my laptop but decided to drive to the isle to warn you instead. My intent was to find Parker." He paused and rubbed his forehead, allowing his lids to close for a few seconds. "If I had been thinking clearly, I would have. I was worried about what he might do to Sabryn, and the next thing I knew, I was here."

"You'd have gone to your brother and given away all our secrets?" Finn looked at Elias. "You should've hit him harder."

"You hit him?" Bronwyn asked her lover.

Elias shrugged. "I had to make him stop, and he wouldna listen."

Kurt wasn't sure how much longer he could keep his eyes open. Even his throbbing jaw wasn't keeping him awake. The faces around him kept going in and out of focus, and he was having difficulty keeping track of the questions being tossed about. He just needed to get the story out so they could let him go to his brother. Or sleep. Bloody hell, how he wanted to shut his eyes and sleep for days—maybe even weeks.

"I would never tell anyone anything about us," Kurt declared.

Carlyle grunted and crossed his arms over his chest. "Us? You're not one of us, mate."

Kurt rubbed his eyes. It was the wrong thing to do. The moment his eyes shut, he felt himself falling asleep. He jerked awake when he leaned to the side. His time was running out. He swallowed, the action proving difficult. "Parker won't stop looking. If he doesn't find me or Sabryn, he'll hurt others. There's enough going on here without adding this."

"And yet you brought it straight to our door," Elias replied.

Kurt took a breath and parted his lips, but the argument he'd had vanished like a puff of smoke. He couldn't even remember what Elias had said. His eyelids wouldn't stay open. He'd been sitting for too long. He needed to get up and get his blood pumping, or he'd pass out. He scooted to the edge of the chair and struggled to stand, but his legs wouldn't hold him. He was reminded of Sabryn watching him—observing but not talking.

All these years, he'd thought she would blast him with her anger and maybe even her magic when he saw her again. But in the end, she merely disregarded him. She had moved on. Maybe she hadn't forgiven him for hurting her, but she wasn't holding on to the same feelings he was. And that cut deep—deeper than he'd been prepared for.

It wasn't as if he didn't deserve it, though. She didn't know the whole story, and he prayed she never learned. If she did, she'd likely kill him.

"I need to rest," he told the room. "Give me half an hour to sleep, and I'll answer the rest of your questions."

Finn faced him. "After all you've just told us, you want to sleep?"

Kurt tried to answer, but everything went black for the second time that day.

CHAPTER FIVE

Sabryn could only watch as Kurt pitched forward and crashed into the coffee table as he passed out. Everyone else sprang into action, checking to make sure he was unharmed as they moved him to the sofa. She remained sitting.

"Fek me," Finn murmured as he straightened. "He passed smooth out."

Carlyle ran a hand through his hair. "He said he hasn't slept in four days."

"I can't believe he stayed awake for as long as he did and drove here," Bronwyn replied.

Song looked around the room. "Now what?"

That's when five pairs of eyes turned to her. Sabryn slowly got to her feet. "We wait for him to wake, I suppose."

Elias stepped in front of her when she started out of the library. "He's the Brit from DC."

"Is there a question in there somewhere?" Sabryn asked.

Carlyle came to stand beside Elias. "We're not asking for

details."

"Good," she said before he could say more. "Because you're not getting them."

Finn joined them. "We jus—"

"What?" Sabryn interrupted. "How long have you three known who he was?"

All three jerked back as if struck.

"Since he arrived," Elias replied.

Finn gaped at her. "You think we'd keep something like that from you?"

"You were alone with him." Sabryn looked at each of them, then shrugged. "What else was I supposed to think?"

Carlyle calmly said, "You're supposed to trust us. We're family."

"Then why didn't anyone come get me when he arrived?" Sabryn asked.

Bronwyn moved between them. "All right. Tempers are running hot this morning. I think we all need to take a breather and calm down."

"I doona know," Elias answered Sabryn. "It wasna done out of malice, no matter what you might think. Something told me to protect you."

Sabryn smiled through her watery gaze and glanced at the ceiling. "Would you have told me?"

"Of course," Finn stated vehemently.

Carlyle nodded once, his turquoise eyes serious. "Without hesitation."

Sabryn wanted to believe them. She had no reason *not* to believe the boys. They had battled together, laughed together, argued together, and created a family between them. They had always had each other's backs. She had never questioned them—not until Kurt arrived.

"You're the glue that binds us," Finn told her.

Sabryn swallowed past the lump of emotion in her throat. Her irritation and ire had nothing to do with the boys and everything to do with learning Saber's true identity. She dashed away a stray tear and looked at her five family members. "I'm sorry. I shouldn't take this out on you. I know you wouldn't leave me out."

"Don't think twice about it," Carlyle told her.

Elias pulled her and Bronwyn into his arms, and then Song, Carlyle, and Finn joined the group hug.

"I'll be happy to toss him out," Finn offered.

Sabryn laughed with the others, breaking the tension.

"He's here," Parker said, standing outside bathed in the morning sunshine, admiring how the light lit upon the perfectly still loch.

The brunette with the large breasts and tight arse leaned her front against the Jaguar. "How can you be sure?"

The first set of Edinburgh Druids had died quickly. Parker had expected the same from these, which is why he hadn't bothered to learn their names. He'd named them for their attributes. This one was Boobs.

"I know my brother. He'll move Heaven itself for Sabryn," Parker replied.

"Assuming she's here."

"Oh, she's here."

Boobs flipped around, thrusting out her ample bosom covered

in the tight shirt and drawing his gaze. She dropped her head back, letting her straight, dark hair puddle on the car. He imagined grasping a handful of it and holding her head back as he thrust inside her until she begged him to let her cum.

"If Kurt cares for her so much, why isn't he with her?" she asked.

"That's a long story. The short version is, he can't." Parker pulled his gaze from Boobs and refocused on the loch. "Not without repercussions."

"From who?"

"It's from whom," he corrected.

Boobs rolled her hazel eyes. "From *whom*?"

"Me."

She smiled and straightened, closing the distance between them with a sultry walk. She didn't stop until her body touched his. "You wield a lot of power."

"You like that, do you?" he asked with a sly smile. Power turned everyone on.

"Who doesn't?" she asked seductively, pressing her breasts against him.

Parker kept his hands in his pockets instead of cupping those delectable orbs that he knew would spill out of his hands. Damn George for sending such a tasty morsel. It had been two weeks since Parker had last bedded someone, and he was horny. He could take what Boobs offered, and he would. Once he saw to what he needed to do. For now, he couldn't take his eyes off the prize. Not when he was so close.

A soft hand came to rest on his chest, her long nails skimming down his shirt. "I'd like to go back with you to London."

He snorted, thinking she was jesting. He quirked a brow when he glanced at her and spotted her serious expression. "Is that so?"

"It is. Why does that seem so farfetched?"

"The truce between our two groups is tenuous at best. George wouldn't appreciate me luring one of her Druids away."

"George has done a decent job of amassing all the fractured groups in the city, but she's not doing anything with us." Boobs leaned harder against him and met his gaze. She bit her lower lip provocatively. "London has power. That's who I want to be with."

Parker's gaze lowered to her mouth, and he imagined those lips wrapped around his cock. He bit back a groan as the image made him throb with need. "You would choose London over Edinburgh?"

"It's an easy choice. You don't see Edinburgh welcoming Druids from outside the city with open arms now, do you? London wants Druids. And I have something to offer them—and you."

Fuck. She was beautiful and willing and would be a nice way to spend a few hours. He pulled his gaze away from her, all the while trying to ignore the weight of her breasts on his arm. "I think you might be right."

"I can be an asset. To you," she whispered huskily in his ear.

Parker's eyes closed as his balls tightened. He started reaching for her when, through the haze of lust, he recalled his orders. He shook off her spell. "We'll talk about it once I have my brother."

Boobs straightened, but her hand lingered on his chest before dropping to her side. "What do you think London will do to him?"

"They'd likely kill him for working with the Skye Druids, but London didn't send me after him."

"Then who did?"

"Diana."

A small frown puckered Boob's brow. "Who's Diana?"

"Our mother."

"Mummy sent you after him? She has *you*. Why would she want a son who chose another group over his family?"

Finally, someone got it. Parker kept those words to himself. He would never say them aloud. To anyone. "Kurt went against her, and he has to pay the price."

"Your mum doesn't fuck around, does she?"

"Not in the least."

Boobs twisted her lips and moved to stand in front of him. She smoothed her hands down his chest before looking at him through her lashes. "Sounds as if she prefers your brother to you."

He tensed, mainly because it wasn't just how he felt—it was the truth. No matter what he did, he could never live up to perfect Kurt. Not even after he'd abandoned their family for his little group of saviors. And in that time, Diana hadn't so much as said Kurt's name.

Parker had begun to believe she had finally let his brother go and accepted him as her heir—he wanted it. Kurt didn't. But just when he was settling into that role, Diana gave him orders to track Kurt down. She even gave him a location as if she had always known where her eldest was.

"He's firstborn," Parker said tightly.

"He matters only if he's alive," Boobs replied, her fingers trailing up to his shoulders.

Parker was all too familiar with that particular fantasy. He had killed his brother a million different ways in his head, but dreaming about it and getting away with it when answering to Diana were two different things.

He looked around the landscape. Though he *was* on Skye, where any number of things could be the cause of his brother's death. Kurt wouldn't go easily, though.

Boobs pressed herself against him again, her voice husky as she whispered, "So, you have thought about it. You have the power. You're handing that over to him as long as you do Diana's bidding. Keep it. It's what those with power do."

It's exactly what his mother would do. She'd probably done it hundreds of times already.

Boobs grinned and threaded her fingers into his hair, pulling his head down to her lips. "And I can't imagine you sharing anything."

He grabbed a handful of her hair and yanked her head back. He said nothing, just stared down at her before kissing her.

CHAPTER SIX

SKYE DRUIDS

Kurt opened his eyes to find himself looking up at a ceiling once more. Though a different one this time. It took him a moment to remember that he had driven to Skye and revealed his identity to the Knights. As the rest came rushing back, he gazed around the library. He didn't remember how he'd gotten on the sofa. His feet dangled over the arm, but at least his eyes no longer felt as if they were made of sand.

He curled his toes, surprised to discover someone had removed his shoes. They had also covered him with one of the throws. The fire popped, bringing his attention to it. He debated whether to roll onto his side and go back to sleep, but as lovely as that sounded, he needed to finish explaining things to the Knights.

Kurt lifted the blanket and swung his legs over the side of the sofa as he sat up. He bit back a groan at the stiffness in his body. He rolled his neck to stretch the muscles and then rotated his arms. His right shoulder popped painfully from an old cricket injury from university. After stretching his arms, he turned his attention to his back, but nothing he did relieved the pain there.

Getting older was bloody hard. He used to be able to sit or sleep anywhere. Now, he had to use an ergonomic setup to stave off the inevitable aches. But he hadn't had any of that the past few days and compounded by a lack of sleep, loads of coffee, and very little food, it was no wonder he felt as if he had been run over a few times. He put his hands on his lower back and arched it. When he still couldn't get it to crack, he twisted from one side to the other, generating several pops that instantly relieved some of the discomfort. A glance out the window showed it was dark. He was surprised they'd allowed him to sleep so long.

He scrubbed his hands down his face, and just as he was about to stand, his neck prickled with awareness. He wasn't alone. Kurt lifted his head and scanned the room. No one was in either chair or behind him, and the doors were closed. He stilled before turning his head to the left. Standing in the corner, hidden by shadows, stood an imposing figure.

Kurt had seen pictures and videos, but nothing could compare to being in the presence of a Fae. Or a Reaper. A Fae Reaper? A Reaper Fae? Kurt wasn't sure what to call Balladyn. He had once been a general in the Light Fae Army before he was betrayed. Then, he'd killed the Dark King and took over the throne before being betrayed again. That's when Death approached him to become a Reaper. Included in that impressive resume was that Balladyn was now the Warden of Skye and deeply in love with Rhona, the Skye Druids' leader.

Balladyn stood as still as a statue, his red-ringed silver eyes locked on Kurt. Tall and foreboding, Balladyn's command and authority seemed ingrained in his DNA. All someone had to do was look at him to know not to fuck with him.

How long had he been there? Did the others believe Kurt needed someone to watch over him? By the flat stare the Fae gave him, it was obvious Balladyn had been told everything.

Kurt swallowed and scrunched up his face at the taste in his mouth. He spotted a glass of water on the coffee table and drained it. After he'd set it back down, he put his hands on his thighs and stood.

"I'm ready," he stated.

"Ready?" Balladyn repeated, his Irish accent both thick and refined. "For what?"

Kurt glanced at the door. "To answer more questions."

Balladyn stepped from the shadows. Kurt tensed as he eyed the towering Dark. The light hit on Balladyn's straight, mid-back-length black hair streaked with silver. He wore dark jeans and a chambray button-down with the sleeves rolled up to his elbows. He dressed like any ordinary bloke on the street, but nothing about the Reaper was average.

"Your deceit hasn't been received well," the Reaper said.

Kurt held his gaze. "I'm aware."

"I double-checked your story. Everything is as you said," Balladyn continued. "There's nothing left of the warehouse."

"I made sure there was nothing left to find. I may have withheld my identity, but I was always fully onboard and aligned with what the Knights were doing."

"They invited you into their group. Embraced you."

Pain lanced through Kurt's chest. "I was proud to be included."

"Yet you didn't tell them who you were."

"I couldn't. I knew they would cut off all ties the moment I did."

Balladyn raised a black brow. "They? Or Sabryn?"

Fuck. It was like being interrogated by Professor Brown at uni. As uncomfortable as it was, it was time for the truth. All of it. "Sabryn. I suppose she told you about our history?"

"She has not."

Kurt was taken aback. "She didn't?"

"That surprises you?"

He nodded, ignoring the queasiness that suddenly developed. "I assumed she had told the lads. Is that why you're here, then? You want me to tell you?"

"It's none of my business. That's between you and Sabryn. I'm here to get information on your brother."

"Of course," Kurt said with an inward shake of his head at his idiocy. "You're trying to find him. Let me get my laptop."

Balladyn held up a hand to halt him. "We can handle it."

So, this was how it would be. Kurt hadn't let himself think past Sabryn's anger to what might happen—not just with the Knights but with the other Skye Druids. They had leaned heavily on him— all of them. He had taken great pride in being able to lend his expertise in getting them out of jams as well as to keep them safe. That was likely all over now. He didn't want to walk away, but he would, knowing they were all safe.

"Right," Kurt murmured as the impact of his actions began to crash down on him. He cleared his throat and tried to focus, but the dark feeling swelling in his chest made it difficult to breathe. "Ah…Parker's being driven around in a racing-green Jaguar F-Pace. He'll stay somewhere expensive."

"Thank you."

"Diana won't stop sending others for me," Kurt said as Balladyn headed for the door.

The Reaper halted and swung his head to Kurt. "Our concern is the London Druids on the isle. If more come, we'll take care of it."

"I can make it all go away."

Balladyn turned to him. "By turning yourself over to your brother, I suppose?"

"It's why he's here."

"Do you wish to return to your family?"

Kurt rubbed his forehead as he snorted. "If you checked my story, then you saw the lengths I went to in order to stay ahead of Parker and away from them. That should be answer enough."

"Yet you're willing to give yourself up now."

"If I had been thinking clearly, I would've reached out to Parker the moment I knew he was headed to Skye. I wouldn't have come here. I would've gone directly to him."

Balladyn briefly twisted his lips. "You say you weren't thinking clearly."

"I wasn't. That's what days without sleep will do. I even left my mobile at the last safe house."

"Did you ever stop to think that maybe you came here not only to warn us but also to reveal your identity? And maybe redeem yourself?"

Kurt glanced away. "I hadn't."

Balladyn grunted and continued toward the door. Kurt opened his mouth to stop him, but no words came out. He watched the Reaper walk out and leave the door open. He looked out into the foyer, but no one else entered the room. He picked up the faint sounds of music drifting through the house.

Another spike of nausea made him wince. The amount of caffeine he had put into his body had done a number on his stomach. He was hungry, but the idea of eating anything made him queasier. The only way to stop the cycle was to make himself eat.

Kurt raked his fingers through his hair and walked around the couch to the open door. Once in the foyer, he looked left to where a large, round table sat atop a circular rug. A vase full of flowers rested in the middle. Beyond that was the front door. Finally, he was inside the manor instead of looking at it through pictures the other Knights had sent.

He gazed across the foyer to another set of double doors that led into the front sitting room, where Elias had brought him last night. He turned his head to the right and spotted the stairs. Farther down the hall was the dining room and then the kitchen.

Kurt headed in that direction. As he reached the stairs, he paused and lifted his gaze. Sabryn's room was on the third floor. Was she there? Maybe they were in the war room they'd set up on the second floor. Or she might have left the manor, not wanting to be near him. He'd made a right muck of things and wasn't sure he could get himself out of it.

It had become increasingly difficult to stay behind the screens and watch his friends battle evil over the last year. Sure, he had his part to play, but he would've rather done it beside them. He might have very well blown that chance, and he only had himself to blame.

No amount of reasoning excused his dishonesty. While he had helped the Knights over the years, he was doing nothing but damage to them now. And Diana would see that continued. Unless he struck another deal with her. It was the only way they'd leave the Knights—especially Sabryn—alone.

Kurt needed to sit with that idea and work out all the possible outcomes and consequences to be sure Sabryn, the Knights, and the Skye Druids were left alone. Diana would expect him to counter her demands, meaning he had to think of her retaliation. Because there would be retribution.

He continued toward the kitchen. The music grew louder as he did, and delicious smells filled the air. Carlyle's voice rose above the lyrics as he sang along to Michael Bublé. Kurt stopped outside the door and listened, a smile forming. He'd gotten videos of the Knights playing around with Carlyle singing and cooking as Finn, Elias, and Sabryn teased him. It was nice to hear it for himself. Kurt wanted to step inside the kitchen and watch Carlyle, but he feared he wouldn't be welcome.

"It's hard to get food while standing out here."

He jerked around at the sound of Song's voice. Kurt stepped aside and motioned to the door. "Go ahead."

"You have to face the music eventually. Take my word for it. The longer you put it off, the worse it will be."

"I know that for a fact."

She glanced at the door as Carlyle's voice rose. "I imagine it's been difficult being a Knight but not actually with them."

"They shared videos and pictures."

"That isn't the same, though, is it?"

He glanced down and realized he hadn't put on his shoes. He should've put on his shoes. "No, it isn't."

"Look, I could be subtle and try to lead you to things, but it's much easier if I'm frank. Carlyle told me how you've gotten them out of tricky situations. You had their backs, and while you kept your identity a secret, it didn't stop you from joining them. I'm not saying I agree with what you did, but I've had many identities over the years and did some terrible things."

"You were forced."

One side of her mouth lifted in a smile. "My point is that you're here now. If they can forgive me, they will forgive you. Now, come on. I'm starving."

Song took his arm and led him into the kitchen. The moment they were inside, she released him and headed to Carlyle, who grabbed her and danced her around the room before dipping her and giving her a long kiss. He straightened them, then spun Song into a chair to dance back to the stove.

Kurt smiled as he watched them. But it faded when he found Sabryn at the table on her phone.

CHAPTER SEVEN

Sabryn pretended to scroll on her phone, all too aware of Kurt's arrival. She fought the urge to leave but couldn't run out of the kitchen. She'd already done that. Besides, despite the manor's size, she would eventually run into him unless she stayed in her room. Since she'd always detested being confined, that wasn't an option.

But neither could she remain around him.

Song shoved a chair across from her out with her foot. "You'll find sitting down is better," she told Kurt.

Carlyle glanced her way, but Sabryn disregarded him, too. She was very good at ignoring others. So good, her mother used to constantly nag her about it. It seemed she hadn't lost her touch. She probably shouldn't boast about it, but a person needed talents.

Kurt made his way to the table and carefully pulled the chair out more before slowly sinking into it, almost as if he expected someone to yank it out from beneath him. Sabryn might have been contemplating that very thing. It would be delightful to see him fall on his ass.

Goddamn him. She hated being the bitter ex. Why couldn't she have gotten over him? Why did the hurt still linger? The *time heals all wounds* adage was nothing but bullshit. It hadn't. Her wound had festered, each year irritating it more until it was an open sore that would seemingly never mend.

She bit her tongue hard to keep all of that to herself. And kept biting until she tasted blood. Then, she bit harder. She had to forcefully relax her hands because she'd gripped the phone so tightly her knuckles had turned white. All because Kurt had walked into the kitchen.

Couldn't Balladyn have kept him in the library?

Bitter, ha! She wasn't resentful. She was furious. Indignant. Fucking piqued.

And vengeful.

Kurt had hurt her like no other. Now that he was back in her life, she wanted her pound of flesh. To wound as she had been wounded. To have him on his knees, his heart ripped from his chest, and in so many pieces it could never be put back together again. She needed his world to crumble around him as he blindly reached out to someone, *anyone*, for help. Only to have no one answer.

The clunk of the wineglass set before her startled Sabryn. She stared at the red liquid softly swaying in the goblet until it stilled. *She* wanted to be that still. To have control over her emotions and reactions. She had been there once, locking herself away from the world. It had been the only way she could protect herself and face each new day.

And it might be the only way she could protect herself now.

Another clunk, this one heavier, as a wine bottle landed on the table. She glanced up at Bronwyn, who released the neck and moved away. Sabryn hastily returned her eyes to her screen. When she realized she hadn't scrolled in a while, she made her thumb move the images, but she wasn't really seeing anything.

"This is amazing," Song said as she looked at her glass of wine.

Bronwyn glanced at her over her shoulder, her brunette locks moving with her head. "It's one of my favorites. We found an entire case in the wine cellar, so drink up."

"Are you not a drinker, Kurt?" Song asked.

More blood filled Sabryn's mouth as she kept herself from issuing a pithy reply.

"I enjoy a nice glass, but I think I'll pass this evening," he replied.

Carlyle turned down the music. "You look better than you did before you passed out."

"I passed out?"

Sabryn couldn't stop the eye roll at the surprise in his voice. She wasn't just indignant. She was childish. He hadn't faked his exhaustion. He had collapsed.

"Rather awkwardly. On the table," Bronwyn told him.

He accepted the glass of water she handed him. "I appreciate you letting me rest."

"I don't think we had much choice," Carlyle replied with a chuckle.

Finn entered the kitchen with Elias on his heels. Sabryn met Finn's gaze before he looked at Kurt.

"What are we talking about?" Elias asked.

Bronwyn handed both Finn and Elias some wine. "Kurt passing out."

"Ah, that," Finn said and laughed.

Elias pulled out the chair across from her, his own snicker bubbling. "You should've said how tired you were."

"I believe I did," Kurt told them, his voice lighter with every word.

Carlyle shook his head, a smile in his voice when he said, "I must have missed that."

Sabryn hated that everyone seemed to accept Kurt as if he hadn't betrayed them. Sure, he had helped them for a few years or five, but he had also lied about who he was. Could she have dug and demanded an answer? Of course. And the reason she hadn't didn't matter now. What bothered her was that the boys seemed to have forgiven him.

And fuck did that feel like a betrayal.

They were *her* boys, *her* family. They should side with *her*.

And they might very well do that if they knew exactly what Kurt had done. She hadn't told them, though. Everyone had a past and someone who'd broken their heart. Those people were supposed to stay in the past, not show up in the present and slither their way into a perfectly good life.

Bitter, indignant, and downright caustic. Sabryn did not like this side of her.

"Well, I appreciate the few hours you granted me," Kurt said.

There was a beat of silence. Then Finn repeated, "Hours? Mate, you've been asleep for two days."

"What?"

Surprise flickered in Kurt's pale blue eyes, and she hated that she'd noticed.

"You were asleep for fifty hours," Elias confirmed.

Sabryn's attention shifted to her left when Bronwyn sat beside her and leaned over to whisper, "You good?"

It was on the tip of Sabryn's tongue to say, "*Yep*." Wasn't that how someone was supposed to answer that question? No one told the truth because no one wanted to hear it. But she wasn't okay. She was so far from fine that she wasn't sure she'd ever get back to *okay* again.

She couldn't do this. She couldn't stay and pretend like Kurt was one of them. Because he wasn't. And he never would be.

Sabryn started to rise when Bronwyn's hand gently rested atop her arm. Sabryn looked over at the woman who had turned from friend to sister within hours of their meeting. Bronwyn and Song were her girls. They meant as much to her as the boys did—maybe even more.

"You don't run from things," Bronwyn whispered. "Don't run from this."

That wasn't true at all. Running is exactly what she did. Sabryn looked up to answer and saw Elias observing her with a worried expression. And he wasn't the only one. Song kept Kurt engaged in conversation, allowing Sabryn a few moments with the others. They were concerned, and their silent looks told her they were still watching out for her.

She lowered her phone to the table and relaxed again in the chair. Carlyle gave her a wink as he set a plate of food in front of her. Finn slid into the chair on her other side, bolstering her, while Elias sat at the end of the table next to Bronwyn. Carlyle was about to take the chair at the other end of the table near Song and Kurt when the kitchen door swung open, and Elodie, Scott, and Filip walked in.

"Och, that smells delicious," Filip said, drawing in a deep breath. "Carlyle, can you cook for me forever?"

Sabryn reached for her fork as Elias greeted his sister and her beau, Scott. Elodie's glorious blond hair was in a French braid that hung down to the middle of her back, and her blue eyes held a welcoming smile as she was formally introduced to Kurt. Scott held out the chair for Elodie to sit before extending his hand to Kurt.

They exchanged pleasantries. Kurt knew everyone, of course, but no one *knew* him, so introductions were needed. Scott's deep blue eyes glanced Sabryn's way before he turned his head of short, dark hair toward Carlyle, who offered him some food. Elodie sat on Elias's other side, with Scott taking the seat to her left. That left Filip to fill the final chair next to Kurt.

Inevitable small talk kept the conversation moving around the table. Sabryn didn't feel like eating, no matter how good it smelled, but she had skipped both lunch and breakfast, and her head had already begun to hurt because of it. She didn't need a headache on top of everything else, so she put food in her mouth and forced herself to chew and swallow without really tasting any of it.

"How does one become a hacker?" Filip asked.

Sabryn stilled, the fork halfway to her mouth.

Filip's gray gaze darted around the table that had grown quiet. "I suppose I should no' have asked that."

"It's fine," Kurt said as he swallowed a bite of food. "It's not something I went out to learn. I had an aptitude for it. I learned most everything on my own, and the more I did, the more I wanted to do. There are two kinds of hackers, though."

"That's right. I know the…um…shite. What's the name?" Filip asked Scott.

"There are white hats and black hats," Kurt offered.

Filip snapped his fingers. "That's it. Black hat. I've heard of that. I didn't know about the white. Do you promote your services?"

Sabryn wanted to halt the conversation. She needed to stop it, but she bit her tongue instead.

Kurt cleared his throat and drank some water. "Not exactly. It's by referral."

Referral. That's right. Carlyle had said he knew of someone who could help.

As if reading her mind, Kurt said, "Carlyle didn't know who I was."

She was sure Kurt was speaking to her but still couldn't bring herself to look at him.

"I'm sorry, Sabryn. I should've come clean immediately, but I was a coward," he continued. "It was as close to you as I could get, and I took it. Every month, I told myself I'd tell you, but we were doing such good work. I liked being a part of that. With you. And the rest of the Knights. If I…I knew once you knew the truth, that would end."

Finn's voice was soft but firm when he said, "You should've told her."

Kurt set down his fork. "I'm telling everyone now. It might be late, but I'm here. And I'm going to clean up my mess. I don't know how Parker found me. I covered my tracks. No one should've been able to locate me."

"It isn't your mess. It's our mess," Carlyle said.

Scott blew out a breath. "Could the London Druids be involved?"

"It's possible," Song answered.

Bronwyn folded her hands together on the table. "Kurt, are

you sure your brother is here to take you home? If London is involved, they wouldn't do that."

"They'd just kill him," Elodie said.

Elias grunted. "So, maybe it is family."

"Like I said, my mess," Kurt replied.

Sabryn stared at her food, her stomach churning. She wanted to pick up her plate and throw it at Kurt. Instead, she gathered it and walked to the garbage to scrape the contents before rinsing it off and putting it in the dishwasher. The conversation continued, but she wasn't paying any attention.

She turned and headed out of the kitchen. She loved her family. She loved the manor. But she couldn't stay there any longer.

"Sabryn, please. Can we talk?" Kurt called.

But she kept walking. It wouldn't take her long to pack her bag.

CHAPTER EIGHT

He was losing her.

No, that wasn't exactly true. He had lost her years ago.

Kurt watched the door swing closed behind Sabryn. He wanted to call out to her. Run after her. He hadn't in DC, and it had cost him everything. Few got a second chance. Why waste it? He stood, his chair scraping across the tile.

But he didn't get anywhere as Elias, Finn, and Carlyle got to their feet, making it clear they wouldn't allow him to go after Sabryn. Kurt watched what was likely his last opportunity go down the drain. And he only had himself to blame.

The sight of Sabryn withdrawn and guarded was unbearable. Especially after years of easy, fun banter between them via text when she hadn't known the truth. He had hoped... Yet he had known in his heart this would be the outcome. It was why he hadn't told her sooner. If hiding behind a screen was the only way he could be in her life, he had been happy to take it. Now, that was gone.

"Go after her," he told the men.

Elias shook his head. "She just needs a minute."

"She's going to pack her things," Kurt replied.

Finn frowned. "She wouldn't."

Kurt blew out a breath. "It's what she does when she closes off. I invaded her space. Her family. She doesn't feel safe here anymore."

"Elias," Bronwyn called softly.

He looked down at her beseeching face before his gaze darted to Carlyle and Finn. The three left the kitchen together.

Kurt looked at the table. He thought about the few moments of comradery he had shared with the Knights. As stilted and tense as it had been, it had been as great as he had known it would be. But he didn't belong here—not at the manor, not with the Knights, and not with Sabryn.

He dipped his head to the others at the table. "Excuse me."

"Where are you going?" Bronwyn asked as he stood.

They would stop him if he told them he was headed to Parker. So, he told them what they wanted to hear. "I'm going to stay somewhere else. Sabryn shouldn't be driven from those she loves."

"There's that cottage we're working on," Filip offered.

Scott nodded as he looked from his friend to Kurt. "That's right. You can stay there."

"That's a perfect solution," Elodie said.

Kurt tried to smile but couldn't quite get his lips to move. Not only was it somewhere they knew, but it was also warded, and would tell them if he left. But he had no choice but to accept. "I appreciate the offer. Thanks."

"The keys are in the car," Scott said, pushing his chair back to stand.

Kurt slid his gaze to Song. She hadn't said anything, but she watched everything. "Tell Carlyle the meal was as delicious as I imagined it would be."

"You didn't eat much," she stated.

He glanced at his plate, which he had only taken a few bites from, and then left the kitchen to find his boots in the library. He sank onto the couch to put them on, wishing he had remained in the room instead of venturing out. A rumble of thunder broke the silence as he pushed to his feet. As he turned to leave, he spotted his rucksack propped against the door.

The front door opened, and Scott came in, shaking the rain from his dark hair. He spotted Kurt in the library and altered his direction.

"Here you go," he said, holding out the key.

Kurt jerked in surprise when Balladyn suddenly appeared beside him. "Fucking hell," he muttered.

"Those won't be needed," Balladyn told Scott and reached for Kurt.

There was no chance to get away. One moment, he was in the library. The next, he was in a cozy living room with rain beating on the roof and a fire popping in the hearth. He turned his head as a woman with long, red hair walked into the room carrying a book and a cup of something that steamed.

Her green eyes locked on him. "Hello, Kurt. I suppose you know who I am."

He glanced at Balladyn, who remained beside him, and nodded. "You're Rhona, leader of the Skye Druids."

"Thank you, baby," she said as Balladyn walked to her and bent to press a kiss to her mouth.

"Anything for you," he murmured.

Kurt looked away to give them a moment, clasping his hands behind his back and studying the pictures on the mantel. Unease settled unpleasantly in his stomach. He wasn't sure if he was about to be berated, trounced, or booted off the isle. Maybe all three.

"Please, sit," Rhona bade and sat in a comfortable-looking chair beside the couch.

Kurt walked around the coffee table to the sofa as Balladyn stood near the doorway. Kurt lowered himself onto the edge of the cushion and looked at Rhona.

"Would you like some tea? Coffee, maybe?" she offered.

He shook his head. "No, thank you."

"We've located your brother."

With everything that had just happened at the manor, Kurt had momentarily forgotten about Parker. Rhona's statement brought everything back. He rested his arms on his knees and clasped his hands. "Who has he hurt in the fifty hours I slept?"

"No one," Balladyn answered.

Kurt jerked his head to the Reaper before sliding his gaze to Rhona. "That's...unexpected. And not his usual operating procedure."

"We thought it odd, as well," Rhona agreed. "If he was here to hurt Sabryn and lure you out, why hasn't he done it? Or at least tried? Granted, she hasn't left the manor, so that could be it..."

Kurt squeezed the bridge of his nose with his thumb and forefinger as he closed his eyes. "I've not had any contact with my family for over six years." He dropped his arm and met Rhona's gaze. "They shouldn't have been able to find me. No one finds me if I don't want them to. But Parker did. He's stubborn and relentless, but he's not smart enough to know how to locate me."

"Who is?" Balladyn asked.

There was only one person. "Diana." Kurt sat back and shook his head. "My mother always had grand plans for creating an empire. She trained us to be exactly what she wanted and needed since birth."

"Heirs," Rhona murmured.

Kurt nodded. "In more ways than one."

"When did you deviate from her plan?"

"DC." Even saying it aloud was agonizing.

His world had begun and ended in the city. He had seen two futures for himself: the one Diana wanted, and the one Sabryn offered. It hadn't been a choice at all.

Rhona took a drink of her tea before holding the mug in both hands. "What happened?"

"I met Sabryn."

"And?"

Images of the past flashed in Kurt's mind, one after the other, like a slideshow. Sabryn laughing, Sabryn teasing, Sabryn falling asleep on his chest in the middle of a movie. "We had amazing chemistry from the moment we met. I fell for her hard. We were inseparable. At least until her father's accident. Then I…" He drew in a breath at the painful memories. "I wasn't there when she needed me."

"And then?" Rhona pressed.

Kurt stared into her eyes. "I went home. I tried to call her. When she wouldn't answer, I got on a plane. But she was gone by the time I got there."

"So, you looked for her," Rhona guessed.

He winced and nodded. "It's far too easy for hackers to find someone. When I realized she was in London, I wrongly thought she was there for me. I couldn't get home fast enough. Within thirty minutes of landing, I realized my folly. She wanted nothing to do with me. No matter how many times I told myself to let her go, I couldn't. I looked for a way to get back into her life. That came when she and Carlyle met. I knew of him from our mutual association with the London Druids. I used my connections to get my name—well, my hacker name—in front of him. And, as I expected, the Knights reached out when they formed."

Balladyn grunted. "And you had your way in."

"Yet you never told her who you were," Rhona said. "Why not?"

"I wanted to prove that I was worthy. That I was on her side. But as the weeks turned to months and then to years, that became increasingly difficult."

A red brow arched. "All of that just to tell her you were sorry for not being there for her? We both know there's more to the story."

Kurt pressed his lips together and silently scolded himself. Had he really thought no one would piece it together once it was all laid out? He didn't ask how they had figured it out. It didn't matter. He was tired of carrying it around. Tired of the burden that was eating away at his soul. No matter who he told or whether he could make it right, there was no absolution. Not in this life nor any other.

They needed him to fill in the blanks. But he couldn't. Not yet.

"You're right. There is more," he admitted. "And I'll share all of it with you. But I must tell Sabryn first. I don't want anyone else imparting the information before I do."

"We won't share it," Balladyn stated.

Rhona nodded. "It will stay between us three. But we need to know."

Kurt shook his head. "I owe her that much."

"I appreciate what you're trying to do, but you must understand where I'm coming from." Rhona set her cup on the table beside her. "I have a London Druid leading ten Edinburgh Druids, and they have come to my home to do harm. I cannot—will not—sit by and wait for something to happen."

"Parker knows I'm here. If I don't get to him soon, he will strike," Kurt warned.

Balladyn shrugged a shoulder. "All the more reason for you to tell us what we need to know."

"What's your plan?" Rhona asked. "Just hand yourself over to your brother to be taken home?"

Kurt ran a hand over his jaw. "It's the only way I can get him to leave."

"Not the *only* way," Balladyn said.

"You forget I know exactly how stretched thin everyone is. This isn't a fight you need to take on. There's nothing they can do that would make me give up any secrets," he argued.

Rhona rolled her eyes. "Don't be stupid. Of course, there is."

"Then wipe my memory. I know some can do it. I'll do whatever it takes to protect you."

"He's telling the truth," a female voice said from behind Balladyn.

Kurt tensed as a woman with curly, auburn hair walked around the Reaper.

"Forgive us, but we had to know," Rhona told him.

For the first time in days, Kurt smiled. "I didn't even think of that. I'm glad you did."

"This is Reaghan," Rhona said. "She's from MacLeod Castle."

He went still. He was in a room with one of the Druids from

MacLeod Castle? The surreal moment would be branded in his brain forever.

"He spoke the truth," Reaghan said as she walked to the couch and sat beside him, turning her body toward his. "Mostly."

Kurt started to argue, but she held up a hand.

"I detected something when you spoke about DC," Reaghan replied.

The words died on Kurt's lips.

"I think it's time you told us what happened," Rhona said. "As I promised before, this will stay between those in this room until you tell Sabryn."

"Not just Sabryn. I should tell the others, too," Kurt said.

Rhona dipped her head. "Deal."

Before Kurt could start, Balladyn held out a tumbler filled with whisky. Kurt accepted it with a nod of thanks and tossed it back before he began.

CHAPTER NINE

SKYE DRUIDS

"You're no' listening, Sabryn," Elias said.

She folded her jeans and set them on the bed. On her way back to the closet, she glanced at the boys standing in the doorway. "I heard you just fine."

"Obviously, you didn't if you're still packing," Finn replied.

Carlyle moved to stand in her way. "Kurt is leaving. He's probably gone already."

"I heard you." She looked at Elias. "And you." Her gaze moved to Finn. "And you. All six times you told me."

Carlyle's brow furrowed into deep grooves. "Yet you're *still* gathering your things."

"I need a few days."

"That shouldn't require all your clothes," Finn retorted.

Sabryn walked around Carlyle to grab the last pair of jeans before returning to the bed, where she had folded her other clothes. "I need a few days," she repeated.

"Parker is still out there. What you need to do is stay where you're protected," Elias said.

She chuckled and shook her head. "You three act like I'm going to do something stupid. You know me better than that."

"Look, we all knew Sab—I mean, Kurt—was hiding something. Why else give us the name Saber, keep most of our communication via text, and disguise his voice?" Finn asked. "We knew it. And we all accepted it. Even you."

Sabryn stilled before slowly setting aside the jeans to face the three men who had become her brothers. As an only child, she hadn't known how desperate she was for siblings until she'd met them. She looked at each man before nodding. "You're right. We did accept him. We even sat around trying to figure out who he could be. Hell, Finn, you once said Saber might be a woman."

"I did," Finn admitted with a crooked grin.

"Had anyone else come to the door, we would've been excited to finally discover the face of the fifth Knight." Sabryn swallowed, her throat feeling tight. "For all of you, that's exactly what happened. But not for me. I can't…" She searched for words. Finally, she shrugged helplessly. "I can't do anything with him around."

Carlyle drew in a deep breath and then slowly released it. "He knows everything about us. We can't just send him away."

"The fek we can't," Finn said angrily. "Sabryn has been on the ground with us, fighting by our side. If anyone should go, it's him."

Elias leaned his shoulder against the doorjamb and stuffed his hands into the front pockets of his jeans. "Sabryn, you're the glue to all of this. You were here from the verra beginning. All of us would lay down our lives for you."

She looked away and blinked rapidly to keep the tears away. She shouldn't need to hear those words—the bond between them was strong—yet she did. Because Kurt knew as well as she did. He might not have been on the ground fighting with them, but he had pulled his weight in other areas. He'd fit in with them so easily. And that hurt the most. That he *belonged*. Because he was a Knight. Why couldn't it have been anyone else but him?

"You're hurting, and we want to help," Elias continued. "Saying that, Carlyle's right. Kurt knows too much. We can no' just let him go to his family or the London Druids. They'll get everything from him, even though I doona think he'll give up those details easily."

She sniffed and met Elias's blue eyes. "I've already thought of that." Kinda of. In between bouts of rage, screaming into her pillow, and crying, there had been moments of relative sanity where she could look at things objectively. "Regardless of what happens, I can't—and won't—be around him."

"Understood," Elias replied softly.

Carlyle dipped his chin.

"I'll go with you," Finn said.

Sabryn took his hand in hers and squeezed. "Thank you, but I'd prefer to be alone."

"Where are you going?" Carlyle asked.

She returned to the bed and began putting everything into her small rolling suitcase. She'd flown into Heathrow with her carry-on and two big suitcases. Given how often they moved, it had only taken a few months to pare things down. Her closet had once overflowed with clothes—some that she never even wore. Now, she made a capsule wardrobe look maximalist. So much had changed.

Yet so much had stayed the same.

"I'm not sure yet," she answered.

"Mum has plenty of room," Elias offered.

Sabryn shook her head and zipped up the suitcase. "Your mother has her freedom after decades of incarceration for a murder she didn't commit. I'm not about to intrude on that."

"It's a big house," Elias said. "Really big. She'll never see you."

Finn chimed in with, "It's also heavily warded. It's not the manor, but it's close."

"We'd feel better if you were somewhere safe," Carlyle added.

They wouldn't relent, but neither would she. She faced the boys. "Emily needs her time to get acclimated to normal life. End of discussion. Plus, I don't need anyone looking after me."

"Maybe no', but it takes time to ward a house," Elias pointed out.

Carlyle raised his brows. "Maybe not. There's the other Emilie."

"Jasper's mom. Of course," Finn said. "It's a great alternative if you're dead set on leaving right this minute." He side-eyed the luggage. "Which you are."

Elias crossed his arms over his chest, looking very pleased with himself. "Your choice. Emily with a y or Emilie with an ie."

"Fine. Emilie with an ie. You're all assholes," Sabryn said and broke into a smile. "But I love you."

Elias pulled her into an embrace first. Carlyle was next, and then Finn. She hugged each of them tightly.

"I'll drive you," Finn said as she released her.

She started to reply when Carlyle tsked. "We're not asking," he stated.

Sabryn rolled her eyes at their protectiveness but did it to hide the fact that she was tearing up again. Elias grabbed her suitcase, and they walked into the hall and down the stairs. She wasn't smiling, but she felt lighter than she had since Kurt's arrival. Putting distance between them was the only way for her to get through this.

As for the rest? Well, she'd face that once the threat from Parker had been dealt with.

As they reached the main floor, she had her cell at her ear, calling Emilie. Sabryn got two steps when Rhona walked out of the library and faced them.

"Hello?" Emilie answered.

Sabryn's heart sank as Rhona looked directly at her. "Hi, Emilie. I need to call you back in a moment. Sorry. Something just came up."

"Of course. It's not like I'm going anywhere," Jasper's mom said with a laugh. "Talk soon."

The line went dead.

Sabryn tucked her phone in her back pocket as Elias set her luggage down.

"Would you four please join us?" Rhona asked, holding her arm out toward the library.

Us. Did that mean Kurt was in there? Sabryn could excuse herself from the meeting, from dealing with Parker, from all of it. But Parker and the threat he'd brought to the isle had nothing to do with what Kurt had done to her. This went beyond her pain and resentment. It was about protecting Skye and its inhabitants—both those with magic and those without. It was the very reason the Knights had come to the isle. How could she turn her back on that now?

Sabryn was the first to walk into the library. A quick, furtive glance showed her the only other person in the room was

Balladyn, who stood near the fireplace. She walked to the window and waited as Finn, Carlyle, and Elias followed her. Bronwyn, Song, Elodie, Scott, and Filip joined them within seconds. Rhona entered last, closing the doors behind her. Sabryn sagged against the windowsill, relieved that Kurt wasn't there.

Rhona walked to stand in front of the hearth and faced everyone. "We've located Parker."

"I take that to mean we're going to escort him off the isle," Filip said.

Balladyn grunted. "Eventually. We have another plan."

"It's fairly simple," Rhona continued. "I've already shared it with my deputies so they can spread the word to the other Druids on Skye. I've also alerted Theo. He and Ferne are getting the specifics to the rest of our group, who will then move into place."

Scott put his hands on the back of the chair Elodie sat in. "Are we sure we should devote all our resources to this? Doona get me wrong. I know it's important, but we still have two other pillars to find, not to mention closing the rip in the dimensions. As well as The Grey and the monster inside it. Oh, and my dad."

"Believe me, I'm all too aware of everything you mentioned. No one is giving up looking for Luke, and we never will. But after Thomas and the London Druids worked so hard to grab Carlyle, Parker and his Druids are a danger we must contain swiftly. If something else comes up, we'll divert as needed," Rhona explained.

Scott nodded, appeased.

"What's the plan? I can safely say we're ready to show our strength against Parker," Bronwyn said.

Rhona clasped her hands in front of her. "Like I said, it will be really easy. Parker is here to go after Sabryn to draw out Kurt.

We're going to give him what he wants. Sort of. Kurt and Sabryn will have a confrontation to draw out Parker."

Sabryn couldn't breathe as Rhona's words penetrated. She tried to draw in another breath as every eye in the room focused on her.

"I don't know," Carlyle began, a frown forming.

Rhona quickly spoke before he could say more. "It has to be believable, and I think Sabryn and Kurt will ensure it is. The quicker we get this done, the faster we can move on to other matters."

"It's a small group of Druids. Can't we take them on ourselves?" Elodie asked.

Song shook her head. "If the London Druids are here, it's because they were ordered to be. The moment they return home, they will be killed to ensure they can't taint anyone in case they've turned. They have nothing to lose."

"So, they're here to kill Kurt?" Filip asked.

Rhona hesitated a moment before saying, "He doesn't think so."

"That doesn't make sense," Song replied. "His family is part of the London Druids. *He* is part of them. Not only did he go against them, but he's also now on Skye."

Balladyn said, "Carlyle went against them, too. They didn't kill him."

"That's because my psychotic father is leading them," Carlyle said.

Rhona lifted a shoulder. "We have reason to believe the Barclay family either has enough influence for Parker and Kurt to be forgiven, or they have other plans."

"I'm no' doing this unless Sabryn agrees," Elias stated.

Finn crossed his arms over his chest. "Ditto."

"Count me in with them," Carlyle said.

Rhona's green eyes once more slid to Sabryn. "You're the only one who hasn't said anything. What do you think?"

"I think we have our hands full, and this is just one more thing to divide our attention and power." If Sabryn set aside her aversion to Kurt, she understood Rhona's reasoning. It was a plan she'd probably come up with herself. "It doesn't matter how detailed we are, though. Nothing will go smoothly. I think the plan is shit. But I also think it makes a lot of sense. While every part of me objects to the thought of it, it has the best chance of success."

Understanding filled Rhona's eyes before she looked at the others. "We're doing this in town between the co-op and the Tea Talker. We'll divide up between the two with some of us inside the buildings, others on the roofs, and others stationed nearby. Balladyn and I will be veiled next to Kurt and Sabryn." She paused. "We're not going to take this looming danger lightly. The London Druids are here, and they're not hiding this time. We'll do this smart and unified. And if we're lucky, finish it tomorrow morning."

"Fekking right, we will," Finn said with a smile.

Everyone began talking among themselves. Thinking about escaping, Sabryn eyed the door but then spotted Rhona headed her way.

The Druid leader stopped before her. "I know this will be hard for you."

"But it's the best way. I get it." Sabryn blew out a breath. "I didn't mean to snap at you."

"Aye, you did. And it's okay. Kurt will remain at my place until this is finished." She lowered her voice and said, "Tomorrow morning is your time to say everything you never got to say to him. It's a chance few of us get. Use it."

CHAPTER TEN

The wind coming off the water and the drizzling rain made the morning wet and chilly. Kurt was nursing his second cup of coffee, the caffeine doing nothing to help his nerves—or his stomach. Everyone believed the plan was a good one and had a high chance of success. Except he knew his brother. And Parker was nothing if not unpredictable. The only thing they had going for them was that Parker had no idea how many people were luring him and his Druids into a trap.

Kurt brought the paper cup to his lips and sipped through the plastic lid. He had always imagined his first time on the isle would be full of taking in all the sights he'd learned about from the other Knights. He even had a list of what he wanted to visit and experience.

Instead, he was standing under the awning of a building while trying to find a place where the wind didn't reach him. It was a futile effort. There was nowhere to go on the isle to get out of the wind but inside, and he couldn't do that yet. His toes felt icy, and the only reason he still had feeling in his fingers was because they were wrapped around a hot beverage. At least his other hand was toasty warm in his coat pocket.

Early May in London was vastly different than it was in Scotland, which was different than on Skye. He didn't usually mind the cold. Maybe it wasn't the weather but the fact that he was about to face off against his brother that turned his body to ice.

Kurt withdrew his mobile to check the time. One minute to go. He stared at the screen, pondering the sheer plethora of mistakes he had made—not just with Sabryn and the Knights but also with his family. Hell, life in general. He'd left nothing but destruction and chaos in his wake, and no amount of apologies could fix that.

The time changed on his mobile. Kurt put the device back into his pocket and turned the corner of the building as he headed for the Tea Talker. He scanned the area around him, looking for Parker's crew. He had scoured CCTV camera footage until he had likenesses for all eight and then sent them to the group. Scott, Willa, Filip, and Jasper had confirmed they were, indeed, Edinburgh Druids. Yet more proof that George's group was working with the London Druids.

Parker and his Druids were watching, waiting for Kurt to appear. That would draw out Parker. The problems arose in what could happen after. While the Skye Druids and Knights outnumbered Parker and his crew, Kurt didn't underestimate his brother. They had been raised by the same mother, and Diana was cunning. Parker emulated her in every way, which is why Kurt was attempting to imagine what Diana would do in this scenario.

A gust of wind came off the water and slammed into him,

snatching his breath. Kurt turned his head to the side until it passed. When he could look straight again, he spotted Sabryn coming toward him. She held her head high, unfazed by the wind ruffling her short, black hair. Her long, trim legs were encased in black denim, and her thigh-length, vintage brown leather coat was both timeless and modern chic—just as she was. She had it zipped, the fur-lined collar protecting her neck. The leather was well-worn, proving it was one of her favorites.

The thick soles of her boots didn't make a sound as she continued toward him, looking serene and beautiful. To any who watched, it looked as if she hadn't noticed him, but he'd bet one of his Swiss bank accounts she knew exactly how many steps separated them.

He had to stop himself from hurrying toward her. There had always been a pull and magnetism between them. Something he had been powerless to ignore. Even now, he was drawn to her. His mind cautioned that it was nothing but a trap for his brother, but Kurt's heart didn't care. He just wanted to be near her. She might even look at him. And if he was really lucky, she'd talk to him.

Sabryn stiffened slightly. It was barely noticeable, just a quick movement no one else would likely see. But he knew everything about Sabryn. Her reaction, however, reminded him that he was supposed to be scanning the area. Kurt dragged his gaze away from her and scrutinized the faces he saw. That's when he spotted Parker just outside the co-op, leaning against a vehicle parked near the sidewalk. He and Parker had the same coloring, but that's where their similarities ended and the differences began. Parker kept his hair combed without a strand out of place. He was also clean-shaven and impeccably dressed. He didn't understand jeans, nor did he own a pair.

The sight of Parker had warning bells sounding in Kurt's head. His steps slowed as he studied his brother. Something was wrong. There was no way Parker should be here already. And where was his crew? Kurt tried to catch Sabryn's gaze to call off the plan, but she wouldn't look at him. And he wouldn't leave her to his brother. Kurt lengthened his strides, his gaze moving between Sabryn and Parker. His stomach knotted painfully, and every instinct screamed at him not to proceed with the plan.

Sabryn reached Parker two steps before Kurt, and her deep blue eyes met his before she turned her head to his brother. "Well, this is a surprise. And not a good one."

Parker smiled before sipping something from a paper cup. "Isn't it just? Is this when both of you try to pretend you haven't been in contact for years?" He paused, his brows raised as he waited. "Except we all know Sabryn had no idea it was you. Don't we, big brother?"

Kurt looked around him nervously. His instincts had never been wrong, and ignoring them now didn't sit right.

"What do you want?" Sabryn asked.

Parker chuckled as he switched which ankle crossed over the other. "Right down to business. You never did like the niceties, did you, Sabryn? So American of you."

"You aren't supposed to be here," Kurt told Parker.

His brother chuckled and took another sip of his coffee, blue eyes meeting blue. "Ditto."

"I'm not with London anymore."

Parker pinched his lips and lowered the cup. "That is a conundrum. However, Diana has a plan."

"I'm not going home," Kurt stated. "Not now. Not ever."

"Diana won't be pleased."

Kurt slid his gaze to Sabryn to find her eyes on him. She was aware that something was off. They might not get a chance like this again. And while he wanted to get far away from Parker, Kurt decided to use the opportunity they had and prayed for the best. "You've been chasing me for days. It's time to tell Diana I'm done with the family."

Parker's gaze was directed at the co-op doors. "It's hard to believe our ancestors came from such a backward place."

"Backward?" Sabryn repeated, her brows snapping together.

Parker continued as if she hadn't spoken. "The Druids of Skye claim to be the most powerful, but that will soon change."

"Leave," Kurt demanded. "Now."

Parker lifted his left arm and tugged back his coat sleeve to look at his watch. Within seconds, Kurt heard police sirens in the distance. His brother lowered his arm and looked at him, a smile curving his lips. It wasn't long before a vehicle peeled out of the Tea Talker car park and sped out of town.

"Oh, dear," Parker said in mock distress. "That sounds urgent."

Kurt took a step closer. "What did you do?"

"Me?" Parker asked innocently. Then he started laughing, the sound growing louder and louder.

Out of the corner of his eye, Kurt saw someone on the street. He did a double take and stilled when he caught sight of Edie, Elias and Elodie's sister that was supposed to be dead. He jerked his gaze back to his brother and saw Parker's smug smile directed at him.

"You aren't the only one who came prepared," Parker stated.

The minute his words were out, magic shot from Edie's hands and struck the co-op's doors. Glass exploded inward as screams erupted around them. Kurt waited for Rhona and Balladyn to show themselves or get Sabryn away, but they did neither. Those inside the co-op didn't come out either.

Sabryn was suddenly thrown to the ground. Kurt lunged to help her, even as she effortlessly rolled to her feet. He never saw her attacker as Parker rammed into his side.

"This has been a long time coming," Parker said in Kurt's ear.

Then his brother was gone. Kurt tried to turn to go after him but got distracted by something warm and wet rushing down his body. Waves of pain immediately followed. He pressed his hand to his left side, and it came away bloody. The moment his brain registered that he had been stabbed, his legs gave out, and he crumpled to the ground. Kurt pressed his hand to the wound but couldn't seem to stanch the blood flow.

He turned his head to call out to Sabryn but found her attention locked on the Edinburgh Druid she fought. His lips parted, but his voice wouldn't work. He couldn't catch his breath, and his vision was blurring. He reached out his right arm to Sabryn. They hadn't set a trap. They had walked into one. She needed to get to the manor before it was too late. All of their group did.

Someone leaned over him then. Was it Parker? Had he returned to finish him off? Kurt fought with what little strength he had left.

"I'm a doctor," the female said.

Sabryn went out of focus. He managed to whisper her name. Another person knelt beside him, blocking his view of Sabryn. His arm fell to the ground as he grew too weak to even keep his eyes open.

"Stay with me!" someone yelled.

CHAPTER ELEVEN

Sabryn punched the man in the jaw, adding a flare of magic to the blow. He staggered back from the impact. She sent her magic to her foot and kicked him in the chest. He flew back this time, landing on a car before rolling unconscious to the ground.

Just as Sabryn headed to him to make sure he was actually out, a woman with straight, heavily graying black hair came out of nowhere and slapped handcuffs on him. Sabryn whirled around for her next attacker, but there wasn't one. There was also no sign of Parker or Edie, which made her very uneasy.

Nothing about the plan had gone right. She should've walked away the moment she saw Parker, but she had wanted things to be done with Kurt and barreled ahead.

The black-haired woman was yelling into her mobile. Sabryn became aware of voices behind her and turned to see a group of people tending to someone on the ground. She winced as she imagined some tourist being caught in Edie's display.

"Just what we fucking need," she murmured, searching for Rhona or Balladyn.

Cold realization struck when Sabryn comprehended that none of the others were around. She lowered her gaze to the ground and locked on the injured person's boots. Her stomach plummeted to her feet when she recognized them. Sabryn shouldered her way through the group, only to draw up short at the sight of Kurt on his back. A woman squatted next to him, shouting at him as she pressed something against his side. Sabryn couldn't look away from the blood soaking Kurt's side and puddling on the concrete.

The wail of sirens jerked her out of her stupor. She watched in a daze of horror as the ambulance pulled to a stop and EMTs jumped out. The female holding Kurt's wound barked orders to everyone as EMS shoved people aside.

Sabryn stood frozen, her brain refusing to believe what she was seeing as they loaded Kurt onto a stretcher and then loaded him into the ambulance. It wasn't until it drove away that she thought about going with him. She looked around helplessly, searching for something or someone to tell her what had happened.

Shouts from within the co-op drew her attention. She stumbled toward the wrecked door and then inside the store to see more blood. She turned toward the store, only to stop and look back at the retreating ambulance. Did she go with Kurt? Did she help those in the co-op?

Fast-approaching footsteps reached her. Sabryn gathered her magic and spun to attack, only to stop herself as Finn slid to a halt before her.

"What happened? Who's in the ambulance?" he demanded, looking inside the co-op. "Fekking hell," he murmured before rushing inside.

Sabryn didn't move. She was too uncertain, too afraid. She had been on edge from the moment she spotted Parker leaning against the car. He'd been too calm, too confident. Now, she knew why.

"Sabryn!"

The urgency in Finn's voice prompted action. He waved her into the store. She looked for the ambulance, but it was long gone. Kurt didn't need her help right now. Others did.

She hurried into the store and promptly slid on the shards of glass. Once she found her footing, she looked around. Willa and Song were tending to some tourists who had gotten wounded. Jasper and Finn were putting out dozens of small fires around the store. When Sabryn looked into the back of the shop, she spotted Nora in her wheelchair attempting to sweep up more glass.

Sabryn started toward Nora when she heard a crash. She rushed into the back and found Nora's husband, Matt, stumbling backward as their daughter, Kirsi, was locked in a battle with an Edinburgh Druid—and barely keeping her feet. Sabryn leapt over a sack of unsorted mail and dropped down beside Kirsi. The space was tight, leaving little room for fighting, but Sabryn was used to adapting. She stepped in front of Kirsi and threw a quick succession of blasts to throw her female opponent off. The woman staggered back, and just as Sabryn was getting ready to launch more, the Druid bolted.

When Sabryn turned around, she saw Matt leaning against the wall, breathing heavily. He made sure Kirsi was unharmed before stumbling to the front of the store.

"Thank you," Kirsi said.

Sabryn dipped her head. "Anytime."

Sabryn scanned the back for anyone else before following Kirsi to the front. Carlyle had made his way to the co-op by then and used his ability as a fire walker to put out the fires without the tourists noticing.

"What the bloody hell happened?" Carlyle asked as he came up beside her.

Finn turned his back to the tourists and lowered his voice as he said, "We got fekked, that's what. Where are Rhona and Balladyn?"

"Why did Elodie, Bronwyn, Elias, and Scott leave in such a hurry?" Jasper asked.

Willa shrugged. "Probably the same reason Theo grabbed Callum and left after getting a call."

"Did Kurt leave with someone?" Carlyle asked.

Sabryn felt everyone's eyes on her. "Ambulance. He was…" An image of him lying so still on the ground, covered in blood, flashed in her mind. "He was stabbed."

"Stabbed?" Finn repeated.

Jasper's face was lined with worry. "He needs Healers."

"If he was put into an ambulance, he's at the hospital," Song said.

"Go to him," Kirsi told them. "Things are handled here. I'll let you know what I find out."

Finn nodded. "We'll do the same."

Sabryn watched and listened to all of it like a dream, her brain unable to shove away the fog that kept her from thinking or moving. Finn took her arm and guided her out of the store and into a vehicle. She didn't remember closing the door or putting on her seat belt. Carlyle and Finn talked in the front seats, but she didn't hear any of it. Song said something from beside her, but she didn't register that either. Carlyle slammed on the brakes before doing a U-turn and speeding off.

A simple plan. That's what they'd called it. Simple and easy. And they'd had all the bases covered—or so they thought. Yet Parker had outmaneuvered them with Edie's help—someone everyone had believed dead.

She and Kurt had stood with Parker, wary but not afraid. Why should they have been? They outnumbered him and his crew. It should have been an easy takedown but went terribly, horribly wrong. Where was Edie now? Parker?

Kurt had been so sure his brother had come to take him home. And why *wouldn't* he think that? It's what Carlyle's father had tried. But that wasn't what'd happened. A knife. Someone had stabbed Kurt. Was it Parker? Why would he use a knife and not magic? Why would he try to kill Kurt? The brothers had never been close, but to commit fratricide? Had it been done on Diana's orders? Or was this Parker acting alone?

The vehicle came to a rocking halt, and they jumped out and hurried toward the hospital entrance. Finn was the first to reach the reception desk, and they directed him to the ER.

They all took off down the hall, panicky and anxious. Kurt was likely in surgery, and they wouldn't be able to see him until he came out. But Sabryn said nothing, just rushed along with them. Because getting there was the only thing they could do right then.

Finn retook the lead once they reached the ER and chatted with the nurses. They confirmed that Kurt was in surgery. Sabryn grabbed the wall as the room spun from relief at hearing that Kurt had at least been alive when he reached the hospital. Carlyle asked if there was a private place for them to wait, and to her surprise, a nurse led them through a door to a secluded room. When Sabryn entered, it was like being back in DC, waiting in the hospital for news about her dad.

"I still don't understand why Balladyn didn't get Kurt to the Healers," Carlyle murmured as he sank into a chair.

Finn paced, his agitation evident in every stride. "I saw Edie. Fekking Edie!"

"Keep your voice down," Carlyle said.

Finn whirled around, his lips peeled back in a snarl of outrage. "Don't you dare tell me to keep my voice down. Not now. Not after this cockup."

"Sabryn, did you see what happened?" Song interrupted, her voice calm and even.

The boys swung their heads to her. Sabryn looked at her hands. Where had her tea gone? She saw scrapes on her palm but didn't remember getting them. She hadn't even seen Kurt go down. Had he called out for help?

"Hey, darlin'. Let's sit," Finn said, guiding her to a chair before squatting before her.

Carlyle moved to the chair beside her, and Song sat on her other side.

"We were wrong about Parker," Sabryn told them, shaking her head. "I let my guard down. Everyone was in place, I thought…"

Finn squeezed her hand. "We all did."

"I knew something was wrong with how nonchalant Parker was." Sabryn swallowed as she recalled the shock on Kurt's face at the sight of Edie. "If Kurt hadn't noticed Edie, I wouldn't have gotten out of the way in time. That strike was meant for me."

Carlyle sighed loudly. "I think Elodie saw Edie, too, because she shouted Edie's name to me as she ran toward the Tea Talker. It's the only reason I looked for Edie."

"It wasn't long after Elodie arrived at the tea house that Elias and Bronwyn said Edie's name before getting in the car and speeding off," Finn added.

Song shoved her hair away from her face. "I had just gotten Carlyle's text about Edie when the explosion happened. I didn't have time to tell anyone."

"We never had the advantage," Sabryn said. "We weren't the ones setting a trap. We were being lured into one."

Finn put his knees on the floor and nodded. "With half our group being called away."

"That couldn't all have been just so Parker could get Kurt, could it?" Song asked.

Carlyle pulled a face. "I'm not sure I believe Edie would have that kind of advantage over us and not do more. Especially just so Parker could hurt Kurt."

"Maybe there's more going on than we know," Song said. "I've only just met Rhona, but she doesn't seem the type to leave her people in a lurch."

Finn's brow puckered in a frown. "She wouldn't."

"No, she would not," Carlyle reiterated. "I've not seen her or Balladyn, which means something called them away, too."

Sabryn leaned back in the chair. "I never saw Parker go after Kurt."

"This isn't your fault," Finn told her.

She shrugged a shoulder. "I was the closest to them. I might have paid better attention if I hadn't been so angry and bitter. I might have been able to stop it."

"All of us had our attentions diverted. It was a well-thought-out and executed plan," Song stated.

"Maybe," Sabryn admitted. "I still should've realized Kurt had fallen. I didn't know anything until some cop showed up and put my opponent in handcuffs. That's when I saw Kurt. Stabbed."

Finn jumped to his feet. "I'm going to fekking bleed that fekking arsehole."

"You won't be doing it alone," Carlyle said.

Song quietly asked, "How bad was the injury? Was he conscious?"

"There was an awful lot of blood. And, no, he was unconscious," Sabryn explained.

Finn had his hands on his hips, his face lined with anger and apprehension as he faced them. "Is that good or bad?"

"It's not good," Song said.

The door to the room opened, and all four turned to find a woman in her late forties or early fifties standing just inside the room. Sabryn recognized her as the officer who had handcuffed the Edinburgh Druid. She hadn't seen the woman's face, but she recognized the graying dark hair and navy peacoat.

"Hello, everyone," she said in a British accent as she entered the room, her gray eyes landing on Sabryn. "My name is Anne Boyd. I'm the new Chief Superintendent of Skye. I'd like to ask all of you a few questions."

Finn took a seat and crossed his arms over his chest.

"Can this wait?" Carlyle asked.

Anne shook her head. "Afraid not. Who wants to begin? How about you?" she asked, pointing to Sabryn.

"You can start with me," Finn stated.

Anne flashed him a smile. "I'll get to you in a moment. Ma'am?" she called, her attention once more on Sabryn.

Carlyle started to rise, but Sabryn put her hand on his arm to still him. "It's all right," she told him. She got to her feet. "After you, Chief Superintendent."

Sabryn followed Anne into the hall. They walked a short distance before entering another room. Anne held the door for her, and once Sabryn was inside, she closed it and leaned back against it. Sabryn bit back a laugh.

"How about we start with a name?" Anne said.

"Sabryn Beaumont. I'm from the States. Washington, DC."

"How long have you been in the United Kingdom?"

That was a loaded question. Sabryn's visa had run out long, long ago. "A bit."

"I see," Anne murmured as she eyed Sabryn. "What exactly is the nature of your visit?"

"I'm staying with friends."

Anne jerked her head to the side. "The friends in the other room?"

"Another friend, actually."

"And who is this friend?"

Sabryn licked her dry lips, suddenly weary. "I'm staying at Carwood Manor, which you'll find belongs to Bronwyn Stewart. If you need to know more, DI Theo Frasier can vouch for me."

"Ah."

One word, but it held a wealth of meaning. It was Sabryn's turn to eye the woman. She stopped herself from asking what the chief superintendent had meant by that. Years of being on the political scene had taught Sabryn to keep her mouth shut and her expressions neutral.

Anne crossed her arms over her chest. "I've only been here a few weeks, but I've heard many strange things about Skye."

"There's a great deal of history here. Things that will lead to folktales, myths, and legends of all sorts."

"It's more than that. I'm beginning to understand why some of the other chiefs were trying so hard to get placed here."

Sabryn glanced at the abrasions on her palm again. "And why is that?"

"Why don't you tell me?"

"I don't have anything to say."

"Nothing?" Anne pressed. "Not even about the petite blonde who threw up her hands when the co-op exploded?"

Sabryn shrugged. "I was caught in that blast, too."

"Let's not play, shall we? I saw you fighting. Those aren't skills picked up because you're trying a new workout. Those moves are honed and perfected. And I saw the results myself. Except those punches of yours hit harder than anything I've ever seen."

"I can take care of myself. It's a good thing, too."

Anne's arms dropped to her sides. "The stories are true, aren't they?"

"What stories?"

"Druids."

Sabryn glanced at the ceiling. Could this day get any worse? Why was a Brit asking her about something to do with the Scots? "I'm an American, remember? What would I know about any of that?"

"Quite a few reasons, by my guess."

Sabryn threw up her hands before letting them fall. "Fine. We're Druids. Is that what you want to hear?"

"It is. Now, tell me what happened today."

"No."

Anne's brows rose. "Excuse me?"

Sabryn got to her feet. "I was attacked, my friends were attacked, and one of them is in surgery fighting for his life. If you want to know about the goings-on of your island, then talk to your people. But I'm done answering your questions. Please, move."

To her surprise, Anne not only moved but also opened the door. Sabryn walked into the hall.

CHAPTER TWELVE

There was nothing more depressing than a hospital. The hope mixed with grief, dread, and sadness seeped from every crevice. Sabryn couldn't stand being in the building, but she couldn't leave either. She might despise Kurt, but Saber had been a trusted and integral part of her team. The fact that they were one and the same made things that much more difficult.

The door to the private room opened, and Song entered before walking to Carlyle. Chief Superintendent Boyd had spoken to them all, but Sabryn knew they hadn't seen the last of her. Right now, Sabryn couldn't care less.

She sank into a chair in the corner and gazed at the carpet after staring at the wall for the last half hour. Every minute Kurt remained in surgery meant he was closer to dying. She couldn't think about the mixed emotions that thought conjured because she wasn't yet ready to face any of it. She might never be prepared. So, she turned her focus to Parker. Thanks to Kurt, they knew the Edinburgh Druids were working with him.

George and her organization had repeatedly come after those on Skye, and Sabryn had reached her breaking point. It was time George felt her wrath. And once Sabryn handled them, she planned to turn her attention to Parker. The bastard would pay for what he'd done. Slowly and painfully.

Sabryn was imagining all the ways she would make him scream and beg for mercy when the door opened, interrupting her thoughts. Her gaze snapped toward it as Finn rushed inside, out of breath and his eyes blazing with fury. He motioned Carlyle and Song over as he sat beside her.

"What's going on?" Carlyle asked.

Finn leaned forward and lowered his voice. "I finally got in touch with Elias."

Unease slid down Sabryn's spine at the indignation deepening Finn's already dark eyes. "What happened?" she asked.

"His mum's cottage was attacked. Emily was watching Edie's children at the time," he explained.

Carlyle grunted. "So, they were after the bairns?"

"Not by what Elias said. They set a fire outside the house," Finn told them.

Song jerked back in shock. "They were trying to burn them?"

"Maybe," Finn said with a one-shoulder shrug. "That's not all."

Sabryn braced herself. "Go on." She nodded.

"Theo took off with Callum because one of the boats Callum had been working on blew up. Shrapnel went everywhere," Finn said.

Carlyle shook his head, anger darkening his face. "Was anyone hurt?"

"Callum wasn't there, of course, and his father was in the

house. As far as I know, no one was hurt." Finn paused for a beat. "Then there's Ferne's store."

Sabryn glanced at Carlyle. "The bookstore? What happened?"

"Someone broke in and destroyed it."

Carlyle surged to his feet and shoved a hand through his hair. "She was getting ready to open in less than a week."

"This was a coordinated attack," Song replied.

Sabryn nodded. "They waited until we were all together before striking places that would send us in different directions."

"To what gain, though?" Finn asked.

Carlyle sat back down with a sigh. "It has to be Kurt."

"I don't understand why Edie would allow her children to be harmed," Song said.

Carlyle took one of her hands in his. "I don't think she cares about them now that she's working with the evil."

"Then she doesn't deserve them," Song stated angrily.

Finn twisted his lips and nodded. "We can all agree on that. I'd really like to know how she's still alive."

"Stop," Sabryn told them. "We're looking at this all wrong."

"All right. Where should we be looking?" Carlyle asked.

She curled her hands into fists. "Parker."

"So, this *is* about Kurt," Finn murmured.

Song wrinkled her nose. "Maybe it's a combination of everything. Carlyle and I both saw Edie. She should've died in that house. If that was her out there, she's looking for revenge."

"Against all of us," Sabryn pointed out.

Carlyle released a long breath. "Bloody hell. Will this ever end?"

"Maybe that's part of it. They're wearing us down," Finn replied.

Song asked, "Has anyone heard from Rhona or Balladyn?"

Finn shook his head. "Not a word."

"What about Ariah? How's the Tea Talker. Was she hit?" Sabryn asked.

Finn squeezed the bridge of his nose between his thumb and forefinger. "No one said anything."

"I'll call," Carlyle said, pulling out his mobile.

They waited for the line to connect. The conversation was brief, and within a few seconds, Carlyle gave them a thumbs-up to let them know that Ariah, Killian, and Ruby were unharmed.

"Stay vigilant," Carlyle told them before hanging up. "They're good," he announced to the room.

Finn scooted down in his chair and stretched out his legs. "It's weird that they wouldn't attack there."

"I agree. Ariah is a big part of the group, and everyone else was hit," Song said.

Sabryn popped her neck. "Who's to say they're done with us?"

"Fuck," Carlyle muttered and leaned forward, dropping his chin to his chest.

They all jerked to attention when the door opened, and a woman in scrubs walked inside.

"Hello. I'm Dr. Dunn," she said with a thick Scottish accent. "Are all of you with Mr. Barclay?"

Finn and Carlyle stood up. "We are," they said in unison.

Sabryn's heart thudded in her chest as she scrutinized the doctor's face, trying to discern anything that might give her any indication of Kurt's health. They had been waiting for news, but now she wasn't sure she wanted to know.

Song scooted over and placed her hand atop Sabryn's. She

hadn't realized she was squeezing the edge of the chair. Sabryn turned her hand over at the contact, grateful for Song's support.

"The knife wound struck between his ninth and tenth rib, grazing the ninth. That slowed the blade's trajectory into his spleen. There was minor damage to the organ and a small nick in his left kidney," Dr. Dunn said.

Sabryn hung on every word, even as she was afraid to hear the rest.

"It took longer than I would've liked to find and repair the lacerations. If the blade had been longer, it could have potentially damaged his lung, as well. Mr. Barclay is very lucky," the doctor said.

Finn sank heavily into a chair and hung his head in relief.

"Kurt is stable, then?" Carlyle asked hesitantly.

Dr. Dunn's smile was small and controlled. "He is stable for the moment. He lost a considerable amount of blood. We'll be keeping a close eye on him to make sure nothing was missed."

"You mean internal bleeding," Finn said as he lifted his head.

The doctor dipped her chin. "Exactly. He coded on the table but was successfully resuscitated."

Just when Sabryn was relaxing, Dr. Dunn's words had the room tilting. She tightened her hand on Song's while trying to figure out how to get a Healer into the hospital and to Kurt without being seen. That's all it would take to fix Kurt. There was no need for him to lie there in pain, possibly still wounded.

"When can we see him?" Song asked.

Dr. Dunn twisted her lips. "Mr. Barclay will remain in the critical care unit until I'm sure of his recovery."

"One more thing, Doctor," Carlyle said. "An attempt was

made on our friend's life. There might be some who call, wanting an update."

Dr. Dunn looked at each of them before returning her gaze to Carlyle. "That detail has already been handled."

"What do you mean?" Sabryn asked.

"Chief Superintendent Boyd locked Mr. Barclay's file so only I can access it."

"I wasn't expecting that," Finn said.

Carlyle held out his hand. "Thank you, Dr. Dunn."

They were quiet after the doctor left, each lost in thought about how close Kurt had come to death.

Finn broke the silence. "We need to get a Healer in here ASAP."

"Getting one in isn't the issue," Carlyle said. "It's the time it will take as they use their magic. As long as Kurt's in the CCU, we can't get to him."

Sabryn shrugged. "We can't. But Balladyn can."

"That's assuming he'll come if called," Finn pointed out.

Carlyle crossed his arms over his chest and rocked back on his heels. "Rhona and Balladyn wouldn't have just left. They either *had* to leave like everyone else, or someone got to them."

"No way," Finn replied with a firm shake of his head. "He's a fekking Reaper who can veil himself and anyone he touches. And he can teleport. There's no way something on this isle could take him and Rhona."

"That we know of," Song added.

Finn blew out a frustrated breath as he realized she spoke the truth.

Sabryn released Song's hand when Carlyle noticed them. She

flashed a quick smile of thanks to Song and got to her feet. "I can't stay here. I'm going to look for Rhona."

"The fek you are. You're going after Parker," Finn said.

There was no need to lie now. She had attempted it, but the boys had seen right through her. And given Song's expression, so had she. "Fine. I'm going after Parker."

"Not alone, you aren't," Carlyle declared.

Song crossed one leg over the other. "I know you all have good intentions because I have them myself. However, when Kurt wakes, he'll want Parker for himself."

"We'll hold the wanker for him," Finn said with a grin.

Carlyle rubbed the back of his neck. "We set a trap that went badly. We have no idea where Parker or his Druids are now."

"Which is why we need to find them," Sabryn replied.

Carlyle stared at her for a long moment. "They aren't done with us. They'll wait until we're alone or in small groups."

"They can try. I was right fucking there," Sabryn said, her voice breaking. "I was right beside Kurt. I never saw the knife. I never saw Parker…"

Finn stood and moved to her side, concern coloring his face. "That isn't on you."

"I underestimated Parker and overestimated our plan. I all but ignored Kurt because I was angry. Had I paid attention, had I—"

"Don't do that," Carlyle interrupted. "You know that road leads nowhere."

Sabryn looked at the three of them. "We were played today. London and Edinburgh keep coming at us. And now, it looks like they've paired with Edie and whatever she's partnered with. We're running out of time, guys. I can feel it."

Finn and Carlyle exchanged a look before Finn asked, "What do you want to do?"

"I want answers. And I want Parker," Sabryn said.

Carlyle took Song's hand. "We'll look for him. You and Finn stay here."

"You can stay," Sabryn declared. "I can't sit here any longer."

She didn't wait for a response as she strode out of the room and down the hall. Sabryn didn't remember where they had parked or even what vehicle they had come in, but that didn't slow her.

"Wait up," Finn said, jogging to catch her. "You're not going without me. Besides. You'll need these."

She looked over as he jingled the keys. "And where we parked."

"That, too." His smile slipped. "He'll be okay. One way or another, Kurt will be fine."

She sure hoped Finn was right. They walked out of the hospital to Carlyle's SUV. Finn got behind the wheel, something for which Sabryn was grateful. Her mind was too preoccupied to concentrate on driving.

"Where to?" Finn asked after starting the engine.

"There's only one place *to* go."

"The hotel Parker was staying?"

She nodded in agreement.

Finn backed out of the space and put the vehicle in drive. "I doubt he'll be there."

"If he's smart, he won't be. But Parker isn't as smart as he thinks he is. Someone would've seen Kurt being taken off in the ambulance."

"Meaning?" Finn asked as he glanced at her.

"Meaning there will be calls to hospitals. I wish the chief had told me what she planned. I would've asked her to say that Kurt was dead."

Finn slowed to take a turn. "You think Parker would leave Skye then?"

"Possibly."

"Unless he plans to come for you."

Sabryn stared out the windshield. "I hope the motherfucker does."

CHAPTER THIRTEEN

Edinburgh

"It's done."

The words over the line made Georgina Miller smile. She leaned back in her office chair and soaked in the delight. "You came through."

"I always do," Mara stated.

George twirled a pen in her fingers. "How did you do it?"

"The usual way. Men always think with their dicks. Parker Barclay is no different. A few tight shirts, a pushup bra, some flirting, and he was all mine. Men are weak like that."

"Well done. You continue to impress me."

"I told you my devotion is to Edinburgh. Do you still doubt me?" Mara asked, her voice hardening with impatience.

George set down the pen, recalling her vision of being betrayed. "My hesitation is borne of being in a position of power. Trust must be earned, not freely given."

"I want our group to thrive and will do whatever is necessary to prove my loyalty."

"And how do you feel about London?"

There was a beat of silence before Mara said, "They're powerful. We need to tread carefully. As long as they think they control us, they'll never see us coming."

"My thoughts exactly. We've kept up our end of the bargain. It's time London delivers on theirs."

"I have my eye on Elias as we speak."

George clenched her hand. "Don't underestimate any of the Skye Druids, particularly Elias. He has evaded facing judgment, but his time has run out."

"I'll deliver him to you," Mara promised.

"Where's Parker?"

Mara laughed under her breath. "He's calling the hospitals to see if Kurt survived."

"And did he?"

"Based on Parker's continued smile, I would say no."

George forced open her hand. "Keep me updated."

She ended the call and gently set the mobile on her desk. Mara said all the right things and could very well mean them, but George wasn't entirely sure about Mara—or *anyone* for that matter. Her vision hadn't shown her the face of her betrayer. She didn't even know if it was a man or a woman. Which meant everyone was a suspect.

Uniting with London had been risky, and they had already lost several members thanks to Parker's incompetence. But if it brought her Elias, George would sacrifice a hundred—even a thousand— Edinburgh Druids. She would have her revenge if it was the last thing she did. Elias had gone unpunished for killing her brother for far too long.

She had given the justice system time. When they hadn't made a move, she'd delivered evidence. And still, they did nothing. They called it self-defense. She knew better. If the police wouldn't provide the justice she required, then she would find it herself. Elias went on living his life while her brother rotted in the ground.

It wasn't just Elias she wanted to punish. Scott, Filip, and Jasper had betrayed her by joining the Skye Druids once they reached the isle. She never forgave or forgot. George intended to look each in the eyes as they died. She wanted them to know who had sentenced them.

She stood and walked around her desk. Her office was secluded from other sections of the warehouse she repurposed for meetings and other Druid gatherings. It was large enough for their growing ranks but also set away from any areas that might draw attention. Not that those without magic knew about Druids, the Fae, or the Dragon Kings. Most humans were sheep being led by wolves and didn't even know it.

She was nearly to the door when she heard a knock, and one of the Druid guards poked her head inside. George's gaze landed on her as she stepped into the office. "Ma'am. You have a visitor."

"And who might that be?"

"She refused to give a name."

George gave her a flat look. "Then send her away."

"I think you need to see her."

"And why is that?"

The guard moved closer and lowered her voice. "Her clothes say very old money, and her accent is posh British."

"If she's a London Druid, why wouldn't she give her name?"

"Perhaps she doesn't want me to know it. Or she could be hiding."

George glanced toward the door. "Let's find out, shall we?"

The guard dipped her chin and turned on her heel. George returned to her desk to await the new arrival. She had barely taken a seat when another knock sounded.

"Come," George called.

The door opened, and the guard stepped aside to reveal the visitor. The woman was tall and slender with blond hair that brushed her shoulders. Blue eyes looked around George's office before turning to George herself.

"A very basic operation," the woman stated.

George nodded for the guard to leave. Once the door had shut behind her, George eyed the newcomer. She wore a brown, cream, and black plaid silk shirt tucked into slim black trousers, a belt with Gucci's gold, double-G logo, and black heels. Her hand gripped the strap of a designer purse.

"It gets the job done. Who are you?" George demanded.

The woman walked toward the desk and eyed the chairs. "This is when you're supposed to ask me to sit."

"I've not decided if I want you to stay that long."

An amused smile curved the visitor's lips. "I heard you were a woman who went after what she wanted."

"I am."

"Well, Georgina, I think we should be friends."

"It's George. And I still don't know your name."

She shifted her purse into her other hand and held out her right. "I'm Diana Barclay."

George slowly got to her feet, not because Diana was nobility but because she wanted to be at eye level when she asked, "Why are you here if you sent Parker?"

"I'm here on official business from London." Diana dropped her hand to her side.

George narrowed her eyes. If Diana knew what George had just plotted with one of her members, she would likely send the full power of London at the city. "Are you saying Parker isn't on Skye on official business?"

"Not at all. I meant my visit is unrelated to what Parker is handling." Diana held out her hand again and waited.

George shook it but released Diana quickly. When George had planned to betray Parker, she hadn't expected his mother to show up. Could Diana be the one who ended her life?

Diana arched an eyebrow, her smile tight. George motioned to the chairs as she resumed her seat.

"Now, then," Diana said as she crossed her legs. "London wants an accounting of the Druids and the money we've sent."

George opened a drawer and pulled out a ledger.

CHAPTER FOURTEEN

Rhona didn't think she had ever seen so much blood. The Druid prison was painted with it. Her gaze fell on the body of their prisoner. Kerry had been held there since they'd discovered she was the one controlling the killing mist. Few knew about the prison, and only a handful could get past her magic. Once Balladyn added his, it was nearly impossible for anyone to get inside.

But someone had.

"I've looked all over the mountain," Balladyn said as he walked up behind her from the narrow tunnel entrance. "I can't find another entry point."

"They came in just as we did."

"They shouldn't have been able to."

Rhona was confused about what had taken place. "Why kill Kerry? She refused to tell us anything."

"Perhaps the individual or individuals who committed the deed wanted to make sure she didn't change her mind about that."

"You can say the name we're both thinking."

Balladyn put his hands on her shoulders and turned her around. "You believe it's Edie? I'm not convinced."

"How could she have survived the last battle? Carlyle was very clear on what he saw."

"That house isn't in our world, nor is the thing inside it. We have no idea what happens if someone dies there."

Rhona gave in and rested her forehead against his chest. Balladyn's strong arms came around her. He was a leader in his own right, but he never tried to take control—and he probably could as the Warden of Skye. He'd only ever been her partner in the truest sense of the word.

She took a deep breath and lifted her head. "If not Edie, then who?"

"Who else wanted Kerry dead?"

"The list is long if we add everyone touched by her murders. Yet not just anyone could get past our barrier."

Balladyn released her and walked to the center cell, where Kerry lay sprawled on her back. "She's close to the bars. That means she came toward whoever was here."

"Greeting them, you think?"

"Could be. I don't believe she'd approach someone she didn't know."

Rhona walked to stand beside him. "Good point."

This was the closest she'd been to Kerry since discovering her. It wasn't Rhona's first dead body, but something about the blood was eerie. She had to force herself to look at her ex-deputy. Even then, it was hard to see anything of use with all the blood.

"Where is the wound?" Rhona asked.

Balladyn grunted distastefully. "That's hard to determine in her current state."

Rhona leaned toward the bars, careful not to touch them and get blood on her. "Is that…a rib?"

"I believe so. I also think that's part of her intestines."

"Bloody hell. It's like she was ripped open."

Balladyn glanced around them. "That would explain the blood."

"I wanted Kerry punished, but this…?"

"Extreme? I agree." His head turned to her. "As horrific as this is, I'm more disturbed that someone got through our combined magic."

Rhona worried her lip with her teeth. "I can't stop thinking about that either."

"There's also the fact that we were drawn here before Kurt and Sabryn could execute their plan for Parker."

Rhona reached around to her back pocket for her mobile, only then realizing that she had forgotten it at home. "We need to get back."

Balladyn jumped them to the co-op without question. The moment they saw the destruction, dread filled Rhona. Balladyn dropped his veil as Rhona rushed toward Kirsi.

"Rhona!" Kirsi cried when she spotted her. "We've been trying to find you."

"What happened?" Rhona asked.

Matt exited the back. "Everything."

"Start from the beginning," Balladyn urged.

By the time Kirsi and Matt finished detailing everything, Rhona was sick to her stomach. She didn't know whether to go to Emily, Ferne, Cullen, or Kurt first. Everyone had been hit.

"They drew as many of us away as they could," Balladyn said.

Rhona met his red-ringed silver eyes. "Then Kerry was nothing but collateral damage. How did they learn about our plan?"

"Someone told them," Kirsi replied.

Rhona didn't want to believe that. Everyone in their group had fought together. They all had something to lose.

"What drew you two away?" Matt asked.

Balladyn answered for her. "Someone got into the prison and killed Kerry."

"I need to check on the others," Rhona said. "Do you need anything? Where's Nora?"

Kirsi shot her dad a quick look. "At home. The morning's events tired her."

"I told her she should've stayed home, but my Nora is a strong one," Matt said, his eyes bright with worry.

Rhona looked at each of them. "I'll be around later to check on all of you."

"Be safe," Matt called, right before Balladyn teleported them away.

Rhona was surprised when he brought her to Carwood Manor. "What are you doing? I need to check on everyone."

"We don't know where Parker and his crew are."

"I don't hide. Or run. You know that."

Balladyn sighed as he touched her face. "Believe me, I know. Sometimes, I wish you would, if only to save me from having a heart attack. I'm not keeping you from your duties, my love. I'm merely giving you a moment."

"Do I look that bad?"

"You just learned there might be a traitor in our midst. That would set anyone back."

She grinned. "Even a Reaper?"

"Even a Reaper," he murmured, pulling her against him. He grew serious as he stared down at her. "It's easy to let today's events spiral you out of control. Stay calm, and the others will follow."

"I don't feel calm."

He nodded and glanced to the side. "I don't either."

"You fake it well."

"Centuries of learning."

She flattened her hands on his chest and shook her head. "I don't believe someone betrayed us."

"Maybe they didn't. Leave that for now. Let's get everyone safe, and then we'll find Parker."

Rhona pulled his head down and rose on her tiptoes to press her lips to his. "Thank you," she whispered. "Take me to Emily's first. Then I have a task for you."

"You wish me to bring Kurt to a Healer?"

"It might raise suspicions if he suddenly leaves, especially with the chief superintendent nosing around. I just want to make sure no one bothers him at the hospital."

Balladyn cupped her face in his hands before kissing her. "Consider it done."

CHAPTER FIFTEEN

No matter how often she looked, she found no sign of the green Jaguar in the hotel parking lot. In any other situation, right about now is when Sabryn would've reached out to Saber and asked him to check the CCTV footage to see if Parker had left the island. But that avenue was closed to the Knights now.

She had known they relied heavily on Sabertooth, but she hadn't really thought about just how much until the option was no longer available. What about the future? Did they find a new hacker? She didn't want to think about it, but she would have to eventually. Kurt was an issue for her. A big one.

Six years of working together, of Saber learning their habits and tendencies. Six years of him always knowing how and where to help when they ended up backed into a corner. Was it fair to throw that away for Finn, Carlyle, Song, Elias, and Bronwyn? No, it wasn't. But could she work with Kurt? He had apologized. That should have been enough, but it wasn't. Not by a long shot.

"Let me go inside and ask the front desk if they've seen the little bastard," Finn said as he pulled into a parking spot.

Sabryn turned her head to him. Finn, who'd had the roughest childhood, loved the hardest and the deepest. He was upset by Kurt's deception but had also already gotten over it and put it behind him. After all, he had pointed out that they all understood Saber had been hiding for a reason. The only difference was that they now knew what the reason was. Finn, like Carlyle and Elias, had already forgiven Kurt.

If only she could.

She wanted to. Desperately. If for no other reason than to keep the Knights together.

"Parker likely already thought of that. We wouldn't get anything. And whoever you spoke with would just report it to Parker," she said.

Finn's sigh was tinged with his mounting frustration. "I'm open to suggestions."

"I'm sure there are better uses for our time than driving around looking for his vehicle."

"If that's what you want to do, then we'll do it."

Sabryn twisted her lips. "I don't suppose you know anything about hacking?"

"Sadly, no. Kurt did give Elias someone's name, though. We could reach out."

"I'm having a hard time trusting anyone not already involved in this."

"Kurt trusted them. If he didn't, he wouldn't have mentioned them to Elias," Finn pointed out.

She stared at the hotel entrance before meeting his dark gaze. "Do we really want to bring someone else into this war?"

"Of course not, but we need to find Parker."

"Unless we let him find me."

Finn's face scrunched up before he shook his head. "Fek, no. That's not an option, so don't even consider it."

"He—" she began.

"No!" Finn exploded. "Kurt is lying in a hospital bed. I won't have you there, too."

She had been so lost in her suffering that she hadn't thought about how the others might be handling the situation. Everyone put on a brave face but was secretly hurting in different ways. She put her hand on his arm and held his gaze. "I'm not trying to get myself killed."

"It sure sounds that way to me."

"You know me, Finn."

He barked a laugh and slid his gaze away for a heartbeat. "That's right. I know you go headlong into battle without hesitation. We got our arses handed to us a few hours ago, which means we need to be more careful going forward."

"I agree, but I can't sit at the hospital any longer. I have to *do* something."

Finn patted her hand before putting the vehicle in reverse and driving away. She lowered her hands to her lap and noticed how his fingers gripped the steering wheel too tightly. Sabryn quickly glanced at his face to find his lips pressed into a firm line. She didn't ask him where they were going. It would be pointless because when he was like this, he didn't talk.

Surveying the hotel would've been just as dreadful as sitting at the hospital waiting for Kurt to wake. Skye wasn't that large, but it wasn't easy to search. If they knew where Rhona was, they could ask her to reach out to her five deputies, who could spread the word through their segments to look for the Jaguar.

Finn's cell rang shrilly, drowning out the music he had turned down earlier. He picked up the phone from the cupholder and showed her the screen with Rhona's name before answering and putting it on speaker.

"Rhona?" Finn asked.

"It's me," she replied.

Sabryn leaned her elbow on the center console. "Are you and Balladyn okay? We've been worried."

"We're fine. I left my mobile and didn't realize it until recently."

Finn glanced at Sabryn before asking, "What happened with you and Balladyn?"

There was a brief pause before Rhona answered. "Someone or something got through my and Balladyn's barrier at the prison and killed Kerry."

"Shit," Sabryn murmured in shock.

Balladyn and Rhona's combined magic was incredibly powerful. The idea that someone could get through that was deeply concerning.

Finn grunted. "I'm not too broken up by Kerry's death. She deserved it."

"You're not the only one who has said that," Rhona admitted. "But her death was very painful."

Finn shrugged carelessly. "She brought a lot of pain and death to others."

"She did. The problem is whoever got into the prison," Rhona replied.

Sabryn briefly met Finn's gaze. "Do you have a plan?"

"Other than to make sure everyone is safe? No. Balladyn and I were just at the co-op. Kirsi and Matt filled us in on everything." Rhona sighed. "I'm now at Emily's to survey the damage to the cottage, and I sent Balladyn to the hospital to watch over Kurt. Where are you?"

Finn shifted in his seat. "We just left Parker's hotel. The Jaguar wasn't there. We decided not to go in."

"That was probably a good idea," Rhona said.

Sabryn heard the weariness in Rhona's voice. "They have us scrambling. We're worried about each other instead of focusing on Parker."

"Because that's what people with feelings do," Finn snapped.

Sabryn realized her mistake the moment the words were out of her mouth. For a man who had never had a family, Finn was particularly protective of anyone he brought into his circle. And that circle had grown when the Knights followed Elias to Skye. Which meant more people could be hurt or taken from him.

"Sabryn's right," Rhona admitted. "But, Finn, so are you. Could Parker have left if he believed he'd succeeded in killing his brother?"

Finn slowed and pulled off the road, throwing the SUV in park. "Possibly. Kurt was sure Diana was trying to get him home, though."

"Sabryn? You know their family better than any of us. What do you think?" Rhona asked.

"I *barely* know them. I never met Diana, and my time spent with Parker was limited. The three months Kurt and I were together were spent developing a romantic relationship. Neither of us spoke about our families much." A sudden thought came to Sabryn. "Although, I do remember that he and Parker bickered constantly. More than most siblings. I asked about the cause once, and all Kurt told me was that it was family pressure."

Finn rested his elbow on the door. "What kind of mother would send one son to kill another?"

"If that's what Diana did," Rhona pointed out. "We don't have any facts. We believed Kurt because it's his family, but he also said he hadn't spoken to them in years. A lot can change in that time."

Sabryn rubbed her hands together. "We need to come up with a plan in case Parker wants proof of Kurt's death. Do we need to check on Ferne? What about Callum?"

"Killian and Ariah are with Callum. Once Theo got word about the bookstore, he rushed to Ferne. Callum and the others fished the debris from the boat out of the water and then headed to the co-op to help Kirsi and Matt finish cleaning up. I just spoke with Theo. Ferne was so distraught he had to physically carry her out of the bookstore. He's headed to the manor with her now," Rhona explained.

Finn tapped the steering wheel. "What about Emily and the kids?"

"They're all fine. Scott and Filip surveyed the extent of the fire damage while Elias helped Emily file the police report. Elodie and Bronwyn already took the children to the manor. It's where we should all head."

"We'll be along eventually," Sabryn said, looking at Finn. "We're going to return to the hospital and stay with Song and Carlyle until Kurt's released."

Rhona said, "Understood. Remember, Balladyn is there, too, should you need him. He's likely veiled inside Kurt's room."

"Okay. Be safe," Sabryn replied before disconnecting.

Finn blew out a breath. "I'm going to admit something to you, but I want you to promise you won't tell anyone else. Especially not Carlyle or Elias."

"I promise," Sabryn said.

He turned his head to look out his door window. "We've faced many criminals and malicious people, and we've always won."

"We're winning here."

"Barely." His head swiveled toward her. "We're holding on by a thread. You can't deny that."

She shook her head. "No, I can't. New enemies are popping up everywhere we turn, but we keep fighting for what's right. And, somehow, we come out ahead."

"We've scraped by, it's true. But I don't think we'll be that lucky for much longer."

"What do you mean?"

He glanced down. "Can you honestly tell me you believe we'll all come out of this alive?"

"Yes," she answered, her concerns growing.

Finn raised his brows. "Really? Against London? Against George and the Edinburgh Druids? Against Parker? What about The Grey? And don't forget Edie. Or whatever else might arise along the way. Because that's what's been happening. Our luck will run out."

His voice rose with every word. They were all overwhelmed by their enemies' ruthlessness and the power with which they continued to strike. There was a measure of relief with each victory, but it never seemed to last long.

"I have to believe we'll survive this," Sabryn told him. "Because to think otherwise is unfathomable."

"It's going to be me."

His statement took her aback. "What?" she asked softly, hoping he didn't mean what she thought he meant.

Dark eyes met hers. "I'm not going to live."

"Of course you are. Why would you say that?"

He hung his head. When he spoke, he sounded resigned. "I've felt it for a few weeks now. When Carlyle vanished, I thought… I…"

"I know. Me, too," she said as she rubbed her hand on his arm, offering comfort. "But he's here. He won."

"It was close. Too close. Every battle is becoming harder and harder to win."

She shifted to face him and gently turned his head to her with her fingers. "Finn O'Connor, I want you to hear me. I'm not going to let you fall. Ever. None of the Knights will. We're a family, and we stick together. Plus, our family is bigger now. Do you know what that means?"

"What?" he asked wearily.

"It means there are more people to watch out for you. It means we get stronger with every person who joins. No one is going to fall. No. One," she stated firmly.

He flashed her a sad smile. "Not even you can stop death."

"Try me," she challenged, lifting her chin to prove her point.

All the while, she was crying inside. She knew what it was to have family and lose them. Finn held on because he finally had something he'd always yearned for. She held on because she knew she wouldn't survive losing another family.

When he didn't smile, she licked her lips and spoke the truth they both needed to hear. "I need you."

"I'll always have your back. You know that." Finn sniffed and shot her a halfhearted grin. "Back to the hospital, then?"

He'd firmly shut away his trepidation once more. It was useless to continue talking about it because Finn wouldn't. She straightened in her seat as he pulled back onto the road. She'd had no idea he was carrying such fear with him, but she knew now. Sabryn intended to watch Finn a little closer. Out of all the Knights, he was the one who liked to get close to his enemies in battle. Next time, she would stay by his side.

Neither spoke on the way back to the hospital. It wasn't until they were inside the building that Finn touched her arm to stop her. She turned to him, a brow raised in question.

"Talk to him," Finn said.

She knew exactly who *him* was. "Leave it."

"I can't. You're hurting, and it kills me. You don't see how he looks at you when you turn away. There's still something between you."

"You're wrong. Whatever was there died in DC."

CHAPTER SIXTEEN

When they reached the waiting room, Finn headed to Carlyle. She watched the two of them for a moment before making her way to Song and sitting beside her. It felt like it should be after midnight, but it was only early afternoon.

"No luck with Parker?" Song asked.

Sabryn shook her head. "He wasn't at the hotel. We decided to come back after talking to Rhona."

"Carlyle just hung up with her. You should return to the manor and rest. Carlyle and I will stay."

It was the perfect excuse for her to leave. Why, then, didn't she take it?

Another image of Kurt lying on the ground flashed in her mind. Sabryn squeezed her eyes shut, but there was no getting the picture out of her head. When she lifted her lids, she saw Carlyle in the chair across from her, scrutinizing her with his turquoise eyes.

"The chief stopped by to say that a couple of plainclothes police are here, one stationed inside the CCU," Carlyle told her.

Before Sabryn could reply, Dr. Dunn entered and smiled a hello. "I wanted to let you know that Mr. Barclay is still heavily sedated, but things have looked good the past few hours. We'll keep him in the CCU for twenty-four hours at least."

"When can we see him?" Finn asked.

"I'll have a nurse come get you shortly," the doctor said before walking away.

Carlyle and Finn shared smiles, their relief easing the tension in their faces. Sabryn was happy Kurt would live, but it didn't solve the issue of his deception or what to do with him. She sat, debating options for the rest of the next hour until a nurse's arrival pulled her out of her thoughts.

"Only two at a time," the woman informed them.

Carlyle stood and motioned at the rest of them. "We'll all go together, but two of us will remain outside the CCU."

The nurse nodded in agreement, and then they followed her up to another floor and past many doors in the brightly lit hallway. Sabryn gagged at the scents of sickness laced with antiseptic and the undertones of some artificial fragrance. She concentrated on putting one foot in front of the other until they stopped. She saw a large sign noting they had reached the CCU.

"Only two of you," the nurse reminded them.

Carlyle and Finn looked at her, waiting. Sabryn forced a smile and motioned for them to go ahead. Within moments, they were through the doors. She took a deep breath and leaned her shoulder against the wall before resting the side of her head on it.

"Is it his duplicity you can't forgive? Or the relationship that didn't work out?" Song asked.

Sabryn looked into her friend's dark eyes. "Maybe a little of both."

Song leaned back against the wall. "That makes sense. Are you upset the boys seem to have…" She paused, seemingly searching for the word.

"Forgiven him?" Sabryn offered. At Song's nod, she shrugged. "Maybe a little."

Song grinned. "That makes sense, too."

"I thought I had let go of the past."

"Sometimes, it's the past that can't let go of us."

Sabryn grunted and shifted so they were shoulder-to-shoulder. "I'd say it's because there was no closure, but does one ever really get that?"

"Depends on who you ask. But if you want that closure, now you have your chance."

"I don't want to dredge up the past."

Song ran her fingers through the length of her thick, black hair and glanced at her.

"Please," Sabryn said. "Say what you want to say. You're one of us, which means you don't have to hide anything."

"I'm not sure I *should* say it."

Sabryn shrugged and crossed her arms. "I can take it. Promise."

"All right. I was going to say there's no dredging up the past when it seems to walk beside you at all times."

My god. Was it that obvious to everyone except her? Why hadn't the boys said anything? But they wouldn't. They probably hadn't noticed it. Or if they had, decided it would be better to keep silent about it.

"I shouldn't have said anything," Song said.

Sabryn touched her arm. "No, no. I'm glad you did. It shocked me, is all. I thought I hid it well."

"You do. So well, you didn't even realize it."

Sabryn leaned her head back and sighed. "I've been such a fool. You're right, though. Now is my chance to get some closure."

"Kurt wants to talk. He's made that clear," Song added.

"I don't think I want to hear what he has to say. But if I want *him* to listen, I need to extend the same courtesy."

Song leaned over and lowered her voice. "I'll get the boys away to give you some time."

"Now? Kurt isn't even awake."

"Maybe that's the best time to do it. He won't interrupt you, and you don't have to hear him."

Sabryn considered it. "You have a good point."

Song pulled out her mobile and sent a text. Within moments, Carlyle and Finn emerged.

"Song needs some food," Carlyle said. "I didn't even notice the time. Why don't you come with us to get something to eat."

Sabryn wrinkled her nose. "I can't eat now. Go ahead. I'll stay."

"We won't be long," Finn promised.

After the three of them left, Sabryn entered the CCU and got directions from the nurses to Kurt's room. The CCU had a church-like quiet about it, broken only by the soft voices of those working there and the continuous beeping of monitors coming from the individual rooms. She didn't look into the other rooms as she passed. By the time she reached Kurt, her breathing was quick, harsh even to her ears. Sabryn paused outside his room and stared at the ajar door. Then, before she could change her mind, she slipped into the room.

Only to come to an immediate halt. The lights were dimmed, bringing attention to the brightly lit monitors recording his vitals. She barely saw them once her gaze landed on the bed and the large man lying so still and pale upon it.

Sabryn took a hesitant step forward. She dealt in magic. She knew how to shield herself and retaliate against it. But knives? Since when did a Druid resort to using such weapons? And why?

Her feet moved of their own volition, bringing her closer to the bed. Kurt's hospital gown was opened to the front, revealing his chest and the bandages covering his wound. Her eyes lingered on the Celtic warding tattoo on the right side of his chest. The covers were pulled up to his wound, and his arms lay outside the blanket, an IV line taped to his forearm.

Sabryn lifted her gaze and saw the oxygen tube. She stared at his face, waiting for his eyes to open, but the only movement was the steady rise and fall of his chest. She had come in to say her piece, but now that she stood beside him, the words wouldn't come. She and Saber had had thousands of conversations. And she'd never had an inkling that she might know him. Kurt hadn't revealed anything to make her suspicious. But he had gone to great lengths to keep his identity hidden. But why? And why work with the Knights?

The Saber she had come to know didn't mesh with the Kurt she knew from DC. He and Parker had fit in easily with the political crowd, those who seemed enthralled with the money and rank the brothers brought. It hadn't been a hoax, either. The Barclays were extremely wealthy, and both Kurt and Parker had lived that lifestyle.

Yet in the quiet of her apartment when it was just the two of them, Kurt had shown her another side of himself. The one who loved eating ice cream out of the carton and preferred sweats to a suit. The man who liked to grow his own herbs and cook his own food. The man who would rather visit the corner pizza place than any Michelin-star restaurant.

He'd been two different people back then, and she hadn't been bothered by it. Yet now, it agitated her. Was this more about her than anything Kurt did or didn't do? The last thing she wanted to do was look closer and find out, but she required answers. She didn't want to cart her past around anymore. She wished to release the weight and move on. And while it was easier to keep things as they were, she forced herself to delve into the *why*.

The answer came quick and hard.

She had trusted Saber. He had portrayed himself as a friend—someone who would always be there for the Knights. And he had delivered on everything. She'd spent sleepless nights texting with him. Both had shied away from talking about their pasts, and she had been glad for it. Now, she wished she had pushed to see what he might have said.

Saber wasn't some hacker hiding from the law or nefarious individuals wanting revenge. He was her ex-lover, who had broken her heart and then walked out of her life without a goodbye.

"Which one of you is the real Kurt?" she whispered. "The wealthy Brit, wining and dining me? The guy who loved to thrift shop in ripped sweats? Or the hacker who hid away and saved our asses more times than I can count? Or are you the man being hounded by his family? I wonder if you even know."

Emotion surged, clogging her throat and making it difficult to talk. "Why did you leave me?"

She lowered her eyes to the hand closest to hers and reached out her pinky to touch him. Just before her finger brushed the back of his hand, her phone vibrated. Sabryn jerked away from him and pulled out her mobile. The number was blocked. She shot Kurt another glance before striding from the room and answering the call.

"I'm surprised you picked up."

The sound of Parker's voice chilled her blood. Sabryn glanced around the hallway and kept her voice low as she asked, "Where are you? I'd like to have a little chat."

"I bet you would," he said with a chuckle. "Don't bother looking. You'll never find me."

"I'm pretty resourceful."

"Not without your trusty hacker doing your bidding."

Sabryn saw the *Exit* sign and hurried into the stairwell for privacy. "You always were a little shit, but I never figured you for a murderer."

"You shared Kurt's bed for three months. That doesn't make you an expert on him, me, or our family, so don't bother trying."

His comment hit home. "Why are you calling?"

A ferry horn sounded through the phone. "I wish I could've seen your face when you found Kurt on the ground. I won't bother asking if he's dead. You wouldn't tell me the truth."

"Oh, I'd be delighted to tell you. How about we meet up somewhere?"

He laughed softly. "Are you that eager to die?"

"Who says I'll be the one dying?"

"You chose the wrong side of this quarrel."

She snorted and rolled her eyes. "I choose the side of good, of right. And I will every time."

"Don't think I've forgotten how you said one of your ancestors was from Skye. Tell me, do you believe that will make the Druids accept you? Is that why you're so keen on dying for them?"

"You must not have gotten enough hugs as a child."

"Did Kurt tell you the real reason we were in DC?"

The question made her freeze. Dread tightened her chest, making it difficult to breathe. She knew she should hang up. That everything Parker said would be a lie. And yet, she stayed on the line.

"I didn't figure he'd tell you that the London Druids singled out your family," Parker said. "We were sent to see which of us you'd fall for. Everything we said and did was to gain your favor."

Sabryn reached for something—anything—with her free hand to keep from falling. She ended up stumbling into the wall as the pit in her stomach grew.

"You went right for him." Parker sniggered. "We had a bet, you know. To see which of us could get you into bed first. We both intended to have you."

She closed her eyes and bent over, gagging.

"You were the one who got us close to your father."

Sabryn's legs gave out. She crumpled to the floor, shaking her head in denial.

"Kurt never deviated from orders. Until you. You must have been an amazing shag for him to refuse to finish the mission. I was the one who had to step in. Granted, it wasn't my finest hour, but I got the job done. Your father never even saw it coming."

She was rocking back and forth now, tears coursing down her face.

"All because he wouldn't work with London." Parker tsked. "He had his chance. He could've ensured his family's protection for generations. I just thought you had a right to know the kind of man you've been working with all these years."

The line went dead, and the phone tumbled from her slack fingers. Parker's words rang in her head.

CHAPTER SEVENTEEN

Sabryn was there. Beside him. Kurt peeled his heavy eyes open and scanned around him to see her. A bellow rose in his chest when he saw only an empty room. He tried to rise but was immediately halted by stabbing pain.

"Be at ease," said a deep, Irish voice.

Balladyn appeared beside him, gently pushing him back onto the bed. It was then Kurt heard the incessant beeping. He looked over at the monitor and then took in the room as a whole. Gingerly, he touched his left side and winced from the small movement. He remembered the sidewalk, Edie, and the explosion. And that Parker had attempted to end his life.

"I can't stay here." Kurt winced at his dry mouth and the sound of his broken voice.

Balladyn quirked a brow, his red-ringed silver eyes gazing down at him peevishly. "Do you not believe I can protect you?"

"Need to find Parker." Fuck, it hurt to talk. His throat was raw and scratchy, making the simple act of forming words laborious.

The Reaper's brow rose even higher. "In your condition? That would be folly." He held a cup with a straw in it to Kurt's mouth. "Drink. You sound awful."

Kurt gratefully sipped the cool water and let it soothe his parched throat. "Was Sabryn here? I thought I heard her voice."

"She was."

Two words, but the silence that came after was worse. It allowed him to imagine all kinds of ghastly things. He braced himself and asked, "What happened?"

"She got a call. I could tell by her tone that it wasn't from someone in our group. I followed and heard her speaking to your brother."

Kurt pushed himself up, regretting it immediately. Agony cut through him as sweat broke out on his forehead. Balladyn caught him when he began tipping sideways. The Reaper raised the top of the bed so Kurt had something to rest against. All of that sapped what little energy he had.

"Where is she?" he asked.

"Gone. I don't know what Parker told her, but she was distressed. I got Carlyle, Song, and Finn, and they took her to the manor."

"Distressed?" Kurt repeated softly, trepidation tightening his stomach. "What did he say?"

Balladyn hesitated, his eyes troubled. "He told her why you two went to DC."

Kurt's worst fears came crashing down around him. He gripped the bed as the room spun wildly. Dimly, he heard Balladyn talking, but none of the words registered. He had to get to Sabryn. If he didn't tell his side of the story, she would never speak to him again. She still might not. But she needed to know. He'd wasted too much time fearing what might happen and had given Parker the ammunition he needed to drive a permanent wedge between him and Sabryn.

Everything became crystal-clear then. Kurt knew exactly what he had to do. He buried the pain and pulled off the oxygen tube before ripping the IV from his arm. Nurses came running into the room almost immediately. He tossed aside the covers and saw that Balladyn had veiled himself. Or maybe he had left. At this point, Kurt didn't care. He had something to deal with and getting out of the hospital was the first step.

"What are you doing?" a male asked.

Kurt put his bare feet on the cold floor and stood. To his surprise, his legs held him better than expected. "Leaving."

"You can't," a middle-aged woman stated as she approached.

Kurt snorted as he tried to find the ties to his hospital gown to close it over his nudity. "You can't stop me."

She took the edges of the gown from him and snapped it closed, her face tight. "You're right. We can't stop you, but you need to sign a waiver before you leave."

"Then you'd better get it to me because I'm walking out now."

"Walking?" the younger male nurse asked with a frown.

Kurt met his gaze. "Walking."

The woman turned on her heel and strode out, telling her male counterpart, "Keep him here until I get back."

"There's no' much left of your clothing, mate," the man said.

Kurt shrugged, instantly regretting it as a wave of nausea assaulted him. "I don't care."

"Let me get you some socks, at least."

Kurt hugged his left arm to his injured side and looked longingly at the bed. His legs trembled like he had run miles. He wiped the sweat from his brow with the back of his hand and noticed his shallow breathing.

"Why no' let me put these on for you?"

Kurt blinked and found the man standing before him again. He nodded because that seemed the acceptable response.

"Here," he said, taking Kurt by the arm and gently turning him toward a chair. "Bend your knees while I help guide you into the seat."

Sitting. Yes, that's exactly what he needed. The moment Kurt gave his legs permission to bend, there was no controlling himself. If the nurse hadn't been there, he would've fallen hard.

"Leaving is a really bad idea," the man said with a shake of his head as he kneeled before Kurt and put on the socks. "You only recently got out of surgery. You need rest."

"I'll get it."

His body was a contrast. He was sweating, but his feet and hands were cold. The socks warmed his feet, but…

The nurse stood as the female rushed in with a stack of paper. Kurt somehow managed to sign them all, though the signature looked nothing like his.

The woman sighed in exasperation. "This goes against the doctor and hospital. Why not wait for Dr. Dunn to come by?"

"No, thank you," Kurt replied, fighting another wave of nausea.

He tried to stand, only to have the male grab his arm and turn him toward the wheelchair. Kurt was more than happy to let them wheel him out the front of the hospital. The overhead lights blinded him the moment they pushed him out of the room. He shut his eyes against the piercing light and kept them that way until they were inside the lift.

His thoughts centered on Sabryn and the anguish—and anger
—she likely felt. There were a million ways he could've told her the
truth. He could've written a letter, phoned, or texted. But he had
wanted to say it to her. Only now, he could admit that he'd made
that plan because his subconscious knew he'd never go through
with it.

The lift doors opened, and they wheeled him out of the
hospital's sliding doors. The midday sun was hidden behind clouds
as birds sang loudly. Expression grim, the female halted, locked the
brakes on the chair, and then folded up the footrests.

She looked at him and then handed Kurt a small see-through
plastic bag. "Your wallet, mobile, and keys. And might I just say
you don't look well enough to stand?"

"Thank you," Kurt said, taking the bag.

"I can wait until your ride gets here."

Kurt put his hands on the arms of the chair and scooted to the
edge of the seat before pushing himself into a standing position.
He couldn't straighten, but he was on his feet. "No need."

The nurse turned at the sound of someone behind him. A
hand gripped Kurt's shoulder, and the hospital vanished, replaced
by Rhona and Balladyn's cottage. He turned his head to see
Balladyn.

"Couch or bed?" the Reaper asked.

Kurt didn't relish attempting to get up and down in either.
"Chair."

Balladyn nodded and helped him over to Rhona's favorite
chair. "I'll return shortly with a Healer."

"There isn't time. I need to find Sabryn."

Balladyn's staid expression didn't change. "You didn't kill
Sabryn's father."

"I didn't stop it either."

"That's not what you told us."

Kurt shifted to try to take some pressure off his left side. "I wasn't successful. That's not stopping it."

"But you *tried*. You'll have a chance to tell Sabryn your side of the story. *After* you're healed."

Kurt wiped more sweat from his forehead. "Take me to the manor. I've waited long enough. *She's* waited long enough."

"I can't bring you looking like this," he stated, moving his hand up and down to indicate Kurt. "You're getting paler by the moment."

"I'm surprised you didn't side with the nurses and make me stay."

Balladyn walked into the kitchen and returned with a glass of water. "Why would I do that? You gave me the perfect excuse to leave. Now, the Healers can do their jobs."

Kurt wrapped his fingers around the glass, but he needed both hands to steady it and bring it to his lips. All the while, Balladyn watched him.

"You always seemed like an intelligent man," Balladyn said.

Kurt snorted a laugh and lowered the glass, not even bothering to try to set it on the table for fear of dropping it. Bloody hell, he was weak. "A backhanded compliment?"

"A smart man would get healed to face his enemies."

"I'll face them."

Balladyn's expression said what he thought of that. "Take the healing now. If you don't, Sabryn will get to Parker while you're… recuperating," he said distastefully.

Kurt leaned his head back against the cushion. "My brother isn't who I'm concerned about. Sabryn will likely get to him first no matter what, and if that happens, Diana will send everything she has after Sabryn."

"You're going after your mother?"

"It's the only way to stop this."

Doubt filled the Reaper's face. "You really don't believe your brother came after you on his own?"

"Parker doesn't go to the bathroom unless Diana tells him to."

"All the more reason for you to get healed. You'll need to be strong to face whichever of your enemies you confront."

Kurt gave him a sad smile. "Once everyone learns the truth, no one will want to heal me."

Balladyn crossed his arms over his chest. "The truth, Druid, is that Rhona is in charge."

"She can't force a Healer to use their magic."

"We'll see about that. Sit tight. I'll be back."

The Reaper vanished in the next heartbeat. Kurt closed his eyes, no longer trying to hide his pain. Sitting was excruciating, but the mere thought of trying to move made his stomach turn. If he'd just had surgery, then there were still painkillers in his bloodstream. If it was this bad now, how much worse would it be when they wore off?

He knew Balladyn hadn't brought him to the manor because of Sabryn, and Kurt wasn't angry about it. The Reaper was protecting his friends. It proved again that Kurt was never meant to do more than peer into this world from the sidelines. He hadn't fought with the Knights, eaten with them, bonded with them. He'd kept himself separate, a wall between him and everyone else.

After so many years of hiding in a room of monitors, he didn't know how to be a part of something. Maybe he was never supposed to. He had been at his best masquerading as Saber, aiding the Knights to keep them safe while giving them whatever advantage he could. He might have been raised to mingle with the nobility, but he had found solace in cutting himself off from the world. Not everyone should be out among the masses, and he was proof of that.

Diana had gone too far this time. She always went too far, but Kurt had made excuses for her in the past. No more. He hadn't targeted their family in any way. Why would she come after him now? There had to be some kind of connection between Carlyle and Song's recent trip to London and Diana sending Parker after him.

Kurt groaned when he realized he needed to empty his bladder. He began the slow and painful process of getting to his feet. Once he stood, he used anything he could touch to help him stay upright. Step by measured step, he made it to the bathroom. Then, he began the arduous trip back.

He paused in the kitchen with his hands on the back of the chair to rest. Sweat dripped down his face, and he regretted not staying in the bathroom. He thought about pulling out the chair when his legs started trembling again, but he needed to lie down.

Something wet rolled down his side and onto his leg. He looked down at his wound and saw that blood had soaked through the gauze and into the gown. He attempted to pull out the chair when his legs went out from under him.

CHAPTER EIGHTEEN

Kurt came to in a strange, dark room. He was tired of waking up in unfamiliar beds. But for the moment, there was no pain, so he didn't move. The lamp beside him had been dimmed, leaving a soft glow that allowed him to see a dresser and the open door. He listened for voices, but the house was silent.

He recalled his wound bleeding and surmised that he had busted some stitches with his movements. He must have passed out because he had no memories after standing in the kitchen. So, where was he? And how did he get here? Unless…was he dead?

Surely, the afterlife would be something better than a bedroom. Kurt gradually moved his left arm, anticipating the pull from his injury, but he could raise it without pain. Next, he attempted to roll onto his right side. Success, again without pain. He shoved down the covers and pushed up onto his right elbow to find he was naked. His bandages were gone, and the only indication of a wound was a puckered, pink-hued section of skin.

"Looks like the Healers did their work," he murmured.

Kurt swung his legs over the side of the bed and grinned at not losing consciousness. He pushed to his feet to see how steady his legs were. When he was sure he wouldn't fall on his arse, he walked to the door and peered into the hallway. There were three other doors, all open, and a light coming from the opposite end.

He quietly crept down the hall, searching for other occupants, and passed a bathroom and two bedrooms before reaching the kitchen and a living area past that. Nothing looked familiar, nor did it appear as if anyone was home. He walked to the nearest window and checked outside but couldn't see much in the darkness. He then headed to the front door and opened it to find the porch bright enough to shine upon the entry and a few feet past it.

Kurt closed the door and ran a hand down his face as he considered things. He retraced his steps to the kitchen and spotted a piece of paper beneath a magnet of Neste Point on the fridge.

Found you unconscious and bleeding. I'm sure you won't be upset at being healed.

The cottage is heavily warded with Druid and Reaper magic. Will be by soon to fill you in on the plan.

B

Kurt read Balladyn's note twice. He tried not to read too much into the fact that he had been moved from Rhona's place, but it was hard not to. It wasn't enough that he had left the manor. They wanted him farther away.

Would he get a chance to talk to Sabryn? He hoped so. Kurt was glad Rhona had pushed him to tell her everything, because while he was far from faultless, he knew Parker well enough to know that his brother had twisted things just to cause Sabryn pain and make things harder for Kurt.

Balladyn said he would return, and Kurt believed him. He looked down at his nakedness and saw he still had dried blood on him from the attack and the surgery. There had to be clothes somewhere. But first, a long shower.

He made his way to the bathroom and turned on the tap, putting it as hot as he could handle it. Then he stood beneath the spray and let the water pelt his body for a long time before washing. It felt so good, he could've remained in there for hours, but his fingers were already pruny. Reluctantly, he turned it off.

As he reached for a towel, he heard something that made him still. Kurt listened for a heartbeat but didn't hear it again. He wrapped the towel around his hips and quietly slipped out of the bathroom. Another sound came from the direction of the kitchen. He crept down the hall once more, but this time, magic filled his palms.

He stepped into the kitchen, ready for battle, and saw Sabryn. She had her back to him as she stirred sugar into a mug. He dropped his arms, shock running through him. She tensed as if sensing him but sipped the liquid.

"You're the last person I expected to see," he said.

She finally turned to face him. "I asked for privacy."

"For?"

"Get some clothes on," she stated as she turned her head to the side as if the very sight of him sickened her.

Kurt glanced at the floor before walking to the bedroom he had woken in. There, on a stool, was his rucksack with the few items of clothing he had stuffed into it. He dressed and raked his fingers through his wet hair, but he didn't leave the room. He had begged Sabryn to hear him out. Whether she came to listen or deliver the words she needed to say, he was getting some time alone with her. For the first time in years, there was nothing standing between them. Not Parker, not miles, and certainly not any screens.

It terrified him.

None of the scenarios he had crafted had ever led him to this. He wasn't sure what to say to her. The truth, obviously, but would it be enough? He might not have been the one to kill her father, but he hadn't been there for her. He'd left her to deal with the aftermath of her dad's death alone. There was no justification or excuse that could make that right. And he didn't intend to try.

He'd wanted the facts revealed, and they had been, thanks to Parker. Though this wasn't the respite he had hoped for. Instead, Kurt carried another type of weight now. And this one wouldn't so easily be shucked off.

Kurt drew in a deep breath and readied himself for whatever would happen, then went to find Sabryn. She sat in a rocker in the living area, drinking her beverage. Her deep blue eyes briefly met his before she focused on something across the room.

The fact that she didn't immediately lay into him made him leery. He wanted to get closer, but her body language warned him against it. Instead, Kurt sat in the overstuffed chair farthest away from her. He tried not to stare, but he couldn't take his eyes off her. He knew the way she walked and ran and her battle stances from six years of watching her through CCTV footage.

But he also knew every inch of her face by heart. He knew the mischievous look she got when she was about to do something playful. The sound of her mirth and how she snorted when she laughed too hard. He knew that she loved to have her feet rubbed, was extremely ticklish, and had an affinity for olives.

He hadn't forgotten anything about those months in DC. Not their first date, their first kiss, or the first time she stood bare before him in all her amazing glory. He'd never known such passion existed. Experiencing it had changed him; it had shaken him to his core and made him take stock of his life and where he was going. He'd known then that if he wanted to be with her, he had to get away from his family. But he'd realized all of it too late.

Too late for her father.

And too late for them.

Sabryn set the mug on the table next to her, folded her hands in her lap, and lifted her gaze to him. "Where's Parker?"

"I don't know. I can find him, though."

"Yes, you will find him for me."

Kurt didn't bother warning her against going after his brother. He'd let her have Parker while he tracked down Diana and put an end to everything before his mother could strike again. "All right."

"Just like that?" Sabryn asked.

He shrugged. "You have a right to your vengeance."

"Are you telling me you don't want retribution? He stuck a knife between your ribs. In case you don't know, Parker was a hair's breadth from killing you."

Kurt squeezed his bare toes into the rug at the realization that he had come so close to dying. "I didn't know. But, yes, I want revenge."

"Well?" she asked tersely.

He didn't know this dance, so he was treading carefully. "You want me to look now?"

"I'm waiting for you to try to talk me out of going after him."

"I don't have a reason to talk you out of going after Parker."

Her eyes narrowed. "Bullshit."

"I know you well enough to know there isn't anything I could say anyway."

Her smile was icy when she said, "You *think* you know me."

He knew her better than she knew herself, but he was smart enough not to say that out loud. "I know all the Knights. It was my job to watch over all of you."

"You spied on me."

Kurt swallowed. His throat was tight. "I did."

Her eyes widened, and she laughed. "The truth. Color me shocked."

"I intended to come clean about everything," he began.

Her voice dipped low with barely controlled fury when she asked, "Really? And when were you planning to do that? In another six years?"

"Admittedly, I let too much time pass."

"You don't say?" she quipped.

He didn't blame her for her antagonistic behavior. She was handling herself better than he would. "My plan was to show you what I could do as Saber. And once you accepted me, tell you everything."

"But you didn't."

Kurt shook his head and rested his hands on his thighs. "I gave myself three months. When the time came, I convinced myself that I needed to show you more of what Saber could do. Before I knew it, a year had passed. Then two. Then six. The longer I let it go, the harder it was to say the words."

"As often as we exchanged texts, why not tell me that way?"

"I tried a few times. I had it all written out. But I could never hit send. It isn't the kind of thing someone should read. You needed to hear it from me."

She blew out an irritated breath. "There's a thing called a phone. You might have heard of it."

"The only thing I can tell you is that I wanted to say it standing in front of you. I tried to do it at the manor."

"Don't you dare," she warned, her tone dripping with fury.

He raised his hands, palms out in surrender, before returning them to his legs. "I wanted you to hear it from me, and I'm sorry I was too afraid to burn that final bridge between us. More than that, I'm sorry Parker spoke to you first."

"It should've come from you. You owed me that, at least."

"I owe you a lot. I know it isn't much, but I'm truly sorry, Sabryn."

She rolled her eyes. "Fine."

Fine? *Fine!* It was so far from *fine* that it wasn't even in the same hemisphere. Kurt had known she was already lost to him, but he still felt her slipping away. And it was crushing, devastating. But he had no one to blame but himself.

"I want to hear your side. Tell me what happened in DC," she demanded.

His heart pumped faster, blood rushing in his ears. He was staring at the love of his life, cutting the final cord, and she wanted him to talk about DC.

"As you stated, you owe me," Sabryn said.

Kurt nodded bleakly. "The London Druids have charged their members with locating Skye Druid descendants around the globe and pulling them into the organization. The moment they learned that an American senator had ties to Skye, plans were made. The elders wanted your father. The thought of a United States senator in their pocket was exhilarating. They decided it would be easier to pull you in first. That way, you could convince your father to join."

"Which is where you and Parker came in."

"It is," he admitted.

She picked at a nail. "You bet on which of you could get me into bed first."

Bloody fucking hell. He'd forgotten. Of course, his brother would share that. Kurt felt the expanse between them growing even more. "We did," he admitted, the words like ash on his tongue. "Everything was a competition to Parker. One of us was supposed to seduce you."

"I made that really easy for you, didn't I?"

"When Parker and I did it before—"

Her blue eyes blazed with fury. "You've done this to others?"

The revulsion in her tone twisted his gut. "It's how we were raised. I know that doesn't mean much to you, but I'm trying to explain."

"Oh, I'm just dying to hear what you'll say next."

Kurt had never felt good about the things he'd done, but he hadn't known shame until Sabryn entered his life. He ran a hand down his face and finished what he had begun. "I was supposed to seduce you and make you fall for me so you would follow me to London. Instead, I fell for you."

CHAPTER NINETEEN

Sabryn was going to be sick. Why put herself through hearing the horrid specifics yet again? Maybe she was a masochist. She gripped the arm of the chair to keep from rubbing her chest where it ached. It felt as if her heart were being torn out. It didn't matter what Kurt said. She couldn't believe any of it. She tried to snort in response, but no sound came out.

Instead, she sat there staring, waiting for him to continue.

"I, ah, I went off script as it were," he went on, leaning forward to rest his forearms on his thighs. He rubbed his hands together before looking at her. "Parker didn't like that. Diana gave me some freedom, but I took too much. I needed time to figure out a way to tell you what was happening and get us out."

"Secrets piled on top of secrets," she murmured.

He dipped his chin. "My mistake was enjoying my time with you instead of planning."

"That wasn't your only mistake."

He winced, and she smiled because she wanted to hurt him.

"You're right, it wasn't. Being with you showed me another way to live. I thought I could persuade Parker, and the two of us could stand against Diana." Kurt shook his head. "Parker became belligerent. We got into a shouting match that ended in a physical fight. He got in a good hit and stormed out of the hotel. I tried to call Diana, but she didn't pick up. So, I went looking for Parker."

Sabryn's voice was surprisingly calm when she said, "He got to her first."

"Yes. I spent the next few hours trying to find him and talk to Diana. I located Parker first. Or rather, he returned to the hotel. I knew by his expression that he had done something but couldn't get it out of him. That's when I called you."

She had been in the middle of a girls' night with her friends and missed the call.

"I drove around for hours, searching for you. I ended up at your apartment, waiting outside like some bloody stalker. When I saw you exiting the cab, I got out of my car. Two men moved from the shadows and headed toward you. That's when Parker appeared. He told me that as long as I stayed away from you, the men wouldn't harm you."

The news unsettled Sabryn. She should've been more aware of her surroundings. "You could've called out."

"I knew the men. I'd seen them work. I couldn't take that chance," he told her.

She stared at the top of Kurt's bowed head. How many times had she run her fingers through those thick caramel strands? How many times had she wound her arms around his neck? Kissed his lips? Felt him moving inside her? How many times had she screamed in pleasure? How many times had she lain against his naked flesh as they slept?

"Diana demanded we return home immediately," Kurt said. "I spent the next hours arguing all the reasons I needed to remain. I reminded her of why we had been sent to America to begin with and listed why you would be an asset to the London Druids. I went on at length about the advantage our organization would have if we had a senator and promised her I could finish the job. But she knew it was a lie. She ordered me to board the jet. I hung up on her." He issued a short laugh and sat up. "It was the first time I'd ever done something like that. It was bloody freeing. Then, it was my turn not to answer calls."

He went silent, his gaze distant as he fell into the past. She almost left him there because this was harder than she'd thought it would be. Sabryn had known he would have a different story than Parker, but she hadn't foreseen such specific details.

"And?" Sabryn nudged.

Kurt drew in a sharp breath and met her gaze. "Parker and I fought again. With words, fists, and magic. We obliterated our suite and the rooms on either side of us. Then, suddenly, he pulled back and laughed. That's when I heard the wail of sirens. He turned on the telly, and a reporter spoke about a car accident. Your father's crash. They said his driver was intoxicated."

"Martin never drank," she stated, remembering how her father's driver of over seven years had had his name dragged through the mud.

"It was Parker and Diana. I knew nothing about it. I swear."

"But you knew they would do something," she maintained.

His throat bobbed as he licked his lips. "I never imagined they would take *that* step. You and your father were assets."

Her stomach curdled. She alternated between wanting to

vomit, cry, and hit something. "I should have been in the car with Dad. I canceled our lunch because I was hungover."

"That was the only saving grace of that day. Parker flew into a rage when he discovered you had escaped the attack. He never saw the strike that knocked him out cold. The next time Diana rang, I answered the call."

"Is this where you tell me you bargained for my life?"

He briefly looked to the side. "Yes, because I did. In exchange for your life, I promised to return to London and cut off all contact with you. The jet was already waiting. I packed up my and Parker's things and dragged his unconscious body onto the plane. I kept him unconscious because I was honestly afraid of what I might do to him. Once we landed, I told Diana I was done. I was packing when she came into my room. That's where we made a second deal."

"What kind is that?"

"The kind where she left me alone, and I didn't go after her."

Sabryn didn't hide her amusement. "From what you told me about your mother, she isn't afraid of anyone."

"I know many secrets she doesn't want getting out. In exchange for me keeping quiet, she allowed me to leave."

"Until she decided she wanted you back."

His lips twisted. "Yeah."

"Is it because she learned we've been working together—well, sort of working together?"

"Maybe."

Sabryn gave him a flat look. "She didn't check up on you?"

"I got to walk away. That was the deal."

"One she's going back on. She sent Parker to kill you!"

Kurt shifted uneasily in the chair. "Then her secrets will be revealed."

"Is that it?"

"What do you want from me? My heart? My soul?" he demanded in frustration. "Because you have them already! I did everything I could to keep you alive."

Sabryn jerked to her feet. Just as she parted her lips to speak, something banged against the cottage. They both froze, their heads turning toward the sound.

"What was that?" Kurt asked.

She shook her head and shrugged before heading to where she'd heard the thump. Sabryn hesitated only a second before peering out the window. The cottage sat cloaked in raven-black night. Not even the moonlight was visible. She had never been scared of the dark, but something about this made her skin crawl.

Another thud came near the window, making her lurch away. Kurt strode to the door and opened it. Immediately, a gust of wind that howled with the fury of the cosmos yanked the door from his hand until it slammed against the wall. The wind held the door still as it swooped aggressively around him. He held up his arms to protect his face and turned his head one way and then the other.

"Get back!" Sabryn yelled, but Kurt couldn't hear her.

She raced to his side and shoved him out of the wind's path. It slammed into her, sending her careening to the side, but Sabryn managed to grab the door handle and keep her footing. Hair whipped into her eyes, preventing her from seeing anything as she worked to get behind the door.

The wind's hold was unyielding, but she wasn't giving up. She looked out into the obsidian night and found herself reaching for the wind. It had never been her enemy. She, like every Druid in her family, was a wind talker. But she had shut out the wind within days of coming to Skye because of its never-ending screams of danger.

"Sabryn!"

She looked at Kurt, who was flattened against the wall, staring at her. His lips moved, but the wind snatched his words so she could only make out some.

"…to…saying?"

A gust brushed past her face and wound around her arm as if trying to pull her outside. Kurt wanted to know what the wind was telling her, and it obviously wanted to impart something to her. It had been difficult to close herself off to it, but once she had, it became a habit. So much so that she sometimes forgot she had the ability.

How many times had it attempted to warn her of danger? Had it tried to tell her Parker's true motives? Had she nearly cost Kurt his life because she had grown tired of hearing its warnings? The implications made her sick.

But she'd deal with that later. Right now, she needed to listen.

Sabryn focused on opening her mind. Robust magic swirled delicately through her. She closed her eyes and lifted her face to the wind, reaching out to it. Once she opened that door again, she was assaulted by deafening screams. Pressure built until she thought her head might explode. Her ears popped, each time more painful than the last.

She released the door and stumbled back, covering her ears with her hands. Fingers gently grasped her shoulders to steady her, but she barely felt Kurt. The angst and panic in the wind's shrieks reverberated inside her, turning her blood to ice.

Danger!

Not safe!

She's coming for yooooooooooou!

Run! You must RUN!

Kurt shook her. She opened her eyes to see his mouth moving but couldn't hear him over the wind. His hands wrapped around her wrists, and he tried to pull her hands away from her head. She fought back, twisting away from him. If she removed them, she would go deaf. Couldn't he understand that? She dropped to the ground and curled in on herself, thinking of nothing but stopping the agony.

Kurt lifted her torso so she faced him and spoke slowly, carefully mouthing, "*Tune it out again.*"

"I can't!" she yelled over the wind.

"Then lower the volume." He touched the side of her face and raised his fingers to show her that blood was dripping from her ears.

This was likely the result of her ignoring the wind for so long. It would be worse if she shied away from it again. Like it or not, she had to address it. And ask for forgiveness. If it didn't kill her first.

Sabryn shoved to her feet, walked against the current to the doorway, and took two steps outside the cottage. She lowered her hands from her ears and winced as the volume increased. The wind roared and whipped around her with the intensity of a hurricane. Then a gust struck her in the chest, tossing her backward. But she landed against a firm body. Kurt's hands fell to her waist, steadying her.

The wind was angry and…scared. "I'm listening now. I'm here," she whispered.

Sabryn held out both arms to accept whatever the wind

wanted to do to punish her. She had hurt and angered it by shutting herself off to it. Now, she was paying the price. There was no caress, none of the softness she had once experienced with the wind. There was only fury and pain.

Danger!

She's coming!

Run!

You must RUN!

"I can hear you. You don't have to shout anymore," Sabryn tried again.

RUN!!!!

The wind continued to scream, but it wasn't as loud as before. "Run where?" Sabryn asked.

Away. She's coming.

"Who's coming?" she pressed.

You're out of time.

CHAPTER TWENTY

Wariness shot through Kurt when he heard Sabryn's questions over the howling wind. He stared out into the blackness, searching for movement, but couldn't make out anything in the tempest swirling around them.

Suddenly, Sabryn whirled around and shoved at him. "Get inside! Now! Get inside!" she yelled urgently.

The panic in her voice propelled him into action. He wrapped his arms around her waist and held her against him as he walked backward into the cottage. The moment they were inside, they both reached for the door. He put his foot on the wall for added leverage against the continuous onslaught of the wind.

Inch by inch, they moved the door until it was finally closed. He was out of breath, his ears ringing from the abrupt dimming of noise after being in the midst of it. Sabryn didn't stop to rest, though. She locked the door and laid her hand against the wood, likely fortifying the wards. Kurt didn't know who was coming, but he understood danger was approaching and joined her as they moved about the cottage.

"What is going on?" he asked as he leaned over the sink and placed his hands on the pane of glass before muttering the words that would reinforce the existing wards.

Sabryn didn't answer as she raced from one room to the next. Kurt was at the window in the bedroom he'd woken up in when he thought he saw a figure moving outside. Icy fingers of unease slid through him, digging deep as he swiftly strengthened the wards. Only when he was finished did he search the void outside. The night thrashed and throbbed, sightless and savage. The darkness screamed, but nothing moved. He told himself it had been a limb or some debris caught in the storm. But he didn't believe it. Sabryn knew someone was coming. And it looked like they had arrived.

He backed out of the room into the hall, his gaze never leaving the window and the wind-torn blackness.

"Done," Sabryn said as she rushed out of a bedroom.

He turned his head and met her gaze. They stared at each other and listened to the storm battering the cottage.

"Who's coming?" he asked.

Sabryn drew in a shaky breath. "Edie."

"Fuck."

"Yep. Pretty much my thought, too."

Kurt turned to grab his mobile and realized he didn't know where it was. "Call the others. We need reinforcements."

"Right. Of course." Sabryn drew her mobile from her back pocket.

Her hands shook slightly as she tried Elias. The call wouldn't connect. She then tried Finn. Same thing. She next attempted Carlyle without any luck.

"Theo," Kurt suggested. "Try Theo."

She shook her head and lifted the phone to show him the screen. "It's no use. We don't have a signal."

He looked at the absence of bars and turned on his heel to grab his pack from the bedroom. Kurt yanked out his laptop and plopped down on the bed as he flipped it open. The internet was out, too.

"Is there a landline?" he asked.

Sabryn pushed out of the doorway and ran to the kitchen as he jumped up and searched the living area.

"Nothing," she called out a moment later.

He shook his head at her when she came into the room. "Nothing here either. I saw someone outside a few minutes ago, but we might still be able to make a run for it."

Sabryn leaned against the wall. "The wind said we were out of time. Our best bet is to stay here."

"What could Edie want? You've been on Skye for weeks, and she's not come after you."

"Maybe it isn't me she wants. She did team up with Parker."

Kurt jumped when something thumped loudly against the cottage again. "You think she's after me?"

"Makes sense. Like you said, she hasn't come after me."

"I'm not so sure. She didn't do anything to me on the street."

Sabryn shrugged. "Who knows. Maybe she's here because you survived."

"That certainly makes it seem like she's working with Parker."

"Why, though?"

Kurt rubbed his forehead. "I don't know. If Edie is as powerful as Kerry, she doesn't need my brother or the London Druids."

"I think Edie is *more* formidable than Kerry. Either way, you're right."

"Let's set the *why* aside for now. Edie is here, and we have no way of getting word to the others."

"Not exactly," Sabryn said with an impish smile. In a steady voice, she called out, "Balladyn."

Kurt returned her smile. Thankfully, one of them was thinking clearly. But with every second that passed without the Reaper appearing, their grins slipped. It eventually became apparent that Balladyn wasn't coming to their rescue. Whether it was because he couldn't or wouldn't didn't matter. The risks posed to them didn't change.

"Who picked this cottage?" Kurt asked.

Her face was tight with alarm when she shrugged. "It's one of many rented out on the isle. Kirsi's parents know the owners and asked if we could use it."

"So, no connection to Edie?"

"None," Sabryn replied.

He looked out the window into a black so absolute it devoured everything. He couldn't see what kept banging against the cottage. "Do you think the entire isle is dealing with this wind?"

"I didn't ask, and the wind didn't say."

"What did it tell you?"

Sabryn jumped at a repeated thumping on the roof. When it finally subsided, her voice was tight when she said, "I've not been using my ability. When I got to Skye, the wind yelled *danger* in a continual loop. I couldn't get it to say anything else or cease."

"So, you blocked it," he guessed.

She looked away, shame furrowing her brow. "Yes. Tonight is the first time I've listened to it in weeks."

Kurt looked at the dark streaks of drying blood on her face and walked around her to the kitchen. He wet the end of a towel and returned to her. He gently moved aside her hair and cleaned her ears, cheek, and neck. To his surprise, she let him.

He asked, "Was the wind angry?"

"Very," Sabryn admitted in a soft voice. "If I had been listening, I might have saved you from getting stabbed."

He caught her gaze, the rich blue as deep as twilight over the ocean. "Don't go there. What's done is done. We need to focus on what's happening now."

She was the first to look away. He moved to her other side and dabbed at the blood there.

"I don't know if the wind has forgiven me," she told him. "It warned of danger and that we weren't safe. It said she was coming for us and that we needed to run."

"Is that all?"

"Pretty much. Except for the end, when it said we were out of time and told me to get inside."

"The wind said *we*?" he asked her. "As in both of us?"

Her brow wrinkled. "Actually, no. It said *you*."

"As in you," Kurt said, nodding to her.

She shrugged indifferently. "I'm sure it meant you, too."

"But what if it didn't? What if Edie's after you?"

Silence met his question. He finished cleaning her all too soon. He should've taken his time and let his fingers linger on her soft skin. Kurt had no choice but to step away from Sabryn. He folded the towel to give his hands something to do so he didn't reach for her.

"I don't think it matters. We're both stuck here," Sabryn said.

The banging and thumps grew more frequent—some closer to

them than others. It was unsettling not to be able to see what was out there. Kurt tossed the towel onto the sofa and was about to speak when the door started rattling like it was about to come off its hinges.

Sabryn whirled around at the sound. They both stared at the door, waiting to see if something would come through. Their attention shifted to the violently shaking windows. The wind had grown louder as a menacing air settled around the cottage. Things were about to get much, much worse. How long did they have before the windows burst or the door was ripped away? How long until Edie walked inside? They had to get ready. Because, like it or not, they were in the middle of a battle. Kurt might have sat behind a screen for years, but he'd been trained since birth for just such a fight.

He took Sabryn's arm and turned her to face him. "Control the wind."

"I communicate with the wind. I don't control it," she stated as if he were a simpleton.

"And most can only hear it, not be heard *by* it. Yet you can carry on a conversation."

She glanced at the door and watched it bow inward from the wind. "I apologized. Apparently, that wasn't enough."

"Unless this has nothing to do with you being forgiven."

Her head snapped to him. "You think Edie is controlling it?"

"What if it doesn't have a choice but to obey? I think it's worth finding out."

She looked at him helplessly. "I wouldn't even know where to begin."

"It doesn't matter. All you have to do is try. If Edie is controlling the wind, then you have an advantage."

"I'm not following," she said.

He couldn't hold back his flinch when something struck the nearby window. "You communicate with the wind. Who will it listen to if given a choice?" he asked crossly. "Just try!"

She jerked out of his hold. "Fine!"

After a scathing look directed at him, Sabryn closed her eyes. He moved closer to her, ready to spring into action should something come for her. He heard a window crack ominously. They were running out of time.

It was two against one. That would have given them an advantage if they were dealing with any regular Druid, but Edie was far from that. Some otherworldly power helped her, and there was no telling what benefits she reaped. And Kurt really didn't want to find out.

While Sabryn continued to concentrate, he turned to the window cracking next to him and added another layer of warding to keep the split from widening. It was merely a bandage, but he didn't know what else to do.

The thunderous wind suddenly lost some of its bluster. He swung his head to Sabryn. A frown creased her brow as she strained. It was just as he had suspected. The wind had chosen Sabryn, and the battle had changed grounds. He hated that he could do nothing but lend his support when he'd rather be fighting alongside Sabryn. But she was the wind talker. Little by little, it died down until it was gone.

"You did it," he stated proudly.

Sabryn's smile was huge when she looked at him. "Let's check the internet."

"Good thinking." He rushed to his room and grabbed the

laptop, but his excitement died quickly. He made his way back to her. "Still nothing."

She shrugged and headed toward the door. "Then, we leave."

Warnings sounded in his head that it had been too easy. He lobbed the computer onto the sofa and ran to her as he shouted, "Wait!"

But it was too late. Sabryn had already unlocked the door and cracked it open. A loud hissing sound filled the room as the very air was sucked away with a violent gasp, and he was slammed into the door. The force of it lodged him painfully in a crevice.

The seams of his shirt started to come apart as the material was ripped from his body. Kurt bellowed in agony as he was pulled through the gap.

"Kurt!" Sabryn screamed, trying to pull him out.

Somehow, he got his hand on the wall and his shoulder underneath him, but no matter how hard he pushed, he couldn't break the seal of his body from the door.

"Hang on. I've got you!"

He hadn't come back from a knife wound only to be extracted through a gap the size of his palm. He sought the edge of the door with his other hand. Sabryn placed his palm on the frame. Next, she helped him get his feet placed, one on the wall next to the doorframe and the other along the edge of the door. She moved in behind him, molding her body to his back. She squeezed her hands between him and the gap while setting her feet next to his.

"Now!" she yelled.

They both shoved with everything they had, but he didn't budge.

"Magic," Kurt bellowed.

"On three," she shouted. "One. Two. Three!"

He used every ounce of his magic, pushing it from his body and into his palms and feet as he pushed away. He felt a slight loosening in the seal around him and doubled his efforts. Hope filled him when the hold loosened more. And then a little more. Until he could breathe easier again. With one final heave, they broke away.

The minute Kurt felt them falling, he tried to shift so he didn't land on top of Sabryn, but her hold was too tight. They fell hard, the impact jarring them both. He barely realized they were on the floor as his feet were dragged toward the crack when the suction began again. He kicked at the door and slammed it shut, rolling off Sabryn. She blinked up at him, a little dazed.

"Are you hurt?" he asked.

She sat up and gingerly touched her head. "No. You?"

He looked down at his torn shirt and what would be a huge bruise running the length of his torso. "I'm fine."

"I have to be honest. I didn't think about the landing."

"Me, neither," he said with a chuckle. "Thanks for the assist." He held out his hand to help her up.

She stared at it but ignored it and climbed to her feet. "I got the wind to stop. I don't know what *that* is."

"My guess is Edie. She wants something, and she's not going to quit."

"Yeah. She wants us. Here. Alone."

Kurt shot a look toward the door. "She wants us away from the others. We're threatening as a whole. It's a good strategic move."

"One Kerry didn't employ."

"It won't take the others long to realize they can't get ahold of us."

Sabryn wrinkled her nose. "Actually, they might. I told them I wanted to speak to you privately. I think Elias, Finn, and Carlyle are hoping we make up."

Kurt was, too. "In other words, you're saying no one will bother us."

"Precisely. Look, I'm the one who asked Balladyn to bring you here. I'm the one who put us in this position."

"This isn't on you. Edie saw an opportunity and took it. It would've been the same for any of the group who went their separate ways."

Sabryn nodded. "Sure. Like when Ferne and Theo go home alone. Or Callum, when he's all by himself. Then there's Kirsi, who lives by herself above the co-op. And Filip. But we can't forget about Scott and Elodie."

"Okay," he said, holding up his hands in surrender. "I get the point. Edie has had opportunities."

"Then why hasn't she taken them?"

He drew in a deep breath and slowly released it. "That brings me back to you, me, or us."

"You, I can see, since you have that relation to Parker."

"Unfortunately. I take it you think she's focused on me?"

She shrugged. "Makes sense that she'd come for you the moment you were alone."

"Except she didn't. Nothing happened until you arrived."

"Fair point." Sabryn raked her fingers through her short, black hair. "What do we do about it?"

"Find a way out. And quickly."

CHAPTER TWENTY-ONE

SKYE DRUIDS

Carwood Manor

The sitting room was silent as everyone looked at each other after Rhona finished recounting what Kurt had confessed to her and Balladyn. Finn walked to the sideboard and poured several fingers of Dreagan whisky into a glass and downed it.

He refilled it before turning to face the others. "Anyone else?" he asked and lifted the bottle.

"I think we could all use one," Elodie said.

Finn set about getting extra glasses. It was easier than thinking about the lengths the London Druids had gone to in order to bring powerful Druids into their community—and kill. He'd always known they were dangerous. He just hadn't realized to what extent until that moment.

Carlyle stood at the window, looking out into the night, his hands in his pockets. "We knew London had killed before. Ferne and Mason's parents are proof. So are Song's."

"There could be hundreds like that," Elias said.

Carlyle turned to face the room. "Without a doubt. My point is that I always thought London would keep their attention on the UK."

Finn didn't hold back his snort as he handed out the drinks to all who wanted them. "When has Britain ever kept their nose out of other people's business?"

"But America?" Bronwyn asked skeptically.

Rhona took her drink from Finn. "It's about power. It's always been about power for London. The more they have under their control, the larger their numbers, and the more formidable they are."

"They didn't get Sabryn or her father," Willa pointed out.

Finn placed the now-empty bottle aside. Another was waiting. One of the perks of being friends with the Dragon Kings was that there were always cases of whisky waiting. "The fact that the London Druids have been searching for descendants from Skye is alarming."

The manor door opened, and Theo entered, sporting a five o'clock shadow and dark circles under his eyes. He glanced into the library before Ferne called out to him, drawing his attention their way. She rose and crossed to him, greeting him with a kiss. Finn sipped his whisky and eyed the Detective Inspector, who had been with his boss for the past several hours.

"I take it things didn't go well," Jasper said.

Ferne handed Theo her whisky and tugged him into her vacant seat. He sank onto the cushion but didn't even acknowledge that he held the liquor.

Theo bit back a yawn. "The chief superintendent wanted everything, and I do mean *everything*."

"You told her?" Ariah asked in surprise.

Theo shrugged. "I tried evading her questions, but she was relentless. So, aye, I told her everything. She'd already seen some of it herself. There was no point in lying now."

"And?" Balladyn asked.

Theo rubbed the back of his neck. "She said a lot of things made sense now."

"Please tell me she's not going to interfere," Rhona said.

Theo shrugged and tossed back the whisky in one swallow. "I made it clear about the threats we faced and that anyone not a Druid would no' only get in the way but also become a liability."

"I bet she didn't take that well," Finn said.

Theo's dark eyes met his. "She's a copper. What do you think?"

Rhona released a long breath. "I won't deny that the chief helped today, and we needed her. She could be an asset. But that doesn't mean I'm going to open our meetings to her. For the moment, we need to figure out what our next move is."

"If we're going to find Parker, we need Kurt. How long are we going to give him and Sabryn?" Elias inquired.

Rhona briefly looked at the clock. "As long as she needs."

"I don't think we can wait that long," Carlyle replied.

Song lifted one shoulder in a shrug. "Then we don't wait. We found Parker before. We can find him again."

"That was before we knew Edie was involved," Elodie said.

Scott ran a hand down his face. "If Edie's the bigger threat, maybe we should be focusing on her."

"That fire was intense." Song shook her head. "There is no way she should've lived."

Elias finished his whisky and sighed. "But she did. And my guess is she's the one who killed Kerry. If Edie can get past Rhona's and Balladyn's magic, then I think we should concentrate on ending her before she does more damage. She went after her own mother and children, for fuck's sake."

"I agree. The Edie out there now isn't our sister," Elodie said, looking at her brother. "I don't think she has been for some time."

Finn set aside his glass. "Am I the only one who thinks it odd that Edie consorted with Parker?"

"Far from it," Jasper declared. "I said that the moment I saw her on the street."

Ariah nodded, her long, crescent moon earrings tinkling. "Which means we can't just fixate on one of them."

"Great," Filip said wearily. "Two foes at once. Again."

Willa snorted. "Two? Try four. Or are you forgetting Edinburgh and The Grey?"

"When is it time to call in help?" Filip asked as his gaze slid to Rhona. "Who else has to die before you realize we can't do this on our own?"

Finn exchanged a look with Carlyle. They'd had this conversation before.

Rhona didn't get upset at Filip's outburst. She scooted to the edge of the chair and set aside her glass. "We're lucky we have friends who have helped in the past, and we may very well call on them in the future. We're Skye Druids, Filip. Our ancestors were called to these shores. Every Druid around the world can trace their ancestry to this isle. We're not being harassed by multiple adversaries because we have powerful allies. We're being attacked because *we're* formidable."

She drew in a breath and continued. "London wants us out of the way because we have the means to stop whatever nefarious plan they have. Oddly enough, had they kept to themselves, we never would've learned of it and likely would have left them alone. As for Edinburgh, this is all about George and her revenge plot against Elias. The Grey…well, as we've recently learned, it wasn't the first time that enemy attacked Skye. The Druids kept the isle safe before—without help—and we will do it again. Because we have to. And we'll do it ourselves because we're Skye Druids. I don't care that some of you weren't born here. I don't care that others once had affiliations with London or Edinburgh. Like I said, all Druids trace back to Skye. Which makes you one of us."

Elias turned his head to Rhona. "And Edie?"

"Whatever turned Kerry and Edie into what they became is, I believe, connected to The Grey somehow," she answered. "Parker and those like him being pulled into this from the fringes will be dealt with."

Finn raised his brows. "Does that mean we can get back out there and search for that twat?"

"I never stopped," Balladyn replied smoothly.

Bronwyn asked, "Then what are we waiting for?"

"We've gone in blind before. It would be better if we knew more," Jasper pointed out.

Finn had heard enough. "How much more do we need to know? Edie is against us. Parker is with London, and whether he came to take Kurt home or kill him doesn't matter. His attempt on one of the Knights is enough for me. They both need to be stopped."

"They will be," Rhona rejoined. "However, Jasper has a good point. We have gone in blind, and we've gotten very lucky. I don't want to press that luck further than we need to."

Carlyle crossed his arms. "What do you suggest, then? Because, frankly, I agree with Finn. We need to strike before they come at us again."

"What we need is Kurt. I want to give him and Sabryn a chance to talk, but right now, we need details only he can get," Elias stated.

Finn nodded. "Every minute counts. We need them both."

The room grew quiet as everyone waited for Rhona's reply. She looked at Balladyn. At that moment, they heard a loud thump upstairs. Everyone froze. The sound was one they had heard before. Finn looked up at the ceiling before glancing at Elias.

Bronwyn's face paled as she jumped to her feet. "Oh, no," she murmured and raced out of the room.

Elias followed, and Finn was quick to join. Bronwyn raced to the second floor and to the left, only to skid to a halt in front of the second-to-last door on the right. The very room she had used to open the rift between the dimensions and hide her unconscious cousin, Beth, for a time. It was the same rift Ferne had been pulled into. The one they'd gone into to find her.

Finn loathed the room. He abhorred anything to do with The Grey. The entire place terrified him. It was somewhere he never wanted to venture into again.

Bronwyn put her hand on the wall near the door and closed her eyes. Almost instantly, she jerked her hand back. "Oh, god."

"What is it?" Elias asked.

She turned her hazel eyes to him, wide with fear. "It's trying to get through."

Finn didn't need to ask what she referred to. It was the beast that had taken Ferne. The same creature Kirsi was meant to fight in the final battle. A monster that haunted his dreams by its sound alone.

"I thought Callum sealed the tear," Finn said.

Bronwyn nervously wrung her hands. "He did. We all saw it."

"We need to stop whatever is attempting to get in before it gets through," Elias said. "What do you need?"

"I-I don't know. The portal isn't open. None of this should be happening," Bronwyn whispered.

The minute Elias looked at him, Finn raced to the stairs. When he reached them, he shouted for everyone to get up there. The house had held off the beast before, and while he didn't know what the house told Bronwyn, her fear was enough of a message. The manor needed their help.

Finn ran back to the couple. The thud of rapid footsteps grew louder as their friends sprinted up the stairs. Finn looked at the bedroom door, praying they didn't have to go inside. It was bad enough that he stood outside the room. He gave it a wide berth, and there were even times he could almost forget he slept in the same house. If he went into the room today, he wouldn't come out. The truth of it filled his soul.

He winced and backed away when Bronwyn opened the door. Finn found himself staring into the darkened room, his heart hammering against his ribs. In that instant, he was back in The Grey with the eerie silence, faint lighting, and the shadow threatening and moving ever closer.

Someone gripped his arm, yanking him to the side and whirling him around. Finn found himself staring into Carlyle's worried eyes.

"What's wrong?" his friend whispered.

Finn shook his head. "Nothing."

"Don't bloody lie to me," Carlyle bit out, his voice pitched low.

Song put a soft hand on his arm. "Babe."

"Finn," Carlyle challenged, ignoring her.

"I don't like the room," Finn finally admitted.

Carlyle searched his face before his turquoise eyes narrowed. "You're not telling me everything."

"The others are going into the room. They need us," Finn stated.

"Let me help. What is it?" Carlyle urged.

Finn closed his eyes and dropped his chin to his chest. Then, he looked at his friend. "If I go in, I won't come out."

Carlyle blinked before his gaze darted to the room and then back to Finn. "The room, or The Grey?"

"The room."

Song pulled her hair back and tied it off. "You two stay here. I'll be back."

Finn watched her walk away and waited for Carlyle to call her back. When he didn't, Finn swung his gaze to her. "What are you doing?"

"Staying with my friend," Carlyle replied.

Any argument Finn had died on his tongue. He didn't want to go into the room, and Carlyle was giving him a way out.

"When this is finished, I want details," Carlyle said.

"There aren't any."

"Stop fucking lying. We've been through too much for you to do that."

Finn turned to lean back against the wall. "There's not much to tell. I saw something when we were in The Grey."

"What did you see?"

"A shadow."

Their talking ceased when the manor shook violently as if the very earth beneath it trembled.

"Carlyle! Finn!" Elias shouted.

Carlyle put a hand on Finn's chest when he started to move. "Stay out here."

Finn shoved his hand away and headed into the room with his friends.

CHAPTER TWENTY-TWO

They needed out of the cottage, but no matter how hard he looked, Kurt couldn't find a way. He threw open the cupboards in his desperate search as the house groaned and creaked threateningly.

"Think there's a hidden passage there?" Sabryn asked from behind him.

He shut the door and turned to her. "I was—"

"I know," she said over him. "I looked in the bathroom cabinet."

"Looks like we're stuck. Do you have any suggestions?"

"We wait for the others."

He turned his head to look out the kitchen window. "Or until Edie gets tired."

"Can the cottage withstand that?"

"We'll have to ensure it does."

She tucked her hair behind her ear. "Reinforcing the wards every hour?"

"That's a good start."

"But it won't hold forever," she said with a twist of her lips.

Kurt rubbed the back of his neck. "All we need to do is buy our friends some time."

"But we're also giving Edie time. *And* Parker."

"Trust me when I say we can't walk out into that."

Her eyes dropped to his torn shirt. "I'm fully aware. I'm going to start the wards again in the bedrooms."

He watched her walk away before warding the window nearest him. As he made his way to the opposite side of the house, he couldn't help but acknowledge that he had gotten exactly what he wanted: time alone with Sabryn to speak his truth. He had gotten the story out, but not with the words he rehearsed. He'd been so sure he couldn't forget them, but then again, he hadn't been sitting before an angry Sabryn when he practiced.

Once he finished his round of the cottage, he sank onto the sofa and opened his computer. All he needed was half a second of internet to send a message to the Knights. There might have been something he could do if he was at the warehouse with his six monitors, ten hard drives, and as much voltage as he needed. All he had now was a laptop. He had built it, adding power for quick, on-the-go instances, but it was never meant to be his only tool— especially not against magical foes.

And that, it seemed, was where he had gone wrong. He'd never imagined a scenario where he wouldn't have access to all his equipment or the internet, because he hadn't ever believed he would reveal his identity to the Knights. Yet, here he was. He'd been in tight situations before and managed to come through somehow. He wouldn't stop searching for any small thread that might allow him to reach cyberspace.

The *whack* against the side of the cottage caught his attention. He looked up from the screen to find Sabryn sitting on the edge of a chair, her arms wrapped around her middle and eyes darting about nervously. Another smack sounded. He listened closer and heard the wind once more. That couldn't be what was making the noise. Could it?

"Is that…?" he asked.

Sabryn nodded. "It started about ten minutes ago."

"Do you want to try to control it again?"

"I already did," she admitted grudgingly, her gaze darting away. "It won't acknowledge me."

Kurt closed the computer. "Why didn't you tell me?"

She motioned to his laptop with her hand. "You were doing your thing. I tried mine. Tell me you were successful."

"I wish I could."

She leaned forward and blew out a long breath. "I need you to say you were."

He studied her tightly drawn face, pinched lips, and the fear in her eyes. If she needed him to lie, then he would lie. "I got through to the lads. Carlyle, Finn, and Elias will be here as quickly as they can."

She turned her head away and nodded. He was searching for something to say to fill the silence when Sabryn sat up and turned dark blue eyes on him. "I still don't understand why Diana would kill you."

Kurt realized Sabryn needed a diversion, and as much as he didn't want to talk about his family or the past, there were things that needed to be said. "I went back on our deal."

"By being around me?"

"I swore I'd keep my distance."

Sabryn rolled her eyes. "You did. I had no idea it was you."

"Everything is black and white with Diana. There are absolutely no shades of gray. You're either on her side or you're not. By going back on our deal, I set myself against her."

"You're her child," Sabryn insisted.

He shrugged and got to his feet. "She was never very maternal. Are you hungry? I can't remember the last time I had a full meal."

"You want to eat?" she asked in disbelief.

"We're going to need our energy." He looked over his shoulder as he walked to the kitchen. "Unless you plan on sitting the battle out."

She pulled a face. "Right, because that's what I do." She followed him. "I'm not sure how long we can stand against Edie."

"It doesn't matter. I don't plan on going down without a fight, and I know you won't either."

Sabryn said nothing as she opened the fridge and looked inside. "How do you feel about a sandwich?"

"I'll take it."

He got out plates and bread as she pulled the other items from the fridge. They were sitting at the table making their sandwiches when she slid a jar of small gherkin pickles toward him. He hid his smile of pleasure that she remembered.

They ate quietly, the thunder of wind as their soundtrack. They were halfway through their meal when the howling suddenly stopped, and the peculiar silence began again. The windows creaked from being pushed inward to being pulled out. They finished their sandwiches quickly and began another round of reinforcing the wards. Eventually, they would break. They both knew it. But neither was the type to sit around and wait for something to happen.

Not long after cleaning up from their meal, they found themselves in the living room again. Kurt didn't know what was worse: the silence or the howling. Both were unnerving.

It seemed Sabryn was done talking. She curled up in the chair with her back to him, which gave him time to look his fill. After so many years, he was finally close enough to touch her. He *had* touched her. But she was here without a screen and miles between them. He listened to her breathing and remembered when the silences between them had been easy and not the awkwardness that hung there now.

He rested his head on the back of the sofa and smiled as memories of the first time they met filled him. It was at an event at a politician's mansion. Men in suits and women in after-five dresses glittering with jewels. He had stood on the stairs leading down to the room when he caught sight of Sabryn in a body-hugging, deep red dress that showed off her stunning figure. Her black hair had been longer then, coming down to the middle of her back, and it was pulled into a sleek, low ponytail. The only jewelry that adorned her were diamond stud earrings.

She stood out in a sea of black dresses, drawing all eyes to her. A flame among the ashes. Alluring, beautiful, and desirable. She moved about the room, talking to some and waving at others—but always with a smile. He hadn't been able to take his eyes off her. He'd studied everything there was to know about Sabryn Beaumont, but he hadn't been prepared for what he saw.

Her head had turned his way, and their eyes locked. He dipped his head, and to his surprise, she inclined hers. Kurt was headed to her when Parker came from the opposite direction and made his move. Sabryn had quickly and subtly rebuffed him. Kurt hid his smile, but it soon became apparent that she refused everyone.

Two nights later, they were at another event together. This time, she wore a long, sexy royal blue dress that brought out the color of her eyes. She left her lustrous, thick hair free except for one side she pinned back with a glittery clip. This time, when their eyes met, he raised his glass of champagne to her. She raised hers in return while offering him a soft smile. It was an invitation, but instead of taking it, he left the party.

The next night was the theater. He had almost decided not to go—there were plenty of other opportunities for them to meet since he had hacked her digital calendar. Only after Parker left to have some fun of his own did Kurt dress and make his way to the auditorium.

He spotted Sabryn the moment he walked into the building. The sleeveless, black lace dress ended above her knees in a ruffled hem that was both sassy and flirty. The short length and black stilettos showed off her impossibly long, toned legs. He was seated in a box across from her, and though he appeared to keep his attention on the stage and the performers, he knew every time she looked at him.

During intermission, he was at the bar for a drink when she walked up beside him. The air had crackled with barely contained desire when their shoulders brushed, and he turned his head to her.

"You're a new face in town," she said.

He cut his eyes to her. "That I am."

"I'm Sabryn Beaumont. And you?" she asked.

"Kurt Barclay."

She quirked a gently arched brow. "British?"

"Guilty." He shifted to face her, leaning one elbow on the bar. "Are you enjoying the show?"

"Not really. Are you?"

He shrugged. "It's all right."

"You came alone?"

Kurt sipped his drink without breaking eye contact. "My brother is in town somewhere. You?"

"My parents. I'm actually on my way out."

"That's too bad."

"Not if you come with me."

The invitation came as a surprise, but he wasn't about to pass up the opportunity. Kurt set down his unfinished drink. "I'm all yours."

They didn't leave by the front entrance. Instead, Sabryn led him out a side door right into the rain. She didn't shriek or run to escape it. No, she raced into it, her arms out at her sides as she twirled in the deluge. He'd never seen anyone so beautiful. Or free.

Then she looked at him. Desire, hot and feral, raced through his veins. He stalked to her as she came toward him. The next thing he knew, she was in his arms. He backed her against the building wall as their lips met in a passionate kiss. It scorched through him, igniting a yearning for her that would never be quenched. And that was all it took. One press of her lips to his, and he had been hers—body and soul.

She wrapped a shapely leg around his hip as the kiss deepened and became more urgent, passion blazing out of control. He gripped her thigh and slid his palm beneath her skirt to her firm arse. He'd never been so hard or hungered for another as he did her. He never felt the rain or heard the traffic.

There was only Sabryn and desire.

She gently scraped his scalp with her nails as their kiss intensified. Moaning into his mouth, she pressed her body into his. He couldn't get enough of her lips, her body, or the taste of her kisses. He ground against her, ravenous for more.

Shrill sirens split the air and interrupted their kiss. He looked from the police car at the side of the street and around them to make sure no one was watching. Then, he looked down at her. They were both drenched, their breaths ragged. Her swollen lips begged for another kiss. A groan tore free of him when her eyes grew heavy-lidded, and she rocked against his arousal. He was seriously considering taking her right there when she lowered her foot to the ground and grabbed his hand.

She led him to the sidewalk and hailed a cab. It was all he could do to keep his hands off her on the ride to her apartment. He tossed money to the driver as she slid from the vehicle and headed for the steps of her flat, him right on her heels. It wasn't until they were inside that they reached for each other, tearing off clothes as each sought to get the other free first.

Kurt squeezed his eyes closed and shut off the memory. He shifted on the sofa to adjust himself since his cock had gone hard thinking of that night and the passion. It had always been like that between them. They had never been able to keep their hands off each other. He'd made love to her a million different ways and only craved more.

At first, he'd been excited to have a mark as tempting as Sabryn, but that hadn't lasted long when Diana made it clear that it was vital the Beaumonts join the London Druids. Kurt had been ordered to do whatever it took to bring Sabryn into the organization. And he had done everything that was asked of him. The problem was that he'd been unknowingly falling head over heels in love the entire time.

And once caught, there was no escape.

From then on, all Kurt had wanted was a future with Sabryn—one away from Diana, Parker, and the London Druids. He'd even convinced himself that he and Sabryn could be together once she and her father joined the organization. But people talked themselves into all sorts of things when they didn't want to face the truth. Things might have gone differently if Parker hadn't been there.

Kurt sat forward on the sofa and scrubbed his hands down his face. Sabryn didn't so much as twitch. He quietly stood and leaned over to see her face, finding her lids closed. Kurt grabbed the throw and laid the blanket over her. He wanted to touch her hair or her face. It was almost painful to be so close to her and know a vast chasm that would likely never be crossed separated them. To have loved someone as vibrant and amazing as Sabryn, only to lose her… It was unbearable.

But the only one he could blame was himself. He had chosen to follow Diana's orders. He could've stopped it all at any time or at least told Sabryn everything. But he hadn't. And that was on him.

CHAPTER TWENTY-THREE

As Kurt walked away, Sabryn kept her eyes closed until she heard his footfalls fade. For a moment, she thought he might reach for her. Her face still tingled from where he had held her as he cleaned up the blood. She hadn't been able to pull away from him. Honestly, she didn't think she could ever refuse him—no matter how angry and hurt she was.

All it had taken was the lightest touch from him, and she ached to be in his arms again. She craved to have his hands stroking her body. She yearned for him. She always had and always would. Because while she cursed him when she was awake, she was his to do with as he pleased in her dreams.

Sabryn hated that she longed for him even now. She tried to return her attention to counting the minutes since the wind had changed but couldn't pull her mind off Kurt. She found herself grasping the blanket as if it were his body and jerked her hand away as if it had scalded her.

Perhaps he was being considerate. It was something she had always loved about him. He'd always been keenly aware of what she needed and took steps to get it for her. But that had been when they were together. They weren't together now, and no number of apologies or explanations could change the past.

Her position had once been comfortable, but now that her concentration had been broken, her hips ached, and her legs itched to straighten. Sabryn pushed aside the throw and got to her feet to stretch her body. There weren't many places in the cottage she could use to escape Kurt, and she wasn't sure she even should in case of an attack. Instead, she walked to a window and studied it, turning her attention to their wards and how they were holding up under the wind's constant push and pull.

If she dared venture outside, her SUV was within steps of the door. If she thought there was a chance she could make it, she'd take it. But witnessing Kurt nearly being sucked through the crack in the door gave her pause. Especially since there was no rhyme or reason for the changes in the wind.

A glance at her phone showed it was just after four in the morning. Springtime in the UK meant fifteen to eighteen hours of daylight, and the sunrise the past few days had been around 5:30 a.m. That meant they only had a little over an hour before the sun rose, and they could see outside. Once the night had been chased away and they could see, they would have a better chance of escaping.

Sabryn put her hand to the window and felt the glass vibrating beneath her palm. It didn't matter how many times they reinforced the wards. The windows would shatter soon. These panes weren't meant to take such sustained pressure. The question was whether they would burst in or blow out. Either way, she and Kurt needed to get free.

If they could just make it until daybreak. One of the other Knights would eventually get curious and check on her. She was sure of it. It would probably be Finn. And when he couldn't get through, he would gather the others and come in person.

Nothing about what was happening made sense. Why was Edie coming for her and Kurt now? Why hadn't she finished her attack on the street? Sabryn had been down. It would've been simple. Not to mention, their group had been scattered. It would've been the perfect time to strike. Edie clearly hadn't cared about witnesses that day. It certainly wouldn't have mattered if she took a life.

Unless someone told her not to. The same being that had given Kerry and Edie enhanced magic, perhaps? But again, *why?* Sabryn dropped her hand from the glass. That could only mean that the being wanted her and Kurt isolated. If it meant to kill them, it'd had plenty of opportunities. And since Edie hadn't finished them, there had to be another reason. Sabryn whirled around and hurried into the kitchen to find Kurt.

He sat in a chair, his arms braced on his knees. His head snapped up as she entered. He took one look at her and asked, "What's wrong?"

"Something got into the Red Hills and killed Kerry. Something that could get through even Balladyn's magic, and we know Druid magic can't compete with Fae magic."

Kurt's brow furrowed. "That's right."

"Something didn't want her talking, and even though she hadn't divulged much of anything, they obviously didn't want to chance it."

He slowly sat up. "I don't think she ever intended to give away anything. She truly believed in her cause."

"A cause that Edie has since taken up. Kerry said the Ancients chose her, but we know from Ferne that they've been silenced."

"Which means something out there is claiming to be the Ancients and convincing both Kerry and Edie to act on their behalf."

Sabryn nodded. "It can also turn mist into a killing machine and granted Kerry the power to control it. That mist got through all kinds of wards. Add that to the circumstances of Kerry's death, and you have something exceptionally powerful."

"So, why hasn't it broken through the cottage wards?" he asked.

"Exactly," she stated, excited that he saw the same things she had. "I don't think it wants Edie to get to us. At least, not yet."

Kurt sat back in his chair and laid an arm on the table. Sabryn's gaze dropped to the tear in his shirt and the glimpse of skin she got through it. She thought about seeing him in nothing but the towel when she first entered. He'd looked good. Really, *really* good. Damn him. She instantly shut off those thoughts.

"They want to isolate us from the others," Kurt stated.

"I think so, too. And that means something is happening on Skye that they don't want us to be a part of. We're stuck here without any way of contacting our friends or getting out to help."

"Have you tried reaching out to the wind again?"

She shook her head. "Not yet. The last time was…" Sabryn shook her head as she recalled the emptiness of not having the wind respond. "But I can."

"If Edie wanted us dead, we'd be dead. That means she has another purpose for us."

"That doesn't make me feel any better."

He wrinkled his nose. "Me, neither."

"Could Diana be working with Edie?"

"Anything is possible when it comes to Diana, but she had her sights set on running the London Druids. She's always bristled under their control. I can't imagine she would willingly submit to some unknown being. That said, if it said it was the Ancients and offered her the kind of power we've seen with both Kerry and Edie, then…yes, she would. Without hesitation."

Sabryn pulled a chair out and sat. "I don't think I need to ask what Parker would do."

"No," Kurt said with a snort. "You don't. Right before Parker stabbed me, he said that it had been a long time coming."

"He never liked being in your shadow."

Kurt looked to the side and slowly shook his head. "We might not have gotten along, but I never thought…" He trailed off, then sighed. "The excitement in his eyes as he slid the blade in was appalling."

Sabryn bit her lip and looked away, not liking how his words, spoken softly while filled with pain, struck her like a punch to the gut. Kurt had looked his would-be killer right in the eyes. The fact that his assailant had been his brother made the act even worse.

"I can't say for certain if Diana sent him or not," Kurt said, turning his head toward her. "But Parker never deviates from Diana's orders."

"It's been six years since you've spoken to your brother. Can you really say that for certain?"

"I don't suppose I can," he admitted.

She twisted her lips. "Sadly, none of that brings us any closer to knowing what's happening outside this cottage. We need to get to the manor."

"If we're not meant to die, then let's try to leave. Maybe Edie will pull back."

"Or she won't, and we'll die."

He lifted his hand in exasperation. "What choice do we have? We stay, we die. We go, we die."

"I'm the reason you're here. Well, in this cottage anyway," she amended. "I didn't want you at the manor."

"Because it was your space. I understand."

"And I'm the one who wanted to talk alone."

He dipped his chin, one side of his mouth quirking up. "You wanted to yell."

She had wanted to do much more than that. She had wanted to hurt him as badly as she had been hurt. Why hadn't she? "Stop being so understanding. I'm trying to apologize for putting us in this predicament."

"Apology accepted, but I don't blame you."

"I do." She could've had it out with him at the manor or Rhona's place. She *should've* said her piece there. She looked back, trying to remember when she had gotten it into her head that she needed to be *completely* alone with Kurt when she hadn't been able to share the same house before. "I shouldn't have asked to be alone with you."

His brows drew together. "What?"

"I didn't want to be alone with you. Why did I ask to have a cottage to ourselves?"

He shrugged, looking at her helplessly. "I've no idea."

"Why didn't Finn, Elias, or Carlyle point that out?"

"What are you suggesting?"

Sabryn rubbed her forehead. "I don't know. I just…something isn't adding up. I wanted to hear you confirm what Parker told me, but…"

"Not alone," he finished.

She tried to ignore the despair in his eyes. "What if this thing helping Edie can reach us?"

"When did you decide to ask for a separate location? Were you at the manor?"

Sabryn thought back to after she'd been taken from the hospital. "We were driving to it." And she had been an emotional wreck, in turns furious and beside herself. "I wasn't thinking clearly."

"You were upset, and rightly so."

"Being emotional allows someone to enter a person's mind. I never once stopped to think that I should guard myself."

Kurt held her gaze. "Your friends wanted to help and gave you whatever you wanted to help you heal."

"Oh, my god. What have I done?" she gasped. "We have to get to the others. They need us."

He stood. "Then let's go."

It was so easy to remember the man she had grown to love in DC. She saw flashes of him now and couldn't reconcile it with the facts of who he really was. But now wasn't the time to think about that. Their friends were in trouble, and she and Kurt had already wasted hours thinking *they* were the target.

"My car is steps from the door," she said, getting to her feet.

"I'll buy you some time as you get to the vehicle."

She shot him a dark look. "Don't be silly. We're both going."

"I think only one of us will make it. You have the key, and you know the roads."

"We go together," she declared and headed for the door.

"Sabryn," he began.

She halted and raised a hand to silence him, then closed her eyes and listened for the wind. It was still silent, which meant it was in the vacuum again. After its frantic screams before, the hush was unnerving. If the Ancients could be quieted, then it stood to reason the wind could, as well. She had turned her back on her gift for weeks, and now that she needed it, it wasn't there.

"I hear nothing," she admitted.

Kurt was right behind her. "We wait until we hear the wind blowing again to make a run for it."

"It'll change as soon as we're outside."

"Then we'd better run fast."

She turned when she heard him walk away. He returned a moment later and handed her a backpack. "What's this?"

"My laptop. The passcode is Sabryn."

"I don't want this," she said and shoved it back at him. "That's your department."

His face tightened. "Don't be stubborn."

"Then don't give up so easily. Get your ass to the car."

The gusts started again, ending their argument. Sabryn reached for the knob as Kurt quickly shrugged on the backpack. She threw open the door and ran outside. A burst of wind knocked into her side, sending her skidding across the stone path and into the grass. She lost her footing and toppled to the ground, the wind rolling her. Something grabbed her arm. Sabryn looked up to find Kurt holding on to the edge of the cottage with one hand and her with the other.

"Hello, Sabryn."

The feminine voice in her head startled her. She searched the area, squinting through the gusts in the pre-dawn light until she found Edie standing about ten feet from her, untouched by the gusts.

"You know I could rip you both into pieces. But I'll make you a deal. I won't hurt either of you if you leave Skye and go your separate ways. It's that simple. If you don't take the offer, you will die, but not before watching everyone you love perish horrifically."

"Sabryn!" Kurt shouted.

She looked at him and felt his grip slipping. When she returned her gaze to Edie, she found her gone. Kurt yanked on her arm, roughly pulling her to him. The wind died enough that Sabryn could put her feet on the ground and stumble into him.

"Go!" he yelled, shoving her toward the SUV.

Sabryn didn't hesitate as she dashed toward the vehicle. They jumped inside just as the air switched to the vacuum. She pressed the ignition button and threw the vehicle in reverse before jerking the wheel around and sliding on the grass and gravel. Then she threw it into drive and slammed her foot on the accelerator.

She glanced in the rearview mirror, but there was no sign of Edie in the soft light of daybreak. Had she imagined her and the voice? No. The words were distinct, and the meaning was clear. Her heart pounded as she took the corners of the winding road at breakneck speed.

Kurt had one hand on the dash and the other gripping the handle near his head. She took a turn too sharply, and the tires on one side of the vehicle went off the road. She straightened the SUV and pressed the accelerator when they reached a straightaway.

"What happened back there?" he asked.

Everything. "Nothing," she answered.

Sabryn felt his gaze on her, but she didn't take her eyes off the road. One turn took them right into the blinding light of the rising sun. She winced and flipped down the visor, but when that didn't help, she raised a hand to shield her eyes. Her focus remained on the road and taking one curve after another.

CHAPTER TWENTY-FOUR

Carwood Manor

"I don't see anything," Elodie said.

Finn nervously stared at the wall. There was no sign of the massive gash that had been cut through the membrane-like section separating one dimension from the other, but he knew precisely where it began and ended.

"The house doesn't feel right," Bronwyn said as she rested a hand on a wall.

Rhona asked, "Has the barrier been breached?"

"I'd have to open the portal to find out," Bronwyn said, dropping her arm and facing Rhona.

Elias shook his head. "I'm no' sure that's a good idea."

"We have to know if we need to seal any fissures," Balladyn said.

Song walked to the far wall Finn stared at and leaned close. "Is this where it happened?"

"There about," Elodie answered.

The house let out another loud groan, and it was all Finn could do to stay in the room. His palms were clammy, his breath thready. Every fiber of his being screamed for him to get out—of the room and the manor.

"Let's go," Carlyle whispered and tried to push Finn to the door.

"I've not backed down from a fight before, and I'm not going to start now." Finn kept his voice low and glanced at the others to make sure no one was listening. If he left, if he ran, he would never be able to look at himself in the mirror. This wasn't the first time he'd been scared. He hadn't run then. He wasn't running now.

Carlyle's lips flattened. "Nothing is happening. This isn't a battle."

No sooner had the words left his lips than a thunderous boom sounded from the other side of the wall. Everyone stilled, all eyes focused on where the sound had come from.

"Callum!" Rhona called frantically.

Killian said, "He's not here. I've been trying to get in touch with him."

"Why the fuck is he no' here?" Theo demanded.

Balladyn teleported out while Bronwyn splayed her hands on the wall, closed her eyes, and communicated with the house. Elias moved up beside her while everyone else started to spread out and assume defensive stances.

The very air crackled with tension. Finn glanced at the door. Everything in him still screamed to get out, but he couldn't do anything. His friends needed him. Besides, he wasn't facing the monster within The Grey on his own. The Druids around him were fierce fighters in their own right, and together, they were nearly unstoppable.

There was an audible gasp before a crack split the wall. Elias grabbed Bronwyn, pulling her away as everyone else stepped back.

"I have to open the portal," Bronwyn cried.

Elias held her to his chest. "No' until Callum gets here to close any rips."

"There may no' be time for him," Scott pointed out.

Another crack suddenly appeared in the exact spot they had cut through the barrier. Ice filled Finn's veins. Something was about to come through. For him. He tried to move back, but his feet were frozen in place.

"Out!" Rhona yelled. "Everyone out now!"

Carlyle reached for Song and yanked her toward the doorway as the others hurried out. Mist began pouring through the cracks and falling down the walls to the floor—coming right for him. Finn lurched to the side half a step, but it followed him. He tried another direction, but it mirrored him that way, too.

"Finn!" Carlyle bellowed.

The mist was filling up the room fast. Finn realized he was the last one inside and spun around. Carlyle and Elias stood at the door, their eyes wide as they screamed his name. They both stepped back into the room just as something wrapped tightly around Finn's ankle and yanked. He pitched forward and landed hard on his stomach, banging his forehead on the rug. He could hear everyone shouting as he rolled and watched the mist rapidly curling up his calf to his knee.

Within seconds, it was up his other leg. That's when the pain started. He kicked his legs, trying to get it off. When that didn't work, he flipped onto his stomach and attempted to crawl out.

Elias and Carlyle each took one of his hands and hauled him toward the door.

But the mist tightened its hold. Finn clenched his jaw as what felt like millions of needles penetrated his flesh and poured fire beneath his skin, suspending him several inches off the ground while both the mist and his friends tugged on his body. He vacillated between awareness and oblivion as his flesh and muscles burned and the shouts continued.

He looked at Carlyle and Elias and begged, "Don't let go."

"Never," his friends replied in unison.

Song stepped from behind Elias and targeted the mist with her magic. Bronwyn, Theo, and Rhona managed to lean through the doorway and do the same. Finn clenched his jaw to keep his screams in check, but the agony was unlike anything he'd ever experienced. The moment the mist loosened its hold, Finn flew out of the room. A shout tore from him when his legs banged against the floor.

"We've got you," Carlyle said, anchoring one of Finn's arms around his shoulders and standing.

The reply faded on Finn's lips as he passed out. He came awake screaming the moment someone touched his legs as they lifted him.

"Stay with us, Finn," Elias urged frantically. "A Healer is coming."

Each step jostled Finn, bringing more pain as they rushed him down the hall. He tried to stay awake, but when oblivion called, he was powerless to ignore it. And anything was better than the shooting pain running up and down his legs.

The next time he woke, he was laid out on one of the sofas in the front room. He waited for the agony to return, but thankfully, there was nothing. Finn rolled his head to the side and spotted Elias sitting on the edge of a chair, bent over with his arms on his legs and his gaze on the floor. Carlyle paced behind him, shaking his head every few moments, likely having a conversation in his head. Finn was about to say something when Carlyle looked at him and did a double take.

"Finn," he said and hurried over.

Elias's head jerked up, and the moment their eyes met, he surged to his feet. "You're awake."

"How do you feel?" Carlyle asked.

Finn lifted his head and looked down to see his legs covered with a blanket. No one else was in the room. That wasn't a good sign. He lowered his head to the pillow and slid his gaze to his friends. "Where is everyone?"

"Warding the manor," Elias answered.

Carlyle stood at Finn's feet and asked again, "How do you feel?"

Finn took stock of his legs and realized he didn't feel anything. Fear of being paralyzed curdled his stomach. He sat up and threw off the blanket before his friends could stop him.

"Fuck," Elias said.

Carlyle turned away, mumbling, "Bloody hell."

Finn stared in horror at his bare legs that now had thick, dark marks running up them like winding vines.

"We wanted to tell you before you saw them," Carlyle said.

Finn touched one of the markings on his thigh, but there was no longer any pain. He peered closer, frowning when he realized what it looked like. "Is that…?"

"A tattoo? We think so," Elias replied.

Finn let that sink in. He tried to curl his toes and sighed in relief when he could move everything normally. He swung his legs over the side of the couch and looked from Elias to Carlyle. "I was expecting a lot more with the pain I endured."

"So were we," Elias admitted.

"What other damage occurred?" Finn was almost afraid to ask, but it was better to know.

"Nothing," Carlyle said.

Finn frowned. "Nothing? That can't be right. I'm not talking about just the pain, there was a sinisterness to the mist."

Carlyle nodded in agreement. "We saw it go right for you. Ulrik thinks it was because you were marked."

"Ulrik?" Finn repeated, his frown deepening. "Why did you seek out the Dragon Kings?"

Elias sighed and lowered himself back into his chair. "Something similar happened to his mate, Eilish. Her markings are similar to yours."

"Where did she get hers?" Finn asked.

Carlyle shifted uncomfortably. "That's the odd part. Apparently, she was transported someplace when she got them. She didn't see anything but the mist, where it climbed her legs and left marks."

"You've got to be fekking kidding me."

Elias sighed. "I wish we were."

"I take it she's had no adverse effects?" Finn moved his hands up and down his legs from the top of his thighs to his ankles to make sure there was no more discomfort.

"Nothing," Elias confirmed.

Finn shrugged. "I'd really like some pants before we continue this conversation."

Carlyle pointed to a spot behind Finn. He turned to find a pair of his jeans laid across the back of the sofa. He wasted no time getting them on and fastened.

"Whoa," Elias said as he stood and put a hand on Finn's chest when he tried to walk past. "Where are you going?"

Finn met his blue eyes. "First, I'm going to find my boots. Then, I'm going to help ward the manor. Which is where you two should be."

"We're continuing the conversation, remember? You sensed you shouldna be in that room."

Finn glared at Carlyle, but he wasn't surprised he had told Elias about their discussion. He would've done the same.

"You should've listened to your instincts," Elias finished.

Finn ran a hand over his jaw. "It isn't the mist I'm afraid of, but what I saw moving in the shadows of The Grey. I overreacted."

"The hell you did," Carlyle snapped. "Look at your bloody legs."

Finn knew they were worried, and so was he, but he didn't want to know just how much. "I was tattooed without permission. You said Eilish has something similar, and nothing has happened to her. So, I figure I'm fine." Or he would be. As soon as he had some time to himself to let it all soak in.

"The mist went right for *you*. It targeted *you*," Elias stated.

Carlyle released a long sigh. "Nothing about The Grey is good. The fact that something cracked the wall and mist escaped, only to go for you concerns me greatly."

"And me," Elias added.

Finn nodded. There was no use denying it. "It does me, too. But the pain is gone now, and I have the use of my legs. We can worry all day about things that *could* go wrong, but it won't change what's happened. Right now, our focus needs to be on keeping the manor strong so nothing like this occurs again. When and *if* something happens because of my marks, we'll handle it."

He held their stares for a long minute before both men relented. They were headed toward the door when Sabryn threw it open. Her hair was tangled, and her eyes were wide. She looked at each of them before bending over to brace her hands on her knees and drawing in huge gulps of air.

"Thank god," she murmured.

Kurt walked in behind her, his hair also in disarray and his shirt torn.

"We were wrong," Sabryn said as she straightened and threw a look over her shoulder at Kurt.

Elias frowned as he glanced at Finn and Carlyle. "About what?"

"We thought the manor was being attacked, and that's why we were confined," Kurt answered.

Carlyle's lips twisted. "Actually, we *were* attacked."

"And what the fek do you mean you were confined?" Finn demanded.

Sabryn looked between the three of them. "You first."

CHAPTER TWENTY-FIVE

Kurt let Sabryn tell Carlyle, Elias, and Finn what'd transpired at the cottage, then remained silent as he listened to the details of what had unfolded at the manor. The experience of being with everyone was still new to him. To be right in the middle of things instead of hearing about it after or when the Knights needed a way out of a situation. But he still didn't feel he had a right to voice his opinions.

"Is the crack still there?" Sabryn asked.

Elias shrugged. "Bronwyn slammed the door after we got Finn out."

"I was too focused on Finn to look," Carlyle added.

Kurt slid his gaze to Finn, who kept his expression calm, but his hands were fisted tightly.

"We need to know if it's still open—" Sabryn began.

Carlyle nodded. "We need Callum. We know."

Kurt's attention slid to Sabryn. Her body was tense. Some of that should have eased once she knew everyone was safe, but it hadn't. She kept looking around as if checking to see if anybody was near. And he wasn't the only one who noticed.

"What is it?" Finn asked.

Sabryn waved away his words. "It's been a long night. I'll be back."

"Where are you going?" Elias asked.

She halted and then looked back at the four of them. "I need to see the room."

"Why would you go in there?" Finn demanded angrily as he surged to his feet.

Instead of answering, Sabryn walked out of the room. Kurt looked at the others before everybody rose to follow her—even Finn, though it was evident he didn't want to go near the room. They reached the second floor and started down the hallway. Kurt spotted Sabryn standing outside a door, her hand on the knob. She glanced at them.

"Don't!" Finn bellowed, right before she pushed it open.

Kurt raced to her, stumbling inside with Carlyle and Elias on his heels. She stood in the middle of the room, staring at the opposite wall and the large crack that ran diagonally from left to right.

"Did you no' hear us?" Elias asked furiously.

Carlyle grabbed her arm and hauled her out of the room. Kurt took one last look at the crack before pivoting and walking out, closing the door behind him. Sabryn yanked her arm from Carlyle and glared.

"What is going on with you?" Carlyle demanded.

Her face shuttered. "Nothing."

"You're lying," Finn replied.

Sabryn blew out a breath and motioned for them to follow her.

Kurt wouldn't be left out. He brought up the rear as they headed to Sabryn's room. She opened the door and stood there until they were all inside. Then, she softly shut it and faced them.

On the drive to the manor, Kurt had been as worried as Sabryn about everyone. It had never dawned on him that something else might be wrong, but now, there was no denying it. Had the wind communicated something to her?

"I'm leaving," she announced.

There was a beat of silence as they let her words penetrate.

Elias was the first to speak. "Do you mean the manor?"

"Not just the manor," Sabryn answered. "I'm leaving Skye."

Carlyle made a sound in the back of his throat. "What the bloody hell are you talking about?"

"I'm fine," Finn told her. "Look at me. I'm walking. The tattoos don't even hurt."

Her smile was sad as she turned to Finn. "You're okay this time. But what about next time?" She focused on Carlyle. "And what if it's you next?" Then she looked at Elias. "Or you."

Kurt waited for her to glance his way, but she didn't. And that was like a knife to the heart.

"We'll deal with it," Carlyle said.

Finn nodded and crossed his arms over his chest. "Like we always do."

"You make it sound as if this is the first time one of us has gotten injured. We all know that isna true," Elias argued.

Kurt asked, "What's really going on, Sabryn?"

She drew in a deep breath and released it with a sigh. "I believe what happened to Finn was a warning."

"From?" Elias pressed.

"Your sister."

Kurt frowned as he thought back to the cottage. "We didn't speak to her."

"She spoke to me," Sabryn admitted as she walked to the bench in front of the bed and sat.

Unease curdled his stomach. "When? What did she say?"

"When we made a run for the SUV. You grabbed me when the wind knocked me off my feet."

He frowned, thinking back to when it'd happened. "I didn't see her."

"You couldn't have. You were holding on to the side of the house and focused on me." Sabryn shrugged. "Edie ordered me to leave. Said if I didn't, I would die, but not before watching everyone I love perish."

Fury ripped through Kurt. He could barely keep his anger in check when he said, "I fucking knew something happened. Why didn't you say anything?"

"I'm saying something now," she answered calmly.

Finn raked a hand through his hair. "Maybe my head is still rattled from everything, but what the fek are you thinking? What will running away do?"

"Why you, specifically?" Elias asked.

Kurt nodded. "That's my question, too."

"I don't know." Sabryn shrugged, showing her frustration. "I didn't get a chance to ask that."

Carlyle blew out a breath and moved to sit beside her. "We all know the risks anytime we go up against someone."

"We've had our victories, and we've been badly hurt. All in all, we've come out ahead. That kind of blessing runs out eventually." Sabryn looked at each of them, her gaze lingering.

Finn pulled a face. "So, you're just giving up? Throwing up

your hands and walking away because Edie threatened us? I don't buy it."

"You don't need to," she replied softly.

Elias stalked to the window before turning and leaning a shoulder against the wall. "I still want to know why she chose you."

"You'd have to ask her," Sabryn said.

Kurt ran a hand over his mouth. "She trapped us. If she wanted you gone, she could've killed you then. But she didn't."

"Precisely," Carlyle said. "That's what we need to focus on."

Finn walked to the chair near the hearth and lowered himself into it. "What all did Edie say?"

"I told you," Sabryn said as she looked away.

Kurt shook his head. "There's more. You might as well tell us. We won't stop until you do."

"Tell us all of it. Every word," Elias pressed.

Sabryn rolled her eyes and rubbed her palms along the tops of her thighs. "Edie said Kurt and I have to leave the isle and go our separate ways."

"And if we don't, you'll die after watching the rest of us be killed?" Kurt asked.

Her dark blue eyes met his. "Yes."

"Why didn't you tell me?" he asked in confusion. "Especially since she added me into the ultimatum."

She briefly leaned her head back before shrugging. "I don't know."

But he did. She didn't consider him part of the Knights. So, in her eyes, it didn't matter what he did.

"All I know is that she kept us there while something was happening here," Sabryn said with a shrug.

"If she wants you off the island, why not just kill you? Like Kurt said, she had both of you trapped," Finn said.

Elias's lips flattened. "We're missing something."

"It's clear that Edie doesn't want Kurt and Sabryn together." Carlyle looked at each of them. "That's where the answer lies. Let's figure out why."

Sabryn surged to her feet. "Don't any of you get it? She threatened you, and to prove her reach, she hurt Finn. She got into the manor!"

"*She* didna do anything," Elias said.

Sabryn's face tightened with anger. "You know what I mean. It might not have been Edie herself, but it's whatever gave her the added powers."

"Maybe we should have a chat with Edie," Finn suggested.

Elias wrinkled his nose. "The last time Elodie and I tried to talk to her, it didna go well."

"You're her brother. I'd listen to anyone before Parker," Kurt said.

Carlyle nodded in agreement. "I think we should give it a try."

"No," Sabryn stated firmly.

Kurt dropped his arms and met her gaze. "Aren't you at all curious why we've been ordered to leave and go our separate ways?"

"It's obvious it came from Diana," she answered.

Kurt frowned and twisted his lips. "You think Diana is mixed up in this?" He shook his head. "I'm not so sure. If she sent Parker to kill me, then she would've had Edie finish it. We weren't hurt. Even if you argue that the wards kept Edie out, she had ample opportunity to get us when we ran to the vehicle. She didn't. In fact, the wind died enough for us to make it."

"If your mother isn't involved, then this is coming from whatever is ruling Edie," Finn said.

Kurt raised a brow as he stared at Sabryn. "I'm not going anywhere. If they want me off Skye, they'll have to kill me."

"We're stronger together," Carlyle told her.

Finn got to his feet. "We won't have to face this alone. We have the rest of the group, too."

"Well?" Elias asked her. "What's your decision? Are you going to walk away and leave this fight? Or are you going to dig in your heels and find out why they've targeted you and Kurt?"

Sabryn closed her eyes and pressed her lips together. Then she took a deep breath and sat straighter as she lifted her lids. "Don't make me regret staying. I'll never forgive any of you if something happens."

"It won't. We'll make sure of it," Carlyle stated.

Kurt rubbed his hands together. "Now that that's taken care of, I need to find my little brother. I think it's time we have a talk."

"We need to look for Edie, too," Elias said.

Carlyle headed to the door. "We have to fill the others in on what's happened."

"You do that," Finn told him. "I'm going to see if they've located Callum. None of us is safe if the monster can break through the dimensions."

They left, leaving Kurt alone with Sabryn. He waited until the others were down the hall before swinging his head to her. "Why didn't you tell me about Edie on the ride over?"

"I already told you. I was worried about everyone here."

He almost asked if Edie had really told her they needed to part ways, or if Sabryn had added that in to ensure he left. He had hoped she might find it in her to forgive him, but that wouldn't happen. And he didn't blame her. There was no need to wonder and worry now. The truth was out, and he accepted the outcome. She would never push him out of the Knights. Using Edie to make him leave was understandable, even if it did bring him to his knees.

"Is there something else?" Sabryn asked.

He'd gotten the time alone with her that he wanted, but he hadn't said everything he needed to say. Fear had kept him silent. He'd had his chance, and he'd blown it. He needed to move on, especially since she apparently had.

"No," he said and headed to the door.

There were no goodbyes or farewells. He couldn't get the words past his lips, so he kept walking. He paused when he reached the stairs, trying to remember where he had left his rucksack. Kurt descended the steps and spotted his bag near the front door. He heard voices coming from the front room as he walked toward it.

He recognized Elias's as he told the others what had happened at the cottage. Kurt stopped outside the open door and listened as everyone took turns talking and tossing around ideas. He almost went inside, but it was better if he kept his distance. His skills would be needed to fight this battle. Afterward…? Well, he didn't want to think about that.

After a moment, he forced himself to walk past the doors to grab his bag. There were plenty of unoccupied rooms in the manor. He would find one and set up there, once more withdrawing. Maybe that's how it was always supposed to be.

CHAPTER TWENTY-SIX

Callum braced his head against the stone building at his back and rubbed his tired eyes as the new day dawned. His gaze wasn't on the sunrise, though. It was on the house where Kirsi's parents, Matt and Nora, lived. No one saw him in his hiding place, and that's how he wanted it. Skye wasn't safe anymore, and someone had to watch over the Browns.

There was movement in the shadows to his side. Callum jerked his head, looking over, magic at the ready, when he spotted Balladyn ten feet away. It didn't matter how much time he spent in the Reaper's presence, Callum would never get used to him vanishing and appearing.

"Killian said I might find you here." Balladyn walked closer, his unusual eyes darting toward the Browns' home. "Why didn't you come to the manor when we texted?"

Callum drew in a breath and released it with a shrug. "I lost my mobile in the attack."

"We need you."

"You know what happened to all of us. No one was watching Kirsi and her parents," Callum stated. His anger had been simmering for hours, and, unfortunately, it looked like Balladyn would take the brunt of it.

The Reaper stared at him for a long moment. "Nor was anyone guarding you."

"Me?" Callum asked in surprise. "I doona need protection."

"On the contrary, I think you do. You're the only one who can heal the rifts. You're a vital part of our group."

Callum looked away, hating that the Reaper had brought it up. "I wasna able to do anything last time."

"You have before, and we need you again."

Callum's gut clenched at the thought of another split opening between the dimensions. "Where is it?"

"At the manor."

His stomach dropped to his feet in shock as he swung his head to Balladyn. "What? How? When?"

"A lot happened last night. We're still working it all out. Something got through, though we're not sure how. Mist spilled out and went straight for Finn."

Callum pushed away from the wall, his mind recoiling at what he heard. "Is he okay?"

"He's been left with marks on his legs, but otherwise, he appears fine."

Appears. Callum remembered walking through the mist when he went with the others to locate Ferne. He had felt a presence near him. Something dark and dangerous. He would never forget how heavy his feet and legs became the longer he stood in the fog. It was almost as if something had gripped him and tried to keep him there. There hadn't been anything on him but the swirling vapor, yet no one else had been affected.

"Bronwyn hasn't opened the portal to see if there is a rift, and she won't until you're there," Balladyn continued. "But if one has formed, there's potential for other things to come through."

Callum looked at the Browns'. A shape moved past a window. He would know Kirsi anywhere. She had spent the night tending to her mother nonstop. "Mrs. Brown's muscular dystrophy flared up yesterday."

"I see," Balladyn said.

"Mr. Brown and Kirsi tried to get her to the hospital, but she refused. Her nurse came to help them, but Kirsi still wouldna leave her mum's side."

"With Matt's magic fading, Nora unable to use hers with the MD, and Kirsi absorbed in her mother, you stayed to watch over them."

Callum shrugged a shoulder and met the Reaper's gaze. "Someone needed to."

"We'll get you a new mobile so we can stay in touch. Right now, you're needed at the manor. As soon as I drop you there, I'll return and stand guard," Balladyn promised.

"Then I suppose we'd better go."

The next second, Callum stood outside a closed bedroom on the second floor of the manor. He didn't need to count the doors to know it was the one they had gone through to enter The Grey.

"Callum," Rhona said, hurrying toward him from down the hall. "I was beginning to wonder if Balladyn would find you."

He looked at the leader of the Druids as she made her way to him. Her steps were hurried, and there were dark circles under her eyes. Her long, red hair had been hastily fastened into a high ponytail. She smiled at him, her relief evident in how her shoulders sagged.

"I didna ignore you," he told her. "I lost my mobile."

Rhona stopped beside him. "Are you all right?"

He flinched when her gaze dropped to the cut on his lip. Callum turned his head away so she couldn't see it. "I failed the last time I tried to seal a rift."

"Not only could you not see that one, but you were gravely injured while trying to close it. No one blames you for that."

Maybe not, but that didn't alleviate the pressure he felt to get the job done.

There was a beat of silence before Rhona said, "You don't have to do this."

"Of course, I do," he replied, his gaze on the door.

She turned him to face her, and her green eyes locked on his. "No, you don't."

"I just…" He trailed off and glanced away. "I doona want to let you down. I closed it once, but it reopened. I might have done something wrong the first time. What if that happens again?"

"Then we'll deal with it. Just as we do with everything that comes our way."

She was right, and he knew it. It was time to stop worrying and do what he could. Callum gathered his long hair behind his head and tied it off with a leather string. "I'll try my best."

"That's all anyone can ask."

He opened the door before he changed his mind and stepped into the empty room, his gaze drawn to the opposite wall and the large crack. He still remembered how he had reached up to the cut membrane and run his hand over it. He hadn't known he could close the tear until then. "It's the same shape as the one we cut through the membrane separating the dimensions."

"Exactly the same?" Rhona asked apprehensively.

He nodded and walked to it, running his hand along the fissure. "I remember how the angle curved slightly as it traveled toward the floor."

Callum peered into the split and saw that it went through the plasterboard. "Are you sure only mist came out?"

"It's all we saw, but we were focused on getting Finn out since he was screaming in agony."

He turned his head to her. "Balladyn said the mist left marks."

"More like tattoos. It burned through Finn's jeans into his skin from his ankles to his hips."

"Shite."

Rhona nodded, her lips pinched. "He passed out from the pain, but when he woke, it was as if nothing had happened. The Healers took away his pain, but there wasn't anything for them to repair. He's not the only one to have such marks, either. Ulrik's mate, Eilish, had something similar happen."

Callum frowned. "She went into The Grey?"

"Neither she nor Ulrik are sure *where* she went, but Eilish told me it was misty and had dim lighting. She did experience some pain from the fog, but other than ending up with tattoos on her legs, she's been healthy. Is that because she's mated to a Dragon King and essentially immortal, or because the marks didn't do any lasting harm? We may never know."

"I take it the thought is that Finn will be okay, too?"

"We hope."

Callum returned his attention to the splintered plasterboard. Behind it were the stones used in the construction of the manor.

He had walked through the tear weeks ago and sealed it on his way out. They were the ones who had cut through the barrier. Maybe that's why he had been able to close it.

"What are you thinking?" Rhona asked.

Callum took a step back to look at the crack as a whole. "I can no' tell if there's a tear or no'. I see this," he said, pointing to the wall.

"But you don't know if there's something to seal."

"Exactly." He looked at her. "I need Song."

Rhona drew out her mobile and sent a text. "She's on her way upstairs now."

Callum returned to studying the fissure. He wished he knew more about his ability. It might come from his family, but he couldn't ask his mother since she had left, and his father would never give him a straight answer, so it was pointless.

"You're always welcome to stay here," Rhona said into the silence.

"Bronwyn tells me that every time I'm here."

"It might be safer."

Callum knew she was referring to his lip. It was odd how everyone assumed his injuries came from him instigating fights with others for most of his life. No one had thought to ask him— not that he would've told them. It was his shame to carry. It was bad enough that Killian had guessed. And Kirsi. Now, the rest of their group knew. Whether someone had told them or they figured it out didn't matter. Everyone knew about the abuse. Thankfully, no one asked him to give voice to it, and he wanted it to remain that way.

"I'll think about it," he said as two sets of footsteps approached. He wouldn't, of course, because his father would make an appearance and disrupt everything. But it was the only thing Callum could say to end the discussion.

Song and Carlyle entered the room before Rhona had a chance to respond. Callum turned to face the couple.

"It's good to see you," Carlyle said with a nod.

Callum returned the gesture before shifting his gaze to Song. "Shall we try again?"

She gave him a welcoming smile. "This rift should be easier than the last since we won't be balanced on a roof."

"That's true." Callum glanced at the wall. "Can you see anything?"

Song narrowed her eyes and examined the fracture in the plasterboard. His gift was closing rifts, but hers was seeing them since they were invisible to everyone else. Song was the only reason they had learned about the one on Skye. There could be—and probably were—others around the world, which was a terrifying thought.

The tear he had closed was one they had cut through, which was probably why he could see it. Others had created the rifts, which likely explained why he couldn't discern them.

"I don't," Song finally answered after a thorough examination.

Rhona's brows drew together. "I don't understand. We all saw it open last night."

"If the proof weren't on Finn's legs, I'd be questioning it." Song's dark gaze slid to Carlyle. "I don't like this."

He grunted and moved to the wall beside Callum, leaning his face close. "The evidence is here and on Finn's legs."

"Are you telling me that something can tear open a rift between the dimensions and then close it?" Rhona asked.

Callum shrugged. "It stands to reason it could. My concern is no' that it happened, but that it happened inside the manor, exactly where we cut through the wall to get into The Grey."

"Exactly where we cut?" Carlyle asked, his gaze probing.

Callum nodded and glanced at Rhona. "Aye."

"Finn didn't say anything," Carlyle mumbled.

Song asked, "You think he noticed?"

"He was staring at it hard enough." Carlyle blew out a breath. "Yeah, I think Finn noticed it was the same."

Rhona's face pinched in concern. "Why didn't he say anything?"

"He's dealing with some PTSD from our visit to the other side," Carlyle admitted reluctantly.

Callum debated talking to Finn to see if they suffered from the same issues. Finn had likely kept quiet for the same reason Callum had. But one other person had it even worse—Kirsi. The monster from The Grey had been plaguing her dreams and visions since she entered its dimension.

Song swung her head to Callum. "Bronwyn is pretty rattled about all of this, too."

The manor had protected them all at various times, but its connection was through Bronwyn. Callum scanned the room. "We've put a lot on the house. We should add some wards to help it defend itself."

"We had the same thought," Rhona said. "We've already started, but it's a huge house, and we could use your help."

Callum dipped his chin. "Of course."

"I'm going to go ahead and reinforce this room," Song said.

Carlyle turned and walked to the doorway. "I'll get the hallway."

"Sounds good," Rhona said before walking away.

Callum watched the couple begin their work, but his attention was constantly drawn back to the crack.

"What is it?" Song asked.

He shook his head. "I'm no' sure. Something isna right."

"What do you mean?" Carlyle asked, poking his head inside.

Callum pointed at the crack. "I see the evidence here, and all of you witnessed it. While I think it's possible something can tear through dimensions and close up behind itself, why would it? It left others visible."

"You think it's because it wanted Finn?" she asked.

Carlyle leaned a shoulder against the doorjamb. "Finn didn't want to enter the room. It was like he knew something was going to happen."

Callum thought about the times Kirsi had been terrorized by the monster from The Grey. He had always thought it was because she knew she would eventually have to face the creature, but now he wondered if he had been wrong.

"Sabryn said Edie warned her," Song said.

Callum looked at her. "What kind of warning?"

Carlyle explained what had happened to Sabryn and Kurt at the cottage when the manor was attacked.

When he finished, Callum asked, "What if what we're seeing is a trick? What if there isna a tear at all?"

"But we saw it happen right before our eyes," Song insisted.

Carlyle grunted. "Not to mention the mist."

"The killing mist could get into houses," Callum reminded them.

Carlyle stilled for a heartbeat before shaking his head. "It was never able to get into the manor, though. Besides, we ended that."

"No, you stopped *Kerry*. That's different," Song said.

Callum shrugged. "Edie took Kerry's place. Who's to say she can no' also control the mist? What happened to it after you got Finn out?"

"I don't know." Carlyle ran a hand down his face. "We slammed the door and carried Finn downstairs. This is the first time we've been back inside since it happened."

Song turned to the fissure again. "So, it could indeed all be a trick."

"To scare us?"

They exchanged glances and, in unison, said, "Finn."

"Bloody fucking hell," Carlyle murmured.

Callum rolled his shoulders as a cold chill ran down his spine. "The evil is getting stronger."

"And coming for the manor," Song added.

Carlyle walked to the wall and placed his hand beside the broken plasterboard. "Every one of us needs to reinforce the wards in every bloody room, inside and out."

CHAPTER TWENTY-SEVEN

The morning was cloudy, with dark clouds drifting overhead and hinting at rain. The flowers Bronwyn had planted were blooming, showcasing vibrant colors and drawing bees and butterflies alike. Sabryn wished this could be a relaxing day of doing nothing but sitting with nature. Instead, she slowly made her way around the outside of the manor, strengthening wards by adding her magic.

The pain in her neck built until she couldn't handle another second of it. She leaned her head to one side and then the other, hearing it pop. It alleviated the ache for a few seconds before it returned. She needed sleep and her special pillow, or her neck would only get worse. But there wasn't time for a nap—not that she would be able to rest. How could she, with Edie's threat still looming in her mind? Not to mention that the manor had been breached, and, of course, the kicker—Finn's unauthorized tats.

She, like everyone else at the manor, was exhausted. Going a night without sleep was hard but doable. Doing that for several days in a row was simply unfeasible. Perhaps that's how the evil intended to win the war.

Once she finished her warding, Sabryn leaned against the corner of the house to rest. She was desperate for a candlelit soak in a bath, sipping wine and reading on her eReader as her favorite cello playlist drifted through the speaker. But she'd take changing out of her clothes, brushing her teeth, and a warm meal.

She should return inside the manor and see what else she could do to prepare for the next attack. The longer she was involved in this war, the more she wondered how they would win. It felt as if the enemy had every advantage. Yet the Skye Druids had won several times in the past, and they would figure out how to do it again.

Voices reached her, and she strained to hear if it was Kurt. She hated the disappointment she felt when she didn't hear his deep timbre before the voices faded. She tried not to look for him but found herself searching for him anyway. Still, she hadn't seen or heard him since he'd left her room earlier. But she wouldn't ask anyone if they had run into him. They might think she cared. Which she didn't.

At least, she didn't *want* to care.

It was impossible to draw a line in the sand with Kurt when there was so much outside interference. She couldn't discount the years he had been a Knight or the lengths he had gone to for each of them time and again—without ever asking for anything. Those thoughts inevitably led her to consider their numerous—and frequent—text exchanges. He had been a trusted friend, just as Carlyle, Finn, and Elias were.

One of her boys.

Her family.

She had accepted that Saber wished to keep his identity secret and never pressed him for information about his past. She wished she could welcome Saber as Kurt. She wanted to, but the past she carried and the one she had learned from him wiped away any chance of that.

What she hadn't told the boys was that she had considered Edie's demand because it was easier to leave than be around Kurt and the constant reminder of what they'd had and his involvement in her father's death. She wanted him to know how it felt to love someone so much, only to have them vanish without a word. But she stayed because it wouldn't just be Kurt she hurt. She owed it to everyone who had been fighting alongside her to continue.

Sabryn lifted her head when she heard footsteps crunching on gravel. She both hoped it was Kurt and prayed it wasn't. She held her breath until Finn came into view.

He searched her face as he stopped beside her. "You look like you're carrying the weight of the world."

She shrugged. "There is a lot going on."

"Do you think it'll ever end?"

"Sometimes, I wonder."

They shared a wry smile before he pressed his back against the manor beside her. "I know you're going to ask, so let me put your mind at ease. I don't feel the tats."

"I was going to ask," she said with a chuckle.

"I've been thinking about why Edie wanted you and Kurt off the isle."

She looked at the sky, watching a gray cloud drift past. "Come up with anything?"

"Only that you two must be important for her to want you gone."

"Or they want us to *think* that."

He rolled his head to her, piercing her stare with his deep brown eyes. "You're a wind talker."

"I am. And you're a Bleeder. What of it?"

"Why didn't you say anything when we learned about the pillars? You could be the sky pillar."

Sabryn snorted. "Just because I can hear the wind doesn't make me the *speur*."

"That's the Celtic word," Finn mused. "I couldn't remember it. I think you should see if you *are* the *speur*."

She turned toward him, bracing her shoulder on the stone. "All right. Let's say I am. We figured out the sky pillar is somewhere at the Fairy Glen."

"That's right."

"We were there. I didn't feel any kind of call to it. Wouldn't you think I would be drawn to it if I were the *speur*?"

Finn flattened his lips and sighed. "I don't know. How often did Ariah go into the forests before realizing she was the earth pillar?"

He had a point there. Ariah was a forest child, but even she didn't know she was the *talamh*.

"You know I'm right," Finn said as he faced her.

"Let me get this straight. You think I'm the *speur* pillar because Edie wants Kurt and I off Skye?"

Finn grinned and crossed his arms over his chest. "Why not?"

"Then how does Kurt fit in? You can't say he's the water pillar, because he isn't a water dancer."

"I've not figured out how he fits into it all yet, but I will."

Sabryn gave him a crooked smile. "Because neither Kurt nor I are part of this, other than as backup."

"You're not even going to consider it?"

"There's no point. Besides, I'm not from Skye."

He pulled his head back, frowning. "What does that have to do with anything?"

"Ariah was raised on Skye. Kirsi was raised on Skye."

"You think the water and sky pillars will also have been raised on the isle?"

She quirked a brow. "You don't?"

"I think we're all called to fight this evil. It doesn't matter how or why we answered the summons. It could be any of us."

Their phones buzzed at the same time. Sabryn pulled out her cell and saw a text from Kurt.

I FOUND PARKER.

"Well, I know what we're doing next," Finn said eagerly.

Sabryn looked up from her screen, a pit in her stomach. "When did he leave?"

"He didn't. He's been working out of one of the attics."

"I didn't see him."

Finn twisted his lips. "He was with me warding the house. He made it a point to keep his distance."

"Oh." She should be happier about that than she was. Why did everything have to be so confusing when it came to Kurt?

"You have a right to be upset about what happened in DC," Finn said.

Sabryn should feel justified by his statement. Instead, all she felt was confused and torn.

"No one will blame you if you stay behind."

She scoffed and pushed away from the stone. "Not likely. I have a few choice words for Parker."

Finn wore an easy smile as they walked together to the cars. He gave no hint that what had occurred with the mist bothered him, but Sabryn knew it was all an act. She let him have his secrets for now—just as he let her have hers.

By the time they reached the Range Rover, Carlyle, Song, Elias, and Bronwyn were already there. Carlyle tossed her the keys to the SUV. She caught them in midair. Kurt strode out of the manor just as she headed for the driver's side. Their gazes met, and he drew up short.

"I can ride with Sabryn," Carlyle offered.

She stopped him with a look. "Don't be silly." She motioned to Kurt and said, "Get in."

Sabryn felt Finn's gaze as he climbed into the passenger seat. She started the engine as Kurt shut the door and put on his seat belt behind her. She looked in the rearview mirror and saw him opening his laptop and typing something. His brow was furrowed, the lines cutting deep from the many hours he spent frowning.

"Where to?" she asked.

He didn't look up as he said, "Head east."

She put the SUV in reverse and backed up before heading down the winding drive with Elias following. Once she reached the main road, she headed east.

"I take it he isn't at the hotel," Finn said, turning to look at Kurt.

Sabryn glanced in the rearview mirror to see him shake his head.

"I'm not sure where he is," Kurt muttered.

She frowned at his tone. "What's bothering you about this?"

He finally looked up, his baby blue eyes meeting her gaze in the rearview mirror. "He's not trying to hide his location."

"Maybe he thinks he killed you," Finn offered.

Sabryn shook her head and adjusted her hands on the steering wheel. "Parker has to know by now that Kurt's alive." She asked Kurt, "How did you locate him?"

"His mobile."

Finn's eyes widened. "He didn't turn off the location services?"

"Seems not," Kurt replied.

Finn sat back. "Trap, then?"

"Possibly," Sabryn agreed.

She caught Kurt's gaze in the mirror. "But it might not be a trap."

"You think my brother's dead?" he asked.

Sabryn shrugged. "Why else would he allow himself to be found?"

"Maybe he doesn't think we'll come after him," Finn offered.

Kurt rolled his eyes. "He was always full of himself. And he might think that. But he's not trying to mask his location."

That bothered her, too. If he was working with Edie, it stood to reason that she would hide him. Unless she wanted him to be found.

Sabryn slowed and pulled over on the next road she found. "We need to talk this out with the others."

She put the vehicle in park and turned off the ignition, pulling out the map of Skye from the center console. They all walked to the back of her SUV to wait for the others.

"What's going on?" Elias asked as he exited the other vehicle.

Sabryn opened the map and laid it across the hood of Bronwyn's older Range Rover. "We need to do a tracking spell."

"To see who's with Parker?" Song asked.

Sabryn shook her head. "I want to make sure Parker is where

we think he is. He isn't attempting to hide, nor has he left the isle. That doesn't make sense to me."

"Because he's working with Edie," Carlyle said.

Finn leaned a hand on the vehicle. "We know she helped him, but that's *all* we know for sure. It could've been a one-time thing."

Elias pulled a face. "He isna going to tell us anything. And even if he does, we can no' believe it."

"I'll get my brother to talk," Kurt replied.

Sabryn tapped the map. "First thing's first. Let's see if he shielded himself."

"Why would he shield his location with magic but not turn off his mobile?" Bronwyn asked.

"Because that's the kind of stupid shit Parker does," Kurt answered.

The seven of them gathered around the map and laid their linked hands upon it. They began chanting. The locator spell was complicated and took years for any Druid to master. Their combined magic made it not only easier but also faster. Sabryn stared at the map as they chanted. It wasn't long before a flash of red like a flare popped up, indicating Parker's location miles from his phone. Then the flare faded, and another flashed on the opposite side of the isle. Then another, and another. There was one more before things went silent.

"Well," Kurt said. "It's safe to say he shielded himself."

Elias grunted. "That doesna tell us if we're walking into a trap, though."

"I think it's safe to assume we're always walking into a trap," Finn pointed out.

Carlyle nodded and gazed out toward the ocean in the

distance. "We shouldn't assume Parker has remained on Skye. That map is only of the isle."

"But that was seven of us using magic," Song said. "I think we were close to locating him, shielded or not. I believe he's still here."

Kurt nodded. "Me, too."

Sabryn folded the map. "Then how should we proceed?"

"If he set this ruse, he'll no doubt expect us to come at him as we did in town," Finn said.

Elias grinned. "Then we split up."

"I like this," Carlyle said. "It's worked for us in the past."

Kurt nodded eagerly. "Then let's give it a go."

"All right," Sabryn said. "Carlyle, come with us. I'll drop you and Finn off so you can walk to where Parker's phone pinged. Elias, come up behind him with Bronwyn and Song. I don't want anyone alone."

They piled into the vehicles and returned to the main road to resume their journey. Sabryn always got nervous before a battle. The moment she stopped feeling anything was the day she ceased fighting. This wasn't just any skirmish, though. This was Parker. The man who had killed her father and attempted to end Kurt's life.

Parker was the kind of enemy who made stupid mistakes like not turning off his phone's tracking. But he was also the kind of foe who occasionally displayed brilliance—like aligning with Edie. He was a wildcard in the purest sense of the word. Anything and everything could go wrong.

Her phone dinged with a text. A heartbeat later, so did Kurt's, Finn's, and Carlyle's.

"It's Rhona," Carlyle said.

Sabryn should have told her what they had planned. It might be better if they had descended upon Parker as a whole, but not this time. She glanced at Finn next to her. "Tell her what's happening but add that we have it under control."

CHAPTER TWENTY-EIGHT

Rhona would be pissed. Sabryn couldn't remember why she hadn't spoken to the Druid leader before they left the manor, but there had been a lot going on. Surely, Kurt had sent the text to everyone. But why wouldn't the others have come out and piled into the vehicles? Especially after everything that had happened. She glanced at Kurt in the rearview mirror. He was still absorbed with his laptop.

No one had said where they were going. She had looked at it on the map, but she couldn't recall where it was. How, then, did she know where to drive? She had stood outside, and not once had she felt the wind. She hadn't tried to listen for it, either. Perhaps it was still punishing her. She hoped it would forgive her soon because she suspected she would need it.

Her father had been a wind talker. One of her earliest memories was sitting on his lap on their back porch as he gently urged her to listen to the wind. Her eyes watered as emotion welled in her chest.

She missed him so much. It didn't matter how much time passed. She still longed to call him and ask for advice. He'd never been too busy to give it, either. What would he say now? What might his sage words be?

Likely that she visit her mom.

"Here," Kurt said, breaking into her thoughts.

Sabryn pressed the brake and stopped the SUV. She looked behind her, but Elias must have already turned off while she was deep in thought. She hated getting so lost in her head that she couldn't remember portions of a drive. It always amazed her that she didn't wreck during such occasions.

"See you there," Finn said as he opened the door.

Sabryn grabbed his arm to stop him. She looked behind him and met Carlyle's gaze.

"What's wrong?" he asked.

She shrugged, trying to put into words what she felt. "I'm not sure."

"We have Parker. We can't let him slip through our fingers after what he did to Kurt and your family," Finn said.

He was right, of course. Parker needed to be punished. There wouldn't be anything to tie him to her father's death, but there *were* witnesses to Parker stabbing Kurt. The chief superintendent could file charges. But would they stick? Not if Diana or the London Druids had any say in it. The only place for Parker was in the Druid prison deep in the Red Hills.

All three of them stared at her. Sabryn forced her fingers to loosen on Finn's arm. "Be careful. If th—"

"We know it's a trap," Carlyle said. "We'll be prepared."

They were gone before she could reply. She watched her friends disappear over the hill.

Kurt said, "Keep following the road for now. Parker hasn't moved."

She lifted her foot from the brake, and the vehicle began to roll forward. She rested her foot on the accelerator but didn't press down. "How far?"

"About a mile."

She suddenly didn't want to go down the road and pressed the brake again. "We shouldn't do this."

"What?" Kurt asked, lifting his head to look at her through the rearview mirror. "Why not? I thought you wanted Parker as much as I do."

"I do," she insisted.

His brow puckered. "Then what's the problem?"

"This is a trap."

"We know it is. And you came up with a plan."

She scowled. "Not much of one. No one disagreed with it or wanted to change it."

"What is going on with you? You always come up with plans the Knights go along with."

"Something isn't right."

Kurt sighed and looked out the passenger window. "Nothing has been right on Skye for some time."

She couldn't argue that point, but that didn't help her shake the sense of imminent doom. Not that she hadn't experienced it before. It just hadn't been so overwhelmingly dire as it felt now.

"What's the wind saying?" Kurt asked.

"I don't hear it."

There was a beat of silence. "Because you aren't listening again or because it isn't talking?"

"I really don't know. I didn't hear it when we were outside looking at the map, but I wasn't trying then, either."

"Try after we park."

She nodded because…what else could she do? Still, she didn't drive farther. "You really found your brother by tracking his phone?"

"You make it sound like you don't believe that's what I did."

"That's not what I meant," she hastened to say. "I just…I'm just trying to sort through everything."

He snapped the laptop closed and set it on the seat next to him. "Why don't we get out here?"

Sabryn happily put the vehicle in park and shut off the engine. Kurt had already exited. He stood beside her, one hand on the door, the other on the side of the SUV. She looked into gentle, pale blue eyes that held more emotion than words ever could. The navy ringing the irises only made them more brilliant.

Those were eyes she had once trusted beyond all measure. Eyes that had burned with desire. Eyes that hungrily watched her from across crowded rooms. Eyes that had crinkled as he laughed at one of her corny jokes.

She missed the man behind those eyes. She longed for that kind of connection again, burned for it. After tasting such bliss, nothing could ever come close again.

He leaned toward her. "You think I didn't want to find him when I first came to Skye because I didn't immediately search for his phone?"

Sabryn shrugged. It was a good question. "Why didn't you?"

"I had gone days without sleep. I wasn't thinking clearly about anything but getting here to you."

"Yes, of course. I forgot about that." *How* had she forgotten that? He had passed out in front of her.

Kurt stepped back and dropped his arm to give her room to get out. "I'm on your side, Sabryn, whether you believe it or not. Everything I've done since DC has been to make up for my part in what happened there. I'll apologize for the rest of my days in hopes you might forgive me one day."

"Don't. Please," she begged as she unfolded from the vehicle and closed the door. "Let's just focus on Parker."

Kurt turned and pointed. "He should be over that hill."

Sabryn didn't like that the SUV sat out in the open. She glanced around to see if there was a place to hide it when she saw that the road just ended. She couldn't have driven farther even if she had wanted to. When she glanced at Kurt, he was already a few steps ahead of her. She hurried to catch up. The seven of them would be enough to take out Parker and whatever Edinburgh Druids might still be around. It would be another matter entirely if Edie showed up.

"I don't suppose you can hack a satellite to see if your brother is alone," Sabryn joked as they walked.

Kurt kept his gaze forward. "I could. I didn't think of that."

She frowned. He *always* thought of things like that. *Always.* Sabryn halted, her heart racing as disquiet curled inside her. Nothing felt right.

He walked two more steps before pausing and looking back at her over his shoulder. "What's wrong? We've given the others plenty of time to get into place."

She searched his face, though for what, she wasn't sure.

"Sabryn?" he asked worriedly as he faced her.

"Something isn't right."

He walked to stand before her. "You forgot to listen to the wind."

Shit, she had. What was wrong with her? She inwardly gave herself a shake to clear her mind of all the problems and worries circling inside her, then closed her eyes and opened her ears. The wind came at her from all directions—some of it soft like a butterfly's wing and other gusts that whipped around her in an angry, urgent frenzy.

But not once did it speak.

She stayed there for several minutes, waiting and listening. Then she spoke to it. "I'm sorry I shut you out. I need your help. Please."

Sabryn repeated the words several times, but it didn't reply. She sighed and opened her eyes. "It won't talk to me."

"It would've been helpful, but we'll make do," Kurt said.

They proceeded forward, but her apprehension grew with every step. Something was very, *very* wrong. Why couldn't anyone else sense it? She had to stop going along with things before it was too late.

"Wait," she called to Kurt as they reached the top of the hill.

But he was looking down into the glen. "There's Parker."

Sabryn reached for him, but her fingers grabbed air as Kurt headed toward his brother. Parker sat alone atop a picnic table. He was the only one around, which seemed particularly odd. She frowned. When she looked across the shallow valley, she spotted Elias, Bronwyn, and Song. Sabryn turned her head to the side and caught sight of Finn and Carlyle. All of them were headed straight for Parker. Sabryn looked at their target, noticing that his eyes were on her. He smiled.

"Stop!" she yelled to her friends. "STOP!!!!"

But no one seemed to hear her. She raced down the hillside after Kurt, screaming at her friends. The wind snatched each word from her mouth, so it never reached them. She ran as fast as she could but couldn't catch Kurt, who was just a few yards ahead of her.

Then, she saw the mist pouring over the hill behind Elias. It stretched like fingers as it slid down the slope toward the trio. There was more behind Carlyle and Finn. When she dared to look over her shoulder, she saw the mist there, too, rushing right for her. She tensed, waiting for it to grab her, but it gave her a wide berth and went straight for Kurt. It wrapped around his ankles and moved up his legs without him realizing.

Everyone had mist creeping up their bodies except for her and Parker. His laughter filled the valley, getting louder and louder the longer it went on. She stopped shouting at her friends and turned to magic. She released a volley at Parker and cheered when it struck him. Yet it did absolutely no damage.

She didn't have time to wonder why as she called more magic into her hands and threw another round at him. He didn't even try to move, and just like before, the magic struck him without effect.

He laughed louder, goading her. "You never learn," he said.

That drew her up short. She looked at the Knights. The mist had consumed them. She could no longer see their faces. Kurt reached out a hand toward his brother, but that, too, disappeared within the vaper.

"I warned you."

Sabryn's head jerked to the side to find Edie. "Let them go."

"I gave you a warning you chose not to heed. I told you what would happen."

"No," Sabryn said, shaking her head. She couldn't—*wouldn't*—believe it. "Let them go!"

"Sabryn!" Kurt yelled.

Kurt's shout drew her attention. She looked over to find him on his knees—at least, she *thought* it was him.

"They're only the first," Edie whispered in her ear.

Sabryn jerked away and readied her magic, but Edie was gone. Everyone was gone. Her friends. Parker. Everyone. She spun in a frenzied circle, waiting for the next shoe to drop.

"You were warned." Edie's voice drifted on the wind.

The truth of what had just happened hit her then. Sabryn dropped to her knees as anguish sank its claws into her chest and ripped out her heart. The grief was sharp, the sorrow suffocating. It was the kind that echoed louder than any scream. All of her fears had been laid bare. She was alone. She'd had the chance to save her friends and had only led them straight to their deaths.

"Sabryn?"

She jerked at the sound of Rhona's voice to see the rest of their group descending into the valley. Terror coursed through her veins as she reached out her hand. "Get back!" she warned.

But the mist was already rising from the ground. It swallowed them in an instant before disappearing into the earth once more. Sabryn stared in stunned silence at what she had just witnessed.

The hush around her was ghostly. The mist hadn't just taken her friends. It had taken every living thing. The birds, insects, and the animals. She leaned forward, her hands sinking into the grass as she dug into the ground, hoping the mist would take her, too.

CHAPTER TWENTY-NINE

The earth suddenly moved beneath Sabryn. Something grabbed her hands, tugging her into the rocky soil. She scarcely had time to breathe before her face was in the dirt. She closed her eyes and braced herself, ready to be suffocated, only to feel a spray of water and hear the roar of crashing waves. Her lids lifted, and she found herself on all fours on a beach. She cautiously sat back on her haunches and nervously looked around as waves rolled against her legs, soaking her.

The wet sand crumbled beneath her as she stumbled to her feet and rubbed her hands on her pants to get the sand off. She watched as the grains rose toward the sky instead of falling to the ground. Sabryn looked around for whoever had brought her here, only to find herself staring at the co-op across the street. There were cars along the curb, but no one was in them. Nor was anyone walking down the sidewalks. She became hyperaware of every sound and movement around her, and while it appeared like she was the only one there, she didn't feel as if she were alone.

"What do you want?" she demanded, turning in a circle.

Edie and Parker were likely nearby, and Edie had promised her a painful death after everyone else died. Pain snatched Sabryn's breath when she thought about Elias, Finn, and Carlyle. And Kurt. A tear rolled down her face.

"You won! Are you happy?" Sabryn screamed.

She walked backward, her eyes scanning the buildings for movement. "You promised a painful death. What are you waiting for? Let's get to it!"

There was no answer.

Sabryn narrowed her eyes as she seethed. "Come on, bitch. Or are you all talk and no action?"

She had been sure that would get a response, but Edie didn't say anything. Sabryn blew out a frustrated breath and spun to look at the ocean. She tilted her head to the side and frowned when she realized the waves were rolling backward as if someone had reversed a recording. Upon closer inspection, she discovered *everything*—including the wind—was moving opposite of the way it should.

"I know someone's here," she stated as ire pushed aside her fear. "I can feel you. Who are you, and what do you want?"

A pinprick of light appeared over the water and brightened as it grew. She had to raise her hands to shield her eyes before it blinded her. Sabryn turned her head away, but not even that was enough. She squeezed her eyes shut and wondered if this was how she would die. Then, just as suddenly as it had begun, it ceased.

She opened her eyes but was hesitant to lower her arms. She had stormed into battle so many times—but always with the other Knights. She hadn't been alone in so very long. It had been important that the boys believed she was strong and independent.

She had never wanted them to know just how reliant on them she had become.

None of that mattered now, though. She was well and truly alone. She had ignored Edie's threat, and all her friends paid the ultimate price. There was no way she could save Skye on her own. It would fall to The Grey or whoever was vying for control. Once the isle fell, it would be up to the Dragon Kings, Warriors, and MacLeod Druids to right things.

Sabryn dropped her arms and turned to face her foe. Her heart skipped a beat when she saw dozens of people standing over the water, their feet never touching it. They stared silently at her, watching her as if she were a specimen in a zoo.

"You're no animal, Sabryn," said a deep, Scottish voice.

It wasn't a voice she recognized. She scanned the faces, trying to determine who'd spoken, when she saw movement to her right. A man with a long, gray beard stepped away from the others and moved toward her. Her mouth went slack as she recognized him from pictures Rhona had shown her.

"Corann?" she asked skeptically.

He dipped his chin in acknowledgment and watched her with his dark brown eyes.

This couldn't be happening. Could it?

"How?" she whispered in shock.

"With great effort. We doona have long, lass."

She shook her head and took a step back. "There's no way you're going to convince me that you're really Corann."

"You're right to be wary. The evil around the isle is developing at an alarming rate. Faster than it ever has before."

"And what are you doing about it? Absolutely nothing."

He glanced at the ground. "We've been hindered."

"We." She looked behind him to the others. "And who are you, exactly?"

"Who do you think?"

She rolled her eyes. "I thought we didn't have time to talk. Obviously, that isn't true, or you wouldn't be so damn cryptic."

His face tightened before he said, "We're the Ancients."

"Of course you are," she replied sarcastically. "As soon as I give you my trust, you'll turn into whatever's controlling Edie. I get it. You wanted me to feel pain by killing my friends. Now, it's my turn. I'm not stupid enough to take the bait."

Corann's gaze was steady and patient as he held hers. "Every Druid who dies joins the Ancients, lass. We managed to speak through Ferne recently so you would all know we were being silenced."

She crossed her arms over her chest and quirked a brow, waiting for him to continue.

"What we're doing now, we do at great peril to ourselves. We've been waiting for an opportunity to reach one of you."

"And you chose me? How lucky am I?" she retorted caustically.

Corann pressed his lips together. "Lass, everything you just experienced was only a dream."

"Liar." How dare he say such a thing and give her hope?

He sighed and shook his head. "I had hoped we wouldna need to show you every conceivable outcome, but it looks as if you're giving us no choice."

"Wait. What?" she asked worriedly, right as he snapped his fingers.

The beach was gone. Sabryn was once again in the glen. Her stomach clenched as she watched her friends being engulfed by the mist. The ground sucked her into it, only to toss her back to the beginning once more. This time, she raced toward Carlyle and Finn, shouting at them to stop. She saved them from the mist until the last moment.

On the third repeat, she convinced Kurt not to go into the glen, but the outcome remained the same. The fourth time, she began shouting before she even saw her friends, urging them to fall back. She and Kurt made it to the SUV, only for him to be taken by the mist inside the vehicle. She clung to his hand, but the vapor eventually took him.

Over and over again, she suffered through witnessing the same event. She lost track of how many times she endured it all, but no matter what she tried to change, it always ended the same: with everyone's deaths.

"Stop!" she begged, too drained and spent to go through the hope and loss even one more time.

Finally, the loop stopped, and she was back at the beach. She crumpled to the sand and stared blankly out at the ocean.

Corann lowered himself beside her. "I'm sorry you had to endure that again."

"You make it sound as if it was only once. You gave me hope each time that I might save at least one of them, only to snatch it away. It was unbelievably cruel. But then I *was* forewarned that my death would be painful."

"I'm no' here to kill you, lass."

She snorted, her gaze still on the water. "Riiiiiight."

"You had to be shown the outcomes. All of them. It was the only way you could learn." Corann was silent for a moment. "This is when you ask...*why?*"

Sabryn briefly closed her eyes. "Fine. I'll play along. Why?"

"Because you can win. You're just going about it wrong."

"Gotcha."

He sighed loudly. "Your friends are alive. Everything you experienced was simply a dream."

"Sure, it was." She wouldn't let hope back into her heart. The pain was tenfold when it was snatched away. And it had been repeatedly taken from her.

"Sabryn," he began.

She turned her head to him. "Where's my father? If all Druids become Ancients, where is he? Why isn't he talking to me?"

"He didna think you'd believe him."

"But I'd believe a man I've never met? You're delusional."

Corann's voice hardened slightly when he said, "Evil will triumph if you doona move forward. There's only one way to win. You've known it from the beginning, but you willna allow yourself to do it."

"Okay." She was done talking, done listening.

Just *done*.

"We're out of time." Corann got to his feet.

She looked up at him to find his lips pinched and his brow grooved with deep lines of worry.

"If you want to keep the Knights alive, then you must do it as a unit. *All of you.*"

The message was clear. She needed to forgive Kurt. "That's not possible."

"Then you've doomed us all," he replied softly.

CHAPTER THIRTY

"Why won't she wake up?" Carlyle asked fearfully.

Kurt kneeled at Sabryn's head. They hadn't moved her after she collapsed. He held her head between his hands and stared into her face, silently willing her to wake.

"We have to do something," Elias stated for the third time.

Finn's fingers were at her wrist, feeling her pulse. "Her heart is racing."

"We need to get her inside," Carlyle said.

Footsteps hurried across the gravel toward them. Song, Bronwyn, and Elodie turned the corner and drew to a halt.

"What happened?" Song asked.

Kurt smoothed Sabryn's hair back with his thumb. "She doesn't faint."

"Do you think it's Edie?" Bronwyn asked.

Elias shrugged. "Maybe."

"She did warn Sabryn away," Carlyle stated.

Kurt glared at all of them. "Enough. We don't know what's happening."

Finn said, "I can find out."

As a Bleeder, Finn could take feelings from others. He had learned to use that skill against his opponents, which is why he liked to get close to his enemies when fighting. There were drawbacks, however. He couldn't stop the feelings he encountered. But this was Sabryn. If Finn was willing, Kurt wouldn't stop him.

"Do it," Kurt urged.

Finn wrapped his hand around her wrist. He jerked back almost immediately. "Fek!"

"What is it?" Carlyle demanded.

Finn's voice shook when he said, "She's scared and grieving."

"This has to be some form of mental warfare," Elodie said.

Elias's nostrils flared. "It's just the sort of thing Edie would do."

A fresh wave of panic seized Kurt.

"It makes sense," Bronwyn agreed. "There's no one here, and Sabryn wasn't ill."

Carlyle looked on helplessly. "We can't help her."

"Yes, we can," Kurt said. "We may not be able to reach her mind, but we can protect her body with our magic."

He didn't wait for the others, just lowered his forehead to hers and let his magic flow from him to surround her. If he couldn't reach her with his voice, his magic would. Sabryn had always been sensitive to other's magic. Yet she lay so still that he had to keep checking the pulse at her neck to make sure she was alive.

Time ceased to exist as, one by one, their magic joined his to cocoon her in a protective bubble. With every second she remained unconscious, more dread filled Kurt. Sabryn was fire and determination. She was the spark that lit a room. The strength that kept him going when he wanted to give up. She was beauty and love. Wonder and brilliance.

He didn't just love her. He *belonged* to her—every breath, every heartbeat. There wasn't a part of him she hadn't claimed. In her love, he had discovered a promise of something pure and steady. Something uniquely theirs.

"Please, come back to me," he whispered.

Sabryn's chest rose as she took in a huge gulp of air. Kurt froze before slowly lifting his head and looking down into her dark sapphire depths. The resentment was gone, her ire softened. For a heartbeat, it was just the two of them.

"There she is," Carlyle said as he grabbed Sabryn's hand.

Kurt sat back as they pulled her into a sitting position. He stared at the back of her head, wondering at the changes he had seen. He was almost afraid to meet her eyes again and find those dark feelings had returned.

Finn dropped his head back and looked at the sky. "Fek me. I don't need another scare like that."

"I agree. Doona do that to us again," Elias told her with a chuckle.

Bronwyn dropped to her haunches at Sabryn's feet. "Are you hurt? What happened?"

"We should get her inside the manor," Carlyle said.

Carlyle, Elias, and Finn helped Sabryn stand. She remained silent as they walked her to the front of the house. Kurt watched them go. Right before they vanished around the corner, Sabryn looked back at him. Their gazes clashed for a moment, and then she was gone. He blew out a breath and climbed to his feet so he could lean against the house. His eyes pricked with tears, so he closed them and lifted a silent prayer of thanks. When he opened his eyes, Song stood before him.

"Good thinking, using our magic as a shield," she said.

He shrugged. "It probably didn't do anything."

"Maybe it did. Maybe it didn't. We should probably ask."

"I'll be along in a minute."

Song looked in the direction the others had gone. "Did you tell her?" Song swung her head back to him. "Did you tell her you love her?"

"I didn't really get a chance."

"You should tell her."

He thought back to his conversation with Sabryn at the cottage. "I don't think it will do any good. Besides, she knows."

"If you didn't actually say the words, how can you be sure?"

He hated to admit that Song had a point.

"Come on," Song said. "Let's find out what happened to her."

Kurt paused as he looked at the vehicles.

"There will be plenty of time to find your brother," Song said. "Sabryn fainting is cause for worry." She walked away.

He followed and entered the manor two steps behind Song. She walked to stand beside Carlyle in the sitting room, and Kurt took his place slightly behind the chair Sabryn had claimed. He rubbed his thumbs along his fingertips, recalling the warmth of her skin and the silky texture of her hair.

Suddenly, Sabryn turned and looked at Kurt over her shoulder. "We can't go after Parker."

CHAPTER THIRTY-ONE

Edinburgh

The world became distorted through the windscreen as rain pelted the glass incessantly. As the wipers swiped it away, all was clear again for an instant. But it didn't last. It never did. Beth had learned that the hard way.

She had always been an optimist, someone whose glass was half-full. If the world gave you lemons, you made lemonade. That's the type of girl she was. Life was one escapade after another, waiting to be revealed. It was all about the timing.

Or so she had once believed.

She'd had blinders on. There were stretches of time when she wished she still wore those rose-colored glasses, but they were fleeting periods. She knew the truth now, and there was no going back. She gazed at all the people hurrying through the rain, under umbrellas and raincoats, with no idea what was happening around them. Their rose-colored glasses were firmly in place and would never be dislodged. Even when the world crumbled to dust.

They were fools. Sheep led by imbeciles with neither power nor wisdom. Very few had any idea what life was or why anyone was even alive. They only cared about the latest fashion, the next tech gadget, or the luxury flat they couldn't afford. They popped out children on autopilot like candy from a machine, thinking it furthered the human race.

It was utter shite.

Beth's gaze shifted to her reflection in the passenger window. She touched her brown hair, now growing out from the pixie cut she had favored for so long. It had fit her facial structure, but that haircut was for the naïve, immature girl who had accidentally blundered into truth and reality.

She stared into her pale brown eyes before observing her heart-shaped face, the pouty lips Sydney had loved, and the cheekbones she had gotten from her mother. That girl was gone forever. Beth couldn't name what she was now, but she was different. And certainly not just a woman or a Druid.

"There she is, ma'am."

The sound of Madeline's voice jerked Beth out of her musings. She turned to the front seat, where her formidable bodyguard sat behind the wheel. Madeline's black hair was in its usual slick bun, and she wore all black, all the time. There wasn't a stitch of color in her very limited wardrobe. Not a pink bow on her panties, no white lace on a bra. Not even colored stitching on her socks. Just drab, basic black. Yet it worked on her.

Tall and intimidating, Madeline was as loyal as they came.

For the moment, at least.

"There," the bodyguard pointed.

Beth followed Madeline's finger to see a slender, stylishly clothed, middle-aged woman stride from the Balmoral Hotel. She had an old-money air about her as she paused to speak to an attendant. Her straight, blond hair was cut to emphasize her classic features, the length hitting just past her shoulders.

Everyone around the woman hurried to anticipate her needs. She never had to ask for anything. She didn't even pause as a gray Rolls-Royce pulled up, and the door was opened for her. She slid inside before the car sped away.

Madeline discreetly pulled from their spot along the curb and followed. The Rolls drove straight to the warehouse where George conducted business. Madeline found a place to park as they watched the woman exit the car and enter the warehouse.

"That's twice in two days," Madeline said.

Beth lightly drummed her fingers on the door's armrest. "And you're sure you heard her accent?"

"I'm positive. I know a posh Brit accent when I hear it. The London Druids are here."

"So it seems."

"What do you want to do?"

Beth drew in a breath and released it, considering. She had an agreement with George in order to get revenge on Bronwyn and take Carwood Manor. But the need for retaliation wasn't as strong as it used to be. She had gotten Sydney out of that horrid mental institution and removed all the drugs from his system. But it had cost her.

After all of that, she hadn't held on to him. Because he no longer factored into her future. She had loved him. She was sure of that. And she could still recall having such feelings. But she couldn't remember what they felt like any longer.

George was using her, just as Beth was using George. And the Druid would attempt to betray her. It was inevitable. Because Beth had the one thing everyone wanted.

"I don't know," she finally answered Madeline.

She turned to look at Beth. "I'm not sure you need George and her Druids anymore."

Beth watched her bodyguard's dark eyes dart to the side. Unable to help herself, Beth looked at the large, thick book beside her. There was no title—no wording at all on the cover. The leather was smooth in places as if thousands of hands had caressed it before daring to view the pages. She had been one of those.

Everyone coveted the book. It had been fought over, stolen, hidden, found, and fought over again—a never-ending cycle—but the book only showed its true power to a select few.

All who heard about it became obsessed with finding it, believing the legend that it held all the answers.

Those who obtained it and peeked inside became entrapped.

Few were strong or brave enough to walk away from the tantalizing lure.

One look. That was all it took for the power within to seduce and entice her. It had changed the course of her life. There were spells from both *mies* and *droughs*. The book was a bible, a grimoire, and a compendium all rolled into one. Everything a Druid could ever want to know or learn sat within its thick pages. It did, indeed, hold all the answers.

But the price for the answers was steep.

Each time she read from it, it stole a piece of her. She both yearned to read more and recoiled at the thought. She was well and truly within its grasp. The only way out was through. She didn't know what she would become, but it no longer mattered. It had too much of her now.

"Beth?"

She tore her gaze from the book and looked at Madeline. "You're right. We don't need George."

"Do you want me to find out why the London Druids are here?"

Beth lifted the book from beside her and set it on her lap. She could feel the power radiating from it, urging her to open it and absorb more of its knowledge. It wanted to gift her ancient spells that hadn't been spoken in thousands of years.

She flattened her hands on the cover and closed her eyes. The book pulsed as if it had a heartbeat, like a living, breathing thing. How could it be anything else? It held the knowledge of Druids long past, where there hadn't been black and white, good and bad, *mies* and *droughs*. A time when there were shades of gray, and a Druid was just a Druid without being labeled.

Someone weaker than her wouldn't have gotten this far. The book had shown her all those who had come before and ventured to learn, only to die when it became too much. She was the exception. She would take all the knowledge, hold all the power. All she had to do was open the cover again.

Her hands trembled. The magic within her was more potent than ever. She thought about Sydney standing in her office, his brown eyes searching hers as he looked for the woman she had been. He wasn't the same, either, though. Both had been altered irrevocably. She thought about him walking away without a backward glance.

It was only then that she realized she didn't need him. She didn't need anyone but herself. She didn't even need Madeline.

She'd wasted so many years chasing one boy after another, defining her life by relationships she may or may not have had. That's what blinders did.

Beth lifted the book's cover and heard the leather creak softly. The book's influence seeped from its pages and the very ink written upon it. She didn't need to flip through it to look for what she wanted. The book already knew. The pages turned themselves, flipping rapidly until they suddenly stopped.

She gazed down. The words were written in a language she didn't understand, but her eyes were pulled toward the drawing of the Fairy Glen. The letters blurred, rearranging before clearing so she could read them. She scanned the page and the two following it before softly closing the book, her hands still gripping it firmly. Beth knew from experience that it would be hours—maybe even days—before she could release it again.

At one time, she'd believed it some sort of spell. Now, she knew it was the book exacting its price from her. The fear that knowledge had once brought grew less and less. Soon, she wouldn't tremble before opening the book, she wouldn't set it aside, and she wouldn't stop reading. That day was much closer than she'd expected.

"What did it tell you?" Madeline asked, her voice soft and eyes wide with excitement and a little fear.

"We need to return to Skye."

Madeline's brows rose. "Now?"

"Now."

She nodded before facing forward and pulling the car back onto the road.

CHAPTER THIRTY-TWO

Alcohol hadn't helped. A hot shower hadn't helped. A change of clothes hadn't helped. Nothing could get what happened out of Sabryn's head. She wandered around her bedroom, a shiver sliding through her every time she thought about her encounter with Corann.

She had gone over every detail a million times in a million different ways over the past few hours. She was tired of thinking about it, but she couldn't seem to help herself. Her feet took her to the window, where she looked out to find it raining. Everyone kept saying it wasn't the rainy season yet. Hard to believe when it rained all the time.

She became immersed in the droplets on the glass panes. Sabryn followed one as it haltingly made its way to the bottom. Her thoughts eased as she focused on a second bead. But as it worked its way down the glass, her mind tumbled back to a rainy night in DC.

She had felt good after one too many drinks, some good

conversation, and flirting. If it had been any other night, at any other time, or with any other person, she never would have walked into the downpour and spun around like a child.

She remembered stopping and seeing his heated gaze. Water dripped from his thick lashes and the ends of his hair onto his expensive suit. She didn't know which of them moved first. Maybe they reached for each other. All she knew was that she had been standing alone, and then she was in his arms.

His hold had been firm and strong, his eyes hungry, needy. Heat spread, sliding through her blood until she burned with it.

"Sabryn," he whispered.

He spoke her name reverently as if he might explode if he *didn't* say it. Then his lips were on hers. The kiss was wild, heated. Passionate. She felt his desire, tasted his hunger, and returned all of it.

She slid her fingers up his chest, over his shoulders, and into his thick hair. Somehow, she ended up against a wall with his deliciously hard body—and even more deliciously hard erection— pressed against her. She had never been so turned on, had never felt such yearning. Such aching need. One touch from him, one kiss, and she had come alive.

He left trails of heat where his fingers skimmed along her body. She lifted her leg to wrap around his hip and bring him closer. His palm caressed her thigh, moving around to cup her ass and fit her against his crotch. They moaned in unison at the contact.

They couldn't get enough of each other. Kissing, stroking, rubbing. Her panties were soaked, and it had nothing to do with the rain. Her body ached for him. She could think of nothing but him and yearned for nothing but to have him inside her.

Sabryn drew in a shaky breath and turned from the window,

hoping to stop the memory. Thinking about what she had been put through wasn't much better than thinking about Corann. She put a hand to her forehead and fought a wave of tears. She blinked them back and lowered her arm when she regained her composure. Her gaze slid to the door as she alternated between thinking about her first kiss with Kurt and what Corann had imparted, then walked out of the room before she changed her mind.

The upstairs was quiet as she traversed the hallway. She reached the stairs and ascended to the attic, her bare feet not making a sound. She was surprised to find the door open. Sabryn paused and peered inside, spotting the table and chairs Kurt was using for a desk. She looked in the other direction and found stacked furniture, most covered with sheets. A daybed had been pulled apart from the rest, and a crinkled blanket and a pillow rested on it, telling her it was Kurt's bed.

Sabryn grimaced. She was the reason he was up here. Anyone else would've told her where to go, but not him. She took a measured step inside and searched for him. Then another. After the third step, she found him to the left.

Kurt stood with his feet apart, his hands in his pockets as he stared outside. She wondered if he was thinking of that long-ago night as she had been. When they first kissed. And slept together. They'd had a lot of firsts that night.

He stiffened, and she realized he had seen her reflection in the glass. He turned to face her, his expression guarded. They stared wordlessly at each other. She wished he would speak first, but she was the one who had invaded his space.

"Do you have a moment?" she asked.

He nodded once. "Always."

This was so much harder than she'd thought it would be.

Sabryn glanced around. "There are plenty of bedrooms to choose from."

"I was giving you space."

She met his gaze, taking in the man before her. Six years of talking, and he hadn't once told her who he was. He hadn't even hinted at it. Hadn't tried to talk about her past lovers. He'd said nothing. If he hadn't lost so much sleep running from Parker, Kurt likely wouldn't be here now. And she never would've discovered Saber's identity.

"I almost contacted you over the years," she admitted. "There were times I even dialed your number, ready to demand closure."

"Why didn't you?" he asked.

She shrugged and swallowed. "I think because I realized that no one actually gets the closure they need. We have to figure out how to move on. It's a learning/growing/healing thing."

"That makes sense."

"Would you have told me the truth if I had asked?"

His chest expanded as he drew in a breath. "I don't know. I'd like to think I would have. I'm sorry, Sabryn. For all of it."

"You had years to drop hints or point me in a direction where I might figure things out. Why didn't you?"

"If being Saber was the only way I could be in your life, then I was going to take it. I wanted you to know all the facts because you deserved it. But that also meant I might lose you completely. Saber could keep you safe, unlike when I was Kurt."

She wrapped her arms around her middle, her emotions still shredded. She had demanded details from Kurt at the cottage, but she hadn't actually listened when he spoke. This time, she did. And there was no denying the misery, regret, or truth in his words. If it weren't for Corann and the Ancients, she didn't think she would be here listening right now.

Did she dare believe what the Ancients had told her? Could the outcome really hinge on whether she forgave Kurt? She thought back to their years in the Knights. They had all worked seamlessly. It had only fractured after she learned his identity.

Hope flared in his eyes. It was how he held himself still, waiting for her reply. He hadn't been the one to kill her father. Granted, he had known what'd happened and hadn't told her, but he *had* tried to stop it. And he had kept her alive.

"We wouldn't have made it this long without you. You've done an excellent job keeping us safe."

His shoulders dropped slightly as if in relief. "Are you okay from earlier?"

She looked at the ceiling and twisted her lips before dropping her arms. "I relived all of your deaths, thousands of times, for what felt like lifetimes. I'm far from okay."

"What do you need?"

Your arms around me. She almost said the words, but they got lodged in her throat. She didn't think she'd hesitate if this were Saber. And she wouldn't if he was the Kurt from DC. Frankly, she was tired of carrying around the anger.

Sabryn walked to him. He enfolded her in his arms without a word, holding her tightly to his chest as she wound her arms around his waist. Tears burned her eyes as she nestled her cheek against him. It felt good to be held again—no, it felt good to be held by *him*.

She basked in Kurt's warmth and strength. The safety of his embrace. With one simple hug, years of pain were eased. And the forgiveness she had withheld sat heavy on her tongue.

"I forgive you," she whispered.

With a sharp inhale, his arms tightened. As he released the breath, he rested his cheek against her head and stroked a hand down her hair. Those three words had relieved his burden, but it had also lightened hers.

The longer Sabryn was in his arms, the more relaxed she became and the more the tension eased from her muscles. They remained locked together for a long time before she lifted her head to look at him. The stark yearning and unadulterated longing she saw in his eyes made her heart miss a beat. Kurt wouldn't make the first move. He had bared his heart before, and she had slashed it to pieces. Yet here he was, holding her because she needed it. She could pull out of his arms now, and he wouldn't stop her. That wasn't who Kurt was. But there was no way she could walk away. Not now.

Maybe not ever.

She didn't want to deny what was between them any longer. They had already been separated for too many years. She rose onto her tiptoes and pressed her lips to his. For a heartbeat, he didn't move. Then he sucked in a breath and slanted his mouth over hers. The desire erupted, singeing every inch of her.

One of his large hands slid around the nape of her neck to hold the back of her head as he deepened the kiss. Her body throbbed, ached. For him. The blaze of passion became a wildfire that would rage for an eternity.

His tongue swept into her mouth, tangling with hers in a timeless dance of longing and need. She moaned into his mouth when his hands caressed down her back to her hips before he lifted her. She wrapped her legs around his waist, bringing her throbbing center against his arousal.

He turned and pressed her against the wall before tearing his lips from hers and pressing hot kisses down her neck. Her eyes rolled back in her head as he rocked against her sex. She clawed at his shirt to get to his skin, finally finding the hem of his tee and dragging it up his chest. He leaned back so she could tug it over his head and off one arm, then the other.

Sabryn sighed when she saw his bare chest and the Celtic warding the size of her hand. He had been lean and buff before. Now, he was chiseled in all the right places. She spread her hands over his pecs and then to the thick sinew of his shoulders and arms.

"Wow," she murmured in appreciation. "I want to see the rest."

He gave her a crooked grin and lowered her legs to the floor. "Only if I get to see you."

"Oh, you'll get to see me," she teased as she walked backward to the daybed. She let her gaze wander over the wide V of his shoulders that tapered to a trim waist and an eight-pack that left her mouth watering.

Kurt's baby blue eyes burned with a craving that made her stomach quiver excitedly. "I lost a piece of clothing. It's your turn."

Dear god, she had missed him. Missed *this*. The sparks, the banter, the easy way they fit together. She pulled off her shirt and tossed it aside. His nostrils flared when his gaze lowered to her chest. She smoothed her fingers across the swell of one breast and the lace against it. "Like this, do you?"

"I'd like it better off you," he stated in a low, ragged voice.

She grinned. "Your turn."

He yanked off his denim in record time, leaving him in boxer briefs, his arousal tenting the fabric. "Yours," he all but growled.

This game had started off fun, but now that so little separated them, she was ready to end it. It took her two tries to get a hold of the waistband of her sweats. She was about to remove them with as much gusto as Kurt had his jeans, but then she saw how his breathing had quickened, and his eyes followed her hands as he anxiously waited to see more.

Sabryn moved her fingers to either side of her waist and cocked her hips to one side as she pushed the garment down. His lips parted. She repeated the performance for the other side and saw his hands clench before he flexed his fingers. It would be fun if she wasn't also breathing hard, watching his cock jump.

She bent forward and pushed her sweats down to her ankles, showing off her cleavage as she did. Then she stepped out of the pants and kicked them aside with her toes. It had been years since a man had seen her in only her underwear. She didn't hide away from Kurt's perusal. Instead, she stood proudly and let him look.

"Bloody hell, woman," he murmured. "You're beautiful."

He started toward her, and she held up a hand. "Not yet, Romeo. You've still got on some clothes."

Kurt looked down at his boxers and quirked a brow at her. His lips curled into a crooked grin. She thought he might rip them off, but she should've known he would treat her to the same show she had given him. He cupped his hand over his arousal and stroked it.

"Not funny," she told him. "You're supposed to remove it."

"Then come take it off," he challenged.

She took a step.

He tsked. "I think it's only fair we even things up since you had on more clothes than I did."

"Oh, really?" she asked, amused.

He continued to stroke himself, drawing her gaze to his thick length. She wanted him inside her. She squeezed her legs together and bit back a moan.

"Remove your panties," he said.

The words didn't register at first. Sabryn blinked and looked up at him. Panties? He wanted her panties removed? That wasn't what she'd expected him to choose, but she didn't care. All of it was coming off eventually. She hooked her thumbs into the lacy thong and tugged it down.

"Wait," he commanded. "Turn around."

She grinned and slowly turned.

He moaned and swallowed loudly. She kept her back to him as she shimmied the panties over her hips and let them drop to her ankles, then stepped out of them. Kurt was pressed against her back in the next heartbeat. Warm breath brushed her ear as he ran his tongue along the shell.

"I dreamed of you every night." He placed a kiss at the base of her neck. "I heard your voice during the day, and when I closed my eyes, I held you against me." Another kiss behind her ear. "It was all that kept me going." He spun her to look at him. "And keeping you safe."

The warmth of his hard body left her lightheaded. She smoothed her hands down his chest and over his flat stomach to the waist of his boxer briefs. She held his gaze as she peeled them down. Sabryn dropped to her knees as his rod sprang free of the material. She wrapped her hands around him, and he released another long moan.

His fingers tangled in her hair, but he held her back when she went to take him into her mouth. She looked up at him.

"I'm barely holding it together," he bit out. "If your mouth touches me, I'm finished. And that's not how I want this to go."

She looked longingly at his arousal as he pulled her back to her feet. With deft fingers, he unhooked her bra.

CHAPTER THIRTY-THREE

Kurt forgot to breathe as Sabryn let the bra drop to the floor. He knew every inch of her body, but his eyes raked over her as if he were seeing her for the first time. Statuesque. Supple. Striking. Everything about her was stunning. She had always been agile, but now those muscles were toned, giving her athletic build more definition.

Her taste was still on his tongue, but it wasn't enough. It was never enough. He wanted her scent on him. He wanted his scent on her. He wanted…her. All of her. He didn't know what had changed, and right now, he didn't care. All that mattered was that he had been granted this time. He wouldn't waste it.

Dark blue eyes watched him. Her lips were swollen and wet from his kisses. Her breathing was shallow, and the pulse at her throat raced. Perfect, round breasts waited for his touch. Her dark pink nipples were already pebbled, and he couldn't wait to wrap his lips around the peaks. His gaze drifted lower to the soft swell of her hips. He lingered on the juncture of her thighs and the neatly trimmed patch of dark curls before looking down her long, shapely legs.

He couldn't stand not being against her, not feeling her soft curves and silky skin against his. He put his hand on her lower back and pulled her closer. She placed her hands on his chest, her fingers splayed.

Body to body. He inhaled the sweet smell of her skin—a scent that was hers alone. This was how it was supposed to be. How it was always supposed to be. He was one of the few who had been gifted love. The kind of love he had once believed was nothing but a fabrication. She had shown him it was real. She had given him happiness beyond anything imaginable. The flowers smelled sweeter, the birds sang louder, and the sun shone brighter.

He reached up with his other hand and touched her cheek, making sure she was real and not another figment of his imagination. Her eyes closed at his touch before she leaned into his palm. Then, her long, black lashes fluttered open, and she met his gaze.

Desire swelled, hot and thick. He threaded his fingers into her hair and tilted her head back. Her lips parted expectantly. He dropped his gaze to her mouth, his balls tightening with a need only she could quench. She was the drug and the remedy, and he didn't want it any other way.

His head lowered until their lips were nearly touching. He refused to let her look away. He wanted to profess his love, something he hadn't done before, but he wasn't sure now was the right time. "You are everything to me. The sun. The moon. Everywhere I looked, everywhere I went, you were always there."

Then, he kissed her. Deeply. Passionately.

Hungrily.

He poured every ounce of his feelings into the kiss. And she returned it just as fervently. The time for talking was over. He had dreamed of holding her again for too long. Kissing her, licking her. Loving her.

Concentrating was difficult as her hands roamed over his shoulders and back. Her touch scorched him, made him burn for more. He backed her to the daybed and then gently pushed her to sit. He followed her down, only breaking the kiss when he knelt between her legs and kissed along her jaw and down her throat. She dropped her head back as he licked her collarbone. He left a trail of kisses down her chest to the valley between her breasts, then cupped one of the beautiful globes and ran his thumb around her hard nipple.

"Yes," she whispered, curling her fingers into his hair and dragging his head to her breast.

He flicked a tongue over the peak before licking around it. He fastened his lips on it and gave it a soft pull. Her back arched, and she held his head tighter. She moaned, long and low. He knew how sensitive her nipples were and spent time teasing them until she was panting.

"Please," she begged, trying not to rock against him.

His answer was to move to her other breast. Her soft moans grew louder, her breathing more ragged. She kept whispering his name, and it drove him wild. When he could stand it no more, he cupped her sex and dipped a finger inside her. He lost all train of thought when he felt how wet she was. She rubbed against his palm, seeking friction.

He wanted to thrust inside her and give them both the release they sought, but somehow, he held back. He slid the finger into her slick heat and moaned when her body tightened around him. Fuck. He wouldn't last. He was going to cum right then.

Kurt looked at her. Her head was tipped back, her eyes closed, and pleasure filled her face. He gently laid her back on the mattress and continued to thrust his finger into her core. Her eyes opened, her gaze briefly meeting his before she moaned and curled her fingers into the blanket.

"So, close," she panted.

He added a second finger. A sigh fell from her lips. Her body was flushed with desire, giving her skin a beautiful glow. He leaned down and licked her clit. She gasped, her body tightening. He smiled as he continued to lick and thrust his fingers. Within seconds, she shattered.

Her body spasmed around his fingers. The sight of Sabryn climaxing was spectacular. Her mouth dropped open on a silent scream, her back arched, and her body jerked with the waves of pleasure. He didn't stop until she lay limp. His cock was harder than it had ever been. He brought it to her center and rubbed it in the folds of her labia.

Sabryn was floating, her body languid and satisfied. Right until she felt the blunt head of Kurt's arousal. Then, the hunger returned with a vengeance. She opened her eyes to find his gaze locked on her sex and his rod as he slid it against her. The head reached her entrance but didn't go farther. His face was tense as he stopped himself from pushing deeper.

A moan escaped her when he brushed against her sensitive clit.

His gaze jerked to hers. He was still for so long, she wasn't sure he would move again. Then, he returned his cock to her entrance and slid inside her.

She bit her lip at the exquisite feel of her body stretching to accommodate him. He pulled out until only the head remained, then slowly slid back inside, each time going a little deeper. He gripped her outer thighs as he rocked back and forth. Delicious heat began unfurling and spreading through her once more.

The play of his muscles as he controlled his movements was mesmerizing. As was the feel of him sliding in and out of her. The pace was languid but oh, so incredible. She closed her eyes and felt him thrust deep, then slowly withdraw again until just the tip of him remained. Over and over, he filled her fully, utterly. Completely.

She had never dared to imagine they would be joined this way again. There was a connection between them that was primal. Ancient, even. As if their souls recognized each other. Even now, after everything that had happened, she craved his touch, ached to be with him. He felt so good, so right. And he had from their very first time. There had never been any awkwardness, no hesitation on either of their parts. Sex had always been easy and glorious between them.

His fingers flexed into her thighs. She forced her lids to open and saw the strain lining his features as he stared at where their bodies were joined. That's when it hit her that he was drawing out his pleasure, drinking in every drop. She clenched the walls of her sex and heard his breath hitch. She repeated it and watched as he squeezed his eyes closed.

She licked her lips and ran a hand down her stomach to slip into the folds of her sex. Her finger brushed against his cock, and his eyes flew open. His lips parted as he watched her tease her clit. His hips gradually moved faster. He angled her hips, allowing him to hit a particularly sensitive spot that made her groan. His gaze met hers again. She was drowning in his pale blue eyes as the pleasure tightened.

Suddenly, he grabbed her wrists and held them over her head. His face was close to hers once more, and she couldn't resist lifting her head so their lips touched. The contact made him groan as something broke inside him. He became wild, driving hard and deep inside her, just as she needed it.

"Just like that," she told him.

"You feel so fucking good."

She met his thrusts, their bodies finding a rhythm. He released her wrists and found her mouth again. His tongue dueled with hers. The room was filled with their harsh breaths and the sounds of their bodies meeting.

A swell of desire spilled through her. She tore her mouth from his to drag in a deep breath.

"That's it, beautiful," he murmured.

She shifted her hips, wanting him deeper. "Kurt. I need…"

"I know, sweetheart."

She gripped his hips and tried to get him to move faster. "Please," she begged.

"Cum for me. Now," he ordered.

She screamed his name as pleasure rippled through her. Waves of heat weighed down her limbs, but she clung to him when she heard his moan and felt his body jerk as he orgasmed. She felt his seed spill into her, and a second mini climax took her.

"My god," he whispered.

Sabryn opened her eyes to find him staring down at her. His breathing was still as ragged as hers.

"You're…" He trailed off and swallowed. "You're stunning. The most beautiful creature in the entire universe."

Her heart clenched as she cupped his cheek. There were so many things she wanted to say, but she couldn't. Too many years of fear and heartache locked them away.

His face fell, and he nodded as if he understood her silence. "I wish I'd held on to you."

She put a finger over his lips. "Don't."

"You're the only thing that ever meant anything to me. You were the one person I never wanted to hurt."

Their bodies were still locked together, their limbs tangled, but there was nowhere else she wanted to be. She traced his full lips with a fingertip. "You're here now."

He relaxed, telling her that he had braced himself for her to shove him away. A fleeting frown furrowed his brow. "I am."

"I don't think it's by accident. I don't think anything regarding us has been an accident."

"What do you mean?"

She drew in a deep breath, her heart finally slowing. She could shrug off his question and curl up against his chest, maybe even drift off in the space between sleep and wakefulness. But there would be time to enjoy post-sex later. What she had to say was too important, and while she hadn't come to the attic to have sex with him, she was glad they had.

"Sabryn?" he pushed.

She met his gaze. "I didn't share everything with the others."

"There's more?" he asked worriedly.

"There is."

His chest expanded, and he slowly released the breath as he stared at her. "Will you tell me?"

"Yes."

"Should we, ah, get dressed?"

She smiled and shook her head. "If it's all right with you, I'd like to stay just like this."

"Actually, it'd be more comfortable if I could at least get all the way on the bed."

Sabryn looked to the side to see his knees on the edge of the bed. This time, she laughed. His smile was blinding as the corners of his eyes crinkled.

CHAPTER THIRTY-FOUR

It wasn't long before they were lying facing each other on the daybed. Kurt wanted her on his chest, but he didn't want to ruin whatever was happening between them.

"All right," he said, giving her the pillow and curling his arm under his head. "What did you leave out?"

"What happened to me?"

He wasn't sure he liked the sound of that. "What do you mean?"

"How long was I out?"

"Ten minutes, tops. Maybe more like eight."

She pulled a face. "It was…"

"Lifetimes, you said."

Her lips pressed together, and she nodded somberly. "That's what it felt like. I grieved, and they gave me hope, then I had to grieve again. It was an unbearable cycle. Nothing I did changed anything."

"How do you know it was Corann and the Ancients?"

"I recognized Corann from a picture Rhona showed me, but I still doubted him. I needed proof."

It tore him up that she'd had to endure all that alone. "What did he give you?"

"The fact that they never harmed me." She paused. "And the lesson they gave. It was cruel and prolonged but needed."

"You didn't mention a lesson before."

She shrugged. "I left that out."

"Why?"

"Because it involves you."

He blinked, taken aback. "Me?"

"In every scenario where we went after Parker, I did the same thing every time, all without knowing it."

"Which was?"

"Not trusting or accepting you."

Kurt touched one of the many earrings running up the curve of her ear. "You have your reasons."

"Had."

"Excuse me?"

"I *had* my reasons."

Past tense. He searched her face, drowning in the deep, fathomless blue of her eyes, as dark as the ocean. And just like those great bodies of water, there was so much more to Sabryn than most realized. She hungered for love and a family but was slow to trust. Yet it was a wonderous, precious thing when she did because her special brand of joy, love, and loyalty was like no other. He should know since he had lost it.

Sabryn drew in a deep breath. "It took those thousands of times, watching everyone die—including you—for it to finally hammer home."

"I don't bl—"

"I know," she said over him, putting her fingers against his lips for a heartbeat. "The boys were right, though. We accepted Saber and his secretive past without hesitation."

Kurt adjusted the arm beneath his head. "But there's a history between us that can't be overlooked."

"I'm not."

He was more confused now than before. "I don't understand. Does this mean you still hate me?"

"No," she said with a small laugh.

"You should."

She gave him a flat look. "Lifetimes, remember? I had a lot of time to hold on to that anger, happily lay all the blame at your feet, and think about our conversation at the cottage that finally led me to a way to forgive you."

Sabryn might have forgiven him, but Kurt wasn't sure he could forgive himself. "I should've done more."

"The past is done and over. It's time we both move on. You need to let it go. We found our way back to each other."

He laced his fingers with hers and brought her hand to his mouth so he could kiss her knuckles. "I can't let go completely with Parker and Diana out there."

"We'll take care of them eventually. However, I think there's something to Edie's need to get us off Skye."

"I don't suppose the Ancients told you what that might be, did they?"

She looked away, her brow furrowed. "Not in so many words. But they need us both to stay."

"And they thought commandeering your mind was the way to go about that?"

"Apparently," she replied with a shrug.

He sat up and leaned on a hand as he digested everything. "So, we don't go after Parker the same way. We knew tracking his mobile was a trap."

"It didn't matter how we went after him if we weren't a team."

"If we had gone, Edie, Parker, and the Edinburgh Druids would've killed us all," she said when he parted his lips to speak.

Kurt scooted back to lean against the daybed arm. "Bloody hell."

"The evil has grown very powerful."

"While others on Skye are losing their magic. Do you think the malevolence is taking it?"

She shrugged helplessly. "The Ancients didn't say anything about that, but I'd believe just about anything after what I went through."

"All of that just so you'd forgive me?"

"Yes. Because they need us both on Skye, remember?"

He ran a hand down his face. "They want us here, but Edie wants us gone. And neither gave you a reason?"

"None."

Kurt looked down at the rumpled blankets that smelled like sex and Sabryn. "Have you forgiven me because you want to or because you feel as if you have no other choice?"

"Look at me," she told him.

He slid his gaze to her. He was beginning to wonder if the Ancients or the evil hadn't taken over his mind. Because he wasn't sure any of this was real.

"You deceived me," she stated in an even tone.

Kurt's stomach clenched painfully. "I did."

"You lied to me."

He dipped his chin, icy fingers closing around his heart. "I did."

"You didn't tell me my family was in danger."

"No," he said around a lump of emotion.

She reached over and took his hand. "But you tried to stop your brother. When that didn't work, you made a deal with Diana to spare my life."

"Your father still lost his."

"I blame Parker and Diana for that."

He rubbed his thumb over her fingers. "How can you be sure I wasn't part of it?"

"I see it in your eyes. And then there's the six years you've protected me and the boys. If you still sided with Diana, you wouldn't have gone out of your way to help us as much as you did."

"Actually…" he began.

She put her finger on his lips and raised her brows. "I believe you. And if I didn't, I have a feeling the Ancients would've seen to that, as well. It's important that we're a true team like we have been. And that can only happen if there's forgiveness."

"I think I expected to grovel for a lot longer."

"I'm sure we can work something out," she said with a grin.

He loved Sabryn's teasing side. "I have no doubt you'll think of something."

Her expression grew serious. "I'd like nothing more than to spend the next few hours in bed with you, but…"

"Does this mean we're going after Parker?"

"It means we're going for a drive."

He cocked his head at her. "Is that safe?"

"No place on the isle is safe. Not even the manor anymore. The sooner we deal with our nemesis, the sooner things can return to the way they were."

"Which nemesis? We have several to choose from?"

She climbed off the bed and reached for her clothes. "I don't know the answer to that yet." When he didn't move to get up, she paused and looked at him. "Are you coming?"

"I was just admiring you," he said, then got to his feet and pulled her against him for a quick kiss.

She pushed him away, but there was a smile on her lips. "Meet me downstairs," she called before walking out.

He stared at the doorway for a long moment. Once he was dressed, he grabbed his laptop and rucksack and made his way to the main floor.

"Going somewhere?" Carlyle asked as he came out of the kitchen.

Kurt scanned the entryway for Sabryn. "A drive."

Carlyle's eyes narrowed as he stared. "You look…"

"Like a man who's just had sex," Finn said as he came up behind Carlyle.

Kurt ran his fingers through his hair. He'd forgotten to check it before he came downstairs.

"Ready?" Sabryn asked, descending the steps.

Carlyle and Finn looked from her to Kurt.

"Nice color you have in your cheeks," Finn told her.

She barely looked his way as she said, "Thanks. Are you coming?" she asked Kurt as she walked past.

Carlyle and Finn gave him wide smiles and a thumbs-up. Kurt waited until Sabryn was out the door before he returned the grin. She had already started the engine when Kurt climbed into the SUV and buckled his seatbelt.

"I used the spell," she said, backing up.

He hesitated, wondering if he had forgotten a conversation they were having. "What spell?"

"To ensure I don't get pregnant."

That had been the last thing on his mind. He should be glad that one of them had thought of it. He glanced at her and tried to imagine what she would look like with her belly rounded with his child. He cleared his throat, but he couldn't stop thinking about her being pregnant. "Where are we going?"

"I just had an urge for a drive. Since you're a London Druid and forbidden from venturing to this beautiful isle, I thought I'd point out some landmarks. Maybe something will strike us as what we're out here looking for."

"Or why Edie wants us gone."

"That, too," she said and glanced at him.

"Should we have brought the others?"

Her head swung to him before she looked back at the road. "Do you want them here?"

"What I meant to ask was, is this something the others should be involved in?"

"We're just driving right now. If we find something, we'll give them a call."

He stared out at the afternoon sky. "If we brought them, you'd have had to tell them what you left out."

"I will eventually, but it was something the two of us needed to work out first. Can we talk about Parker?"

"Of course. Do you have a plan?"

"Not even close. I was thinking we should forget about him."

Kurt's brows rose as he turned his head to her. "Forget about him? Are you serious?"

"I know you want revenge for his attempt on your life."

"My vengeance toward Parker is for your father's death, not for my stabbing."

Her face softened. "I think he's a diversion for the real issue."

Kurt hadn't considered that. "You mean Edie."

"Possibly. We had a good plan to get Parker, and that almost ended in your death. We knew we were heading into a trap by tracing his phone. And if I hadn't fainted and had my mind invaded by the Ancients, we'd all be dead."

"Hard to argue any of that. But even if we stop going after Parker until later, that doesn't mean he'll stop coming after us."

Sabryn turned on the blinker and slowed before turning. "He's not made a move on us since the first encounter. We're the ones who went after him."

"Because I didn't want him coming for you. Where are we?" Kurt asked as he looked at the magnificent landscape.

Pictures couldn't do the isle justice. No photo could ever capture the brilliance of the green, the vivid blue sky, the dark, gloomy clouds, the gray of the stone, or the essence of Skye itself. It was no wonder the Druids had been drawn here. Everywhere he looked left him spellbound.

He spotted the blue water through the steep hills and couldn't take his eyes off the landscape. It wasn't until Sabryn parked that he finally looked at her. She said nothing as she climbed out. He wordlessly followed, trailing behind her on the road.

"If we take the path ahead, we'll end up at an overlook above Glen Conon. You have to see the waterfalls. They are magnificent," she said.

"I'd like that."

She nodded but walked past the path.

"I thought we were going to the falls," he said.

"We will. Just not today."

He fell into step beside her as they headed toward a steep mound that looked like the ruins of a castle. "You've not said where we are."

"We're at the Fairy Glen."

Of course. He'd seen in it pictures, but it was different being there. He swept his gaze from side to side as they walked the path between the narrow hills. "This has to rank high on your favorites of the isle."

When she didn't reply, he realized she had walked ahead. Kurt caught up with her and tried to pull her to a stop, but she kept walking. He finally moved in front of her and saw her gaze pinned past him—her unfocused gaze. That's when he felt the wind against his cheek. She took his hand then and guided him toward the ancient rowan trees and the ruined, moss-covered foundation stones.

CHAPTER THIRTY-FIVE

The wind was all around her, mild at times, and fierce—almost angry—at others. But no matter how hard Sabryn listened, it didn't talk. Panic thumped against her ribs as her mind raced and her stomach churned sickeningly, putting her into fight-or-flight mode. Only Kurt's comforting hold grounded her.

She stopped and closed her eyes. Her chest was heavy, making it difficult to breathe past the scream swelling within her. Kurt said nothing as he moved in front of her once more. She felt his presence and eagerly reached out with her other hand. Her palm connected with his chest as he moved closer.

Solid. Steady. Unfaltering. She should've realized he was Saber. Maybe a part of her had. Sabryn drew in a shaky breath and opened her eyes. His pale blue orbs were locked on her, a small frown furrowing his brow.

"You're the sky pillar," he stated.

Her stomach roiled with dejection and the last bits of hope

that faded like the stars at dawn. "I…I thought I might be. I was drawn here."

"You're the only wind talker we have. It has to be you," he insisted.

She swallowed and looked away. "I can no longer hear the wind. I haven't since we encountered Edie at the cottage."

"Something must be blocking you. Like the Ancients are being blocked."

"The Ancients spoke through Ferne. They got into my head. They're not as blocked as we were led to believe."

He gently turned her back to him. "Think about the lengths they had to go to in order to reach Ferne and you."

"I thought you didn't believe it was them."

"But you did," he reminded her.

Sabryn sighed and shook her head. "I don't know anymore."

"Why are we here?"

"I don't know that either. I didn't even realize I was headed here until I parked."

He rubbed his hands up and down her arms. "You were drawn here. That has to mean something."

"It means I was hoping I might be the sky pillar. I didn't know I wanted it until I learned I wasn't it." And did that ever make her sound pathetic?

Kurt covered her hand on his chest with his. "Everyone wants to be special. And you are."

"Don't worry. I'm not going to fall to pieces. You don't have to try and bolster my ego."

"I never imagined you were. I'm simply stating a fact. Look at what you created with the Knights. If you need a reminder of how special you are, think back to all the people you've helped over the years."

She pressed her forehead into his chest. "Thank you."

He kissed the top of her head and wrapped her in his arms. "So, this is the Fairy Glen. I can see why one of the pillars would be here."

"Rhona called the pillars gateways to protect against forces outside the living," Sabryn said as she lifted her head and looked around him. "The basalt outcropping is named Castle Ewing because it looks like a ruined castle." Her gaze lowered to the foot of the castle to the large spiral of stones. "The Skye Druids are the pillars."

"You can't know that."

She lifted her gaze to his. "Corann brought the young Druids here and told them the story, remember? I detailed it for you after Rhona, Bronwyn, Elodie, and Ariah remembered. There must have been a wind talker with them that day. And we need to find whoever it was so they can take their place as the sky pillar."

"I'm not so sure. In case you forgot, Edie wants us gone. What if it's because you *are* the pillar?"

"You're wrong, but I'll play Devil's Advocate. If I am the sky pillar, why is Edie so keen on having *you* gone?"

His lips parted to answer, but no words came. After a moment, his brow furrowed. "I don't know."

"Exactly. It was a ruse. One more distraction."

"You think even the Ancients getting into your head was a distraction? They told you I needed to stay, too."

She walked around him to stand at the beginning of the stone spiral. "I think the Knights are integral to the battle. The only way that happens is if we're a true team as we were before you came here. That's why the Ancients went to such extremes."

"But back to what Edie threatened. When a foe like that specifically targets someone, it means something." He moved to stand beside her.

"Maybe it doesn't," Sabryn said, turning her head to him. "Maybe it was all a smoke screen. What if most of what we're dealing with is meant to keep us looking everywhere but where we really should be?"

He grunted. "Is the mist going after Finn also something to divert our focus?"

"Possibly. I don't know. All I am sure about is that I'm not the sky pillar."

"Well," he said with a long sigh. "I'm glad."

She chuckled as she faced him. "I'm dying to hear why that is."

"Think about what Ariah and Killian went through. He was targeted to stop her from discovering she was the earth pillar."

"You not up for an attack?" she teased.

He wore a serious expression and pulled her against him. "I can handle it. I was talking about my worry doubling for you. I couldn't cope if something happened to you."

"It's a chance each of us takes when we go into battle. We're taking it just by being on Skye."

"Believe me, I know. You've no idea the worry I've sustained, sitting behind a screen miles from you and waiting for one of you to update me. And the times you were injured…" He looked away, his Adam's apple bobbing as he swallowed. "It was the worst."

"You're in the middle of it now."

He lowered his gaze to her, his expression earnest and somber. "There's nowhere else I'd want to be."

It felt weird, but also very, very right to be in Kurt's arms again. The easiness they'd had between them in DC was back, almost as if the last years hadn't happened. She took his hand, and they retraced their steps to the car park.

"I know why I was drawn here," she said.

He nodded to a family walking past. "Why is that?"

"To show me I wasn't the pillar so I can concentrate on other matters. Everyone has a part to play on this gameboard. Some might view us as nothing more than pawns in a chess game, but they'd be wrong."

"Why is that?"

She glanced at their linked hands, an inward smile spreading through her to chase away the last of her sadness. "Pawns are crucial to creating a strong structure that provides a solid foundation for attacking and defending. They're also good for controlling the center of the board. Their strategic placement can significantly impact a game's outcome."

"I think I need to learn chess."

"Our enemies showed us what they planned by dividing us. We need to come up with a strategy for when it happens again. Because it will happen again."

"Agreed."

They released each other when they reached the vehicle and then climbed inside. Sabryn felt good about things for once. Well, *good* was perhaps the wrong word. She felt better about them than she had in a long time. She was still disappointed about not being the pillar. Being on Skye, fighting alongside the others, and knowing she had ancestors from the isle had made her believe— *hope*—that she might be it. But Kurt was right. It was better that she wasn't. She was a Knight. Her attention needed to be with them.

She started the engine and looked up as she put the vehicle in reverse, only to freeze when her gaze collided with Edie. "Kurt," she murmured.

"Drive," he directed.

Sabryn's foot remained on the brake as Edie stood ten feet from the SUV. The smirk on her face infuriated Sabryn. She put the vehicle in drive. She could gun it. Run Edie over and end her threat once and for all.

"She's not worth it," Kurt said.

Sabryn tightened her hand on the steering wheel. "She's killed. She'll kill again."

"But you're not a murderer. If you run her down, that's exactly what you'll become. We know Edie's working with the evil. If she dies, it'll find another, just as it did when Kerry got caught."

Fuck. He was right. Sabryn huffed a breath and returned the gearshift to reverse. Edie's laugh iced her blood. She had known Sabryn wouldn't do anything. It had been a test, and Sabryn had failed.

"We need to get out of here," she said, flooring the accelerator. She jerked the wheel to the side, narrowly missing a parked car, before throwing the SUV into drive and speeding through the car park. She saw the exit and headed around a row of vehicles.

"Sabryn!" Kurt shouted.

There was no time to react as something slammed into them from the side. Glass exploded and metal screeched as the SUV flipped once, then twice, before rocking to a violent halt. Her ears rang, and glass tinkled as it fell. She swallowed feebly and tried to make sense of what'd just happened. A look outside showed everything was upside down. No, not the world. *She* was upside down.

Kurt. She swung her head to the side and spotted him hanging with his arms by his ears. She couldn't tell if he was unconscious or… She couldn't even think the word. She couldn't see any blood, but the entire passenger side of the vehicle was crumpled inward.

She reached for him, only to wince as something pulled at her side. Sabryn gasped at the pain and lifted her head to find the keys she had tossed into the cupholder now embedded in her side. Sweat beaded her brow as she cautiously placed her shaking hands over them and called to her magic. She drew in a breath and gripped the keys. Her magic slid down her fingers, giving them strength as she yanked them out and tossed them aside.

She pressed her hand against her tender side as blood welled. This time when she reached for Kurt, she was able to reach him. She gently touched his face.

"Kurt? Can you hear me?" she asked.

She needed to feel for a pulse, but to do that, she needed to reach him better. That meant unbuckling herself. Sabryn used her blood-covered hand to reach for the button, but her fingers kept slipping. They couldn't stay like this. They were sitting ducks, waiting to be attacked again. She kept pressing against anything she touched, hoping she would find the latch. Finally, she did. The seat belt released, and she fell awkwardly against the roof of the SUV.

Sabryn glanced outside the cracked windshield as she scrambled to Kurt. She brushed aside his hair and felt for a pulse. When her fingers found it, she nearly collapsed with relief. She hated to move him in case he was injured, but she had no choice. If she didn't get him out now, they would both die.

"Kurt," she whispered, crawling over piles of broken glass to get into a better position.

Sabryn got on her knees and had just reached around to release his seat belt when she heard footsteps moving casually around the vehicle. Sabryn instantly stilled. Was it Edie? Were Parker and the Edinburgh Druids with her?

Magic pooled in her palms as she waited with bated breath. The person stopped outside Kurt's window. She slowly moved to the side, trying to see the individual. There were no sirens, no indication that anyone had seen the accident or called the authorities. Sabryn spotted her cell lying just out of reach. It must have fallen out of her back pocket when the SUV rolled, and she had no idea where Kurt's was.

"There's nowhere for you to go," Edie stated. "You should've heeded my warning."

Sabryn released magic simultaneously at the seat belt buckle and Edie, then fired off another round at Edie instead of softening Kurt's fall. Both her shots landed against Edie's lower legs, causing the Druid to howl in rage-filled pain. Sabryn used that time to grab Kurt under his shoulders and try to pull him through the driver's side.

She was nearly out when magic struck her torso. The force of it made her lose her hold on Kurt. Sabryn lay back and saw two Edinburgh Druids coming at her from either side. She flung out her arms and launched a volley of magic at them. One found its mark, but the other went wide. She left Kurt inside as she shimmied out of the vehicle and did a backward roll to get to her feet as Edie joined the other female.

CHAPTER THIRTY-SIX

Kurt came to when something heavy hit the vehicle, jerking it. He opened his eyes to the sound of grunts and groans. Battle. He tried to sit up by using his hands, only to wince and yank them away. He stared at his palms dotted with broken glass. A quick survey showed that the SUV was upside down, and he was lying against the roof, looking up at both seats—empty seats.

"Sabryn," he whispered.

Another crash against the vehicle caused more glass to rain down on him. Kurt raised his arms to shield his face and flipped onto his stomach. He removed as much of the glass from his hands as possible while trying to see who was locked in battle outside. They kept moving around the car, which made it difficult to see. He turned and crawled across the glass to finally get a better look. His gut clenched when he spotted Sabryn locked in combat with Edie and another woman.

The passenger door was crumpled inward from the impact. It was also ripped, the jagged metal sticking up, making it impossible for him to get through. Blood dripped from the metal above him. He looked in time to see Sabryn's torn shirt and bloodied back. Kurt glanced at the windscreen. It was splintered in hundreds of spiderweb cracks. One good kick could break through it, but it would bring attention to him, and he didn't want anyone to know he was conscious yet.

He looked toward the back of the SUV to find more torn steel and smashed glass. Then turned over his shoulder. The driver's window was completely gone, but the door was intact. He twisted himself around once more before crawling out of the vehicle. The SUV was only a foot or two away from another parked car. It shielded him for the moment, but he couldn't help Sabryn from that position. He remained low, looking around to make sure no one was coming up behind him. When he was sure no one was there, he got to his feet.

Magic slammed into the SUV, shaking it. Sabryn grunted when she landed hard on the ground. He took a step, and the world tipped and swayed aggressively. Kurt grabbed hold of the car just to remain on his feet. He wouldn't be much help to Sabryn like this. They needed the rest of the Knights. He reached for his mobile, but found it was no longer in his pocket. He wasn't even sure if he had brought it. But he had his computer.

He hesitated. Either he crawled back inside the SUV for the laptop, or he helped Sabryn. There wasn't time for both. Boots slid across the asphalt as Sabryn grunted in pain. His decision made, Kurt walked around the back of the vehicle and called to his magic. It slid through his veins and along his skin to collect in his palms. He raised his arms and took aim at the women.

Edie saw him right as he released the magic and ducked, but the blonde fighting her wasn't so lucky and took the full force of both strikes. Sabryn was on one knee, bruised, bloody, and breathing heavily, but still in the fight. The blonde fell to the ground, shrieking in pain. Kurt raced to follow Edie as she ran between two vehicles.

"No, don't," Sabryn called after him.

There was no way Kurt would let Edie go. He shouldn't have stopped Sabryn from running her down earlier. He caught sight of Edie's short, blond hair and fired off a round of magic. It struck a car window and sprayed the air with glass.

"There's no hiding, Edie," he called.

She laughed in answer.

He followed the sound between more cars and farther away from Sabryn. The other Druid was down. Sabryn could take care of her and contact the others while he tracked Edie. Kurt stilled, listening for her. There was no more laughter, no footsteps. Only silence. He squatted and peered around a hatchback, but Edie wasn't there. He looked the other way, hoping to see where she had gone. A part of him worried that Edie had doubled back and returned to Sabryn, but he would've heard her footsteps. If he couldn't hear anything, that meant she wasn't moving.

"You came looking for us. Well, you got us. Why hide now?" Kurt goaded.

"Who said I'm hiding?"

The voice came from behind him. Kurt whirled around as he surged to his feet. He fired off a round just as Edie's magic struck him in the left shoulder, spinning him so he smacked into another car. Stabbing pain ran down his left arm. He lifted his right arm on her next shot, but her magic went right through his block. He twisted to minimize the hit and only felt a glancing blow across his chest.

"You don't belong here," Edie said as she walked toward him, serene and confident.

He was thankful the car was there because it was the only way he remained upright. "Too bad. I'm here."

"I gave you an opportunity to leave."

"Why is that?" he asked.

Her blue eyes narrowed on him. She looked so much like her siblings that it was hard for him to separate her from Elias and Elodie.

"You'll never know now. Don't say I didn't warn her," Edie said, lifting her hand.

Kurt's life flashed before his eyes. The things that had been, the things that were, and the things that would never be. All the stuff he had meant to do but never got around to. Everything he had always wanted to say but never did. So many regrets. The chief among them being the time he'd lost with Sabryn.

Magic surged through him, answering an unspoken call. "You might best me, but you won't win. Your side is doomed."

"Not this time," she said.

Kurt saw movement over Edie's shoulder and spotted Sabryn creeping up behind her. His fingers curled inward as he felt the weight of the magic in his palms. He dove to the side and fired off a round from both hands. One went wide. The other impacted the shot meant to kill him. He hit the ground hard, his eyes on Sabryn as she attacked Edie from behind, sending the Druid sprawling onto her stomach.

A jolt of shock slammed through him, fast and electric, locking his limbs and stealing his breath at the sight of Sabryn. Wind whipped around her as she held her arms out at her sides and stalked toward her foe. Edie sprang to her feet and whirled around to lob several rounds of magic, but Sabryn blocked every one. Or the wind did. Kurt wasn't sure which. When he heard voices and saw people returning to the car park, he struggled to stand.

They couldn't get any closer or someone could get hurt. Kurt raced toward them, waving at everyone as he shouted for them to get back. A few stood at Sabryn's SUV, looking inside to see if anyone was injured.

"Call the police!" Kurt shouted to anyone who would listen. "Ask for DI Theo Frasier. Tell him to get here immediately!"

There was a gasp, and then the crowd ducked as the deafening crunch of steel filled the air.

Kurt nervously looked over his shoulder for Sabryn. He spotted her dark hair before it disappeared behind a van. He wanted to get back to her. He returned his attention to the onlookers. "There's a dangerous criminal over there," he cautioned them. "Everyone needs to stay back until the authorities arrive."

He had to repeat himself three more times before anyone listened. Each time he tried to get to Sabryn, someone attempted to head to their cars. He realized he wasn't keeping anyone anywhere when another window broke and the group took two full steps back. He couldn't see Edie or Sabryn anymore. He had no idea who was winning, and that was killing him.

"Stay!" he bellowed to the group and then ran to help Sabryn.

His steps slowed to a walk when he passed multiple cars that had been moved from their spots and now rested at odd angles—a few crunched badly. The screech of metal on metal filled his ears. He looked up in time to see a small SUV sliding across the asphalt at him. Kurt put his hand on the bonnet of a vehicle next to him and leapt on top of it, jumping across two more as the SUV crashed into the spot where he had been standing.

A gust of wind whipped his feet out from under him. He slammed into the bonnet, his head smacking the windscreen hard enough to make his ears ring. He pushed himself onto his hands and knees and feverishly scanned the car park for Sabryn. She and Edie's battle had taken them through several rows of cars and was headed straight for the road.

He vaulted to the ground, ignoring the aches and pains in his body, and headed toward Sabryn. The closer he got to her, the harder the wind blew. He had to grip the cars he passed to push himself to the next one and then the next, growing ever closer to the women. Fear coiled around him, sinking its razor-sharp teeth into his heart as he sought a glimpse of Sabryn. Kurt tucked his head against the force of the wind and clawed his way from vehicle to vehicle. He had to move quickly twice, lest he end up squished between two automobiles. And all the while, the wind steadily gained strength. He wouldn't be able to stay on his feet for much longer.

He looked up when he heard someone scream. But it wasn't Sabryn. It was Edie. The wind had her pinned against a car. Kurt turned his head toward Sabryn, who stared at Edie with unblinking eyes. Her arms were out at her sides once more, her palms facing the other woman and fingers moving as if she were playing an instrument—or directing the wind.

Each time Edie attempted to move, a blast of wind slammed into her, making her cry out again. The sight rooted him in place, horror and disbelief tangling in his gut. But Edie refused to give up. She kept fighting against Sabryn—and was gaining ground. Sabryn wouldn't be able to keep Edie immobilized forever.

Kurt didn't want to break Sabryn's concentration, so he quietly made his way closer. Edie watched him as he raised his hand, ready to deliver a round of magic into her, when he paused and recalled his words. They knew Edie was working with the evil. They didn't have to spend time hunting her, which is exactly what would happen if he took her life. The evil would find someone new. It would keep finding someone new until the final battle took place.

He was torn. Killing Edie would give them a victory now, but would it mean a later defeat? The sound of sirens ended his debate. Kurt lowered his arm as Edie began to laugh, the wind haltingly sweeping the sound around him. He ignored her and headed toward Sabryn.

Kurt glanced over his shoulder when he heard his name and spotted Theo and Chief Superintendent Boyd just outside the wind. There was no time to tell them anything. Kurt tucked his head and kept going, gradually making his way up behind Sabryn. When he reached her, he slid his hands along her arms until his body was molded to hers.

"Sabryn," he whispered in her ear. "You need to stop the wind. We have spectators. Theo and the police are here."

She turned her head to the side as if searching for him. He pressed his body into hers as she leaned back against him. But the wind continued its howling. He linked his fingers with hers and tried to turn her hands. She fought against him, lifting her arms once more.

"Sabryn, it's me," he said into her ear. "I'm right here, baby. You trapped Edie. You did it."

The wind softened a degree.

"That's it. I'm right here with you."

The wind steadily decreased until it was only a soft breeze. This time when he lowered her arms, Sabryn let him. Kurt didn't stop Edie when she slipped away the moment she was free, a smug smile on her face. He wanted to go after her, but he wouldn't leave Sabryn.

Theo hesitantly walked up from the side, his face tight with concern.

Kurt met his dark gaze and said, "We need a moment."

Theo took a long look at Sabryn, nodded, then turned around and walked back to speak to someone.

Kurt wrapped his arms around her, their hands still linked. "Sabryn, baby? Can you hear me?"

When she didn't answer, he moved to stand before her. Her eyes were vacant and unblinking. He cupped her face in his hands and lifted it until her gaze met his. "Come back to me," he urged. "Come back."

He kept repeating the words, never looking away until she finally blinked.

"Kurt?" she whispered in bewilderment.

"I'm here."

She touched the side of his face. "You're bleeding."

"So are you."

CHAPTER THIRTY-SEVEN

The cold sank into the marrow of her bones. Sabryn was in sweats, covered with a blanket, and drinking whisky while sitting cross-legged on the sofa in the library with a fire roaring in the hearth. And she *still* couldn't stop shaking. She remembered little of the fight after seeing Kurt get struck by Edie's magic.

"Sabryn?"

She startled at Rhona's voice. A look around reminded her that the room was filled with those waiting to hear her account of things for the second time that day. What was happening to her? First the Ancients and now this?

Sabryn swallowed and tried to remember what had been asked. Oh. Right. Rhona had asked her what drew her to the Fairy Glen. "I don't know."

"I already told you that's what she said to me," Kurt replied.

He stood beside the hearth, looking haggard and worried, his arms crossed. His gaze rarely left her. Elias, Carlyle, and Finn wore similar expressions. Finn had parked her in the middle of the couch and sank next to her while Carlyle took the other side. Elias stood behind her with Bronwyn to his right, and Song to his left—her family shielding her.

"We're only trying to figure out what happened," Ferne said.

Kurt ran a hand down his face and turned away.

Sabryn huddled under the blanket. "I left something out about my interaction with Corann and the Ancients. And I did it because I wanted to talk to Kurt first." She detailed what Corann had told her about forgiving Kurt. "After what I experienced and saw, I knew he was right. I went to Kurt and told him all of it."

"That's when you left the manor for your drive?" Theo asked.

She tried not to feel interrogated, but it was difficult. Especially when every eye in the room was focused on her. "I wanted to get out and show Kurt around Skye. Yes, my first stop was the Fairy Glen. And no, I have no idea why. I heard the wind and tried to communicate with it when we got there."

"It didn't respond?" Willa asked.

Sabryn sipped the whisky and let the warmth slide down her throat to settle in her stomach and spread. She shivered again despite it. Finn shifted closer. When he did, a muscle in Kurt's jaw clenched. "It did not," she replied. "I thought I was being punished for ignoring it."

"I'd have blocked it out, too, if it was yelling at me all the time," Ariah stated.

"I, uh…" Sabryn paused and swallowed. "As the only wind talker among us, I thought I might be the sky pillar."

Elias twisted his lips and said, "You were no' the only one to think that. We talked about the possibility, too."

"Are you?" Rhona asked.

Sabryn shook her head. "Hard to hold that position when I can no longer hear the wind."

A weird vibe ran through the room, making her frown. She was missing something.

"What happened at the glen?" Jasper asked.

Sabryn looked at Kurt and found his gaze on the floor, his brow furrowed in what seemed to be a permanent frown. She took another sip of whisky to fill the silence. "Nothing much. I told Kurt about the pillar, and he said he was glad I wasn't it since it put a target on Ariah."

"Not just me," Ariah said, running her hand along Killian's thigh. The two shared a look, unspoken words passing between them.

Sabryn shrugged. "Then we headed back to the SUV and debated why Edie wanted us off the isle if I wasn't a pillar."

"I'm wondering that myself," Filip murmured.

Jasper leaned against a bookshelf. "It could be a diversion."

"That was Sabryn's thought," Kurt replied.

Carlyle shrugged. "It's a good one. It means we'd be running around wondering why you two were targeted instead of focusing on other matters."

"We had just gotten into the SUV when I looked up and saw Edie." Sabryn squeezed the glass as she recalled Edie's smile. "She was close enough that I...well, there's no easy way to say this," she said as she looked from Elias to Elodie, "I considered running her over."

Kurt dropped his arms and hooked his thumbs into the front pockets of his jeans. "I cautioned her against it since we knew Edie was working with the evil."

"We jailed Kerry, and it found a replacement," Rhona said as she nodded. "We spent a lot of time trying to figure out if there was someone else before we learned it was Edie."

Elodie shifted in the chair, her mouth pinched. "And, in the meantime, our sister hurt others. I don't blame you for thinking that way, Sabryn."

"Nor I you, Kurt," Elias stated. "Our goal is to stop anyone from harming others. It's what we've done for years. It's what we have to do here."

Finn absently rubbed his leg as if his jeans bothered his newly tatted skin. "Except Edie is just a pawn. We're going to spend weeks fighting against those like her when we should be preparing for the big battle."

"I'm no' going to sit by and watch innocents die while doing nothing," Scott replied.

Song said, "That isn't what Finn meant."

"We can have this discussion later," Rhona said and nodded at Sabryn. "Please, finish."

Sabryn drained what was left of the whisky, and Carlyle took the glass from her, allowing her to tuck her hand beneath the blanket. "Kurt's point of letting Edie live was valid. I knew we had to get back to the manor, so I sped through the car park. I was close to the exit when something hit us."

"What?" Theo asked.

When she shrugged, everyone turned to Kurt.

His pale blue eyes locked on her. "I only saw a blonde."

"Magic, then," Willa said.

Theo blew out a breath. "It bloody well tore the SUV apart. I can't believe Kurt didna have more than a cut on his temple."

"The force of whatever struck us caused the vehicle to flip

twice," Sabryn said. "The only reason we stopped was because we struck another car."

Callum spoke from the back corner. "You were being toyed with, then. Just as we were last time."

"Edie and the other Druids weren't playing with me." Sabryn brought her knees up to her chest. "They were intent on killing me. I think their aim was to kill, but the strike on the SUV didn't do as much damage as they had hoped."

Elias placed his hands on the back of the sofa near her head as he leaned over her. "Or maybe it did precisely the damage they were going for."

"What do you mean?" Rhona asked.

Elias straightened and walked to stand in front of the fire as he directed his gaze to Sabryn. "I think all of it was engineered to see your response."

"Me?" Sabryn asked in disbelief.

Elias's brows snapped together as he looked first at Finn and then at Carlyle.

Sabryn regarded each of them in turn. "What aren't you telling me?"

"Finish your story," Rhona urged softly.

It was the kind of voice a parent used with a frightened child. Calm, gentle. Apprehension gripped Sabryn. "I tried to get Kurt out of the vehicle but was struck by magic. I had no choice but to leave him and deal with Edie and the other Druids."

"At some point during that, I came to," Kurt added. "I went for both Edie and the Druids, but Edie saw me and ducked."

Sabryn nodded. "He gave chase when Edie ran, and I was able to catch my breath. I started to follow them when the blonde attacked me again."

"I tried to corner Edie, but she got behind me." Kurt shrugged as he shifted his feet. "Edie had just landed a strike on my shoulder when I saw you," he said to Sabryn.

"I saw that." She'd felt rage so profound that it scared her still. She had never felt anything like it before.

Finn lightly touched her leg. "Then what?"

"I don't know. The next thing I remember is Kurt holding me as sirens wailed," Sabryn told them. The room grew quiet as if nobody knew how to reply. She caught Kurt's gaze. "What happened? What did I do?"

He hesitated for just a beat before he said, "You were controlling the wind, and you had Edie pinned against a vehicle with it."

"That's…" Insane? Impossible? Ridiculous?

"I saw it, too," Theo added.

Sabryn shook her head. "I have no memory of any of that."

"The last thing you saw was Kurt being injured," Jasper said. "What did you feel?"

She looked at him, her heart racing and her hands fisted beneath the blanket. "Fury."

"And then?" Carlyle whispered.

Sabryn tried to swallow to wet her dry mouth. She lowered her gaze to the blanket as another shiver went through her. "Nothing."

"You could've killed Edie," Kurt stated softly. "I've never seen such a display of power."

Her gaze jerked to him. She wanted his arms around her again. Needed his warmth to envelop her. But she didn't move, and neither did he. "Did I hurt anyone?"

"I kept everyone back," Kurt answered.

Rhona leaned forward in her chair. "Have you ever done anything like that before?"

"No," Finn, Elias, Carlyle, and Kurt said in unison.

"At least no' as long as we've known her," Elias added.

Rhona's green eyes turned to her. Sabryn shook her head. "Not that I'm aware of."

"That kind of power couldna come out of the blue, could it?" Scott asked.

Ariah shrugged. "I didn't know I was the earth pillar until I stumbled upon it."

"I'm not the air pillar," Sabryn stated. "I don't know what happened, but I'm not the pillar."

Elodie shot Sabryn a smile. "Skye does weird things to people. I should know."

"I've never heard of a wind talker controlling wind," Bronwyn said.

Rhona drew in a deep breath. "Neither have I. I wish Corann had kept records."

"I can search the Druid chatrooms," Kurt offered.

Elias nodded. "That's a great idea."

"It won't take long. I just need to put in a few keywords," Kurt explained.

Rhona dipped her chin. "That would be helpful. Let's get on that."

"I need my laptop, which is…" Kurt trailed off and grimaced. "I had it with me."

Finn pushed to his feet. "There are plenty around here. I'll get you mine."

"Mine was custom built for hacking, but I'll take anything right now," Kurt said.

Killian offered, "Make a list of what you need to build a new one, and we'll get it."

Kurt nodded his thanks.

Sabryn was ready for the interrogation to be over, but given how Theo kept staring at her, she wasn't sure it was.

"Why both Kurt and Sabryn?" Theo asked.

The room went silent as everyone stilled, their gazes moving to him. Sabryn pushed back into the sofa and instantly regretted it when the injuries on her back screamed in protest. She'd refused the Healers, as had Kurt.

"Why did Edie say both of them needed to leave the isle?" Theo asked.

Song tilted her head. "We decided it was a diversion."

"But Edie could've just said Sabryn. She didna have to say both," Theo pointed out.

Jasper crossed his arms over his chest. "That's true. What are you thinking?"

"I'm thinking Edie knows something." Theo's gaze shifted from Kurt to her. "Are you sure your power has never manifested before?"

"Positive," Sabryn replied.

"What about your family?" Theo pushed.

She shook her head but did a double take when Kurt's face went slack.

"What is it?" Carlyle asked him.

Kurt's expression filled with confusion that turned to bafflement. His jaw worked as he struggled to find words. "When Parker and I were getting ready for DC, I saw a folder on Diana's desk. She had traced the Beaumont family tree." He paused and ran a hand down his face. "I saw a drawing of a woman with wind swirling around her. Diana snapped the file closed before I could read the page."

"It could be nothing," Elias said.

Finn twisted his lips. "Or it could be something."

"Wind talkers run in my family," Sabryn said. "My father was one. So was my grandfather."

"I'd forgotten about that drawing, but it wasn't just of a wind talker," Kurt said.

Sabryn sighed. "Looks like we need to talk to Diana."

CHAPTER THIRTY-EIGHT

Edinburgh

The rain never stopped. Diana didn't know how anyone lived in the horrid city. Everything was damp and dreary. And Scottish. She couldn't wait to return to London.

She drummed her nails on the sofa arm as she stared out the window to the distorted world beyond. She wouldn't be here if she hadn't sent Parker to find Kurt. Now, she had lost both her sons. Though she didn't have concrete proof—yet—she was sure Georgina planned to double-cross the London Druids.

Diana had already visited the leader of the Edinburgh Druids twice without much success. Georgina—because she refused to call a woman George—was cagey and shrewd. It was no wonder she had become a leader. Diana wanted to dismiss her, but she knew that would be unwise, and Diana made it a point to never underestimate anyone. The Edinburgh Druids were a larger group than London had initially estimated.

Georgina needed something from the London Druids, and they needed the Edinburgh Druids to deal with Skye. It was the perfect exchange. At least, it should've been. She propped her elbow on the sofa and rested her chin on her knuckles as she attempted to sort through what might have happened with Parker. He'd never disobeyed her before. Not once in all his years. He had been the perfect child. Kurt had started out that way, too, but he had always tested her by questioning orders and disobeying.

Kurt was too much like her. It's why she had given him more room than Parker. If she had treated her youngest the same, Parker would likely already be dead. He was great at following orders, but not so great at making decisions.

Eventually, Kurt would've returned to the family, one way or another. She had grown tired of waiting, and her plans required him. She had given Parker Kurt's location. It should've been an easy grab, but she had forgotten just how clever her eldest was. He had led Parker on a merry chase around Scotland for days. She never should've sent Parker to Skye. Especially not with the Edinburgh Druids.

Her mobile rang from its place atop the coffee table. She leaned forward to see who was phoning and steeled herself when she saw Thomas Oliver's name.

"Hello?" she answered.

"Diana."

Her fingers curled into the leather sofa. She hated how he said her name—part sneer, part suggestive. She didn't know why she had ever allowed him into her bed. The affair had been short and benefited both of them, but Thomas was one of those men who never let a woman forget. When he was very forgettable.

Yet he thought his prowess something for the history books.

When a man aged and the rotating women on his arm remained young, it said a lot about the person.

"Yes, Thomas?" she replied, keeping any hints of rancor from her tone.

"I expected you back in civilization by now."

She pushed to her feet and walked to the window. "Things aren't finished here."

"You mean your wayward sons haven't been located."

He tsked at her as if she were a schoolgirl. She curled her fingers into a fist and fought to remain calm.

"You didn't just lose one. You lost both. That's not befitting someone I've granted such power to."

She couldn't wait to shove his face into the ground with her foot. "Oh, I have my boys," she lied. "I was trying to sort out what's happening with the Edinburgh group. But I'll alert the pilots to depart in the morning."

"Explain yourself," he snapped.

"I believe Georgina is endeavoring to double-cross us."

"Well," he said after a brief pause. "That will not do. Dig deep. I need specifics so I can put her in her place."

Diana glared at the window as her anger festered and grew. "Of course."

The line went dead. She dropped her hand and closed her eyes. Few had been able to stir her emotions like Thomas Oliver. She was one of only a handful who knew he ran the London Druids—and remained part of the small group who still held that information.

It couldn't leak out to the rest of the London Druids. The elders had always led them, which had to continue—even if it was just for show. Thomas gave the elders plenty of power in exchange for their silence. Thomas had always been able to discover what someone wanted, what they craved. And he gave it to them.

She was no exception. He'd seen her drive and recognized her ambition. It was one of the reasons they had become lovers. But he hadn't been malleable enough for her, and she hadn't been a fire walker.

Yet, Thomas still turned to her for important matters. He believed her utterly devoted to him and his cause. And she let him think that. It had allowed her to continue climbing the ranks within the organization, but she wasn't finished yet. There was much more to be done.

The phone rang again. She almost didn't look at it before answering. The number was unknown, but the area code came from the Isle of Skye. Her heart missed a beat at the thought that it might be Kurt. It had been years since she had heard his voice.

Her finger trembled when she accepted the call. "Hello?"

"Hello, Diana."

She squeezed her eyes shut at the deep timbre of her eldest's voice. Her free hand reached out for something to steady her and made contact with the cool pane of glass. Kurt's call wasn't just unexpected, it was astonishing. She had never allowed emotion to rule her, and she wasn't about to let him know how pleased she was. If he'd rung her, he needed something.

"What a surprise to hear from you," she replied.

"It shouldn't be. After all, you broke our agreement."

The hard edge to his voice steadied her. He was angry, but she had anticipated that. "I need to point out that *you* broke it first. Just shy of three months after we struck the bargain."

"You knew?" he asked in disbelief.

She sighed. "Did you honestly think I wouldn't keep tabs on

you? I released you, son. I didn't cut you out of my life as you did me."

"You," he began furiously, then paused and drew in a deep breath. "You had Sabryn's father killed and were intent on ending her. I didn't want to be a part of our so-called family."

His voice was measured, the words carefully chosen. But she heard the resentment all the same. She could tell him the truth, but he wouldn't believe her. "Shall I remind you that you rang me? I take it you're annoyed that I sent Parker for you."

"Annoyed?" he asked with a bark of laughter. "Yeah, I'm bloody *annoyed*. Tell me what I want to know, and I won't kill him."

Diana's stomach dropped like a stone to her feet. "You aren't a killer, son."

"No, apparently, that's just Parker. Or is it you, too?"

"Me?" she asked uncomfortably. She turned to head back to the sofa since this was a conversation best had sitting.

Kurt snorted. "Always playing the innocent. That act is getting old. Why not just admit that you sent Parker to get me, and when I wouldn't come, you told him to end me?"

End me.

The words echoed in her head. Her knees buckled, but she grabbed the arm of the couch and fell upon the cushions. "That is not what I did."

"Sure, it isn't. Parker doesn't do anything you don't tell him to do."

"Kurt, listen to me," she stated, her blood turning to ice. "I sent your brother to fetch you, yes. We knew you wouldn't come easily, and you led him on a merry chase. I recognized there was one way to get you to come to him."

"Oh, he got me to Skye. Then he drove a knife between my ribs. It was by sheer luck alone that he didn't penetrate my lung."

Diana bent over, her eyes closing. She refused to accept what she was hearing. This couldn't be happening. Not to her family. She had gone to such lengths to ensure it would never happen. And yet, it was.

"I didn't," she whispered hoarsely. "I would *never*. Not with you or Parker. He was only supposed to bring you home."

"Did you mention that I needed to be alive?" Kurt asked sarcastically.

She wiped the tears that trailed down her cheeks as she straightened. "He knew that."

"He didn't."

Her plans, carefully thought-out and orchestrated, were going up in smoke. And she hadn't even realized it. "Does that mean you're holding your brother?"

"You have no idea what's going on, do you?"

The derision in his voice was like being doused with ice water. Diana shut off the worry and concentrated solely on him. "Meaning?"

"However influential you believe you are, however powerful you think the London Druids are, you don't stand a chance."

She drew in an unsteady breath, her exasperation mixing with disquiet. "I don't need to hear how formidable the Skye Druids are."

"I'm not talking about them. I'm referring to the evil growing here. The one we're fighting on a daily basis."

We. He considered himself a Skye Druid now. She probably should've seen that coming.

"It's an evil you can't even begin to imagine," Kurt continued.

"It's coming from another dimension and is bringing a battle that has played out in Skye several times before. The Druids have beat it back every time. Now, it's our turn. This is when you admit that London—i.e., you—is working with the evil."

"London wants to wipe out Skye. That's what I know."

"I should've known you wouldn't admit it."

She wouldn't let him provoke her. Though, it wasn't easy. "I know nothing about what you speak of, and that's the truth. Whether you believe it or not."

"If Skye falls, it won't matter how many Druids London has at their disposal. Life as you know it will be over."

That was simply not an outcome she would consider. Yet she couldn't ignore what her son was telling her. "Don't be dramatic."

"How's this for dramatic, Diana? Parker has joined the evil. We don't have him. Yet. I'll make sure none of us kills him when we do find him, but that comes at a price."

She swallowed as she leaned back against the sofa. Kurt was a great many things, but he wasn't a liar. If he said he didn't have Parker, then he didn't. She hadn't been able to get ahold of her youngest in days. Could Parker really have aligned with this supposed evil? Was that what Georgina kept hidden from her?

Or was it something even worse?

"And what might that price be?" she asked, proud that her voice wasn't shaking.

Kurt drew in a deep breath. "I want to know everything you discovered about the Beaumonts. And I mean *everything*."

CHAPTER THIRTY-NINE

The silence that met his demand wasn't surprising, but Kurt was still disappointed. He had thought his mother might listen. Maybe that was the little boy in him. The one still clinging to the past instead of facing who she was.

The library was silent, save for the crackling fire, as the entire room held their collective breaths and waited to hear what Diana would say. The mobile sat heavy and cold in Kurt's hand as he stared at the screen, waiting. He lifted his gaze to Sabryn.

She sat silent, clearly anxious. He hated that the answers lie with Diana. And he loathed that he hadn't realized it sooner. If there was time, if he had his laptop, he would have done his own research and wouldn't have to be at Diana's mercy. Since that option wasn't available, he was prepared to do *whatever* it took to get answers.

Because he had sat on the sidelines for too long.

Because he had kept silent for too long.

Because the woman he loved needed the information.

Kurt took a breath, ready to deliver another threat, when Diana's voice came through the speaker.

"All right," she finally answered.

He scowled at the screen as he tried to visualize his mother's face. She had caved so easily. Too easily. This call should have been the first of several as he debated with, pressured, and coerced her. She had already decided, but she had always required his arguments before. His misgivings doubled as he tried to figure out her motives for capitulating so quickly. If it were anyone else, he'd have said she was being a mother. But that wasn't Diana. She was, first and foremost, a Druid seeking power. And somewhere down the list she was a mum. But that was nowhere near the top.

Kurt shifted his weight from one foot to the other in agitation. Diana wouldn't have given in so quickly unless she wanted something. "Thank you."

"Don't thank me yet. This isn't a conversation to have over the phone."

He shot a furious glare at the ceiling. "I'm not returning home."

"That's a good thing since I'm not there."

Diana always knew just how to push his buttons and send him into a rage. He fought against falling into that pattern. He was no longer a son who sought his mother's approval. He had forged his own path.

"Then let me be clear. I'm not leaving Skye," Kurt declared.

"I didn't expect you would."

There wasn't time for these games. He ran a hand through his hair in frustration. "You expect me to believe you'll come here? The very place that would mean your death by London?"

"It seems so."

The world tilted as disbelief rang warning bells in his head. He couldn't have heard her correctly. Sabryn dropped her feet to the floor and sat up straight, her brow furrowed. She had heard Diana, too, then. Which meant he hadn't imagined it. That didn't make believing his mother any less alarming.

"Why?" he asked.

Diana issued a resigned sigh. "It's my only move."

"That isn't strictly true."

"Do you want the information or not, son?" she retorted in a clipped voice.

Kurt would do anything to help Sabryn—even return home if that's what Diana required. "I do."

"Then expect me within three hours."

"Three?" he repeated in shock.

Diana made an indistinct sound. "Travel from Edinburgh shouldn't be too difficult. I'll charter a helicopter."

The line went dead before his brain fully grasped what she'd said. Kurt tucked his mobile into his back pocket and raised his brows, unsure what to think about the conversation.

"Edinburgh, huh?" Finn asked.

Carlyle scowled. "We should be worried if she's in Scotland."

"But is she here on her own or because London sent her?" Song asked.

Rhona pushed to her feet. "Diana sent Parker to Scotland, so it makes sense she followed. We have less than three hours to prepare."

"There's no preparing for Diana," Kurt told the room. "Nothing she does *doesn't* forward her agenda."

Ferne shrugged a shoulder. "Do we even know what that agenda is?"

"Seems pretty cut and dried to me," Filip said.

Elias shook his blond head. "I'm no' so sure."

"What do you mean?" Theo asked.

"Both of her sons are on the isle. That can no' be good for a London Druid, no matter how high-ranking they are," Elias said.

Kurt glanced at the floor. "Nothing matters to Diana but getting the power she wants."

"Does that match up with her coming here?" Bronwyn asked.

Sabryn got to her feet and folded the throw. "It doesn't matter. She's coming. That's what we need to plan for."

"I agree," Rhona said. "Do we bring her here?"

Kurt was horrified at the thought. "Absolutely not. I doubt the manor would allow her entry anyway."

"Where, then?" Finn asked.

Carlyle said, "It's not going to matter if we're somewhere private or public, as we've already learned. Tell us what you need, Kurt, and we'll be there."

"She'll land at the Ashaig." Rhona looked at Kurt. "It's a single airstrip. Public, but not very busy."

He twisted his lips. "Sounds like the perfect place. She can hand over the information and leave directly."

"We should strategize in case she doesn't," Elodie cautioned.

It was bad enough that Parker was on the isle. Kurt wouldn't let Diana stay. "She won't. I'll make sure of it."

Sabryn set the blanket on the sofa. "Perhaps I should meet her alone. It is data on my family she's giving us."

"You're not talking to her without me," Kurt stated.

Elias looked between them. "I'm no' comfortable with the two of you alone."

"We can be scattered around the airfield as backup," Finn said.

Sabryn shook her head. "Not everyone. We've seen what happens with that."

"Just the Knights, then," Rhona suggested. "The rest of us will remain here at the ready in case you need us."

Sabryn thought about that for a moment and then nodded.

"One of us should alert Kirsi," Elodie suggested.

Callum pushed away from the wall. "Her mum is ill. Balladyn took my place watching over them while I was here."

"We'll leave her with her parents for the time being," Rhona said.

Sabryn walked out of the library, and Kurt followed. She was still too pale for his liking. He caught up with her a few steps into the foyer. She didn't look at him as she continued toward the stairs. He put his hand on her lower back, needing to touch her, wanting that connection.

He glanced over his shoulder and spotted Elias, Bronwyn, Carlyle, Song, and Finn behind them. Sabryn led them to her room, and they reached for the door handle at the same time. He was alarmed by how icy her hand was. Clearly she had yet to fully recover from the Fairy Glen. He wanted her to remain at the manor, but he knew she wouldn't, so he didn't even broach the subject.

She entered the room and headed straight for the bathroom. The sound of water met his ears as everyone else filed inside. Finn shut the door, and they waited for Sabryn. When she finally exited the bathroom, she was rubbing her hands together as if to warm them.

"I'm new, so maybe I'm missing something, but shouldn't we have remained with the others to plan?" Song asked.

Carlyle put his arm around her and drew her against him. "You're not missing anything."

"I needed a break," Sabryn said.

Bronwyn sat against the headboard. "Since it's just the Knights, it might be easier to plan things between us."

"Us?" Elias repeated. "I'd prefer if you remained here, love."

"I know," she said with a smile. "But I'm going."

Sabryn sank onto the edge of the bed. "What if it's another trap?"

"I don't think it is," Kurt said.

Finn leaned a shoulder against the wall. "Why not?"

"Diana was too…" Kurt searched for the right word. "Too astonished by my call. If this were a setup, she would've anticipated me."

Song leaned into Carlyle. "She could be acting."

"And it's been six years since you've spoken to her," Finn pointed out.

Before Kurt could answer, Sabryn said, "We need to be ready for anything. Kurt and I will greet Diana."

He nodded his agreement when she looked his way.

"The airfield isna large, and neither is the single terminal building," Elias explained.

Carlyle said, "That will make it easy to surround."

"We should get there early," Bronwyn said, rising from the bed and heading toward the door. "I need to change."

Elias frowned. "Change? What's wrong with what you're wearing?"

Bronwyn gave him a pointed look.

"Aye," Elias murmured as he glanced at Sabryn before following Bronwyn out.

Finn lifted a hand in a wave. "That's my cue."

"We'll meet you downstairs," Carlyle said as he and Song trailed the others.

The door shut softly behind them. Kurt slid his gaze to Sabryn to find her watching him. "It's all right if you don't come."

"This is about me. I need to be there."

"I can handle Diana."

She sighed, her lips curving slightly. "I have no doubt about that. Me going has nothing to do with trust and everything to do with wanting the truth."

"I intend to get all of it."

"And I'll be right beside you when you do."

He sat next to her on the bed. "How are you really?"

"Scared. Shaken. Nervous. Panicked." She looked at him. "I don't remember anything."

Kurt laid the back of his hand on her leg and waited until she put her cold palm against his before saying, "We'll get through this."

"Are you sure I didn't hurt anyone?"

"I promise. You aimed the wind at Edie."

She gave him a flat look. "You said the wind moved cars."

"Well, yes, but—"

"No *buts*," Sabryn stated.

He drew in a deep breath and released it as he glanced at their joined hands. "I assure you that no one got near you."

"If they had been closer, would I...?"

"It didn't happen, so why think about it?"

She lowered her gaze to the floor and rested her head on his shoulder. "Why can't I remember?"

"Maybe because you don't want to. It could be your mind protecting itself."

"I'm glad you were there to stop me."

He laid his cheek against her head. "I swear I didn't intentionally keep anything from you. I forgot about the file until—"

"I believe you," she said over him. "Why do you think Diana is in Edinburgh?"

"Your guess is as good as mine."

Sabryn sidled closer. "I can't get warm."

Kurt grabbed the edge of the comforter and pulled it up to wrap her in it before winding his arm around her shoulders and bringing her closer to his body.

"Diana sounded genuinely surprised when you told her about Parker's attempt on your life," Sabryn continued.

"It could be like Song said, and she's acting."

Sabryn lifted her head to look at him. "Is that really what you think?"

"No, but I also don't know if I actually heard the surprise because I need to believe Diana didn't send one son to kill the other."

"I'm sorry."

He pulled her head down so she leaned on him once more. All this talk of family made him think of Sabryn's. "Have you spoken to your mum?"

"Not in a few weeks. She's never really forgiven me for leaving."

"How is her new romance?"

Sabryn chuckled. "Oh, my god. I forgot I asked you to do a background check on him."

"Daniel Sykes. Sixty-two, divorced with three kids—two boys and a girl. He's the editor of the newspaper, though I can't remember the city."

"You most certainly can," she said, jabbing him in the ribs.

He grinned as he heard the smile in her voice. "Denver."

"I still can't believe she moved back to her hometown," Sabryn mused.

"There was nothing left for her in DC after you left."

She nodded absently. "Mom seems happy, though. She's always sending me pics of her and Daniel while asking when I might return home."

His heart skipped a beat at the thought of Sabryn leaving the UK. "What do you tell her?"

"That I've built a life here, but I soften it with a promise to visit soon."

The tension eased out of Kurt's muscles. "You should."

"I will when this war is over."

Neither of them commented on what might happen if they didn't triumph. They both knew the consequences of such an event.

"I should get ready," she said as she straightened.

Kurt stopped her before she got to her feet. He put his finger on her chin and turned her head to his, pressing his lips to hers and lingering as desire flared. He wanted to toss her onto the bed and spend hours loving her body to erase the worry that had taken up residence in her beautiful blue eyes. But they both had to prepare for Diana.

He reluctantly ended the kiss and looked longingly at the bed.

CHAPTER FORTY

The *whop-whop-whop* of the chopper blades filled the space as the aircraft lowered to the ground. Sabryn didn't try to hold her hair down as the wind churned around them. She tucked her still-cold hands into her cardigan pockets and steeled herself for Diana Barclay, Viscountess Bridemere.

Sabryn had been insanely curious about Kurt when they first began dating and did an internet search of his family. There was a plethora of information to choose from, and Diana was front and center for all of it.

Reginald Barclay, Viscount Bridemere, was a tall, handsome man with thick, silver hair, an engaging smile, and the same pale blue eyes as Kurt. In fact, Kurt was nearly the spitting image of his father with the same chiseled jaw and wide shoulders. Even Parker took after Reginald, but he was a pale comparison to Kurt.

The helicopter engine shut off, and the incessant drone instantly quieted. The chopper door opened, and legs clad in off-white trousers swung into view. A moment later, Diana appeared in pointed-toe, cream heels, a blue oxford with the sleeves rolled to her elbows, and a brown belt around her trim waist.

Her blond hair was pulled back from her face in a loose bun, showing off her thick, gold hoop earrings. The button-down revealed a single dainty gold chain. A gold watch encircled her left wrist, a single gold bangle her right, and only her wedding ring adorned her fingers.

Diana wasn't just attractive. She was model-gorgeous, despite nearing sixty. Or maybe because of it. She was regal and assertive. A woman who knew what she wanted and grabbed it without apology. A woman who never asked permission. She was, in fact, someone Sabryn understood and respected.

At least when it came to Diana taking her place in a man's world. The rest? Not at all.

Minimal makeup graced Diana's face, showcasing her natural beauty. There was an air about her that demanded attentiveness and attention. And she got it. She never had to lift a finger for anything. Someone was always there to assist her, just like the pilot, who exited the chopper and helped her down.

Diana turned her head his way and murmured something. The man stared after her like a lovesick fool. Unlike so many others, he recognized that she would eat him alive, but it didn't stop him from desiring her. If Sabryn had met Diana before Kurt, she would've wanted to get to know her.

But Sabryn knew exactly who Diana was now, which made it hard to find kernels of anything but loathing and disgust.

Kurt squeezed her hand before starting toward Diana, Sabryn a half-step behind him. There were no smiles in greeting from any of them, though Sabryn noticed Diana's gaze sweeping over Kurt. At first, she thought Diana was judging him on his jeans and tee shirt.

Sabryn soon realized she might have been hasty in her judgment when she noticed the delight in Diana's gaze. It was that of a mother excited to see her child.

Their trio came to a halt, each staring at the other. Diana's eyes were bright, and there was a hint of a smile on her lips as she stared at her son. Sabryn watched as the woman clasped her hands, almost as if stopping herself from reaching out to Kurt. There was an air of hopeful anticipation from the viscountess.

Diana was the first to speak. "I'm pleased to see you."

"The information, if you please," Kurt replied.

Sabryn glanced over and noticed his tight jaw. This had to be incredibly difficult for him. A brother who had tried to end his life was running about, and Kurt didn't know if his mother had anything to do with it. There was no way he could let his guard down, nor did she want him to.

"Down to business, then?" Diana asked, regret clear as her optimism died.

Kurt dipped his chin. "I think it's for the best. You're not supposed to be here, after all."

"Let me worry about that."

"Because you know nothing will happen to you?" he retorted.

Diana tilted her head to the side and smiled softly. "You've turned into a fine man."

"No thanks to you."

Sabryn inwardly winced at the anger in his voice. Years of resentment and ire were boiling to the surface. She slid her hand into his. His fingers immediately twined with hers, holding her almost too tightly. She felt the tension running through him and wished he didn't have to confront his past for her to discover hers.

Diana briefly looked at their hands before turning her attention to Sabryn. "The haircut suits you."

"The information, Diana," Kurt interjected pointedly.

She quirked a brow at him, her look icy. "Right here? Out in the open like this?"

"Why not?" he asked.

She turned around and held out her hand. The pilot hurried to her and handed over her purse before bowing his head and stepping back. Diana looped her arm through the handle and faced them. "If you want the information, you'll get it while having a meal with me."

"A me—?" Kurt started, incredulous. His face hardened, and his nostrils flared in fury. "Have you lost your bloody mind?"

Sabryn tightened her fingers on his as she told Diana, "Time is of the essence."

"Then we shouldn't tarry," the viscountess replied.

A muscle worked in Kurt's jaw. He swung his gaze to Sabryn, who nodded to let him know she was fine with it. "Where's your car?" he asked Diana as he looked around.

"We can wait for me to find one. Or…" she said, drawing out the word. "I can ride with the two of you."

Sabryn hurriedly said, "Fine," before Kurt could argue.

She turned to walk to Carlyle's SUV they borrowed before glancing toward the building and spotting Bronwyn through the glass doors. They exchanged a look before Sabryn climbed into the driver's seat. Her friends would see them and be sure to follow.

Kurt and Diana climbed inside, with Diana getting into the back behind Sabryn. She started the engine and drove away. Kurt sat stiffly beside her, his gaze straight ahead, and his hands curled into fists. Sabryn glanced at Diana to find her staring out the passenger window. The atmosphere was strained and remained that way as she pulled out onto the road. Sabryn glanced in the rearview mirror and spotted Bronwyn's older Range Rover behind them just as she had expected.

The ride was silent, broken only by road noise. Sabryn was happy when she finally turned into the restaurant's gravel car park. The beautiful old stone building was in the heart of the village with a sign that read *Gasta*. Rhona had introduced her to the eatery, and Sabryn had fallen in love with the old converted mill. They served the best hand-stretched pizzas. Too bad the thought of food made her stomach roil now.

She parked, and the three of them wordlessly made their way inside the building. The history of the place was everywhere Sabryn looked. That's how it was everywhere she went in the UK —so much history at her fingertips to learn and explore. It was both awe-inspiring and alarming.

No one spoke until they were seated at a booth next to a window. Kurt slid in beside Sabryn. Diana was the only one to look at the menu. The smells coming from the kitchen were mouthwatering. Sabryn looked over at Kurt to see him glaring at his mother. She nudged him with her elbow and jerked her chin to the menu when he cut his eyes to her. His lips compressed into a thin line, but he picked up the menu.

Sabryn turned her head away, only to have her gaze collide with Diana's. The viscountess lowered the menu and clasped her hands atop the table. "I warned them to leave you be."

"Warned who?" Sabryn asked.

"Thomas and the elders." Diana twisted her lips. "They rarely listen to me."

Sabryn studied the older woman. Beside her, Kurt sat motionless, his body vibrating with tension. "Why would you warn them?"

"You called her an asset," Kurt stated.

Diana nodded as her gaze shifted to him. "I did, indeed, tell you that. I wanted to make sure the mission was a success. Several candidates were being considered for the undertaking, including Carlyle. It was Thomas who chose you and Parker to go to DC."

"That isn't what you told me," Kurt insisted.

They fell silent as a waiter arrived. Only when he departed did Diana continue. "I had orders."

"We were your bloody family," Kurt bit out, barely keeping his voice from rising.

Sabryn didn't take her eyes off Diana. The woman had come prepared, and Sabryn wanted to hear all of it. "You obviously wish to tell this part, so tell it."

"The London Druids' goal, from the time our ancestors left Skye, has been to attract the strongest Druids into the organization," Diana said. "It would grow the numbers and strengthen us as a group."

"To eventually wipe out Skye," Sabryn said.

Diana dipped her head in acknowledgment. "Yes. That, as well. Over the years, our directive fell by the wayside as the elders fought for control, and others in the organization clashed to be named as elders."

"Until Thomas," Sabryn guessed.

Diana pulled a face. "Until Thomas. I've known him my entire life. We briefly dated long before I met Reggie. Both Thomas and I had big dreams."

"And a thirst for power," Kurt added snidely.

Two beats of silence passed as Diana looked at him. Then she said, "Thomas already had a title, which made him not only an eligible catch within the party, but also someone to be groomed to one day be an elder. The same couldn't be said for me. I wasn't from nobility, nor was my family esteemed or wealthy. It was my expertise with spells that caught others' attention. I was never one to sit back and watch. I wasn't content being in the front either. I wanted to be one of those sitting in a seat of authority. I've never denied it. It's something everyone knows. Even your father."

Kurt snorted. "I highly doubt that."

"Ask him yourself, then," Diana countered quickly. She drew in a breath and slowly released it, once more calm. "I've never apologized for knowing what I wanted or for going after it. It has served me well for the most part."

Sabryn crossed one leg over the other. "I gather you mean Thomas."

"I do. His influence over the elders began when he was just a boy. I made it clear what my goal was. He was much sneakier because he didn't want to be one of the elders. He intended to rule the entire organization. He's cunning in a way you never see coming."

Sabryn traded a look with Kurt. "We're aware of the lengths Thomas will go to."

"Of course. Carlyle." Diana unrolled her napkin and spread it across her lap before looking at them again. "Only a few have knowledge of Thomas's true role in the society, but I don't think it'll be that way for long."

Kurt rolled his eyes. "How does any of this relate to Sabryn and DC?"

"We did get off topic," Diana admitted. "Eight years ago, Thomas came to me with a file of names. He had highlighted the families he was interested in wooing to join London. They were from all over the world, and every family had a special gift. The Beaumonts were at the top of that list."

Sabryn's stomach clenched at the mention of her family.

Diana glanced out the window and shook her head. "But a United States senator? That was reaching. Still, Thomas wouldn't take no for an answer. For two years, every instance of London attempting to gain Senator Beaumont's attention was thwarted. Gifts, women, even invitations to London, hinting about our organization. They were all flatly refused. It infuriated Thomas. He had set his mind to something and wouldn't be denied."

She paused and looked at Kurt. "We were at a monthly gathering. You and Parker were standing with friends, laughing about something. I was waiting for your father after a private meeting with Thomas and others about who would go to DC. I'd done my best to keep you and Parker off that list, and it had worked. What I didn't know was that Thomas had sent Carlyle away, which removed him from consideration. That night, standing outside that meeting, Thomas announced that you and Parker had been chosen to bring the Beaumonts into the fold. I might have realized Thomas's move if I hadn't spent the better part of the time warning them to leave the Beaumonts alone."

"Why were you warning them about my family?" Sabryn asked.

"Because of the magic running in your veins. Your father should've told you when you were a little girl. I can only think that he didn't know."

"Should've told me what?"

Diana said, "That you come from a distinguished line of Druids who didn't just hear the wind, they talked to it. And they controlled it."

CHAPTER FORTY-ONE

Kurt couldn't breathe. The world narrowed, the edges going soft as if even reality wanted to recoil from the truth. It made sense now why London had been nearly desperate for the Beaumonts to join. But it hadn't been the senator they wanted. It was Sabryn.

"Dad would've told me," Sabryn murmured, surprise softening her voice.

Kurt saw her pale face, took in her rapid breathing. His gaze skated to his mother.

"He would've told me," Sabryn said again. "He spoke about our family and magic often. He would've said something."

Diana sat ramrod straight in the chair and smiled at the server when they delivered their food and drinks. There were several beats of silence afterward before she said, "Most Druids are aware that our magic has been diminishing with every generation. Each time one of us has an offspring with a non-magical, our power declines. It's a fact that can't be ignored. Your mother has no magic, and I can pinpoint each of your ancestors who didn't. You never displayed anything to your father when you were young that would've made him think you had inherited your great-great-grandmother's power. I'm sure he believed it had skipped you or had died out in the family altogether."

"But London didn't, did they?" Kurt asked, his fury steadily mounting.

His mother glanced at her untouched plate of food. "Thomas believed that by bringing the family into the organization, he could arrange a marriage to a powerful Druid family and eventually return what made the Beaumonts so special."

"Then why kill them? Wouldn't Sabryn and her father be worth more alive?" he demanded.

Sabryn leaned back in her chair and gazed out the window, deflated. "Why didn't Dad tell me?"

Kurt fought between the need to gather her in his arms and walk away or stay and learn the truth. He felt Sabryn's pain and confusion, and it killed him that he had been party to anything that hurt her.

Sabryn returned her attention to Diana. "You and Thomas conspired for me to marry one of your sons."

"No," Diana replied.

Kurt sat back with a huff. "I thought we were past the lies."

"Thomas needed one of you to woo Sabryn, sure, but he would never have allowed you *or* Parker to have her. He wanted Sabryn for his son."

All the air left Sabryn. "Carlyle?"

Blood rushed in Kurt's ears. He stared at Diana, waiting for her to smile or laugh off her words as the jest he hoped it was. But she didn't. The facts—as horrific and ghastly as they might be—were finally being laid bare. All the years he'd believed he had been protecting Sabryn, when in fact, Thomas had called off any hits because she was with the very person he wanted her to be with.

Kurt rubbed a hand over his cheek and tried to process everything. If he hadn't been looking, he never would've seen the slight tensing of his mother's jaw. It was nearly indiscernible, but he knew her well enough to notice. He saw movement to his side just as her gaze cut away from him.

There was a blur of movement as a man walked up, grabbed a chair from a nearby table, and swung it around. Confusion and then fury filled Kurt when Parker set the chair at the end of the table and sat in it backward, his arms folded on the back of the chair.

"Apparently, I missed the memo that there was a family meeting," Parker said with a cocky smile. His blue eyes landed on Sabryn. "Never expected to see you mixing it up with Mummy Dearest."

"What the fuck are you doing?" Kurt was enraged that his brother would show his face, especially after trying to kill him. He could still feel where the blade had entered his body. Parker was within arm's reach and Kurt felt a great, driving need to punch his brother in the face. Over and over and over until there was nothing left.

Parker shrugged flippantly. "Perhaps I should be asking you that. Or you," he said, cutting a dark look to Diana.

"Leave," Kurt told him. The longer Parker sat there, the more incensed he became. He didn't know how much longer he could control it. "Now. Before I rip you apart."

Parker chuckled and sat up straighter. "We both know that isn't going to happen."

"What do you want?" Sabryn demanded coolly.

"You really don't want me to answer that," Parker replied with a wink.

It was the last straw. Kurt jumped up and loomed over Parker. Sabryn reached over and grabbed his hand to keep him from lunging at his brother, who merely sat there, laughing. Diana, for her part, didn't so much as bat an eye.

"Don't," Sabryn whispered.

Kurt looked at her before scanning the restaurant and finding others watching them. He nodded woodenly and sat.

"What are you doing on Skye?" Parker asked Diana. "Let me guess. You're talking about me."

Kurt glanced at the ceiling as he fought for some semblance of control—and lost. "Not everything is about you."

Parker's smile was tight as he zeroed in on Sabryn. "Then it must be about *you*."

"Say what you need to say and leave," Kurt commanded.

His brother ignored him, just kept his attention on Sabryn as he drummed his fingers on the back of the chair. "I'm guessing the talk has turned to DC. You really made a mistake in not choosing me."

"Nothing about you interests me," Sabryn quipped.

Parker's smile was slow and dangerous. "I bet I can change your mind. All I need is five minutes, and I'll wipe every thought of Kurt from you forever."

Kurt bared his teeth. "You're treading on thin ice. *Brother*."

"Worried, are you?" Parker mocked. He laughed and took a deep breath. "I suppose Kurt told you about DC, but was his story true? Or was mine? Did Diana give you another one? Hmm," he said, tapping his chin in mock contemplation. "Which one should you believe?"

Sabryn remained silent, though her dark blue eyes burned with ire.

Parker sighed dramatically and took a slice of her pizza, biting into it. "Hm. Not bad."

"Would you like to order?" the waiter asked after walking up.

Parker motioned to the table. "I'm going to eat off theirs."

Kurt motioned for the guy to leave. It was bad enough the customers were eyeing them. He didn't want anyone else near, just in case. He studied Diana, who remained conspicuously quiet. What Kurt hadn't figured out yet was if it was because she didn't want Parker to hear what she had to say, or if they were working together. Kurt was betting on the latter.

"Shall we compare DC stories?" Parker asked after he'd swallowed another bite. "I'd love to see where the differences are. I'm sure Sabryn would be interested. For instance, I bet she's wondering who ordered her and the senator's deaths."

Kurt glanced at Diana, who quietly observed her youngest offspring. This was a setup, just as he had feared. Diana and Parker were working together. She had kept them engaged until Parker found them. But he and Sabryn weren't alone. The rest of the Knights were nearby, waiting, for just such an occurrence.

"It was Diana, by the way," Parker continued around another bite. "In case I didn't make that clear."

Sabryn rested an arm on the table and watched his brother. Her anger was banked. She sat calmly, coolly. The exact opposite of him. Kurt was ready to explode. He spent every second meticulously keeping his rage under control. He was rapidly losing the battle, however. Soon, he wouldn't care who was around or might see. He never should've brought Sabryn anywhere near Diana.

Parker looked around the table at each of them, smiling as he finished the slice of pizza. Kurt knew that devious look. His brother was up to something, and whatever it was, it wouldn't be good. Kurt gauged the distance to the nearest exits. He didn't know where the Knights were, and he could only hope they were close enough to assist when the growing tension reached its boiling point.

"Let's take a ride," Parker suggested.

Sabryn shook her head. "No, thanks. You can leave, though."

"It wasn't a request," Parker replied menacingly and stood.

Kurt rose as he and Parker glowered at each other, nose-to-nose. "We're not going anywhere with you."

"Oh, but you will. Unless you want all the innocents in here to die," Parker threatened.

On cue, two people walked into view. Kurt recognized them as Edinburgh Druids. Diana set her napkin on the table and grabbed her purse as she stood. Kurt watched her dig out her wallet and toss some money onto the table before heading to the door.

"After you," Parker said.

Kurt was calculating how he might contain any damage to the restaurant and anyone around him when Sabryn slid out of the booth. She touched his back before walking behind him to follow Diana. Parker grinned knowingly. Kurt would let him win. For now. He stared Parker down for another minute before walking away. Diana and Sabryn were already outside.

"Into the SUV," Parker directed. "Sabryn, be a dear and get behind the wheel. Kurt, you'll be in the front. Diana and I will take the back."

Kurt exchanged a look with Sabryn as they headed toward their SUV. There were plenty of other vehicles in the car park. Kurt scanned them, hoping to see one of their friends. No luck.

"Care to tell us where we're going?" Sabryn asked as they walked.

Kurt put a hand out to stop her. "Your leverage is over, Parker. We're not going anywhere with you."

His brother's laugh made a knot of unease form in Kurt's stomach. Parker walked past him as he said, "If you look really hard, you'll notice that my friends didn't exit with us. You come with me, or they start killing. And the threat will remain until I call them off." He turned and walked backward a couple of steps. "Best get moving," he advised before facing forward and continuing to the vehicle.

"We don't have a choice," Sabryn murmured as she followed him.

Kurt knew getting into that SUV was tantamount to a death sentence. He caught up with her and dropped his voice as he said, "We do, actually."

"We're not alone," she whispered. "Let's see this out."

He wasn't convinced it was the right thing to do, but he couldn't debate with her about it without alerting Diana and his brother that they had brought backup. Kurt swallowed the rest of his argument and climbed into the SUV. He sat stiffly as Parker settled behind him.

Sabryn started the engine. "Which direction?"

"Take a left out of the car park," Parker directed.

Kurt pulled down the visor to look at his brother in the mirror. "Why did Diana tell you to kill me?"

"Oh," Parker said, his face scrunched up in mock distress. "I'm not sure you're ready to hear that." He turned toward their mother. "Unless *you* want to tell him. Go ahead and tell him. He should know the truth."

Kurt waited for Diana to rebuff Parker or defend herself, but she simply said, "Now isn't the time."

That confirmed everything Kurt had always feared.

CHAPTER FORTY-TWO

"What the bloody hell is going on?" Carlyle asked as he drove behind Sabryn and Kurt.

Finn had one hand on the dashboard as he turned to look behind him. "I've no fekking idea. No one is following us."

"I don't like this. Not one goddamn bit."

Finn shook his head as he looked at him. "Nothing good will come of this. Are you sure we should've left Song with Elias and Bronwyn at the restaurant?"

"Not in the least. Call Rhona. I have a feeling we're going to need more help."

The drive with Parker was ten times as tense as when they had driven with Diana. Sabryn understood Kurt's hesitation to go anywhere with his family. The only thing that kept her from losing her cool was knowing their friends had their backs. And maybe if Sabryn willed it hard enough, she could manifest not just Parker's and Diana's defeat, but the Edinburgh Druids', and Edie and the Big Bad.

We will win. We will win. We will win.

She adjusted her clammy hands on the steering wheel. Parker whistled in the back seat as if they were chums off on a fun jaunt. She had never thought of herself as particularly violent before. She had always stood up for those who couldn't—or wouldn't—but today, she could only think about removing Parker and Diana from the face of the Earth forever.

Because they were evil.

They had dared to hurt Kurt.

And they would happily take lives to forward their plans for power.

Her heart had yet to stop pounding. Her stress level was to the max and had been from the moment Diana landed on Skye. If they came out of this alive, Sabryn would need a nice, long vacation. She cut her gaze to Kurt to find him sitting with his hands clenched atop his legs, eyes forward, scowling out the window.

If what Diana had told her about her ability was true, then why get in the car? Why weren't Parker or Diana more afraid of her? Unless what she had done earlier against Edie was nothing more than a fluke. Maybe it was something that happened only once. That could explain their seeming lack of concern.

Parker directed her with one- or two-word directives. Her nerves were frayed by the time she finally pulled to a stop on a grassy slope. Ahead was a white sandy beach and crystal-clear water reminiscent of a Caribbean island. But the boat bobbing in the shallow water sent a chill down her spine.

"What a beautiful day," Parker declared as he opened the door and started to climb out. When no one moved, he ducked back in. "Don't make me force you out."

Kurt met her gaze before grabbing the handle and shoving open his door. Sabryn hesitated for only a moment before exiting. As soon as she was outside, a rush of wind surrounded her. She listened, hoping to hear some kind of warning, even though she knew she was already in danger. Unfortunately, the wind remained steadfastly silent.

"You need to know the rest," Diana whispered as she came up beside Sabryn.

She ignored the older woman and moved to take a step.

Diana's hand fastened around her wrist, holding her firmly. Her gaze was direct as she held Sabryn's eyes. "You need to know the rest."

"Then tell me."

The viscountess released her when Parker moved around the front of the vehicle. He walked backward again and motioned for them to follow him. Once he faced forward, Kurt stopped and shook his head at Sabryn, telling her he wasn't going anywhere.

"Not now," Diana said, leaning close to Sabryn. "I need time to tell you the rest."

It could be a trick. It was likely a trick. Still, the idea of uncovering hidden secrets about her family was too alluring to pass up. She followed Diana and held Kurt's gaze. He frowned at her, confusion filling his face. After a moment, he sighed in frustration and fell into step with her.

"Tell me," Sabryn insisted.

The older woman tucked a strand of blond hair that had come loose from her bun behind her ear. "The power only manifests in Beaumont females, but it co—"

She halted when Parker looked over his shoulder at them. "You three are dawdling. That simply won't do."

"Fuck off," Kurt countered.

The smile vanished from Parker's face as he stopped and slowly turned to look at his brother. "Do you know how many times I've dreamed of killing you?"

Sabryn and Diana froze. She didn't pull away when Diana tugged her closer as Parker walked up to Kurt.

"I always knew you hated me," Kurt said.

Parker nodded, his brows rising. "I never tried to hide it. I should've been born first."

"The power comes at a cost," Diana whispered into Sabryn's ear, dividing her attention from what was happening with the brothers. "A big cost."

Sabryn shot her a quick look. She was torn between Diana and watching Kurt's back. She couldn't do both.

"You blame me for being born before you?" Kurt barked a laugh. "That's so you."

Diana roughly grabbed her arm to get her attention. "Did you hear me?"

"Yes," Sabryn hissed while trying to pay attention to Kurt.

"This might be the only chance I have to tell you, so listen," Diana insisted.

Sabryn jerked her head to the viscountess. "Then talk fast, because I'm not going to give Parker another chance to take Kurt's life."

Diana's eyes narrowed briefly. "The only way you survive your power is if you have a tether."

"A what?" she asked as she darted a look at Kurt, who was still exchanging barbs with his brother.

"A tether. If you don't, you *will* die."

That got Sabryn's attention. "Why? How?"

"There isn't enough time for that," she said urgently. "If Kurt asked for this information, it's because you've already experienced something. Am I right?"

"Yes."

Diana's lips flattened. "That's what I thought. Who brought you down?"

"Down?" Sabryn repeated, then thought about how she had come to with Kurt's arms around her, holding her from behind. She looked at him.

"I was afraid of that," Diana murmured.

Sabryn returned her focus to the woman. "Why?"

Diana never got a chance to reply because her attention moved over Sabryn's shoulder. She heard Diana's quick intake of breath and turned in time to see a man coming up behind Kurt.

"Kurt!" Sabryn yelled in warning.

He pivoted, but not before the man's magic struck. Kurt stumbled but managed to stay on his feet.

"You never could handle your own fights," he taunted Parker.

"Stop this," she ordered Diana.

The viscountess's lips twisted. "I can't."

"Can't or won't?" Sabryn asked furiously.

"Can't. I didn't tell Parker I was here."

Sabryn frowned. "Why should I believe you? You've done nothing but follow what Parker wants."

"Should I have made a scene at the restaurant and took a chance that people might die? You didn't."

Two more men and a woman came into view, each focused on Kurt. Sabryn moved to intervene when Parker tsked, shaking a finger at her as he turned his full attention on her. Magic, warm and robust, flowed through her body before pooling in her palms. The smell of the sea tickled her nose as a steady wind came off the water.

She sidestepped away from Diana to put some distance between them as she prepared to battle Parker. Sabryn glanced at Kurt and found him being pelted by the others' magic. He was shielding himself, but that wouldn't last long. Thankfully, the Knights would come charging in to help any moment now. She only needed to keep Parker occupied until then.

"Things would've been so much easier if you hadn't canceled plans with your father that day," Parker said.

Sabryn shrugged. "That's me. A constant disappointment."

"Not for much longer."

"Diana never sent you to kill me," she guessed.

Parker chuckled as he darted a look at his mother. "What does she call me? Her *perfect soldier* because I follow orders. And I do, but they aren't always hers."

They were circling each other now, each waiting for the other to strike. Sabryn wanted to check on Kurt but didn't dare give Parker any advantages. "You're one of those, then."

"One of those?" he asked snidely, his eyes narrowing.

"The weasel characters. The ones who align themselves to more powerful individuals thinking they'll get the glory and ranking they believe they're entitled to. Except it never happens. They always get their comeuppance in the end."

Parker smirked. "You have me mistaken for someone else. I could explain it, but I just don't want to."

"I'm so grateful since I couldn't give a rat's ass," she retorted.

His face tightened with anger. "I'm glad I get to be the one to shut that smart mouth of yours forever."

"Bring it on."

Parker lunged. Sabryn shielded herself with magic, only to see him throw up his hands to either side. One blast was directed at Kurt, and the other at Diana. It was so unexpected that Sabryn couldn't move for a moment. She watched in horror as Kurt dropped to the ground, unmoving. The Druids swooped in and lifted him before running to the beach.

Sabryn started to follow when magic struck her side, spinning her around. She lost her balance and fell, rolling to her feet. She bit back a cry of pain at the wounds on her back but shoved it aside as she found her footing and lobbed a round of magic at Parker.

They traded shots while Sabryn inched her way toward the shore to go after Kurt. Parker's magic was stronger than the last time she had encountered him, and by the smile on his face, he knew it. She was having trouble blocking him. More of his rounds hit her than not. Sabryn stayed on her feet by sheer will alone.

Then next thing she knew, Parker sent a blast at her legs, knocking them out from under her. Sabryn landed hard on her stomach, one arm beneath her, as her breath left her on a whoosh. She gasped for air and looked up to see Parker leaning over Diana, who was now on the ground.

Sabryn forced herself to her hands and knees. She gathered her magic once more and readied herself to fire at Parker when he was suddenly right in front of her, his hands around her throat and squeezing. She pressed her palms against his chest and released her magic. He grunted but didn't let go.

"Do you feel my power? Of course, you do. I know the secret of Skye. That the Druids here are losing their magic," he said, his blue eyes wild. "And I know exactly where it's going."

His fingers continued to tighten as he cut off her air. She clawed at his hands and watched his smile turn crazed. Suddenly, he grunted and jerked. He twitched a second time before releasing her and spinning around with a bellow of rage. Sabryn's lungs filled with delicious air. She coughed, her hand flying to her throat as she spotted Finn and Carlyle battling Parker. Her gaze swung to Diana, who'd propped herself up on one elbow with her other hand against her side, blood seeping between her fingers.

Sabryn hurried to her, trying to find the wound. "Where are you hurt?"

"Stop. Stop!" Diana insisted, shoving her hands away.

She looked up at the older woman. "You need help."

"And you need to find Kurt." Diana shot a pointed look over Sabryn's shoulder.

She turned to see Parker running into the waves before being pulled aboard the twin-engine boat. The driver gunned the motors as the boat sped off.

"You need him," Diana said.

Sabryn heard footsteps quickly approaching and glanced over to see Finn and Carlyle running toward her. "I know, but we need to tend to you."

"It's nothing," Diana stated. "If you give in to your power again without Kurt, you will die, and the evil trying to take over will win."

Sabryn stilled. "You know?"

"Research into your family also meant research into Skye. The last Beaumont with your ability was the sky pillar. The evil only needs to take out you or your tether. Now, go get Kurt."

Finn headed toward the beach as Carlyle slid to a halt beside them. He was breathing hard, looking from Sabryn to Diana.

"Go. I'm fine," the older woman insisted.

Sabryn nodded and jumped to her feet as she heard an approaching engine coming from the water.

"Come on," Carlyle beckoned, taking her hand. "We called in reinforcements."

Sabryn took one last look at Diana before racing toward the shore, where Callum was pulling up in a center-console boat.

CHAPTER FORTY-THREE

Diana drew in a ragged, painful breath and pulled her hand away from her body to find it covered in blood. Her lungs fought to expand as every beat of her heart sent more blood pumping out of her wounds. She didn't know how many times Parker had stabbed her. She had been too shaken and surprised to even try to stop him. Though she should've expected he would try something since he had attacked Kurt in the same way.

She looked up to see the boat carrying Sabryn and her friends heading out of the bay. It took a great deal of effort to remain sitting, but she couldn't stay down. If she did, she would never get up again, and she needed to call Reggie. She looked back at the SUV. Had she really walked that far? She thought she had been closer.

"Get up and get moving," she ordered herself.

Diana swallowed and used the toe of one shoe to remove the other, then repeated the action on her other foot. Bending her legs to get them under her sent a debilitating wave of agony through her. Sweat broke out across her skin, and the sky spun alarmingly. She fought to stay conscious. Every second counted, and she was wasting too many as it was.

She had fought for everything she had, and she wouldn't stop now. With her teeth clamped together, she pressed as hard as she could against her injuries and got to her knees. She could hear her heart beating in her ears, but as long as she was alive, she could move.

Shifting from her knees to her feet took more concentration and several tries. Her limbs were weak and threatened to buckle at any second, but she eventually stood. After a slight turn, she took a hesitant step toward the Rover. Then another.

Her foot landed on a sharp rock, but she barely felt it. The pain throughout the rest of her body was too intense for her brain to register much else. She made her way, one slow, agonizing step at a time. Each time her body begged for rest, she plowed forward. Because she didn't have a choice. Her husband had to know.

"I'm sorry, Reggie," she mumbled. "You told me not to come. You knew…"

She faltered and pitched to the side. A cry of frustration tore from her lips but became a grunt as her shoulder rammed into something solid. She laid her palm flat on the metal of the vehicle and rested her forehead against it for a moment, thankful that she hadn't fallen to the ground.

"Come on, Diana. You can do this," she murmured. "You endured three births and buried a stillborn. You can get the rest of the way to the door."

With the SUV holding her up, she made her way to the passenger door. There was no point in getting into the driver's seat.

She'd never make it to a hospital. But she had time for one phone call.

Her hand slipped on the door handle. She got it open on the second try, but pulling it wide caused her to lose her footing. Her fingers slid on the handle and she fell. Tears pricked her eyes, but she rolled over onto her stomach. Using her elbow, she pulled herself close to the vehicle as a rush of warm blood seeped through her fingers.

It took both hands to heft herself onto her knees and then her feet. The sight of her purse on the seat made hope flare brightly in her chest, but the act of leaning over to grab it forced a moan of pain past her pursed lips. Still, she looped a finger around a handle and pulled it to her. Once she had her mobile in her hand, she lifted it so it could scan her face and unlock.

Her legs started to shake. She was about to lose consciousness and would possibly never wake again. All she needed was a few moments. Her movements were jerky as she punched her husband's name and watched as the line connected. She shifted to lay the phone on the seat so she could hit speaker when it tumbled out of her hand and across the leather to slip between the seat and the other door.

For a moment, Diana just stared at the door. She gave in to the tears then as her knees buckled and she slid to the ground. She'd used all her energy to get to the SUV for that call, and she had failed. She lay back on the rocky ground and looked up at the darkening sky as her eyes slowly slid closed.

Kurt writhed helplessly as his many wounds throbbed. The magic had struck without mercy, without clemency. It threaded into his veins like ice tipped with fire, curling into his bones with surgical precision. He clenched his jaw as his spine bowed, as if his soul itself were turning on him.

It wasn't just torment—it was desecration. His muscles locked, nerves crackling like lightning beneath his skin. Every breath was shattered as his heartbeat pounded like a drum in a body he no longer controlled. It hadn't just been magic the Druids had thrown at him, it had been a spell unlike any other, one that was slowly unmaking him, peeling away strength, memory, and identity—until all that remained was raw, searing agony.

He didn't scream. Not because he didn't want to, but because he couldn't. All sound died in his throat, swallowed by the wind and the bouncing of the boat against the waves. The magic inside him wasn't just hurting him, it was *learning* him. Breaking him apart, piece by literal piece, with cold intent and an ancient, ravenous hunger.

If only the pain would dim for a heartbeat, if only he had a respite, he might be able to hold on, but there was no reprieve. Just soul-crushing anguish.

He heard voices and tried to fixate on them, but it was impossible to concentrate on anything but his body coming apart. Kurt heard a familiar laugh. Parker. The boat bounced, knocking his head against the side as he rolled. This time, he screamed.

"Does it hurt, brother?" Parker whispered in his ear.

Others joined in the amusement, their voices raised over the roar of the wind and the engines as the boat sped across the water. Where was Diana? Sabryn? *Sabryn.* Kurt had to get up, he had to find her.

Something heavy pressed against his shoulder, keeping him at the bottom of the boat. Fingers dug into his cheeks and squeezed hard.

"Look at me," Parker demanded.

But Kurt couldn't open his lids. He couldn't even jerk his head away.

Parker roughly lifted one of Kurt's eyelids. His brother's face was right above his, wearing a maniacal smile as he bobbed with the boat's movements. "It would've been a lot easier if you'd died the other day, but this works out so much better. Did you honestly think the Skye Druids stood a chance this time?"

The growl of the motor dimmed as the boat slowed.

Parker laughed and released Kurt's eyelid so it fell shut. "All your troubles are about to be over, brother."

"Which way did they go?" Finn yelled over the wind as they all hung on to something, and Callum steered the boat effortlessly across the water.

Killian shrugged.

Callum pointed ahead. "I saw them head this way but lost them after."

"We can't spend hours blindly looking," Carlyle said.

Finn's expression was grim. "Are they taking him to London?"

"No," Sabryn replied. "Parker wouldn't have stabbed Diana if they were."

"He did what?!" Killian asked in shock.

Carlyle looked at her. "Where are they going, then? Why take to the water?"

Why, indeed? She had believed Diana and Parker were working together because Diana hadn't spoken against anything Parker said. Now, Sabryn realized it was because she and Kurt wouldn't have believed anything coming out of her mouth. So, Diana had stayed quiet. It made her and Kurt think she was with Parker and convinced Parker that she wasn't a threat.

Had Sabryn missed something? A comment, a gesture, anything that would have told her Diana was on their side from the beginning. She shut off those thoughts since they would get her nowhere. Kurt was in trouble.

Cold wind whistled past her. She turned her face into it, wishing it would speak to her once more. She had apologized, but it seemed it hadn't forgiven her yet. Maybe it never would. Diana's warning about the Beaumont ancestors rolled through Sabryn's mind. She still didn't know what'd happened at the Fairy Glen. How could she have that kind of ability but not hear the wind? And if there was ever a time she needed the wind, it was now.

"Please," she implored in a soft whisper. "Kurt needs help. Please guide me to where he is so we can stop the evil."

She strained, listening for even the slightest whisper, but there was nothing in the wind whipping past them. She was about to give up when she heard it.

North.

The voice was so unexpected that Sabryn jumped at the sound of it. "Keep going north," she shouted to Callum.

He met her gaze before speeding up the boat. All of them were standing, holding on as they bounced across the waves with land to their right. She scanned the horizon as daylight steadily faded, and the water turned an ominous midnight blue.

A bay came into view on their right. She felt the others' eyes on her. "Where to?" she whispered.

North.

Sabryn motioned for Callum to keep heading north. They turned their heads as one to look into the bay. There were other boats about. Any of them could have Kurt, but she had asked for the wind's help. That meant she had to listen and trust.

If it *was* the wind.

"No," she said between clenched teeth and squeezed her eyes closed.

She couldn't start second-guessing now. Only madness lay ahead if she went down that road.

The bay fell behind them as they continued through open water. The only sounds were the grumble of the motor, the wailing wind, and the thudding of her heart. A glorious sunset with shades of lavender and pink that defied words lay before her, but Sabryn couldn't enjoy it.

The next cove.

Sabryn's heartrate quickened. "They're in the next cove."

Callum nodded and steered around the curve of the isle into a V-shaped cove. There, sitting just inside the inlet, was a boat. Three men stood on one side and tossed something into the water. No. Not something. They threw Kurt.

CHAPTER FORTY-FOUR

Diana moaned as pain jostled her awake.

"Easy, lass," a deep voice murmured. "You're safe now."

She cried out as something was tied tight around her abdomen.

"I have to stop the bleeding," he told her, breathing heavily.

She managed to open her eyes and saw a man leaning over her with dark hair and a bushy beard. Blue eyes briefly met hers before her eyes closed. A cry fell from her lips when his arm brushed against her stab wounds as he lifted her.

"I know, lass, I know. I'm sorry," he said.

He sounded winded, as if he had run a long distance. She began to shiver. He placed her into the back seat of the Rover and draped something over her. She drank in the warmth. She heard the soft *snick* of the door closing near her head, and a heartbeat later, the driver's door opened. She tried to ask him to get her phone, but her mouth felt like cotton. She drifted off, only to be startled awake by the roar of the engine turning over.

"Hold on, lass," he threw over his shoulder. "Do you hear me? I'm going to get you help, but it's going to be a rough drive."

Words were forgotten as she moaned in pain each time the vehicle bounced over a rock.

"Doona dare die on me!" he bellowed.

If only it were up to her. But it wasn't. Not this time.

Sabryn heard the guys talking, but she wasn't listening. Her gaze was fastened on the spot where they had dumped Kurt. Shouts came from Parker's boat as they neared. Callum didn't slow until they reached the other craft. Sabryn dove into the water before their boat even stopped and swam as fast as she could, but it wasn't quick enough. The dark water had swallowed Kurt completely.

Suddenly, a light shone through it. She looked over to see Callum swimming past, a flashlight held between his teeth. Sabryn attempted to follow, but he cut through the water much quicker than she could.

Pressure built in her ears as she descended, but she kept going. She wouldn't stop. Not until she found Kurt. At least that was her thought. Unfortunately, her lungs had other ideas. She was forced to turn and head back to the surface. She gulped in air and immediately went under again. The muscles in her arms and legs burned, but she kept swimming.

She saw something move in the dark depths. A moment later, Callum appeared, towing Kurt by the neck of his shirt. Panic seized her when she realized Kurt wasn't moving. Sabryn immediately turned around and followed Callum up. By the time her head breached the surface, Killian was helping Callum pull Kurt into the boat.

Sabryn heard a motor gun near her. She glanced over in time to see the water churn from the other craft and tried to move. Arms reached down and grabbed her, jerking her out of the water just as the propellors whirled to life where she had been. Out of breath, cold, and unnerved, Sabryn watched Parker and his boat speed away.

"Let them go," Killian said as he did chest compressions. "We have Kurt."

Kurt. She spun around and dropped onto the floor of the boat next to him. He wasn't breathing. She tilted his head back, watching Killian so she knew when to blow air into Kurt's mouth. The instant Killian nodded, she pinched Kurt's nose and blew.

Water splashed, but she didn't move from Kurt. Callum rushed around her to the back and helped Carlyle and Finn into the boat.

"Stop," Finn told them.

Sabryn didn't look up as she shouted, "No!"

"CPR won't help. It's a spell," Carlyle said breathlessly. "They used a bloody spell."

Sabryn stilled as Finn knelt beside her. Carlyle pulled Killian back as Finn searched Kurt's front. She shivered in the cool night air, unsure what to do.

"We need to find the entry point of the fekking spell," Finn said hurriedly.

That spurred them into action. Callum produced a knife and cut away Kurt's shirt. There were wounds on his front, but Finn barely looked at them. It wasn't until Carlyle turned Kurt onto his side that Sabryn saw the ragged entry wound the size of a softball on his right shoulder.

"Fek me," Killian murmured.

Sabryn had never seen such a spell before. "How do we reverse it?"

"We don't," Carlyle said as he looked to Finn.

Finn had already laid his palm atop the injury by the time Sabryn realized what he planned. His face immediately creased in pain as Finn used his Bleeder abilities and took Kurt's feelings from him. Carlyle bade Killian to hold Kurt and then hurriedly moved to Finn's other side to help hold Finn up.

Sabryn smoothed hair from Kurt's face and willed his eyes to open. She couldn't lose him. She looked up at Finn, who was bent to the side, supported by Carlyle and Callum. She couldn't lose Finn either.

She caught Carlyle's gaze. "They told you it was a spell?"

"Not willingly," he admitted.

"Why would they at all?" Killian asked. "They outnumbered us."

Dread slithered through Sabryn. She glanced back, but Parker was long gone. "Why would they tell you?"

"Maybe they know we can no' save him," Callum replied.

Sabryn gently turned Kurt onto his stomach. "I need a light," she bade.

A heartbeat later, a beam from a flashlight shone on Kurt's back. Sabryn bent close to look at the discolored skin. She grabbed Killian's arm and moved the light where she needed it, then pressed on Kurt's back. Puss came from the wound, followed by a thick current of blood.

"Sabryn," Carlyle called.

"Something inside." She sat up and looked at Finn. "Stop him. There's no way he can take all the pain. It'll kill him."

It took all four of them to remove Finn's hand from Kurt. Finn never opened his eyes as he fell unconscious.

"I've got Finn. You tend to Kurt," Carlyle told her.

She turned her attention to Kurt. "I need…tweezers," she said helplessly.

"I got those," Callum said as he jumped up and pulled out a first-aid kit. He rummaged through it before producing the tweezers.

Sabryn took them and began to dig into Kurt's wound where she had glimpsed something metallic. The rocking of the boat didn't help and made her have to repeatedly adjust. One of those times, she felt the tweezers clink against something firm. She redoubled her efforts and was rewarded when she finally clamped the ends around the object and extracted it.

"Will he wake now?" Killian asked.

Sabryn looked into the Irishman's eyes and shrugged. "I don't know."

"Finn doesna look much better," Callum said.

Sabryn slid her gaze to Carlyle. His bleak look said it all.

Emily wandered around the empty, quiet house. For sixteen years, she'd spent her time in a tiny room. The cottage was huge in comparison. Elodie kept telling her it would take time for her to adjust. That wasn't the problem. The problem was her middle child —Edie.

The moment Emily learned about Edie, she had wanted to find her grandchildren. She insisted they stay with her and used the excuse of wanting time alone with them. But the children knew something was going on. She, Elodie, and Elias were trying to make life as normal as possible for them, but there was nothing normal about their parents disappearing. The kids were quiet and withdrawn. She gave them as much space as she dared while also endeavoring to prevent another generation of trauma. Her children had endured plenty. If she had any say in it, her grandchildren would be spared.

Her grandbabies were staying the night with friends, which they needed. But it meant she was alone in the mostly empty cottage. The rooms were blank, waiting for her to find furniture and decorations. Eventually, the house would feel like hers, but she felt like an outsider right now.

A helpless outsider at that.

A war was raging on the isle, and she was sitting on the sidelines while her children and their significant others risked their lives. Emily didn't mind sitting out when her grandbabies were with her, but when she was alone, she knew her time could be put to better use.

The sound of an approaching car caught her attention. The closest cottage was over a mile away. If she heard a motor, then the vehicle was nearly at the house. The cottage was heavily warded by Druid and Fae magic, thanks to Balladyn, and there were also thick bolts on the doors. But she knew that wouldn't keep someone out if they really wanted inside.

Lights moved through the windows and bounced along the walls. A moment later, the engine shut off. She listened and heard two vehicle doors close with several seconds between them. She walked toward the front of the house, staring at it as if she could see through it to who might be approaching. Her mobile dinged at the same time someone pounded on the door.

Emily glanced over her shoulder to the kitchen where her phone was. She kept forgetting the doorbell had a camera. She should look at that since it was likely why her mobile had sounded. Just as she turned to do that, another round of pounding came. She halted and swung back around.

She walked to the door and looked through the peephole to see an older gentleman with an unconscious woman in his arms. The man lifted his head, and she gasped as she recognized his face from pictures. Her fingers hurriedly fumbled with the locks as she threw open the door.

"I need your help," he stated.

Emily stepped aside and let him enter, her gaze going to the woman's blue top soaked in blood. She shut the door behind them, locking it out of habit, and hastened after them. He headed down the short hall to the bedroom and laid the woman on her granddaughter's bed. The woman moaned as her eyelids fluttered open.

He untied a makeshift bandage and then ripped open the woman's shirt to reveal multiple stab wounds. "We need to stop the bleeding."

His words sparked Emily into action, and she ran to get towels and the first-aid kit. She raced back into the room and handed him the items. Emily looked down when the woman took her hand and mumbled something.

Emily shook her head and leaned down to hear better. "I didn't hear you."

"Forgot," the woman said.

"You forgot something?" Emily asked.

The woman nodded, her eyes drifting close as she pinched her lips against a round of pain.

"Hold this."

She lifted her eyes to the man. His dark hair was gray at the temples. He had a beard now, but she still recognized him. "Luke Ryan."

His blue eyes briefly met hers. "Aye. And you're Emily MacLean. The woman bleeding is Diana Barclay."

"As in Kurt and Parker Barclay?" she asked.

Luke nodded.

"Where have you been?" Emily asked him.

He glanced at Diana. "We need Healers."

"Must…tell…her," Diana mumbled.

Emily frowned. "Tell who?"

"Sa…"

Emily looked at Luke, who was busy trying to stop the bleeding.

"Sab…"

"Sabryn?" Emily asked. "You're talking about Sabryn Beaumont?"

There was a hint of a smile that vanished as Diana's eyes cracked open. "Sh…she…"

"Wait until we get your wounds seen to," Emily said.

A tear ran from the corner of Diana's eye. "Can't."

Emily looked at Luke.

His lips flattened, his look bleak. "Get her whatever she wants."

"I'll call Sabryn," Emily said.

Diana's fingers tightened on her wrist. "No…time."

CHAPTER FORTY-FIVE

"Why isn't Kurt waking?" Carlyle asked.

Sabryn took the bit from the tweezers into her free hand and returned to Kurt's wound to look for more. Water dripped from her hair onto his back. She was no longer cold. Fear and anxiety had sweat beading her brow. She wanted off the boat, but they didn't have the time. How long could Kurt go without breathing? How long until he was past their ability to save him?

The sea continued to thwart her attempts, causing irritation to flare. A frustrated scream built until the metal pinged against another particle. Sabryn removed it and immediately looked for more. Thankfully, she found the third, fourth, and fifth pieces easily. The sixth took more time.

With every piece she pulled out and Kurt didn't wake, she returned to look for more. Again and again, she removed metal from his body, piece by tiny piece. Her back ached from bending, her knees screamed for ease, and her neck was straining from being at such an odd angle that she would likely never be able to hold it correctly again, but she would suffer through eons of pain if it meant bringing Kurt and Finn back.

A loud boom caused all of them to freeze.

"What was that?" Sabryn asked.

"That came from the other side of Skye," Callum said as he faced the isle.

Carlyle pointed. "I see smoke."

Sure enough, gray smoke ballooned against the evening sky.

"That looks like it's coming from the Fairy Glen area," Callum stated.

Shock rocked her. Sabryn looked down at Kurt and then met Carlyle's gaze. "They told us it was a spell because they wanted us distracted."

Callum faced her. "Could they be trying to take out the location of the air pillar?"

"Can they do that?" Killian asked.

That was easier than going after her, and with the Fairy Glen gone, Skye would fall. "Get us there," she ordered Callum.

"It will take too long," he said right before he shouted for Balladyn.

Emily dragged in a big breath and held Diana's hand between hers. "What do you want Sabryn to know?"

Diana swallowed with great effort, her face a pasty white. "Fly."

"Fly?" Emily repeated, unsure if that's what she'd heard.

Diana's eyes closed, and she nodded once. "She…has to…l-let…go…"

"I'll tell her." Emily looked over at Luke, who had blood up to his elbows.

"Reggie."

Her attention returned to Diana. "Who's that?"

"Her husband," Luke said.

Emily didn't know how Luke seemed to have all the answers. "Is he on Skye? Shall we get him?"

Another tear leaked from Diana's eyes as she shook her head. She met Emily's gaze, silently beseeching her.

"You want to call him?" Emily guessed.

Diana nodded.

"Do you have her mobile?" Emily asked Luke.

He didn't look up as he pressed more towels against Diana's wounds, causing her to moan. "It might be in the SUV."

Emily released Diana and ran from the house to the Range Rover. She flung open the driver's door and quickly looked for the phone in the console. Then she yanked open the passenger door and scanned the back. She spotted blood on the leather as she climbed inside and checked under the front seats. She opened the other passenger door to get out and heard the clatter of something falling from the vehicle. When she jumped down, she saw a mobile phone. Emily picked it up and raced back into the cottage.

"I found it. I found it!" she hollered as she bounded into the room.

Luke wiped his forehead with his shoulder. "You need to make that call now."

Emily fumbled with the device, bringing it to Diana's face to unlock it. In her haste, she kept hitting the wrong things. Finally, she found Reggie's name and pressed send.

"I got him," Emily told Diana as she brought the phone to her ear. "Wait for him to speak."

Emily knew the moment Reggie answered by the way Diana smiled, and fresh tears fell.

"Reggie," Diana whispered. "Yo-you were…right…"

Balladyn appeared before Sabryn could get her thoughts together. The Reaper looked from Finn to Kurt and then at her. Carlyle, Callum, and Killian succinctly explained what was going on.

Balladyn's long, black and silver hair was ruffled by the breeze as he held his hand out to her. "If you are the *speur* pillar, you need to protect it."

Sabryn numbly handed the bits of metal and tweezers to Killian as she got to her feet. Blood flowed into her cramped legs, providing a rush of relief. She didn't want to leave Kurt and Finn but she had to defend the Fairy Glen.

"We've got them," Carlyle promised.

Balladyn motioned for him to stand. "You need to come, too."

"Go," Callum urged hurriedly.

Carlyle jumped up and reached for Balladyn. In the next second, they were at the base of Castle Ewen, surrounded by Edinburgh Druids.

"Let's hope Balladyn returns with reinforcements," Carlyle said as they moved back-to-back.

Magic surged through Sabryn as she eyed the Druids around

her. They were repeatedly flinging magic at the ground and the monument behind them. They knew the pillar was at the Fairy Glen but didn't know where, so they were going after everything.

"If they keep this up, they'll eventually land a direct hit," Carlyle mused.

Sabryn reared back her hand and let loose a blast of magic at the Druid nearest her. "Then let's not let them."

He chuckled before joining her. Their adversaries kept pelting the area but also directed blows at her and Carlyle. The Druids weren't there on their own. Edie was likely nearby. Maybe even Parker. Sabryn intended to take down Kurt's brother herself.

"Watch out!" Carlyle yelled, shoving her out of the way as he raised a shield of magic.

Sabryn spun around and took his place to fend off more attacks.

Kurt came to with a bellow of pain.

"Easy," said a voice he recognized but couldn't place.

A hand rested on his back, keeping him down. He gritted his teeth as he felt something moving around inside his injury.

"Just a wee bit longer."

Another voice he knew but couldn't name. His head was clouded with agony, making it nearly impossible to string two words together. He followed the leg lying near his head to see someone slumped over at his feet. The boat rocked, making the man's head roll. A jolt of surprise went through Kurt when he saw

Finn. Kurt tried to get up again. This time, another set of hands joined the first to hold him down.

"We have to get them all out. I just need a little longer."

The Irish accent registered as Killian's. At least Kurt was with friends again.

"Sabryn?" he called.

"She's gone now, but as soon as we get you healed, we'll take you to her," Callum said.

Kurt squeezed his eyes closed. "What happened?"

"Too fekking much," Killian murmured.

Finn shifted his leg and grunted.

"I think he's finally coming around," Callum said.

Kurt clenched his teeth as a spasm of pain shot through him.

"I think that's it," Killian declared.

Kurt put his hands against the deck and tried to push up. The agony that movement caused made stars flash in his eyes. Hands helped him sit up and lean back against the side of the boat.

Finn rubbed his head as he slowly came awake. He blinked open his eyes to look at Callum and then Killian. When he spotted Kurt, he blew out a relieved breath and sat up. "Where are Carlyle and Sabryn?"

"Balladyn took them," Callum explained. "The Fairy Glen is being attacked."

"Then we need to get there. Now," Kurt stated, feeling the urgency.

Finn nodded toward Kurt's left arm, which he held protectively against him. "Can you even move?"

"I can stand, and I have my other hand," he retorted.

Finn grinned and said, "Balladyn."

Kurt looked around for the Reaper, but Balladyn didn't appear, leaving a knot of worry in his stomach that steadily built. He turned to Callum. "Drive. As fast as you can."

"Do you see Edie?" Carlyle asked between the booms of magic landing around them.

Sabryn had been searching for her from the moment of their arrival. "Not yet."

"She's here. I know."

So did Sabryn.

Carlyle grunted as magic hit his arm. She shifted in front of him, blocking a strike against her while firing off one of her own. Sabryn smiled when her shot landed, killing the Druid who had struck Carlyle.

"Where the bloody hell is everyone else?" he asked as he stepped to her right to intercept a blast aimed at her.

The ground shook violently beneath them. She stumbled back, wondering if it was an earthquake. Carlyle grabbed her hand and yanked her away from the slope seconds before the rocks would've fallen on top of her.

She's here.

The whisper of the wind was featherlight against her cheek, the voice loud and clear. Sabryn scanned her surroundings, searching. Her gaze jerked to the side when she saw a patch of blond hair. There, walking behind the line of Druids, was Edie. Her lips curved into an arrogant smile as their eyes locked.

Emily's stomach clenched in dread when Diana's eyes fell closed, and her head rolled listlessly to the side. Luke checked for a pulse, and his shoulders slumped as he hung his head. He released the towels and stepped away from the bed until his back hit the wall.

The sound of a voice shouting through the mobile snapped Emily out of her stupor. She glanced at Luke as she brought the phone to her ear. "Hello?"

"Who is this?" asked Reggie worriedly.

"My name is Emily. Diana was attacked."

"Attacked? Where? How? Is she all right?"

The panic in his voice made Emily's throat clog with emotion. "I…I'm sorry. I'm afraid she isn't."

There was a long pause on the other end of the line. When Reggie next spoke, his voice was tight and resolved. "Where is she?"

"The Isle of Skye."

"At the hospital?"

Emily swallowed and took Diana's hand in hers. "There wasn't time. She's at my house."

"I'm on my way."

"I didn't think London Druids could come."

"I don't give a bloody damn about some absurd rules," Reggie snapped. He took a breath and calmly said, "I'm coming to get my wife's body. Now, tell me where she's at exactly."

Emily gave him her name and address. "You should probably know that both your sons are here, as well."

"I know," he replied, sounding as if he carried the weight of the world. "I'll see you shortly, Ms. MacLean."

The line went dead. Emily lowered the phone and stared at Diana.

"You probably shouldna have done that," Luke said.

She turned her head to him. "He has a right to his wife's body. I think it's time you told me how you got to Skye."

"I've been here for weeks." He sighed and pushed off the wall. He grabbed one of the unused towels and wiped the blood from his arms. "You need to get to Sabryn and deliver that message."

"Me?" she asked, taken aback. "It seems you know more about what's going on than I do. I've only just gotten out—I mean, back…" She let her words trail off.

Luke walked around the bed and came to stand beside her. "I know. Lock the door behind me. I'll send Elodie or Scott as soon as I can."

"Why? Diana is dead."

"That doesna mean Parker willna return."

The truth hit her like a wall. "Parker killed her?"

"Yep. Be vigilant," he told her and stalked from the house without another word.

Sabryn might not remember what had happened between her and Edie earlier, but she knew she had been winning—and not because Kurt had told her. She knew it for a fact. It was a feeling in her bones—and in her magic.

"Sabryn!" Carlyle called.

She didn't dare take her attention off Edie. Not when they were about to finish the battle they had begun hours before.

CHAPTER FORTY-SIX

Every bounce of the boat as it zoomed across the water threatened to send Kurt to his knees from the piercing pain. So many questions were running through his head. Where was Parker? Where was Diana? How had Sabryn found him? What had his brother done to him? Yet his need to know that Sabryn was safe dwarfed any necessity for answers.

He held the handle beside him in a death grip, willing the boat to go faster. Callum had the motor at top speed, but Kurt didn't think it would be enough. He could feel it in his bones. They were going to be too late.

All their planning had been for naught. Again. The anger that erupted within him made him want to howl in fury. They had been so careful, so very fucking careful, and still, Parker had managed to be a step ahead of them. Was it because of Diana? Or were Edie and the power controlling her to blame?

Did it even fucking matter anymore?

The Skye Druids had staved off attack after attack, clawing their way to victory one inch at a time. He had honestly believed that would continue. That he would be a part of it. He had never considered that his brother would turn.

A hand landed heavily on his shoulder. He turned and looked into red-ringed silver eyes right before Balladyn teleported him off the boat. The sudden stillness of the ground made him tip to the side with a wave of vertigo. Kurt regained his balance, his heart thundering as he realized he stood on the edge of a storm of Druid magic, tearing through the air in violent, invisible waves. Magic crackled like thunder, the earth scorched and seething around him. And Sabryn was out there in the midst of it all.

He hurriedly scanned the battlefield for her. His lungs seized when he saw her right in the middle. Kurt started toward her, only for Balladyn to hold him back.

He shoved the Reaper's hand off and whirled around, his fury unleashed. "Why isn't anyone helping her?!"

"Hold up," came a shout before Balladyn could respond.

Kurt turned at the sound of Elias's voice and saw him, Bronwyn, and Rhona running from around one of the many hills. He glanced back at Sabryn, impatience hounding him. Every second he wasn't with her meant another second she could be killed. Kurt clenched his hands and fought against going to her.

"Diana had a message for Sabryn," Rhona said when they finally reached him.

Kurt scrunched his face. *That's* what he had waited for? "She can wait. If you aren't going to help Sabryn and Carlyle, I am."

Elias seized his arm and drew him to a halt. "I'm sorry, but Diana is dead. Parker stabbed her."

"No." They must be mistaken. Kurt couldn't have gotten it wrong. Diana and Parker had been working together. He *wouldn't* have gotten that wrong.

Elias's blue eyes were filled with sorrow. "She clung to life long enough to impart a final message for Sabryn. And you need to get it to her."

Kurt didn't have time to think about his feelings about Diana when there was a battle to win. "What is it?"

"Fly."

"Fly?" he repeated dubiously.

Elias shrugged. "Hopefully, Sabryn will know what that means."

"Edie's here," Balladyn announced.

Kurt pulled his arm from Elias's grip and headed toward Sabryn.

The wind began to whistle around Sabryn, its intensity swelling and strengthening. But it wasn't from her. Standing across the terrain was none other than Edie. The other Druids, the blasts of magic striking the ground, and even Carlyle faded away as all of Sabryn's focus was trained on her adversary.

Edie stood with her feet hip-width apart, her arms by her sides, her chin dipped slightly, and her gaze locked on Sabryn. It was time for them to dance again. And this time, only one of them would be walking away.

Edie's lips curled in a taunting smile—challenging and

dangerous. Without warning, she rushed forward, her hands splayed and elbows bent at her sides as the wind whipped to life with a shriek. The air struck Sabryn dead-center, slamming into her chest like a battering ram and hurling her backward. Her skull cracked against the ground, and pain detonated white-hot behind her eyes. Gritting her teeth, Sabryn rolled to her feet, magic flaring through her blood like a war cry.

She was ready when Edie halted and threw out her hands. Swirls of air, dense with fury, coiled tightly around Sabryn, restraining her. She reached for it, calling to it as she had done countless times before. She didn't fight against it, didn't struggle. Instead, she relaxed.

The wind surged again—a raw, snarling force—before it struck. It shattered like waves breaking against unmovable rock the moment it touched her. Edie's gaze sharpened as she advanced, her confidence shifting into something darker.

"I need you," Sabryn whispered to the wind, spreading her hands.

It answered by multiplying the ribbons around her, the air crackling with power and the roar of the currents.

Kurt ran up behind an Edinburgh Druid and kicked the back of his knee. The guy dropped, allowing Kurt time to punch the back of his head and knock the Druid out cold. His shoulder throbbed mercilessly, but he would bear any pain, suffer any torment, to get to Sabryn.

He continued advancing, eyeing the many enemies swarming

the area. Finn and Elias were suddenly on either side of him, fending off attackers who attempted to stop them. More of their friends poured out of the hills to surround the Edinburgh Druids.

The air crackled with magic as it was hurled and blocked across the ancient landscape. The hairs on his arms rose while pressure dropped and static skittered over his skin. Magic slammed furiously into the dirt and sent debris flying in every direction. Each strike of earth, stone, and flesh landed with the force of a drumbeat—low, primal, and terrifying. Bodies were tossed by unseen forces, the screams of the wounded lost in the chaos of battle. The isle shuddered with every blow as if the very land itself recoiled and shrank beneath the strikes.

Kurt saw that Song had found her way to Carlyle and was helping him protect Sabryn. He barely spared the couple a glance as he passed them where they fought side by side. They, along with Elias and Finn, blocked any assaults directed at him. The ground shook, the sky sizzled with power, and anguished screams rent the air. He paid no attention to any of it. The only one that mattered, the only one that caused his heart to clench with both love and fear, was Sabryn.

She stood, her legs braced apart, arms at her sides, and palms facing forward. Three strides past Carlyle, and he felt the edge of a cyclone. The wind kicked up bits of grass and pelted him with tiny stones. The ferocity stung his eyes and snatched his breath. Sabryn's short, black hair whipped around her in a violent dance.

His steps faltered as he saw her. His beautiful, formidable warrior was a magnificent sight to behold. Not the resilient woman before him now, but a powerful champion chosen by fate or magic —or both—to stand as one of the three pillars responsible for Skye's protection.

The wind grew fiercer, angrier. It lashed at his face, yanking him from whatever revelation had been revealed and back to the present. Back to the battle. He might not know what his mother's dying words meant to Sabryn, but he would deliver them. Kurt took a step forward, and was engulfed in the storm.

It screamed. It howled. It thundered and snarled. It both tried to rip him apart and squeezed him until he thought he might asphyxiate. Because it was wind against wind as Sabryn's and Edie's magic clashed, turning the battlefield into a windstorm.

The wind shrieked indignantly around her. Sabryn sensed it turning against her as it had at the cottage. Edie's haughty smile said she believed she had gotten the upper hand again. Her opponent advanced a step, confident in her victory. But Sabryn wasn't giving up yet. She leaned into the wind and pushed her magic into it, gently coaxing it back to her.

"You know me," she whispered. "You know I'm on the side of right."

There is no right or wrong side.

She blinked, unprepared for such a reply. "Of course, there is. I'm protecting Skye and the people here."

What makes you believe that's the side of right?

"Because we're not killing innocents."

And how do you know that's what the other side wants?

Sabryn was taken aback by the question. "Those wanting our land are coming from another world. They have their place. We just want ours."

There was no response this time. The wind whipped at her face, the impact as sharp as a slap. It pummeled into her chest and tore at her clothes with claw-like fingers. And she never pulled away, never flinched. No matter how much it hurt. She only leaned into it.

"You know me. You know my family. You have helped us win before. I'm asking that of you again," she pleaded.

Edie's snarl ripped through the air as she hurled her arms forward. The wind obeyed like an unleashed beast, lashing against Sabryn's skin in brutal strokes that left her burning and raw. Her boots skidded on the grass, the ground sliding away beneath her. Gritting her teeth, she dug her toes into the earth as her muscles strained. But the gale refused to relent, shoving her backward more.

"Sabryn!"

Her heart lurched when Kurt's voice reached her. Or was it a trick? Did she dare look away from Edie to find out? Did she give her nemesis that slight advantage? She was propelled back several feet, no longer directing the wind or influencing it. It was now a weapon in Edie's hands. And it intended to kill her.

"SABRYN!"

This time, she did look. Trick or not, she had to know if it was him. Hair tangled in her lashes, impeding her vision, but she saw him, nonetheless. His chest was bare, and his blond hair whipped around his head as he raised a hand to shield his face from the savage gusts. Pale blue eyes met hers. And Diana's words came back to her.

"The only way you survive your power is if you have a tether. If you don't, you will *die."*

Diana had known Kurt was her anchor, but neither of them

had had a chance to tell him. Sabryn hadn't dared to hope he would revive after they'd fished him from the water. She hadn't allowed herself to think about what life would be like without him.

And now, she didn't have to.

Sabryn felt the explosion of wind as it feverishly whipped about her. She reached for Kurt, their fingers brushing, but the wind dragged his feet out from under him before she could grab him.

"Kurt!" she screamed.

She spun back to Edie. Sabryn's mistake was taking her attention off her enemy. She brought her hands together and allowed her power to swell like wildfire. Magic bloomed between her palms, growing fast and expanding into a pulsing mass of heat and energy. A cry tore from her as she hurled it toward Edie.

Her foe lifted a hand to deflect it, but the force barreled through her, slamming into her and knocking her off balance. It was all the opening Sabryn needed.

She turned against the churning wind and ran. Her heart pounded like a war drum. The stones of the spiral snagged at her feet, but she didn't stop. Then, finally, she gripped Kurt's hand, solid and warm. Relief crashed through her the moment their fingers locked. She had him. And she wasn't ever letting go.

They shared a smile as she helped him to his feet. A second later, the wind swirled around them and tossed them to the side to be pinned against the base of Castle Ewen.

Kurt grunted as she landed hard against his chest, his bare back crushed against the structure. The wind pushed against her back like a weight, lodging her against him.

"Fly!" he shouted.

She wasn't sure she'd heard him correctly. Sabryn attempted to ask him, but the wind snatched her words the second they left her lips.

He slowly, steadily moved his hands up her back to cradle her neck while his eyes remained locked on hers. Then he angled her head so her ear was near his mouth. "Diana said you have to fly."

CHAPTER FORTY-SEVEN

Kurt bit back a shout of pain as rocks dug agonizingly into his back, tiny grains burrowing into the sensitive flesh of his open wound. His body convulsed, and he remembered the agony of when the spell had first been cast on him. Sabryn was being crushed against him, making it impossible for him to drag air into his lungs. He wanted to curl in on himself, shrink away from the torment.

Yet he knew this was exactly where he was supposed to be.

He had delivered Diana's message, at least. He caught sight of Edie's triumphant expression, as if the battle—and the war itself— were over. She didn't notice that his friends were thrashing the Edinburgh Druids. But then again, they were expendable.

Kurt fought against the pressure of the wind and lifted his head to stare into the dark blue pools of Sabryn's eyes. He wanted to cling to her in the hopes he might wake from this nightmare, but the only way out was through. And the only one who could get them through was the woman he loved.

"I don't understand," she said, her words broken by the wailing wind.

He smoothed his thumb over her cheek near her lips. "You will," he told her.

Then he gripped her shoulders and spun her to face Edie.

Sabryn gasped for air as the wind seized her breath. She tucked her head to drag more into her starved lungs while still being flattened against Kurt. The wind was Edie's to wield now, and she used it like the savage, aggressive weapon it could be. The air was thick with pressure and…something else. Something dark and cruel.

Something inhuman.

Power surged and pulsed threateningly. Sabryn looked up to see Edie moving her arms as she forced the wind to obey through brute strength. The wind responded, becoming sharper and more violent. It whipped and thrashed, whined and hollered as it lifted shards of rock and other rubble to hurl at her and Kurt.

A scream rose in Sabryn's throat as she fought to lift her hands, but the wind wouldn't release her. The first bits of rock sliced her exposed skin, leaving trails of blood in their wake. The wind was her friend, not something to be used against her. It was her birthright, a legacy passed through her ancestors. And she wouldn't let them down.

Bold, dazzling magic sparked through her veins. It was wild and fierce, defiant and turbulent. It was hers but magnified by a hundred. No, a thousand. As if she had only ever had a drop of magic before, and now, the entirety of it was available to her. And it wanted to be set loose.

The sheer force of it terrified her. She didn't know what to do with that kind of power. And she didn't know what it would do to *her*.

Edie's maniacal laughter reached her. The wind redoubled its efforts to kill both her and Kurt.

"No!" Sabryn hollered, twisting her hands until her palms faced Edie.

Then she called to the potent magic coming to life inside her. There was a rush as it answered. Words of a spell she didn't know spilled from her lips and formed a cocoon to block the debris but not the wind. Kurt's hands rested on her waist. Sabryn heard Diana's voice filling her head once more.

"*...your tether.*"

His hands were there to hold her, secure her. Ground her. Because he was her anchor. It was Kurt who would keep her secured to their world so she could give herself over to the power. The instant that realization hit, the magic slid pleasingly beneath her skin, gliding over muscle and tendons before twirling around bone. The rich, opulent sensation was like nothing she had ever experienced. It was lush, sensual. Carnal.

Warmth suffused her, and with it, certainty. A belief in herself, in the fate that had brought her to the isle. A conviction of her place among the Skye Druids and her ancestors.

No longer was she being crushed against Kurt. She lifted her hands to find wisps of wind curling elegantly around her fingers. She played with them and coaxed others to her with a mere thought. The wind coiled in her palm, and she paused as it infused her magic. It expanded and contracted as if breathing, and she realized it was matching the rhythm of her lungs. And if she could do that with some of the wind, she could do it with all of it.

Sabryn lifted her head and speared her foe with a look. A flash of unease flitted over Edie's face before she heaved more wind at them. Sabryn watched it barrel toward her and Kurt. It tried to knock her to her knees, attempted to pulverize them. And it might have. But she had been prepared.

She slowly lifted her hands and released the magic-infused wind she held so it mixed with the rest. "I know you," she softly called. "We've danced together before, you and I. You've guided me, urged me. Warned me with words no others could hear. And I shut you out because I was scared. But I need you now. This land and the Druids who call it home need you. Help me, and I will never ignore you again."

There was a hesitation in the air as if the wind were considering her words, weighing them.

"You say there is no wrong or right. I say you're wrong. Your connection to my ancestors saved the isle before. I'm asking—no, I'm *begging*—for you to join me in doing it again. Like those who came before me. We're destined for this."

Together.

"Together. Always together," she promised.

The wind wrenched and pulled away from her, twisting above her in a long, swirling tunnel that unraveled and ripped across the landscape. Sabryn hadn't commanded it. She had asked, and the wind had answered.

But they were far from done.

Sabryn dug deep, pulling at the rich, new magic suffusing her. Then she reached for the wind. Not for control but for connection.

It was automatic, and she didn't question it. Her magic knew what to do, and she let it take her when it needed.

Kurt could finally breathe again. The wind was no longer shoving them into the side of the monument or bellowing in his ears. It gave him a chance to see the rest of the battlefield. He started to release Sabryn when he saw Carlyle in trouble, but her hands came down atop his, stopping him. He sucked in a surprised breath at the rush of wind that crackled pleasantly up his arms, over his shoulders, and around his neck before gliding down his back.

There was a connection between the three of them now. Kurt could feel the wind as if it were a living, breathing entity. He didn't need to hear its words to understand that it had chosen a side. The air pillar had found her place.

Sabryn lifted her head and spread her arms out to her sides. The wind buffeting them was a soft and yielding caress—no longer a weapon against them but for them.

He almost believed things were over. Until he looked at Edie.

Magic poured from Sabryn and spun in a dizzying dance with the wind, mingling and intertwining until they were one. The more she gave, the stronger and more powerful the wind became. They worked in tandem, steadily becoming more potent.

But it kept asking for more. Sabryn felt as if she might blow away at any moment. Only Kurt's hands kept her from vanishing. She tried to tell the wind that, but it refused to listen.

More.

Sabryn hesitated, unsure.

More.

"I can't," she answered.

More!

Kurt's words returned then. *"Diana said you need to fly."*

MORE.

Everything clicked into place then. Sabryn understood Diana's message. The only way to fly was to let go and trust—just as she had asked the wind to do. Sabryn drew in a breath and gave the wind all of her magic. All of herself.

Kurt's hands were no longer on her waist. He was directly behind her, his chest against her back, his arms held out alongside hers, anchoring her not just to Skye but also to this dimension, to her body.

To him.

It took trust that hadn't been there before. The kind of trust Corann and the Ancients had known she would need. She wouldn't have believed them had they told her. She was too stubborn that way. She had needed to learn it on her own.

Sabryn watched the beautiful display of wind as it curled and twisted in dazzling displays before shooting in every direction at once, directed at her enemies.

And, just like that, the battle was over.

She didn't move as the wind returned, swirling around her and Kurt in a soft caress before dissipating. Sabryn thought she would be exhausted after such an emotional, physical, and mental battle, but she felt rejuvenated—invigorated, even. She looked up at the stars overhead, searching for another look at the wind, but it was gone. For now. It would be back whenever she needed it. They had a new bond, a connection as old as the land they fought for.

"Is it over?" Kurt asked.

She leaned her head back against him. "This battle. Not the war."

"That was…" He chuckled softly as he wrapped his arms around her. "That was fucking amazing."

She turned in his arms. "I wouldn't have been able to do it without Diana. She told me I needed a tether. You."

His brows rose on his forehead. "That's why you gripped my hands."

"She warned me that, without you, I could die."

"And the flying?" he asked skeptically.

Sabryn slid her hands over his chest to his neck. "To let go and trust—you and the wind. I did, which is what the wind asked as it demanded more of my magic."

He drew in a breath and glanced around them. "And it took out everyone."

"Everyone?" She looked over her shoulder, searching for Edie.

Kurt took her hand as they walked to the last place Edie had been seen as the others made their way over. Sabryn scanned the ground, but there was no sign of Edie.

"You've got to be fucking kidding me," Kurt murmured.

Something moved in the shadows. Kurt had his hands up when Chief Superintendent Boyd came stumbling into view. Her clothes were torn and dirty, and there was blood on her face.

"She's gone," the chief said.

Rhona limped over, blood coating one arm. "Who?"

"The blonde you were fighting against." Anne swallowed and

swayed as she gazed around her in shock. "She vanished right before a gust of wind knocked me over."

Carlyle grunted as he and Song leaned on each other, both covered in blood and dirt. "We couldn't get lucky enough to take Edie out, could we?"

"She went up against the *speur* pillar and got her arse handed to her," Finn said as he looked proudly at Sabryn. "I will be saying *I told you so* for years."

Sabryn smiled as she turned to stare at the Fairy Glen. It was hard to tell just how much damage had been done to the area in the moonlight, but the evil hadn't succeeded in destroying it—or her. That's what mattered.

Ariah came up beside her and squeezed her hand. "Did you find the location of your pillar?"

"I did," Sabryn said and looked at the base of Castle Ewan.

The wail of sirens could be heard in the distance. They looked at each other nervously.

"Go," the chief told them. "Take care of your wounded. I'll handle things here."

Balladyn stepped forward. "I can help you."

"So can I," Theo told her.

Anne nodded to Theo. "You stay. The rest of you need to go before the others get here. It won't look favorably for any of you to be involved in this after what happened the other morning in the village."

"Thank you," Rhona said.

The chief dipped her head and turned away, Theo at her side. Sabryn watched the approaching red and blue lights flicker as Balladyn teleported them out.

CHAPTER FORTY-EIGHT

Sun poured in from the window across from the bed and onto Sabryn's face, waking her. She drew in a breath and shifted her leg against Kurt's. His arm tightened as he held her against his side and turned his head toward her. She opened her eyes to look out the window and smiled to find herself snuggled next to him.

He yawned and kissed her forehead. "Morning," he said sleepily.

"Good morning," she replied. Happiness swirled through her as sweet as honey.

She watched a bird fly past the window, their melodies filtering through the glass. Last night, she had never imagined she would have such a morning again. She wasn't just alive. She was in bed with the only man she had ever loved.

Their victory had come at a high price, though. Parker's betrayal would have lasting consequences for both Kurt and his father. Then, there was Diana's death to process. Kurt hadn't spoken about it since delivering the devastating news to her. When she tried to press, he had silenced her with a kiss and carried her to bed. They would have to deal with it eventually, though. Diana's body was on Skye, and Reginald was coming to get her.

"Can we spend the day in bed?" Kurt asked, his voice still husky from sleep. "I believe we've earned it."

"We've more than earned it," she said, caressing his abdomen.

He threaded his fingers into her hair. "Do you feel different now that you're the air pillar?"

"In a way. The wind is easier to hear now."

"I'm sleeping with a badass," he said, a smile in his voice.

She chuckled and tilted her head up to see his face. "Is that what you think of me?"

"It's how I've always thought of you."

Sabryn snuggled against him. "Each skirmish is getting worse. There was a moment last night when I was sure we were going to lose. I've never tasted fear like that before."

"But we were victorious."

"We walked away. Which is, indeed, a win. But I won't call us triumphant until we've ended all of this."

He blew out a breath and tightened his arm around her. "We're one step closer to that. We have the air pillar now. We just need to find the water pillar."

"I'm worried about Kirsi."

"I didn't see her last night, but I wasn't looking, either. I woke on the boat and demanded to get to you. I only made it thanks to Balladyn. How the bloody hell do we get anything done without him?"

Sabryn laughed softly. "I wonder if he rolls his eyes when we call for him."

"Does he ever smile?"

"On occasion."

Kurt grunted. "I won't believe it until I see it. I swear he only has one expression."

They shared a chuckle. Her thoughts returned to Kirsi. "I think I need to talk to Kirsi. She's not ready."

"If someone told me the only way to win was to fight a monster and kill it, I don't know if I would be, either."

Sabryn grimaced. "It's information that needed to be shared, but I don't think anyone has talked to her about it."

"Not even Callum? You used to tell me how those two drifted together if they were ever in the same room."

"If Kirsi will talk to anyone, I think it would be Callum."

Kurt adjusted the pillow behind his head. "I'm not saying you shouldn't check on her, though. Especially with her mum being ill."

Sabryn almost used the mention of Kirsi's mum to talk about Diana but chickened out at the last minute. "How does it feel to be in the thick of things with us?"

"Glorious. And bloody terrifying. You talked about being scared, but I don't think anyone was more afraid than I was. Not at the battle, but at the possibility of you getting hurt."

"There will always be that possibility. We were both wounded. Everyone sustained injuries last night—some worse than others. Speaking of, I need to change the bandage on your back."

He lightly ran his fingers up and down her arm. "I don't want to move yet."

"We could hide out in here for a few days," she suggested.

"I like that idea. Do you think we could place food orders with Carlyle? He's a brilliant cook. He could've been a chef."

Sabryn smiled against his chest. "We take full advantage of

his love for cooking. Just be forewarned to check containers in the fridge to make sure you don't accidentally grab one for the cats."

"Where are the cats? I thought I might get to see at least one of them."

"We haven't exactly spent much time here the last few days. And your interest will wane when Basher and Moon get the zoomies at three in the morning and sound like a herd of wildebeests running down the halls."

Kurt started laughing.

"It's not funny. One night, I didn't shut my door all the way, and the two little assholes burst into my room as I was sleeping on my side and used my back like a springboard."

He laughed even harder, which made her smile. This is what she had been missing since DC. A sunny morning lying in his arms, talking about nothing in particular. Just being together in the moment.

Kurt rolled her onto her back and looked down at her, his expression serious as he brushed his thumb across her cheek.

"I love you," she whispered, her chest swelling with the emotion. "Even when I hated you, I loved you. Even when I was cursing you and wanting to hurt you, I still loved you."

His pale blue orbs held a wealth of emotion as he gazed at her. "And I love you. It isn't a sane love. Or a staid one. It isn't simple or rational. Nothing about what I feel for you has ever been. I hurt you before."

"That's in the past, and I've forgiven you." She smoothed back a lock of his hair that had fallen over his forehead.

"It doesn't change what I did. I want you to know I'll never do anything like that again. I'm yours," he continued. "For eternity.

You are my heart. My very soul. I will be by your side for however long you'll have me."

She cupped his face and pressed her lips to his. "I like the sound of eternity."

"For eternity it is, then." He kissed her: deeply, passionately, letting her taste his love and his promise.

EPILOGUE

SKYE DRUIDS

Later that day…

Kurt fidgeted nervously as he and Sabryn walked to the turquoise door. He stared at it for so long that Sabryn finally knocked for him. The door opened before he had a chance to prepare. Emily MacLean met him with a small smile, her blue eyes moving from him to Sabryn.

"Please, come in," she bade them, absently smoothing her hand over her shoulder-length blond hair. "Reggie is already here."

Reggie. His father. The only one who had ever called him Reggie was Diana. To everyone else, he was Reginald. To Kurt, he had simply been Dad. He had dearly missed the long conversations he and his father used to have. While far from happy, the family they had been was forever altered.

Sabryn tugged him inside the cottage as she said something to Emily he didn't pay any attention to. Emily led them through the house, turning back to look at him. Her lips moved, but his brain couldn't make out anything she said. His last words to Diana had been harsh. He had assumed her guilt without allowing her a chance to protest.

All too soon, they stood outside the bedroom. Kurt dug in his heels as his stomach twisted and blood roared in his ears. He couldn't do this. If he saw Diana, he would have no choice but to admit she was dead.

His mother. The woman who had been larger than life and never feared anything. She couldn't be gone. She needed to know what her information had done for them. For Sabryn. She should know that, and he wanted to be the one to tell her. But he couldn't. Because of his brother.

Sabryn touched his chest. He looked into the deep blue pools of her eyes and saw her sadness and concern. "You don't have to do this," she said.

He brought her hand to his mouth and kissed it before linking their fingers. Then he took a step forward and looked into the bedroom. He saw his father first. Reginald sat beside the bed, hunched over, his head in his hands and his shoulders softly shaking. Then Kurt looked at the bed. Diana lay still, a blanket up to her chin. He could almost convince himself she was sleeping.

Memories of long ago ran through his mind: Diana teaching him how to brush down a horse, how she used to play hide-and-seek with him and Parker in the garden. A smile curved his lips when he thought about the time he had thrown mud at her, and she had thrown it right back.

Tears stung Kurt's eyes. Where had these memories been the last six years? Was it a child's onus to always believe the worst of their parents? To focus on the things they swore they would never do if they had children of their own? He'd hated Diana. Yet now, staring at her, he found he would do almost anything to have one more minute with her.

Suddenly, his dad lifted his head and looked at him. The moment Reginald got to his feet, Kurt walked to him. They embraced, both overcome with grief. He had never seen his father cry before, and it spoke to how deeply he had loved Diana.

His dad was the first to pull away and turned his watery gaze past Kurt. "Sabryn. I've waited a long time to meet you."

Kurt eagerly watched as Sabryn walked to his father and put her arms around him. Reginald held her tightly for a moment. It was no surprise that his father liked her. His dad was easy to like and generally liked others.

"Diana told me all about you," Reginald said.

Sabryn glanced at Kurt. "Maybe don't believe everything she said."

"She liked you a great deal." Reginald turned to look at his wife as a tear rolled down his cheek. "She couldn't tell you that."

"Why not?" Kurt asked.

His father's blue eyes swung to him. "I know you're angry at her, but you should also be angry at me."

"You?" Kurt asked, surprised. "Why would I be mad at you?"

Reginald wearily sank into the chair. "You think you knew her, but you didn't. No one did but me. She only let her guard down when we were shut in our room together."

Kurt shook his head in disbelief.

"We both knew things needed to change with the London Druids. I preferred to fight behind the scenes, and she liked being front and center and seen. She wanted to lead, and I wanted that *for* her," his father continued. "It was a perfect partnership in every way. I know others think she married me to control me, but that was never our relationship. From the very beginning we were a team. Every decision we came to, we did together."

Sabryn moved closer to Kurt. "So, you knew about DC?"

"I knew about all of it before it happened." Reginald ran a hand down his weary face. "She wanted to go against Thomas, but it wasn't the time. I cautioned her against it. Maybe we should have." He turned his head to Kurt. "She was a good woman who loved fiercely and did everything she could to keep her family safe. She was strong and determined, but she loved her family above all. Why else do you think she would venture here for you and Sabryn?"

Kurt shook his head, staggered by what he heard.

"You knew Parker had changed," Sabryn guessed.

Reginald shrugged. "I suspected. I wanted her to wait for me so we could come to Skye together."

"I pressed her." Kurt was going to be sick.

"Rightly so, if what I've heard is true. The blame doesn't lie with you, son."

Kurt looked into his father's eyes and fought against a wave of remorse that threatened to swallow him.

Reginald slid his gaze to Sabryn. "You were successful?"

"We were," she answered. "Thanks to Diana. She stayed alive long enough to pass along the last bit of information I needed."

"Good," Reginald said, his voice breaking. His gaze swung back to his wife.

Kurt stared at Diana's face and saw the blood against her pale cheek. The vibrant, beautiful woman who had always been so put-together was gone. "I said hurtful things to her."

"She knew you loved her," his father said.

But Kurt wasn't so sure, and he would spend the rest of his life wondering. "Are you taking her home to bury her?"

Reginald shook his head. "She is home. Skye is where all Druids hail from. I've spoken to Rhona already."

"A fitting place to lay Diana to rest," Sabryn said. "She deserves to be honored. She helped save us last night."

"To save Skye," Kurt added and wrapped an arm around her.

The next day...

Finn tried not to squirm as he stood in the war room, but the jeans rubbing against his legs grew more uncomfortable by the day. Since jeans were the only kind of pants he owned, he was in a bit of a pickle. Worse, he didn't want to tell anyone about his discomfort lest they think something was wrong. Something *was* wrong, but that wasn't the point. He didn't want anyone to worry.

Most had taken seats around the tables. Finn had tried sitting, but he couldn't take it. He curled his hands into fists to keep from scratching. His skin was raw from him scoring his skin from his ankles to his hips with what little he had for nails. He'd done some research and knew tattoos had a healing process, but nothing like what was happening to him.

He looked around the room. Kirsi was missing another meeting, but no one would say anything, not when Nora was so ill. But there was a new face among them. Luke Ryan. After all the searching, Scott and Willa's father had found his way to them.

Finn suspected they had been called to the war room to hear about his exploits.

Rhona walked in, drawing everyone's attention. She nodded to Kurt, who opened a laptop and punched a few keys. A second later, his screen was projected on the wall behind her. In big, bold words, the headline read:

ANCIENT MAGIC AWAKENS: ISLE OF SKYE'S DRUIDS UNLEASH GLOBAL DEBATE.

Below it, the subheading read:

*Unexplained phenomena linked
to newly exposed Druid community.*

"Fekking hell," Finn murmured. "Is that real?"

Rhona released a long sigh. "I'm afraid so. It went live less than an hour ago, and Chief Superintendent Boyd has already been drowning in calls."

"Reporters are arriving on the isle as we speak," Kurt added.

Elias ran a hand down his face. "We're going to be under a microscope."

"The chief is doing her best to protect us, but there isna much she can do," Theo added.

Ariah looked around. "Is nobody wondering how this was leaked? What proof there is?"

Grim-faced, Kurt hit a button, and his screen changed to a video of the battle at the Fairy Glen.

"This has to be London," Ferne said.

Carlyle nodded. "I was about to say the same thing."

"You're forgetting George," Luke added.

Balladyn shook his head. "It doesn't matter who, how, or why. It's amazing that Druids have stayed hidden for as long as they have. Same with the Fae, and especially the Dragon Kings. Maybe it's time everyone knew what was out there."

"In other words, we need to prepare," Rhona said.

Bronwyn shook her head. "Like we needed one more thing to deal with. This is going to hinder us."

"Maybe that's exactly what it's meant to do." Sabryn shrugged from her seat near the front. "Maybe this is the evil and is meant to add another layer of issues."

Elodie threw up her hands. "Well, then we do what we've been doing. We keep fighting."

The world looked different now, as if it had dimmed somehow. Kirsi used her shoulder to wipe at her tears. She should be there for her dad, but she couldn't. Skye was a small place, and it had only taken thirty minutes for news to spread of her mother's death. The sight of her father in shambles as the phone rang endlessly had been too much. She'd said nothing to the nurse as she bolted from the house.

She drew her knees to her chest and watched some seagulls. The boulder she sat on was where she often found Callum, and she had to admit that she had hoped he would be here. She wasn't exactly up for conversation, though, so maybe it was better that she sat on the beach alone.

What was she going to do without her mother? Her illness had lasted a long time, but Nora had always been a fighter, pulling through when others had little hope. This latest episode had been one of the worst, and then her mom was gone before they realized it. Kirsi would have to return home soon. Her father would need help arranging the funeral.

Her head jerked to the side when something brushed her arm. She almost couldn't believe it when she saw Callum sitting beside her. His light brown waves were pulled back in a queue, his amber eyes studying her. The tears welled before she could stop them, overflowing and sliding down her cheeks. He said nothing as he wrapped an arm around her and held her.

Edinburgh

Parker sat with his ankle across his knee as he looked at George across her desk. "You seem surprised to see me."

"I wouldn't say surprised," she replied. "I would put myself more in the confused column. Especially since things on Skye didn't go as you planned."

Parker chuckled. "I wouldn't say that."

George quirked a dark brow. "Mara was the only one to return from the two groups of Druids I sent you. I would definitely say things didn't go as planned."

"London paid for those Druids."

"Those were my people," George stated, her voice rising with her anger. She paused, her glare icy. "No more Edinburgh Druids will die on Skye."

Both of Parker's brows rose at that statement. "Unless you're the one sending them, right? Because you've sent plenty to the isle. In fact," he said, twisting his lips, "several have joined the Skye Druids."

"How dare you?" she began.

He rolled his eyes and cut his hand through the air. "Stop right there. You had no problem handing people over as long as London gave you money."

"And Elias. He isn't here," she snapped.

Parker pursed his lips as he sighed. "No, he is not."

"Why is that?"

"Because I don't care about your little revenge plot."

George's eyes narrowed as she sat up straighter in her chair. "And just what *do* you want?"

"That seat."

She stilled, fear flashing in her eyes. George was so focused on him that she never saw Mara coming up behind her with the knife.

"Your time is done," Parker said.

Mara slit her throat with one swipe of the blade. George grabbed her neck, blood gushing, as her lips worked, but no words came. Parker cleared his throat as he stood and buttoned his suit jacket before waiting for Mara to join him.

"Ready?" he asked her.

She tossed the knife on George's desk, and the two walked out before the leader took her last breath.

Thank you for reading **AFTER MIDNIGHT**. I hope you enjoyed the ending to Sabryn and Kurt's story as much as I loved writing it.

There's a bonus short story featuring Kut and Sabryn. Grab it here:

https://mailchi.mp/donnagrant/aftermidnight

If you want more Skye Druids, then you're in luck! Up next is **KISS OF SKYE**.

BUY KISS OF SKYE NOW
at www.DonnaGrant.com

* * *

And don't miss out on the Elven Kingdoms series. The next book set in Dark Universe, is **MOUNTAIN FIRE**…

BUY MOUNTAIN FIRE NOW
at www.DonnaGrant.com

* * *

To find out when new books release
SIGN UP FOR MY NEWSLETTER today at
https://www.tinyurl.com/DonnaGrantNews

* * *

Join my Facebook group, Donna Grant Groupies, for exclusive
giveaways and sneak peeks of future books.
https://bit.ly/DGGroupies

* * *

Keep reading for a peek of KISS OF SKYE and a glimpse at
MOUNTAIN FIRE …

SNEAK PEEK AT THE NEXT SKYE DRUID BOOK

KISS OF SKYE, SKYE DRUIDS SERIES, BOOK 8

Return to Scotland and *New York Times* and *USA Today* bestselling author Donna Grant's Skye Druids, where magic and danger intertwine and a tale of passion, revelations, and new beginnings unfolds.

BUY KISS OF SKYE NOW
at www.DonnaGrant.com

Keep reading for an excerpt of KISS OF SKYE …

KISS OF SKYE EXCERPT

London

Rowen didn't bother to open her umbrella as she walked from the hotel into the drizzle to the waiting cab. She slid into the seat and gave the driver directions before trying to get comfortable in a vehicle that had held dozens of people that day alone.

She looked out the side window and fought against the revulsion that rose. The cobblestone streets, traditional pubs, and medieval architecture impressed her. She didn't care about the city's long history and royal landmarks meant nothing to her. The city was loud, dirty, and crowded.

And if she heard "you're from across the pond" one more time, she was going to scream.

Rowen loosened her fingers that gripped her purse too tight. She only had a little more time in the country before she could get home. She missed her animals. She missed her routine. She missed her life.

The cab slowed as it pulled to the curb. She tightened the belt of her trench coat and adjusted the strap of her purse on her shoulder. She realized as the cab pulled away that she had left her umbrella. That was the second one. Her thoughts shifted away from the vehicle to her surroundings.

There were many similarities between UK and America, but there were just as many differences. For one, parking lots. Or rather car parks. Similar, but different. She sighed and stared at the striking ancient building before her. The white-gray stone matched other prominent architecture around the city. One talkative cab driver had explained it was called Portland stone that was quarried from the Isle of Portland in Dorset. He had gone on—in great detail—about all the different types of Portland stone, but she had tuned him out.

The stone was used as far back as the Roman era, which made it difficult to determine just how old the building was. But she knew. The sun was behind a building as it sank into the horizon. A few rays found their way between structures and struck the windows of a café to her right, blinding her.

Rowen turned her head away as she made for the building. There was a grand entry in the front where others were entering. There were no guards. Druids didn't need them. All she had to do was get through this night, and then she could go home and deliver her report on the London Druids.

From the moment Rowen had read the email invite, she had wanted to ignore it. There had always been open communication between the London Druid and her group, but not once had they ever been summoned. Granted, they had never invited anyone from London to them. Everyone knew the power London had. They were respected but not feared.

Things had changed, though. Small things at first that had been overlooked or explained away. The incidents became larger and more frequent, making everyone sit up and notice. Others had wanted to travel to the UK, but for some reason, she was chosen. Rowen tried to refuse, but here she was. In a city she loathed about to enter a viper's nest.

The heels of her shoes clicked softly on the pavement as she approached the building. She had expected there to be a grand edifice, but the double domed front doors fit in with all the others. There was a fanlight in stained glass above the door. There was an ornate caste iron knocker and handles that held a touch of mysticism in the design.

As she got closer, she was able to see the stained glass was tree of life with its limbs extending outward and upward while its roots mimicked the branches. She stood before the closed door and stared at the raven head protruding from the door holding the knocker in its beak.

Ravens were powerful symbols and messengers to Druids. The birds were particularly linked to wisdom, prophecy, and the connection between the living and the Otherworld. Moreover, ravens were associated with death and transformation.

Her eyes dropped to the handle that resembled a root. If she had any doubts about where she was, they vanished. Rowen grasped the door knocker and struck the door twice.

Almost instantly, both doors swung open and a petite brunette in her early forties greeted her with a toothy smile. "Rowen," the woman said smiling, the corners of her soft brown eyes crinkling. "We're so excited to have you here finally. Please, come in. I'm Ella, and I'll be showing you around."

For a second, she almost turned and bolted.

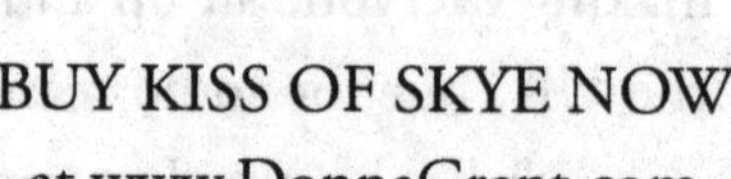

BUY KISS OF SKYE NOW
at www.DonnaGrant.com

GLIMPSE AT THE NEXT DARK UNIVERSE BOOK

MOUNTAIN FIRE, ELVEN KINGDOMS SERIES, BOOK 4

He's the fire I crave—and the danger I can't escape.

I was sent to a land of power and secrets, a place where every step could be my last. Yet, nothing could have prepared me for him.

Tall, imposing, and carved from stone, he was nothing like I imagined. There was something in his eyes—something deep and untouchable—that called to me, making me question everything.

I was only supposed to survive here, to blend in with the shadows. But with every moment spent in his presence, I felt myself unraveling.

His touch ignites a fire I can't ignore, and his gaze has a way of making me forget everything but him.

In a city full of danger, where darkness lurks just beyond the light, I've come to realize that nothing is more dangerous than the way I crave him.

I never planned to let him into my heart, yet I'm unable to stop the pull between us.

And in this world of lies and shadows, I'll have to face what's burning between us before it consumes us both.

New York Times and *USA Today* **bestselling author Donna Grant weaves a sensual tale of forbidden love, fiery passion, and the impossible choices that come with it in the thrilling fourth installment of her Elven Kingdoms series.**

BUY MOUNTAIN FIRE NOW
at www.DonnaGrant.com

ABOUT THE AUTHOR

New York Times and *USA Today* bestselling author Donna Grant® has been praised for her "totally addictive" and "unique and sensual" stories.

She's written more than one hundred novels spanning multiple genres of romance including the bestselling Dragon Kings® series that features a thrilling combination of Druids, Fae, and immortal Highlanders who are dark, dangerous, and irresistible. She lives in Texas with her dog and a cat.

www.DonnaGrant.com
www.MotherofDragonsBooks.com

facebook.com/AuthorDonnaGrant

instagram.com/dgauthor

tiktok.com/@donnagrant_author

bookbub.com/authors/donna-grant

goodreads.com/donna_grant

pinterest.com/donnagrant1